THE EMPEROR'S SECOND WIFE

BY ZOE SAADIA

At Road's End
The Young Jaguar
The Jaguar Warrior
The Warrior's Way

The Highlander
Crossing Worlds
The Emperor's Second Wife
Currents of War
The Fall of the Empire
The Sword
The Triple Alliance

Two Rivers
Across the Great Sparkling Water
The Great Law of Peace
The Peacekeeper

Beyond the Great River
The Foreigner
Troubled Waters
The Warpath
Echoes of the Past

THE EMPEROR'S SECOND WIFE

The Rise of the Aztecs, Book 3

ZOE SAADIA

ISBN: 1537358022
ISBN-13: 978-1537358024

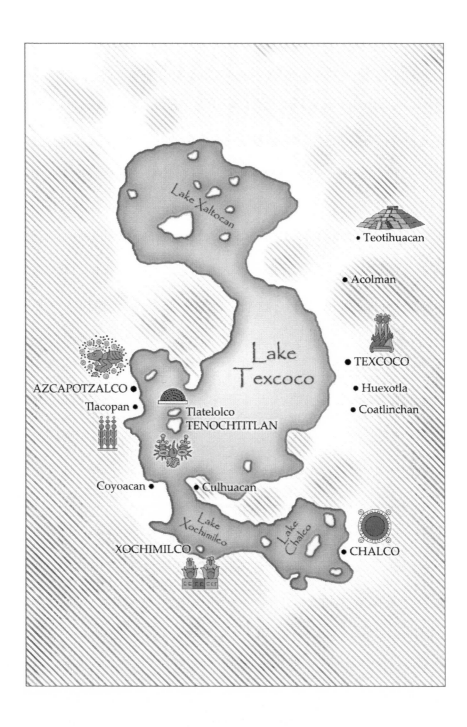

PROLOGUE

Tenochtitlan, 1417
Before the second Tepanec invasion of Texcoco

Iztac eyed the large rubber ball wide-eyed, rolling it between her palms.

"Where did you get this?" she asked the boy, not taking her eyes off the rare object. Tossing it in the air, she caught it back with difficulty. The ball was heavy and unpleasantly coarse.

The boy's eyes sparkled. "You'll never guess."

"Oh yes?" She looked at him, taking in the gentle face, the yet-uncut hair, the slender form of a boy eleven summers old, too small for his years. "Let me think. You went out for *calmecac* lessons this morning. So you must have found it somewhere along the road." She wrinkled her nose. "I wish I could get out of the Palace too, sometimes."

"Such a ball? Along the road? Can't happen!" called the boy victoriously. "Do you think those things are just rolling all over the city?" Pointedly, he rolled his eyes "Haven't you seen a ball game in your life?"

"I've seen many ball games!" exclaimed Iztac hotly. "In Texcoco we have a beautiful court, as large as this whole palace. I watched that game twenty times and more. You don't have such things in Tenochtitlan."

The boy frowned. "I've seen warriors playing more than your twenty times." He peered at her as she tossed the ball once again, catching it with both arms. "You can't touch it with your hands."

"Oh, I know that." She threw the ball, then tried to hit it with her elbow. It slipped off and rolled over the ground. The boy's laughter made her angry. "You can't do any better," she said, kicking the ball impatiently.

"Oh yes, I can." He picked it up, then proceeded to throw it in his turn. His sandaled foot shot sideways, hitting the ball with his hip, sending it back into the air.

Iztac gasped. "I can't believe it. How did you do this?"

"Easily." His eyes sparkled.

"Do it again!"

This time he missed, cursed, picked up the ball anew. She caught her breath, wishing him to succeed. He was so vulnerable, so unsure of himself, this heir to the Aztec throne. Just a boy of a little over eleven summers, kind and well-meaning, with no streak of viciousness to his nature, not a natural warrior. He was as nice as his father, but having a fierce, dominant woman for a mother was his bad luck, decided Iztac, watching the ball flying sideways after a less successful toss of an elbow.

"Let me try," she said, grabbing the coarse rubber as it rolled over the ground again. "Where did you learn to do this?"

"There was this man in *calmecac* this morning. The other boys say he is coming there to teach every few dawns now. He is so old!" The boy rolled his eyes. "He said the warriors should know how to handle a ball, so he took us outside and proceeded to show us." His hands flopped in the air. "Iztac-Ayotl, you wouldn't believe it. He is so old, but he ran and hit the ball with all parts of his body. He made all the boys work. But I was the best. Would you believe that? I did better than the rest of them!" He beamed at her, his pride spilling over.

She hugged him. "Oh, Chimal, I'm so proud of you!"

His shoulders were thin, fragile against her touch. He needed to develop his arms, she reflected. At his age, *calmecac* boys were supposed to be stronger, more fit. Why wouldn't his mother let him join the school like a regular boy?

"So, did this man cut his lessons short when it became too hot?" she asked, moving away and picking up the ball again.

His face fell. "No. They went on. Then he said they would

practice shooting slings." He glanced at the sky. "I suppose they are doing it now."

She kicked the ball angrily. "Why won't they let you attend *calmecac* like a normal boy?"

He shrugged. "Because I will be the emperor."

"It's not an excuse. My brother will also be an emperor, and he went to *calmecac* for many summers. Like you, he attended the lessons, but when he was about your age he went to live in *calmecac* like any other boy."

"Well, your Acolhua people are strange," he said haughtily. "My mother says the future emperor should not mingle with his subjects. She says the emperor can't be treated like a simple warrior. She says they should not be allowed to talk to me like any other boy."

"So then, here you are, stuck in the Palace with no ballgames." She saw his face twisting, and regretted her outburst. He was just a boy, and she was a grown woman of seventeen summers, the Emperor's Second Wife. She was not a girl anymore, and this place was not Texcoco Palace, this boy was not her brother to mess around with, and laugh and tease.

She clenched her teeth against the memories. It pounced on her suddenly, as it always would, threatening to take her, to shatter her oh so painfully erected walls of oblivion. Texcoco Palace, the place she had loathed so much, the place she had thought to be her prison, now loomed in her memory, beautiful and imposing, perfectly groomed, with her trustworthy maids and all that freedom to run about, away from the watchful eyes of her father, the Emperor, or his Second Wife, her mother, having her brother, the best boy in the whole world, for a friend.

She remembered herself complaining to Coyotl that she was just a meaningless princess. Oh, now she knew better. What a delightful existence it was, to be just one of many, to matter to no one. Only as the Second Wife of the Emperor had she had discovered what real imprisonment was.

She took a deep breath. *Stop being such a whiny cihua*, she admonished herself. *You can still sneak to the Palace's gardens whenever you like, and you have this boy to play around with, to run, and even to climb occasionally. Or play with a ball, like now.*

"Come," she said, snatching the ball back from his hands. "Show me how you do this. Stop pulling those offended faces. You are not the emperor yet."

"And you are not the First Wife," he retorted, lips pursed.

"And I will never be this thing. And I don't want it, either. It's such a bore!"

"No, it's not. Chief Wives can order everyone about. No one dares to argue with my mother, ever."

Iztac shivered. "Well, your mother makes a good Empress. Of course everyone obeys her."

Even the Emperor himself, she reflected, her stomach twisting uneasily. Oh but she made such tremendous efforts to avoid getting in the way of this terrible woman.

She shivered again, remembering the first time she had seen Tenochtitlan's Empress, tall and widely built, with her broad face and large, widely spaced eyes, so typical of the Tepanecs. One of Tezozomoc's favorite daughters, given to the Aztec Emperor as a token of good faith. To make sure Tenochtitlan behaved, was Iztac's private conclusion. Such an imposing, domineering, fierce woman. Not that Iztac had noticed any of that at first.

Her arrival at Tenochtitlan had swept by, vague and bleary, like a bad dream. She remembered only the fragments of it. The damp air that assaulted her nostrils, the dismal looking palace with no resemblance to the richness of the Texcoco Emperor's dwelling, the pleasant looking face of Huitzilihuitl, the Emperor, smiling at her, his eyebrows raised in surprise, saying something about her beauty and charm.

She remembered herself breathing with relief when she had finally been led to a private set of rooms, away from the multitude of people peering at her as though she were an exotic animal from the thickness of the highland forests. The Highlands! Oh, she remembered battling the tears, keeping them at bay. She would not cry, not in front of those people, nor in the privacy of her rooms.

Well, those were not her rooms, she was quick to discover. Those were the Emperor's rooms. As the maids rushed to and fro, busy removing her imposing headdress and some of the heaviest jewelry, she had breathed with relief. It was so good to be rid of its crushing weight. But when they began painting her cheeks and lips, dressing her in a light, flimsy robe tied by a colorful girdle, a new wave of latent fear washed through her. Their smiles and giggles told her what would be the last part of the ceremony. She thought of the Emperor's hands removing the light material, and her stomach twisted so violently, she became sick, and the maids hurried to replace the ruined garment with another one.

Smiling grimly, she remembered that she had been spared that part of the ceremony, after all. Huddled in a far corner, with the maids distressed and uncomfortable, she had shut her eyes at the sound of many footsteps, but the cold commanding voice of a woman was the one to interrupt the sudden silence.

"Out. All of you," said the woman imperiously. "Wait at the outer corridor until I call."

The feathers on the delicate headdress of the Empress rustled angrily as the maids and the servants scattered through the doorway. Iztac just stared, mesmerized by the broad face and the large, slightly squinted eyes that gazed at her with the coldness and calm of an ocelot eyeing a forest mouse. Not a decent meal for a predator, but a disturbance nevertheless.

"Get up, girl," said the woman coldly, when the last of the servants was safely away and the room went eerily quiet. "Take a seat over there, on this chair by the podium."

Fighting to get to her feet, Iztac made a tremendous effort not to drop her gaze.

"Well, I think it's time we have our first talk." The woman neared the opposite chair and set there, majestic, the richly embroidered rims of her gown rustling. "Two noble wives of a noble emperor." She grinned coldly. "Huitzilihuitl has many wives, but none of them matter. They are not noble enough, and they are not important." Her gaze grew colder, more difficult to stand. "Well, little princess of Texcoco, how was your journey?"

Iztac cleared her throat, trying to say something. Nothing came out.

"Oh, girl, don't be so frightened," said the woman, but her eyes flickered with satisfaction, telling Iztac that if she was frightened now, she didn't know yet what real fright was. "We can get along. You seem to be a nice little thing. You won't stand in my way, will you?"

Iztac clasped her palms to stop them from trembling, but even the pain of her nails sinking into her flesh did not help. Her mind refused to suggest any kind of an answer, even had her lips been able to form the words.

"You see," went on the woman, unabashed by the lack of response. "There can be only one Empress, so it's important that you should not nurture any ideas of you becoming one. You have the necessary blood, and you have looks." The woman leaned forward, placing her well groomed palms upon the podium between them. "I would hate to see such a pretty girl getting hurt. Your mother is one of my half sisters, another daughter of my father, the mighty Emperor of Azcapotzalco. Your father, the Emperor of Texcoco, was foolish enough to replace her with another Chief Wife, a sister of my husband." The woman shook her head. "Oh, how foolish of him. Texcoco will lose this war. The Tepanecs will take this *altepetl* and the rest of the Acolhua lands. But my father would rule it wisely, better than your father did."

The thought of the Tepanecs swarming Texcoco shores, the thought of Coyotl and the nearing battle, helped.

"My people will not lose," said Iztac, surprised by the clearness of her voice. "They will throw the Tepanecs back into the Great Lake, and then they will cross it to conquer Azcapotzalco itself."

The derisive grin disappeared. "Oh, you are a spirited one. I see." The dark eyes grew freezing cold. "Listen, girl. I didn't come here to talk politics. You are nothing but an insignificant princess, just another one of the minor wives. You understand little, if anything. It would not be appropriate for me, the Chief Wife and the Empress, to spend my time lecturing you on history and politics." The feathers rustled again as the woman tossed her head high. "I came to tell you this, and I will not be repeating myself. You are to stay at the minor wives quarters, and you are not to pursue the Emperor with any of your girlish tricks. He may honor you with an occasional visit, but you are not to bear him a child."

The eyes bored into her, now blazing, burning her skin. "Should you conceive, you will not be allowed to bring this child into our Fifth World. You will be dead long before it happens."

Iztac felt her heart, which had been pounding wildly, going still. Like a wave traveling through her chest, it slipped down her stomach, leaving everything gray, lifeless, dead in its wake. She clutched the uneven surface of the reed podium with both hands, her anger rising, sudden and difficult to control.

"I will take my own life before you have the pleasure of killing me," she said hoarsely. "But I will not do this until I hear of my people's great victories, until I hear how they ruined Azcapotzalco, until I know what tribute they've made the Tepanecs pay." The woman's face swam before her eyes and she blinked, desperate to banish the tears. These were of rage, not of fear, but she was afraid the woman would interpret them wrongly. "I will not bear *your* Emperor a son. If I can help it, he will never touch me at all. If you can make him not come to me at nights, I would be grateful. I don't want to be his Chief Wife. All I want is to go home. All I want is to go away, to run as far as the Smoking Mountain of the Highlands, if you wish to know. I don't want your place, and I don't want your status. And I will take my own life, but not before I hear of my people's victories."

She shut her eyes, her heart pumping insanely, as if trying to jump out of her chest. Like the heart of a sacrificial victim.

"Oh, what a spirited girl you are." The woman's voice reached her, overcoming the pounding in her ears. "I would hate to see you suffer. I would hate to have to get rid of you. The Tepanec blood of your mother is raging in your veins, that much is obvious. You may feel loyal to your Acolhua side, but you are a Tepanec in your spirit." Pausing, the woman smiled coldly, then rose to her feet. "We may come to know each other well over the future summers. If you behave, those may even be pleasant encounters for you. Remember what I said. You bear no children to the Emperor, and you keep away from him." A cold grin. "As a favor from a woman to a woman, I'll make sure he doesn't come to you tonight. You will be removed from these premises shortly, oh proud Acolhua princess. It'll be off to the minor wives quarters for you, to share it with the rest of the insignificant women."

The light paces dimmed, disappearing down the corridor. Iztac shut her eyes once again. She tried to take deep breaths, but they came in with difficulty, convulsive, bringing no relief. The fact that the Emperor would not come to her tonight rang in her ears again and again. He would not be untying the ropes of her gown.

She clasped her palms tight. Oh, the gods were so kind to her.

The memory of the moonlit grass around the pond surfaced, the memory she had managed to tuck away for the past market interval, since her last attempt to find *him* on the Plaza. The memory of his large brown hands, rough and scratched, the hands of a youth used to fighting and climbing, doing all sorts of wild things, yet their fingers long and well-shaped, the fingers of a man good at drawing and painting. Oh, he drew such beautiful pictures. And he had taken his time untying her robe, she remembered, although it would have been enough just to pull the light gown up.

The moon goddess, she thought. *Revered and silvery, but golden for him, with obsidian for eyes.* She sobbed and let the wave of grief take her. Now the tears flowed unrestrained, and she didn't care anymore.

"Iztac-Ayotl, wake up!"

The boy's voice tore her out of her reverie, brought her back to the clear afternoon sky and the rustling trees of the Palace's gardens, two summers later.

"You look like you've just seen a ghost!" He peered at her teasingly. "Have you?"

"No. I was remembering what it was like when I first arrived here."

"Oh, I remember you well." He pulled a face. "You were sparkling like a statue, and you looked like you would faint at any moment."

"I did not!"

"Oh yes, you did. You were so frightened. Like a girl. And you are a girl, a silly girl."

She measured him with a glance full of meaning. "Don't you mess with me, Chimalpopoca."

He giggled, then sobered abruptly. "I'm not saying you are frightened now. But you were back then, all the same." He frowned. "I felt bad for you."

"No, I wasn't." She snatched the ball from his hands. "But I will fall asleep if you don't start playing. Show me everything that this old warrior taught you."

"He is not just an old warrior. He was our Chief Warlord for, oh, ages."

"Oh, the Aztec Chief Warlord! I should have guessed." She drew her breath sharply. *More ghosts from the past.*

"What? What's wrong with him?"

"Nothing. It doesn't matter. Everything is wrong with him. I hate him."

"Why?"

She ground her teeth. "He kidnapped someone. Someone I knew."

Chimal burst out laughing. "Chief Warlords don't kidnap people. No one can tell them 'no', anyway. No one but the emperor," he corrected himself. "Chief warlords take warriors and go out and kill our enemies. You are so silly."

"Yes, I know what warlords do. But he did kidnap this boy all the same." She saw him opening his mouth to argue and plugged her ears with her hands. "I don't what to talk about it, so don't even try! And anyway, why hasn't he died already? He is so old."

"He is not that old. They say he is like three times twenty summers old or something. I've seen people older than him. And he is hopping all over the place. He is teaching history and warfare, but they say he is too eager to get to the training grounds and give them actual lessons on all sorts of weapons." He sighed. "I wish I was allowed to live in *calmecac* like the rest of the boys."

She watched his twisting face, her chest filling with compassion, pushing her own misery away. "Maybe we should try to talk to the Emperor. He is your father after all. And he is the Emperor."

His dubious glance made her hold her tongue. Huitzilihuitl was a kind, pleasant sort of a man, wise and far-sighted. He made good laws, and he judged wisely in the imperial court. He strove to achieve his goals peacefully whatever the cost, avoiding struggles and confrontations. He gave up on the argument with his advisers when they maintained that the cost of building a special construction, to bring fresh water to Tenochtitlan, would be too high. He never argued with their Tepanec overlords. He had preferred to abandon his Acolhua allies, instead. He never argued with his powerful Chief Wife, either.

"I'll try to talk to him about you when he sends for me," she said resolutely.

"Does he see you in private?"

"Sometimes."

She thought about the rare occasions on which the Emperor would send for her, to be brought into his chambers, quietly and hurriedly, as if by stealth. He would look at her guiltily, as though regretting not being able to do it more often. Not wasting his time on talking, he would take her gently and carefully, only to send her away afterward. Neither pleased, nor repulsed, she would leave, breathing with relief, afraid of only one thing – that she may be with child. However, those encounters were infrequent, occurring only once in every few moons, and so far, she hadn't conceived.

That was no lovemaking on either part, she knew. It was a physical act, but for what purpose, she didn't know, didn't care to ask. The lovemaking belonged to the past, to the silvery night and the moonlit pond.

She clenched her teeth tight and forced her mind to focus on the boy, who seemed to be studying her carefully.

"The Emperor sent for me about a market interval ago and this time he wanted to talk," she said, forcing a smile. "So maybe I'll be able to talk to him about you the next time."

The boy frowned. "Doesn't he talk to you every time he sends for you?"

"No. He doesn't talk to me."

"What does he do to you?"

She shifted her weight from one foot to another. "All sorts of things. The things men do to their wives." Uncomfortable under his heavy gaze, she added hurriedly, trying to clear the atmosphere. "He doesn't think I know enough history or politics." She winked. "I haven't been to *calmecac*, either."

"But you did your temple training. All girls do this." He looked away, frowning. "When I'm the Emperor, I'll take you to be my Chief Wife."

She laughed. "I'm too old for you. But your mother will find you the prettiest princess in the entire valley. And the noblest one. Well, anyway, I didn't do my temple training, either," she added in order to change the subject, unsettled by the anger flashing out of his eyes. "Texcoco was busy preparing to fight the Tepanecs back then, so they never got around sending me to the temples."

The pleasant face of Tenochtitlan's future ruler twisted. "Stupid Acolhua Emperor."

"He is not stupid! He beat off the Tepanec invasion, and then he invaded their lands. He beat them three times in three large battles! Think about it. He took towns and villages." She flapped her hands in the air. "He laid a siege to Azcapotzalco itself!"

The boy's eyes flashed. "But he didn't succeed. He took his warriors and ran back to his side of the Great Lake."

"So what? He will regroup, and the Tepanecs will think twice before trying to attack Texcoco again."

But as she said that, she knew it was not true. The Tepanec Emperor enlisted the support of more *altepetls*, even of his old enemies from the towns around Lake Chalco. He was preparing another invasion as they spoke, here in the tranquility of the Tenochtitlan Palace, neutral and perfectly safe. That was what Huitzilihuitl had told her when he had sent for her a market interval ago.

She frowned, remembering how surprised she had been, bidden to sit alongside the Emperor's chair – not the magnificent chair of the main hall, but a pretty affair, nevertheless.

Not daring to touch the offered refreshments, she glanced at the pleasant-looking face of her husband, a man she hardly knew, a stranger. Oh, he looked tired and not at his best. Dark rings surrounded his eyes, and the narrow face had a grayish shade to it.

Uncomfortable, she had listened to him as he talked at length about his Acolhua allies, about his responsibilities to his growing *altepetl* and his Mexica people, about his obligations to Azcapotzalco. The man seemed troubled, and as if in a bad need to talk.

"Your people have proven brave and resourceful," he concluded. "How can one watch the struggle of the worthwhile neighbors and allies without offering help?"

Pondering this obviously rhetorical question, she watched him, swept with compassion. He was a nice man, and he seemed to feel bad for not joining the Texcoco people in their struggle. Tenochtitlan would benefit from taking the Tepanecs down. Thanks to the haughty Empress and her connection in the Tepanec Capital, Tenochtitlan's tribute was not heavy. Still, a tribute was a tribute. But then, Tenochtitlan had benefited from the continued hostilities of its neighbors as well. The traffic of the canoes around their shores grew, with the traders trying to avoid the troublesome areas, detouring through the Aztecs island, instead.

Hugging her elbows, she said nothing.

"Shall I help your father, Iztac-Ayotl?" asked the Emperor finally, gaze imploring, almost pitiful.

"Yes, I think you should," she whispered, unsure of herself. She cleared her throat. "I think none of our *altepetls* should pay a tribute to the Tepanecs."

He shook his head. "I wish it was that simple!"

"But maybe it is, Revered Emperor," she said, feeling the calm flowing through her body. "Your Chief Wife is the favorite daughter of the Tepanec Emperor, but your sister is the favorite wife of my father, the Acolhua Emperor. He put aside his own Tepanec Empress to favor your sister." She allowed herself a tiny smile. "You are obliged to both empires, but while one is aggressive and demanding, the other is fighting a war on behalf of both our *altepetls*."

A smiled dawned. "You are a wise woman, Second Wife. How old are you?"

"I've seen seventeen summers."

"Oh, you are wiser than your years warrant."

She shifted uneasily, aware of the servants. What if someone reported this conversation to the Empress?

He capped his forehead with both palms. "I may do this, you know. I cannot stand on the side any longer. Tezozomoc had demanded our active participation this time, and I cannot do this. I cannot betray my Acolhua allies."

She shivered despite the afternoon heat. "Are the Tepanecs going to invade Texcoco again?"

"Yes," he said. "And this time they will be better prepared."

Clasping her palms tight, feeling them sleek and sweaty against each other, she remembered Coyotl's face glimmering with excitement as he had told her that they were going to beat the Tepanecs, beaming at her, glowing with pride, brave and invincible. They did beat the Tepanecs back then. Already in Tenochtitlan, deep in her private misery, she remembered how excited she had become, for a few heartbeats at least, warmed by the wonderful news; how she had wished she could see her brother, to tell him how proud she was. Then there was more news of Acolhua forces crossing the Great Lake, invading the towns belonging to the Tepanecs. Somewhat accustomed to her new life by then, already being friends with Chimal, she contemplated sending a note to Coyotl, somehow. Oh, but he had promised to come to Tenochtitlan, to visit her. She could barely contain her excitement. It would be so wonderful to see him victorious. Well, it would be so wonderful to see him no matter how.

Coming back from her reverie, she peered at the boy.

"I'll talk to the Emperor," she said, smiling broadly. "He is sure to send you to *calmecac* for good." She winked at him. "And I will miss you. But you will visit a lot. Like my brother did."

There were agitated voices, and a small army of slaves came running, bearing on them, their gesturing shaky, faces flustered. She felt the boy tensing by her side, and she shivered too, recognizing the personal maid of the Empress in the lead.

"Honorable First Son, please follow," cried out the woman, her cheeks glowing red.

"What happened?" he whispered, resisting her pull.

"Oh, your father, the Emperor, he wants to see you. Come!"

Iztac just stood there, transfixed, the sensation of the looming disaster crawling up her spine. Something was wrong. Something was terribly amiss. The look that Chimal shot at her as he was pulled away, confirmed the ominous feeling.

"What happened?" she asked the slave, who still lingered as if undecided, gazing around and at a loss.

The man looked up, as if finding it difficult to concentrate. "Oh, Honorable Second Wife, it's the Emperor," he cried out, wringing his hands. "He is dying."

CHAPTER 1

Tenochtitlan, 1419
(approximately a year and a half later)

The wind blowing from the lake shore brought clouds of dust, making Itzcoatl shield his eyes. Frowning, he blinked to clear his vision. The freshly built long boat he had come to inspect swayed with the small waves, sporting the brightness of its polished, yet-untouched wood.

"It took you longer than expected to deliver it," he said, glancing at the main engineer. "I recall you promised three of these vessels before the end of this moon."

The engineer did not lower his gaze as appropriate for a man of his class. Instead, he stood the Warlord's glare calmly, his eyes old and washed out, but clear, unafraid. A cheeky bastard, reflected Itzcoatl, having difficulty remembering Tenochtitlan without its main engineer, appointed to hold this position by Itzcoatl's father, the First Emperor, Acamapichtli. The man should have retired summers ago, yet there was no one as good as him, and anyway, the old engineer was still full of energy and life, hopping all over the city with his scrolls and his army of assistants, supervising endless projected constructions.

"The first boat took the longest time to build, Honorable Warlord, because of the improvement we made in its prow. The other two vessels will be delivered more quickly. You will have the promised three vessels by the end of this moon, with a possible delay of no more than a market interval."

Itzcoatl studied the broad, wrinkled face for another heartbeat, not pleased with the engineer's obvious lack of fear.

"Well," he said finally. "I will trust your word once again. But I warn you. If those vessels are not delivered in time I will not take it kindly." He measured the long body of the boat with a glance. "And it better be the steadiest canoe I've ever sailed."

"It will not disappoint you, Honorable Warlord," said the engineer, unperturbed. "The length of the boat will not affect its maneuverability." The broad shoulders lifted in a shrug. "Tenochtitlan's previous Chief Warlord was happy with the improvements we introduced into his fleets."

Cheeky old bastard, fumed Itzcoatl, staring the engineer down. Tenochtitlan's previous Warlord had made many changes in the Aztec warrior forces, organizing them as was appropriate for the growing *altepetl* with more and more lands and provinces to govern. He was the one to develop Tenochtitlan's fleets, making it look as if the island-city was anxious to protect itself but, in fact, ensuring the Mexica dominance on their home water and maybe even elsewhere.

"Just make sure you deliver the rest of the vessels in time," he said finally, stepping back onto the dry land.

Speaking of old bastards, he thought, signing to his warriors and the palanquin bearers. That same former Chief Warlord would be sure to linger on the marketplace, at his favorite stall of tortillas by the warehouses, having finished with his *calmecac* lessons for today.

How do I detour by that place and make it look unintentional? he asked himself.

The engineer hesitated.

"What else?" inquired Itzcoatl impatiently.

"If I'm allowed to mention the matter, Honorable Warlord," the man cleared his throat, "the water undertaking. Everything is ready. The plans are drawn, the lists of the most needed materials are written down, the preparations are done. My people are eager to start." He shifted from foot to foot, his wrinkled face frowning, losing some of its unperturbed composure.

Itzcoatl felt his interest piquing. "Do you have the drawings ready? Is it truly possible?"

"Oh, yes!" The old man's eyes lit. "We can build a construction to bring fresh water to Tenochtitlan. It is possible and can be achieved. It was possible at the time of your Revered Father, our beloved First Emperor. If not for the Tepanecs, he would have commenced this project." The broad shoulders lifted briefly. "Now that the situation has changed, we can start implementing those plans. We will need plenty of material, but I suppose the Empress can make the arrangements."

Itzcoatl frowned. "You are overstepping your authority, engineer," he said coldly. "The royal house will let you know when it is the time for you to know. You are an engineer, not an adviser. My father and his Chief Warlord valued your opinion, but neither are responsible for the welfare of Tenochtitlan anymore. Do not forget your place, engineer. At your advanced age I would think one could have learned a measure of patience."

Something flickered in the depths of the dark eyes before the man dropped his gaze. "Of course, Honorable Warlord. I apologize." But there was no apology in the old man's low voice.

To cool his anger, Itzcoatl turned toward the wharves, eyeing the warehouses and the people rushing about. The main engineer was not at fault, he knew. He had said nothing to warrant this sharp reprimand. Many things had changed since the reign of his father, Acamapichtli. Thanks to the wise rule of its First Emperor, Tenochtitlan did not crash under the weight of the heavy Tepanec tribute. On the contrary, the Mexica *altepetl* prospered, gaining more and more independence.

Yet, even Huitzilihuitl, the Second Emperor of Tenochtitlan, Acamapichtli's son and Itzcoatl's half-brother, could not afford the expense of the water construction, although, by then the tribute was reduced to one fourth, thanks to the Tepanec Empress. No, their beloved *altepetl* still had not enough resources and available manpower to enjoy fresh water of the mainland.

However now, with Texcoco conquered and given to Tenochtitlan as its tributary, the situation should change. Huitzilihuitl had been dead for more than five seasons, with his son, a mere boy of thirteen summers, ruling in his stead, guided ably and firmly by his Tepanec mother.

Itzcoatl shivered. Oh but this woman made his nerves prickle. So tall, so imposing, so haughty and sure of herself. Had she hastened the death of Tenochtitlan's Second Emperor? Well, of course he had his doubts, along with many of the nobility. Yet, he kept those thoughts to himself. So far, he was in good graces with the Empress, who had promptly confirmed him the position of the Chief Warlord, needing him and his influence among the warriors.

Watching the queue of canoes waiting to pass the first bridge, he noticed one parting from the rest, lurching toward the low bank of their wharf. The face of the paddling commoner glowed red, and even at this distance, Itzcoatl could see his lips moving, muttering angrily.

A young warrior, standing on the prow, swayed rhythmically with the vibrations of the boat, his legs wide apart, broad face set. Nearing the wharf, he did not wait for the canoe to touch the bank, but leaped out with the grace of a man used to running and climbing, somehow inappropriate in a warrior with an obsidian sword. Yet, sure enough, the exquisite weapon was tied to the young man's plain, unadorned girdle.

As his companion, a warrior as tall but more narrowly built, talked to the owner of the canoe, Itzcoatl narrowed his eyes, displeased with the men landing anywhere near his precious new boat.

Gesturing to his personal guarding warriors, he frowned. "Get rid of them."

The engineer and his assistants tensed. "Well, Honorable Warlord, if our presence is not required—"

"No, it's not. All I require is the prompt delivery of two more of those long boats before this moon runs its course."

"It will be done, Honorable Leader."

Their eyes wandered back toward the lone canoe, and now Itzcoatl's sharp eyes picked out the figure of a young girl, crouching in the back of the boat.

"You, get off this wharf right away," he heard one of his warriors shouting.

The tall newcomer whirled around, startled. Eyes flashing, he peered at the nearing guards, hand tightening around the hilt of his sword.

"Stop staring and get back into your boat," shouted the same warrior again, hastening his step.

The young man's jaw tightened. "What's wrong with us landing here?" he asked in a slightly accented, Tepanec-sounding Nahuatl.

"Everything is wrong with you landing here." The warrior didn't bother to look at the young man, glaring at the owner of the boat, instead.

The fisherman looked up, pale and frightened. "I told them so, Honorable Warrior," he muttered, cringing under the stern gaze, while struggling to steady his vessel which bumped against the planks of the wharf. "But they wouldn't listen. The warrior did not want to wait in the queue."

The other youth rose to his feet, standing there easily, not perturbed by the vibrations of the boat.

"Oh, so the honorable visitors didn't want to wait." The guard turned back toward the first youth. "With this attitude you will not survive your visit here, foreigner. And now, get back to your boat before I have you sent for a swim."

Even from a distance, Itzcoatl could see the knuckles of the young warrior's hand whitening as it tightened around the hilt of his sword. For a moment, his eyes lingered on the beautiful carvings that covered its handle.

"You will end up in the water first, warrior," said the youth in a low voice. "Or, more likely, here, spilling your guts over these planks." The young man's eyes brushed over the rest of the group.

"Oh, you are done for, you filthy provincial," cried the leading guard out, tearing his sword from his girdle with a swift, powerful movement.

However, the youth's sword was out as promptly. Holding it with the ease of a man used to its weight, he took a step aside, obviously making sure his back was protected by the wall of a nearby warehouse.

"Kuini, don't!" The other youth leaped out of the boat, making it sway and almost topple. Hurriedly, he made his way toward the guards. "Wait, please," he said, catching his breath. "I think there is a misunderstanding here. This is our first visit in Tenochtitlan, and we have not been aware of certain customs of your *altepetl.*"

"Oh yes, that's obvious," muttered one of the warriors, but the fierce glance the young man shot at him made him quail.

Fascinated, Itzcoatl fought the urge to come closer. It would have been beneath his dignity to pay attention to a petty quarrel his warriors should have been able to take care of. Curtly, he gestured to his palanquin bearers.

"We apologize if we broke any law by landing on an inappropriate mooring," the young man went on, his voice level and well trained. "No offense was intended and no harm meant. Please, step aside and let us return to our boat."

Oh but this youth had learned oratory, and he had evidently used it before. Curious, Itzcoatl glanced back. How would one come to learn the subtleties of politeness without losing one's face?

The young man clearly expected to be obeyed, he realized, taking in the slender face and the Acolhua accented Nahuatl. A noble youth of Texcoco origins? No, there was nothing familiar in this face. This youth's companion, still pressed against the wall and ready to fight, looked more familiar, with his broad Tepanec face and the widely-spaced eyes. *Where had he seen a face like that before?*

Stepping into the lowered palanquin, Itzcoatl heard the leading guard growling, "Just leave these moorings at once." But the man's voice bore none of its previous mocking disdain.

Interesting, he thought, making himself comfortable upon the embroidered cushions. Since taking part in the conquest of Texcoco, he hadn't met Acolhua noblemen. Those who survived must have been keeping low, not traveling over the countryside, visiting all sorts of *altepetls.*

Who were those youths?

Sure enough, the imposing figure of the previous Chief Warlord leaned against the wooden stall in the shade of the large tree. Eating heartily, the old warrior conversed with the food stall's owner, obviously enjoying himself.

Ordering his palanquin bearers to stop, Itzcoatl got out, stretching in the warmth of the high spring sun. One of the worst complaints against his high position was this necessity to be carried around. A warrior of many summers, he liked to walk, reaching his destination faster than the swaying palanquin would allow.

"What an unusual pleasure! Greetings, Honorable Warlord." The stall owner smiled widely, unabashed. The cheeky commoner was used to high company, reflected Itzcoatl, slightly put out.

"It is, indeed, a pleasure," said the former Warlord, measuring Itzcoatl with the twinkling, slightly challenging gaze. "A rare one. The great leader's busy day does not leave much room for an idle pastime, I presume."

Following this man's leadership for almost half of twenty summers, fighting alongside him for the last few of them, Itzcoatl could not imagine that broad Tepanec face without the mischievous twinkle. Unless twisted with rage, of course. This man was a ruthless warrior and an authoritative leader, yet, the light humor was always there, bubbling near the surface, spilling out at the slightest provocation, or even without it.

"Well, no, it usually does not," he said, grinning. "Will you honor me by drinking a cup of *octli* with me?"

"Yes, of course." The tall man straightened up. "Bring us some food and a flask of *octli* to that table in the shadow," he said to the fascinated owner. "And make it the best of your stocks or your commoner's limbs will be the ones wrapped into your tortillas next time."

The food owner returned the challenging grin, unafraid. "Of course, Honorable Leader. My food and drinks are always of the best quality, as you know. I value my honorable customers' satisfaction above all." The man's squinted eyes flickered cheekily. "A man of your caliber would never honor my poor corner of the marketplace otherwise."

"Oh, don't push it, you cheeky frog eater," laughed the ex-Warlord, turning away and leading the way toward the mats spread under a tree.

"So," he said to Itzcoatl, squatting with an obvious relief. "To what do I owe this honor, oh busy Leader of the Warriors? Or was it that you just came here to sample the wonderful tortillas of the marketplace? They don't serve anything as delicious in the Palace these days."

Against his will, Itzcoatl smiled. "No, they don't serve a simple food in the Palace anymore. The amount of spices alone could make you fight for breath."

"The best spices from all over the Tepanec Empire, I presume."

"Oh yes, the very best."

Taking in the darkening face of his converser, Itzcoatl let his gaze wander, eyeing the warriors playing a bean game next to the nearby table. The ex-Warlord may have been a man with no title these days, but he still had many followers and aids ready to do his bidding.

"So, how are our warriors' forces? Giving you no trouble I trust. "

"Our warriors are as fierce, as warlike, as invincible as always." Returning his gaze to his companion, Itzcoatl studied the broad Tepanec face. "I was honored to receive a responsibility over the fiercest, the bravest, the best trained warriors around our Great Lake."

"Oh, yes. I was privileged to lead these men for countless summers." The older man's face softened. "Your revered father was a great man."

Itzcoatl shrugged. "I can barely remember him. He was too busy to pay attention to his illegitimate children."

"The responsibility for Tenochtitlan left its First Emperor no time to sleep," said the ex-Warlord somewhat defensively. "He had to ensure his legacy, while making sure this *altepetl* remained free and well, to enjoy the fruits of his work."

"And yet, we are losing our independence rapidly now."

The broad face darkened. "Yes, we are."

A pretty maid neared, balancing a large tray in her hands. Swift and delicate, she began serving their plates and cups, arranging them neatly on the crude surface of the low table. The stall owner lingered nearby, supervising her activity.

"How is our new emperor?" asked the former Warlord when both the girl and the man moved out of the hearing range.

"He is doing well." Pushing his irritation away, as always when being reminded of his half-nephew, the emperor-boy, Itzcoatl picked up his cup. "His mother is there, to give him advice when he needs it."

"Most of the time I suppose, given his tender age." The older warrior seemed as busy with his drink.

"Yes, of course."

"Luckily, she still thinks she needs you."

Itzcoatl felt the taste of the spicy beverage growing suddenly bitter. "Yes, she does."

"It won't last, you know that."

"Why not?"

The older man picked a tortilla. "What makes you so valuable also turns you into a threat. And you do have the necessary blood."

"My blood is of no consequence. My mother was not noble enough."

The twinkle was back in the large, widely spaced eyes; the twinkle and the challenge. "The blood is not the only thing that matters. What you have is more than enough."

Pushing his sudden excitement away, Itzcoatl forced a shrug. "I don't have such aspirations."

"Of course." The man's grin widened. "Yet, Tenochtitlan could do well with a strong, dedicated ruler of enough years and experience."

"Not according to the Empress."

"No, not according to her."

The silence hung, uncomfortably heavy this time.

"I made sure Tlacaelel, Huitzilihuitl's First Son, has moved out of the Palace, unobtrusively and unofficially, of course"

"Why is that?"

The old warrior shrugged. "Away from attention. Away from trouble. So the fate of his father will not fall upon him."

Itzcoatl felt his muscles tightening. "Nothing will happen to him. He is not important. He is nothing but a youth of what? Twenty summers? He doesn't merit your trouble, or anyone else's."

The grin of the former Warlord did not waver, but his large eyes darkened. "He is a born warrior and a talented youth. He is a threat, just like you are. But you can take care of yourself." Another shrug. "So what are the Empress's policies now?"

Itzcoatl frowned, not mistaking the suddenly light tone of his companion. "Nothing that contradicts her mighty father's policies."

"The tribute the Acolhua *altepetl* is paying must be of a great help."

"Yes, it is." The memory of the engineer surfaced. "It may even pay for our water construction, the one my half brother, Huitzilihuitl, was forced to forgo." He grinned. "The main engineer, a cheeky old bastard, had the gall of bringing this up, trying to make me hasten the process."

The older man's smile widened. "The main engineer? Oh, the old frog-eater would certainly love to build the water construction before it'll be his time to embark upon his journey through the Underworld. And he deserves this honor, too."

"This man received too many honors from my father and you. He doesn't know his place."

"Oh yes, the engineer was always an untamed beast. I made him a warrior once upon a time, when we were young." The brown eyes sparkled, their amusement spilling against Itzcoatl's gaping face. "He fought in quite a few campaigns, very well at that. But then your father made him go back to engineering. He thought the man could serve him better in that capacity." A fleeting smile flashed. "The Emperor turned out to be correct, as always."

Itzcoatl lifted his eyebrows. "Tenochtitlan must have been a strange place back in your days."

"Oh yes, it was." The amusement of the old warrior drained off. "Well, it could be a good thing, this water construction. I imagine the Empress will get the consent of the Tepanecs. There is no reason she should not, now that she's made Tenochtitlan behave." The man's cup made a hollow sound banging against the table. "Like the last of the unimportant provinces, fawning and groveling and hurrying to do as bidden. Ruining all that Revered Acamapichtli had done, reducing everything he had achieved into nothing!"

Yes, thought Itzcoatl, forcing himself to finish his drink, concentrating upon the burning sensation running down his throat. *This man is right. Our current Emperor is just a child, and his mother is the daughter of the mighty Tepanec ruler, who does not understand her Mexica subjects. But what one can do about it?*

He studied the furious face of his companion, taking in the sun-burned, weathered features. This man was one of Acamapichtli's most trusted leaders, serving the First Emperor loyally and faithfully, investing all his energy and immense willpower, pushing Tenochtitlan to become an *altepetl* that mattered.

Even under Huitzilihuitl, Acamapichtli's son, this man was trusted to carry on his policies, until his doubtful adventure in the Acolhua capital had created a breach between the Emperor and his Chief Warlord. The embarrassing incident faded in the stormy events that followed, with Acolhua forces beating the Tepanecs off, then invading their own lands, casting the Mexica capital into painful dilemmas. Yet, after some time, Tenochtitlan's Chief Warlord had resigned, pleading his advanced age and the failing health, but not before making the Emperor agree to his choice of successor for the important position, naming Itzcoatl, the illegitimate son of Acamapichtli and Huitzilihuitl's half brother, a good warrior and a promising leader, for the position.

Oh, I owe this man much, thought Itzcoatl, picking a tortilla, pleased with his own calmness in contrast to the agitated state of the old leader. *But I still don't know if I can trust him, if he means what he says. Should I go with his wild ideas of switching the government, or should I try to please the Empress and hope for the best?*

"Tenochtitlan is prospering," he said mildly. "It may be able to retain its independence, if it acts wisely."

"But it does not. It doesn't act wisely!" The older warrior ground his teeth. "We should have never joined the Tepanecs in the Acolhua War. We should have stayed neutral. As it was, our greediness made us lose a worthwhile ally. The tribute Texcoco is paying will bring us no good. In the long run, we will lose, just like the Acolhua people, but in the worst way. The Tepanecs conquered them, while us they will swallow slowly and painlessly."

For a while they drank in silence, watching the warriors as they cast their beans, joking about the figurines that were to be moved up the crude wooden board.

"Well, it's too late to regret it now," said Itzcoatl finally. "We are alone, and we cannot stand up to the mighty Tepanecs, now any more than we could under the rule of my father. Yet, we are stronger and much better off than we were then. Our situation is not that bad."

The dark eyes bore at him, reminding him of the raids under this man's leadership. Sometimes things would go wrong, despite the thorough planning and their leader's brilliant ability to find all sorts of unusual solutions to unexpected troubles, and then the warriors knew better than to cross this man's path.

"It suits you to see the pretty facade and nothing else, doesn't it? It feels safer, I'm sure."

Itzcoatl felt his own jaw tightening. "I'm accountable to no one save the Emperor these days." It came out calmly, and he marveled at the fact, feeling his insides shrinking from rage.

They glared at each other for one heartbeat, then another.

Finally, the older man shrugged. "Well, I suppose you are entitled to your opinions, Warlord," he said, resuming his eating. "When you are as old as I am you may understand better."

With an effort, Itzcoatl drained his cup, then placed it carefully on the table.

"I do understand you well," he said, calming down as always when the other side backed off. "Didn't we always understand each other?" He shrugged. "The untimely death of our Emperor set off a chain of events that none of us could have predicted or prevented. But I will always be of service to you, oh former Chief Warlord and the most trusted adviser of my revered father. I know where your loyalty has always been."

The older man grinned. Still immersed in his food, he seemed to sink into his thoughts, his expressionless voice ringing strangely, as if belonging to someone else. "We should be ready for the day the Acolhua people will rebel."

This time Itzcoatl's cup banged against the table. "The Acolhua will never rebel. The Tepanecs squashed them too thoroughly. I fought with them; I've seen what they have done. Texcoco will never again be an Acolhua capital. Even if their people have some spirit left, they have no one to lead them."

Back to his usual self, the older man nodded, eyes sparkling. "And this is exactly the problem that could be solved under favorable circumstances."

"How?"

"I'll tell you how in a due time." Ignoring Itzcoatl's glare, the former Warlord refilled both of their cups. "I'm going away for a market interval or so. Upon my return I will seek your company." The man's large brown palms rested on the table as he leaned forward, his gaze dark, penetrating. "If you have greater ambition than being just a first-rank leader, you will have to commit yourself, Chief Warlord. You will have to choose your side."

"And what side are you on, besides your own these days?"

The older man grinned, not taking offense. "My own side is not very interesting these days. Awaiting one's own start of the journey through the Underworld is a boring thing, and I want to see the fruits of your father's, and my own hard work coming to life before it happens." The thick eyebrows lifted in their turn. "You, on the other hand, have much to gain from those last activities of mine. So make up your mind before my return."

"I daresay I should not inquire to the nature of your destination."

"Yes, I suppose it is nothing you would want to hear about. One needs to clean one's head sometimes, and the mountainous air of the eastern shores will do nothing but good to my failing health."

The mountainous air? wondered Itzcoatl, returning to his food. *Is he going into the dubious highland areas again?* The impossible old man had strange family connections in the lands of the savages, or so the rumor had it, and it would be so much like him to concoct his wild schemes, calling on all sorts of unexpected help.

Do I trust him or don't I? he asked himself painfully. *And do I tell him about the last, most tempting offer of the Empress?*

CHAPTER 2

Iztac stared at the Chief Warlord, wide-eyed. Safe in doing so, she didn't try to conceal her interest, forgotten in the vastness of the reception hall. She had a bad feeling this morning, forced into her best clothes, crowned with the uncomfortably heavy headdress, yet the feeling dispersed when she was brought into the main hall. The matter seemed to have nothing to do with her. Promptly forgotten, she began looking around with a genuine interest.

Suppressing a grin, she remembered herself as a young girl, sneaking into the main hall where her father would receive all sorts of delegations before the war with the Tepanecs broke. She had to disguise herself as a maid, thrilled by the sense of danger, by the feeling of adventure. Coyotl had been so agitated, catching her doing this. And it was not that she was overly interested in politics. She was just bored.

Yet now, here she was, sitting in another reception hall, beautifully dressed and formally invited. Or, maybe, forced to attend. She didn't know for sure. Since the death of the Emperor, five seasons ago, her days passed in complete boredom, stuck with a bunch of silly women, the other minor wives, devoid of any interesting company, even that of Chimal. She missed him, her playmate of two summers, the cute little boy, almost a younger brother, now an official Emperor.

How could they elevate a child into the Emperor's chair? she asked herself again and again. But, of course. She knew the answer to that; knew who was ruling Tenochtitlan now, knew who made the Aztecs join the Tepanecs against *her* Texcoco, sending hordes of those fierce warriors into the Lowlands, to defeat her people. Oh, this woman was an abomination! She should have died instead of Huitzilihuitl.

It was more difficult to force her thoughts off the hideous events that followed the death of the Emperor, with the Tepanecs and their throng of allies, even their enemies from Lake Chalco, washing Texcoco shores like a lethal wave, relentless, unstoppable, deviously cunning. Through the days that followed, she had heard all about it, the way the Tepanecs had tricked her people into thinking they would attack in the north, sending only a part of their forces there, but launching their main attack from the south, catching the Acolhua people oh-so-terribly unprepared, taking their towns and villages like ripe fruits. Texcoco was conquered shortly thereafter, but all she could think about was Coyotl. Was he still walking among the living? Her father, the Acolhua Emperor, was dead, but no one seemed to know what happened to his heir. Coyotl seemed to disappear from the surface of the Fifth World, but not in any traditional way.

She felt her beautifully polished nails sinking into the flesh of her palms. It helped to divert her thoughts, to forget that now her beautifully noble Texcoco was given as a tributary to none other than Tenochtitlan. What a farce! The Tepanecs didn't even want the *altepetl* itself. They took a few of the provinces and gave Texcoco away, to reward the Aztecs, who had finally decided to behave. Oh, those people were beyond contempt, all of them, the Tepanecs and the Aztecs alike.

Returning her gaze to the Chief Warlord, she winced. The imposing man was watching her. Previously, he had sat on his reed chair, comfortable and at ease, looking at the Emperor patiently and good naturedly, like a man would look upon a boy. Well, Chimalpapoca *was* a boy, but he was also an Emperor now, crowned with the emperor's headdress and anointed with divine ointment.

Yet, now the young Emperor was talking, but the narrow eyes of the Chief Warlord rested upon her, with that same expression of patience and mild interest of a person who would rather spend his time elsewhere, doing more important things.

Oh gods! She shivered, for upon meeting her gaze, the eyes of the man flickered, and his lips twisted into a hint of a grin, an amused, suggestive sort of a grin. It was as if he were already familiar with her, as if they had already shared something.

Dropping her gaze, she clasped her hands together tightly. Having never met the man, she knew, of course, who he was. Itzcoatl, Acamapichtli's illegitimate son, one of many, sired by the Emperor's concubine, a slave woman acquired on the markets of Azcapotzalco. Oh, how vile! The fruitful slave had bore the Emperor enough children to survive into adulthood, two of them so prominent and able that the royal house could do nothing but accept them, both exceptionally good warriors and leaders. And now, here was one of them, sitting in front of the new Emperor, looking at him with an impudent amusement, staring at her, the previous Emperor's Second Wife and Acolhua First Princess, like a man would stare at a pretty girl on the marketplace.

"We would need to expand our fleets," she heard the man saying, looking back at Chimal once again. "Now that we are a power to be reckoned with, we should strengthen our shore defenses and our power on the water."

"Who would dare to attack us?" asked the Emperor's mother, not bothering to glance at her son.

The boy's gaze flew at her, expectant and somewhat frustrated, and Iztac's heart squeezed. He should not be here, she knew. He should be playing about and going to school with other boys. He was too young to be concerned with these things. However, what haunted her most was the fact that he took his responsibilities seriously, trying very hard to do what was right, to be a good Emperor, but his mother did not appreciate that, brushing his efforts aside and ruling Tenochtitlan all by herself. He was a necessary decoration, a facade.

"No one would dare to attack the faithful allies of the mighty Tepanec Empire, Revered Empress," said the Chief Warlord smoothly. "Still, a large altepetl such as ours should be prepared for any eventuality." He paused, looking at her sincerely. "The tribute Texcoco is paying would cover the cost. They had been prompt in their payments so far."

"The long boats?"

"Yes, Revered Empress. Twenty more of the large canoes would see Tenochtitlan suitably protected."

Iztac listened, now genuinely interested. She had never seen those ships, but she had heard about them. Half twenty of men could sail in those canoes comfortably. It could carry considerable weights, even building materials for the pyramids and the temples. Chimal had told her all about it when they'd managed to meet briefly, some market intervals ago. He had toured the wharves and came back greatly impressed. He said those canoes were so long, one could go from one edge to another spending twenty or more paces. She had had a hard time believing him.

"There is another matter," The Warlord was saying, addressing the Empress, seeking her gaze under the shade of the imposing headdress. "Tenochtitlan needs fresh water. Our late Revered Emperor chose wisely not to engage in such undertaking. The costs were prohibitive. However now, with the flow of the tribute coming from the Acolhua *altepetl*, we may consider building a construction to bring fresh water from the springs of the main land."

The Empress's contemplative gaze rested upon the thickset warrior.

"But how can we build something like that?" exclaimed Chimal, almost jumping from his throne, his excitement spilling.

"Chimalpapoca!" said the Empress curtly, not bothering to turn her head, and the boy sank back onto his chair, shoulders hunched, face falling.

The woman still watched the Warlord. "The advisers were not happy with this project when it was proposed for the first time."

"They maintained the cost was too high, Revered Empress," answered the Warlord calmly. "But the circumstances have changed. Now we have Acolhua tribute to rely upon." A hint of a smile stretched the thin lips as the eyes of the man deepened, clouded, turned unreadable. "Many circumstances have changed. Our Emperor. Our relationship with Azcapotzalco."

The Empress narrowed her eyes. "You are bold, Chief Warlord," she said, but a tiny smile played upon her lips now.

"I apologize if I angered you, Revered Empress." The man

returned her smile, not afraid in the least.

Of course, thought Iztac, biting her lips, rigid with fury. Tenochtitlan could do no wrong since their active participation in the conquest of Texcoco. The favorite tributary of the Tepanecs, ruled by the grandson of Tezozomoc himself. How vile! She ground her teeth.

The Warlord was getting to his feet, bidden to leave the revered presence. She watched him, a widely built man of, perhaps, two times twenty of summers, his broad back straight, his calves well developed, face sunburned, confident, radiating power and well-being. He reminded her of that Aztec Warlord who had come visiting Texcoco three summers ago. Arrogant and sure of himself, the master of the world. So certain of the impunity belonging to his high status that he had dared to take a boy being led to the court of a lawful Emperor, just because he felt like doing it.

Her stomach twisted again. He had saved *him*, only to take him away from her afterward. Was he still alive, that wild Highlander, who would steal hot tortillas to make her happy and who would kiss and make love to her in the most wonderful of ways?

Deep in her reverie, she looked up, and her heart missed a beat. The Warlord slowed his paces and stood in front of her, measuring her with that same amusedly appreciative gaze.

"So this is the exalted Tepanec princess?" he asked, smiling into her eyes. "I'm so happy to meet you at last, oh Honorable Second Wife of our late Emperor."

The exalted Tepanec princess? She stared at him, speechless, unable to think, her stomach hollow, heart making wild leaps inside her chest.

"Yes, this is our pretty Iztac Ayotl, the granddaughter of the mighty Tezozomoc," she heard the Empress saying. "A good Tepanec blood is flowing in her veins, sprinkled by the Toltec and Acolhua additions aplenty."

"Oh, what an honor," said the Warlord, but his eyes did not reflect a flicker of reverence, a spark of adoration. Instead, they measured her openly, satisfied as if she were a piece of merchandise the man had acquired, not displeased with the high cost.

She swallowed.

"I most sincerely hope to come to know you better, Honorable Princess," he went on, unabashed. "It would be a delightful experience."

His paces rang hollowly on the polished stone floor as he went away, leaving the spacious hall, determined and full of purpose, the way the warriors always walked.

Iztac blinked, trying to make her mind work, until her gaze brushed by Chimal, startled by the unconcealed rage that now twisted the boy's gentle features.

The Empress rose to her feet. "Come with me, Iztac Ayotl," she said, calm and unperturbed, strolling toward the main entrance, her maids trailing behind. She glanced at her son. "Stay here. The advisers were sent for, along with the elders of the districts. I'll be back with you in a short while."

Iztac got to her feet with difficulty, her fear overwhelming. That woman had never addressed her by name. The times the Empress had deigned to talk to her could be counted on the fingers of one hand. Her limbs stiff, stomach twisting, she followed into the brilliance of the daylight, down the polished stairs and along the well-swept paths of the gardens below.

"Well, Acolhua princess," said the Empress. "It has been a long time since we had a private conversation, has it not?" She picked a flower and sniffed it idly, not put out with the lack of response as it seemed. "How much time has passed? Three summers? Oh, so many things have changed since the day you arrived here." The full lips twisted in the hint of a smile. "I remember this day well. My father was about to conquer your pitiful *altepetl*, but your people surprised him. Oh, they did." A shrug. "Yet, here we are, with your Texcoco conquered nevertheless, paying a heavy tribute to Tenochtitlan, of all places; their emperor dead, their lands subdued."

As always, it had an effect. Iztac clenched her fists. "It took the Tepanecs two summers to do it, and my people were betrayed!"

"Betrayed by whom? By the Mexica Aztecs, you mean? Are you criticizing Tenochtitlan's Emperor?" It came out openly amused.

Iztac said nothing, too enraged to try to cover her slip.

"They say the heir to Texcoco throne may still be alive," went on the Empress, conversational. "Some say he had fled as far as the Highlands. I hope those rumors are not true, although it would be amusing to think of the Acolhua emperor-to-be living with the savages."

The woman went on, spilling more venom, but Iztac did not hear any of it. *Coyotl might be alive and in the Highlands.* Oh gods! The Highlands? Why would he go there? Why would he venture into the heart of the Acolhua enemies, unless... She bit her lower lip, afraid to believe it just yet.

"Well, enough gossiping about your people, Iztac Ayotl," concluded the woman. "You were lucky to find yourself here, in Tenochtitlan. You belong to this royal house now. A good turn for you." A brief nod of the royal head concluded the tirade. "You'll be given to our new Chief Warlord on the day of the Flaying Festival. He is eager to have a princess of such an exalted bloodline. He will agree to do many things to achieve that honor. He'll serve my son more loyally, thanks to you." The woman stopped, turned around, threw the flower away. "Your Acolhua blood is not as precious these days, but your Tepanec side makes up for this lack. The granddaughter of the mighty Tezozomoc. Oh, both your bloodlines are impeccable."

Unable to breath, Iztac stared into the broad, well-kept face, taking in every crease, every spot, every cavity where the yellow powder had been applied less carefully. Or maybe the paint was just running in the high-noon heat.

The large, speckled eyes returned her gaze coldly. "Don't stare at me like that, girl. You will do it. You have nothing else to do and nowhere to go."

"I won't. I won't do it." It came out hoarsely. She found it difficult to recognize her own voice.

"Of course you will." The eyes of the woman grew colder. "And don't threaten to take your own life, the way you did on our first encounter. You have no strength to do this. You have some spirit, but you are not a strong woman." The Empress shrugged, resuming her walk back toward the Palace. "When you think of it, Itzcoatl is not so much beneath you. He is the son of the First Emperor himself. Born to the slave concubine, I must admit, but the son of Tenochtitlan's First Emperor nevertheless, a half-brother of your previous husband. And who knows? Maybe it's better to be the Chief Wife of the Honorable Warlord with royal blood, then one of the minor wives to the mighty Emperor. You may like this diversion, girl."

Her cloak swayed calmly as the Empress mounted the stairs once again. "Don't follow me. Go. Go to the minor wives quarters and think how nice it would be to have a set of rooms of your own."

It took a long time for nightfall to come. Iztac paced the terrace, watching the setting sun, willing it to sink faster. Just to spite her, it stuck above the trees at the western part of the gardens, refusing to move. To glance at it over and over didn't help. She had been pacing this terrace since the early afternoon, since the moment she had come back from that hideous interview with the Empress.

"Iztac-Ayotl, why don't you come in?"

She didn't halt, didn't turn around, recognizing the voice of Ihuitl, one of her fellow minor wives, a princess of Cuauhnahuac. There used to be four of them here, sharing the spacious quarters and the Emperor's infrequent favors, with more minor wives located elsewhere. Yet, since Huitzilihuitl's death, there were only three of them left, with the fourth woman given away only a few market intervals ago, married off to the ruler of this or that province.

"Come, sister. You've been pacing this terrace for ages now. It's annoying. Come on in."

"Leave me alone," said Iztac, not slowing her pace.

The young woman muttered something and went in. She was actually a nice little thing, sweet and not malicious. Unlike the other woman, the one who had been given away. Iztac frowned, remembering the viciousness of their verbal fights. The stupid woman hated her, the haughty Acolhua princess with no finesse, was the way she would put it, ready to inform her, Iztac, and the whole world of her feelings and opinions. That is, until one day Iztac just kicked the annoying *cihua*, pushing her so hard that the woman fell over a reed podium, wrecking the whole thing. The incident had silenced the mealy-mouthed gossiper for moons. If she still shared her thoughts regarding Acolhua royalty among the Emperor's wives, she was careful not to do so in her, Iztac's, presence.

Acolhua princess, thought Iztac bitterly. *A Tepanec princess now, curse their eyes.* But this was just too much. She would not play along nicely. Not this time. She was given away once and it was one time too many. Had only that highlander boy kept his promise! She clutched her fists tight, fighting the welling tears. No, she wouldn't think of him. Whether he was dead or alive, it was of no consequence to her. And the same went for Coyotl, she knew, blinking the tears away. Whatever happened, she would never see either of them again.

The sun had long since disappeared, and she slowed her agitated pacing and listened. The muffled voices reached her. No, of course both of the silly women were still wide awake, chattering, immersed in their meaningless conversations. *Oh gods, let them fall asleep quickly.*

By the time the Palace went quiet, Iztac's nerves were as taut as an overstretched bowstring. Forcing her thoughts to relax, she measured the dark midnight sky with a glance, then listened carefully. Not a sound. Peeking inside, she eyed the sleeping women, watching their blankets as they rose and fell, then listened to the darkness below.

It took her no time to tuck her skirt into her girdle, then to tie her sandals to it. Taking a good grip of the railing, she went over it, pleased with how easy it came back to her. She hadn't climbed walls for all eternity it seemed.

Carefully, she sought out the ledge, having enough time to study this wall in daylight, waiting for the sun to disappear and for the silly women to calm down. The gardens waited below, quiet and deserted, still she made her way carefully, keeping away from the moonlit patches of the open earth, not venturing out until she'd reached the other wing of the Palace.

Scanning the open shutters of the second floor, she tried to calculate which windows belonged to the Emperor's quarters. She had visited those rooms so rarely, and not via climbing walls.

Eyeing the moonlit terrace, she remembered passing it on her way to visit her previous master, recollecting how the urge to run out would well up every time. She bit her lips and banished the unwelcome memories.

Well, if the terrace was there, then the Emperor's quarters should be to its left, two or three shutters removed. A cold sweat covered her back at the thought of climbing into the wrong opening, stumbling into the Empress's quarters, instead. Taking a deep breath, she crossed the open ground, her paces light, satisfactory soundless.

This wall was even easier to climb, the moon shining strongly, lighting this side of the Palace. She prayed no one would pass by. Breathing heavily, she clung to the bulging stones. Yes, those were the Emperor's quarters all right. She slid in and stood there for a while, catching her breath, eyeing Chimal's muffled form as he slept snugly, buried in a pile of blankets and pretty cushions, curled into a ball, one hand tucked under his cheek, the other shielding his eyes. She watched him for a while, smiling. He was such a spoiled baby. Who would sleep with so many cushions?

"Chimal, wake up," she whispered, kneeling beside him and shaking his shoulder.

He murmured and tried to bury his head deeper under his palm.

"Wake up." She shook him harder. "I need to talk to you."

His eyes opened, but he didn't jump up the way she would have. He just lay there, staring at her, eyes so wide-open she thought they might pop out of their sockets.

"Iztac-Ayotl!" he cried out, and she shut his mouth with her palm, frightened.

"Hush," she gasped, then moderated her tone. "Don't scream. You'll bring the whole Palace here."

He squirmed free from under her palm and sat upright, wide awake now.

"What are you doing here?" he breathed, his small, pleasant face a mask of astonishment.

"I need to talk to you."

"About what?"

"Something very important. You have to help me. I need your help."

His eyes grew larger. "To do what?"

"Your mother wants to give me away to Itzcoatl, your Chief Warlord." Pursing her lips, she took a deep breath. "I won't have it. I need you to prevent that."

His face twisted, fell. "Yes, I know."

She gasped. "How long have you known?"

He dropped his gaze. "A few dawns. Maybe a market interval."

"And you didn't tell me?" Having difficulty containing the suddenness of her rage, she clasped her palms tight.

His gaze flew at her, frightened, imploring. "How could I tell you? I never see you. We never meet anymore. I'm not allowed—"

"You are the Emperor," she interrupted angrily. "Emperors can do whatever they like. They don't act like frightened little boys."

The eyes peering at her filled with tears, and her heart squeezed.

"Well, I'm not saying that you are a frightened little boy," she said, trying to calm down. "But you have to let them know that. They are treating you like a boy, but you are the Emperor of Tenochtitlan. They can't tell you what to do all the time." She frowned. "This morning I wanted to punch them, the way they looked at you, the way they interrupted you all the time. Your mother and that filthy commoner warlord, too."

"He is no commoner," he said, biting his lips. "He is my uncle."

"Who said so?"

He dropped his gaze. "My mother."

"He is not your uncle. He was your father's *illegitimate* half-brother, having a slave for a mother. He can't treat you like an annoying boy. But he did this. He did!"

He shifted uneasily. "My mother knows what to do. She says I have to learn a lot, and until then I'm to listen and not to talk."

Oh, she could just kill the vile woman!

"Well, your mother knows her way around politics, and you should listen to her. But not all the time. You are the Emperor. Not her."

He began looking relieved. "You are not angry with me, Iztac Ayotl?" he asked, looking at her searchingly.

"No." She fought a smile. "Well, maybe just a little. But mainly I'm angry with them."

"My mother?" he gasped, appalled.

"Yes, but don't tell her." She winked. "She won't take it kindly."

"No, of course I won't tell!"

She grinned. "And I'm angry with your precious new warlord, too. He didn't show you proper respect." She snorted. "Some uncle!"

That made him giggle. "You are wild, Iztac Ayotl." He looked up at her curiously. "And you are scratched and covered with dust. What did you do?"

She eyed her reddish, dirty palms, then shrugged. "I climbed here, you silly boy. Do you think we would be talking here in peace and quiet if I tried to come in, passing all your guards and servants?"

His eyes grew to enormous proportions. "You climbed here? But it's so high!"

"It's not that high."

He jumped to his feet and ran toward the window. "You have to show me how you did this!" he cried out, then shut his mouth with his hands and listened attentively.

She came over and listened, too. Nothing, save a slight breeze, interrupted the darkness.

"I'll show you on my way out," she whispered, relaxing. "But not before you promise not to let them give me away."

He grabbed her arm. "Don't go. Not yet."

"I have to. Before someone notices."

"Please stay. Only for a little while. Please!"

She shook her head, amused. "Well, only for a little while." Warmed by the openness of his joy and relief, she smiled. "And maybe I'll come again, from time to time. What do you say?"

"Oh, yes! And you will teach me to climb walls, too."

"Well, it would be difficult. We would need it to be broad daylight for that." She frowned. "And anyway, the first thing is to make sure I'm not given to that *uncle* of yours."

"I will, I will make sure of that," he said ardently. "I will not let them give you away."

"What will you do?"

"I'll think of something. I promise." He shifted his gaze. "I'll be allowed to take a wife when I've seen fifteen summers. It's less than two summers away."

"Yes, not a long time to wait. But why would you want this? It's no joy."

His gaze was firm on the polished tiles of the floor. "I'll take you to be my Chief Wife."

She could not hide her smile. "I'm too old for you. I've seen almost twenty summers."

He straightened up angrily. "No, you are not. I counted and you've seen only seventeen, maybe eighteen, summers."

"Eighteen. I was born on the year of One Rabbit."

He studied the floor tiles. "It's not so many summers apart. I'll be old enough for you in a short time." His voice shook. "Why wouldn't you want this?"

She listened to the wind rustling in the bushes. "I don't know, Chimalpopoca. I suppose it could be a good idea. I'm not sure your mother would have it, though. And anyway, it's a long time to think about it now."

Watching the dark trees of the gardens, she suppressed a shrug. He was a nice boy. Kind and sweet, and good-natured, just like his father. He would make a good Emperor once he broke free from his mother's clutches. But was it possible? The power-hungry woman would never let him rule independently. There were rumors maintaining that she had hastened the death of this boy's father because the Emperor had planned to change his policies against his Empress's better judgment.

Iztac shuddered. Oh, she could believe these rumors, oh yes. This woman could do anything. And yet, they were in her power now, Chimal and her, as well as the rest of the Palace, the whole of Tenochtitlan ruled by Tezozomoc's daughter. How ridiculous.

"Well," she said, shaking her uneasiness off. "We'll see about that, eh? When you are older." Swinging her leg over the windowsill, she suddenly felt uncomfortable to pull her skirt up under his heavy gaze. "I'll come again, I promise. Once in a market interval, and I hope we won't get caught."

His eyes flashed at her out of the darkness. "Don't forget. You promised."

She heard the urgency in his voice and again the thought that he was growing made her uneasy. Working her way down the wall, uncomfortable with the edges of her long, fluttering skirt, she decided that it might be, actually, not such a bad idea. The Chief Wife of the Emperor. Oh, they could rule Tenochtitlan together, come to think of it.

CHAPTER 3

Kuini watched the warrior, who stood leaning against the cold stones of the Great Pyramid, enjoying its shade. Immersed in his conversation with two other warriors, the young man's eyes kept darting around as if making sure he was not being watched, and this was precisely what drew Kuini's attention. This, and the youth's way of holding himself, simply but still somewhat royally, with this imperceptive light dignity Coyotl always seemed to radiate.

A group of people that looked like commoners with their dusted cloaks and rather carelessly tied hair, stood in the sun, immersed in their own conversation, but Kuini had long since noticed the careful side-glances the two of them kept stealing at the young warrior's back. Amused, he watched the bulging under their cloaks. Those people carried clubs, he knew, but were careful to conceal them. Interesting.

With the clamor of the Central Plaza raging all around, Kuini shifted his gaze back to the Great Pyramid. Some pyramid, he thought disdainfully, remembering the beautiful constructions of Texcoco, with their stone or even marble stairs and the glittering temples atop of them. Tenochtitlan's Great Pyramid had two temples, but those were not as impressive, and the pyramid itself was lower and generally not as polished. As for the Plaza? The large square was a mess of activity with not a hint of the aristocratic, delicate beauty of the Acolhua capital. No, this *altepetl* seemed to be too busy to bother with appearances.

Shrugging, Kuini wiped the sweat off his forehead. Tenochtitlan disappointed him greatly. Only this morning they

had sailed the Great Lake against the rising sun, nearing the
island-city from the east, watching it rising from the dawn's mists,
bright and cheerful, with traces of smoke curling everywhere and
the silhouette of the Great Pyramid dominating the sky, casting
the distant shore's hills into complete insignificance.

The incident with the warriors on the wrong wharf fading, he
had watched the still-angry fisherman navigating their canoe into
the wide canal, maneuvering it skillfully in the queue of many
other boats, halting patiently every now and then, waiting for the
wooden partitions of the bridges to be removed. Glad to be able to
reach the dry land at last, they had paid the man with a pelt and a
necklace – the previously agreed upon price – and watched him
sailing away, still muttering bitterly.

He remembered glancing at Coyotl, seeing the set expression of
the pleasant face. Still tense from the previous encounter, the
Acolhua nobleman seemed to be impressed, but mostly with the
businesslike air of the place, reflected Kuini, proceeding down the
wide road, the damp scent of the canal haunting his nostrils.
People rushed all around them, hurrying up the wide roads,
sometimes halting to converse with those sailing along. A floating
city!

He recalled Dehe, tense and hardly breathing, hurrying by his
side, clutching to his arm, hurting it with the desperation of her
grip. He didn't want her coming along. The girl was better off
staying in the Highlands, settled in this or that village. She had
nothing to do in Tenochtitlan but to be a burden, an additional
aspect of distraction.

However, the easy-going, anxious-to-please little thing Kuini
had grown to like through his last days in Huexotzinco seemed to
disappear, leaving behind the adamant *cihua* who had flatly
refused to be escorted anywhere, protesting her helpfulness, not
above reminding them that without her aid Coyotl might have
been making his way through the Underworld in those very
moments.

Well, she might have been right about that, he thought,
shrugging, remembering the day they had fled Huexotzinco, with
Coyotl's forehead still wide open and his arm beginning to swell,

hardly able to walk or talk coherently. Luckily, the girl had waited for them, ready with ointments and brews to make him cool. Somehow, she knew what the trouble was without a need for an explanation. Brisk and sure of herself, she had led them away through the trails even Kuini found difficult to recognize, finding a good place with another brook and another cave to spend some days there until Coyotl felt better thanks to her smelly, bitter-tasting brews.

Oh yes, the Lowlander might have died without her, Kuini was forced to admit, and so he could not argue too forcefully. It was either banish her brutally or take her along, and so here she was, clinging to him with the force her thin, fragile hands did not warrant, afraid to breathe, as it seemed. Oh but he should have been more insistent about making her stay in the Highlands.

Then, upon leaving the wharves, their disappointment grew. Tenochtitlan stretched ahead, clusters upon clusters of wooden warehouses and dusty roads and alleys, swarming with people. The persistent scent of the lake enveloped them, penetrating their nostrils with its swamp-like odor. The Great Pyramid towered to their west, swimming in the damp, misty air. They exchanged glances. That's not how they imagined the beautiful island-city of Acamapichtli.

"I suppose now we go looking for that uncle of yours," said Coyotl, shifting his weight from one foot to the other.

"Yes, I suppose so."

It took them some time to find their way out of the busy wharves areas, wandering around, reluctant to ask questions, afraid to attract attention. Dressed like youths from provinces, simple warriors with plain cloaks and daggers, they were not supposed to draw glances, still their swords was an oddity in provincial warriors, setting them apart from the crowds, making them uneasy.

And then, another disappointment. Locating the spacious dwelling of the former Chief Warlord hadn't helped. The sturdy slave guarding the gates refused to let the strange, dust-covered trio enter. No amount of reasonable talk, or even threatening, helped. The Honorable Leader was out, and no word could be sent to him.

"Then we'll just sit here in front of that gate until he comes in, and then you'll see how pissed he will be with you," growled Kuini.

"Then I'll call for his warriors, and they'll beat you senseless before throwing you away from that gate," said the guard, unimpressed.

"You just try to do that!" hissed Kuini, moving closer.

"Listen, why can't you just send a word to his main servant?" asked Coyotl, pushing himself between them. "It would be easy enough to do that, and he may know about us. Your Honorable Master is expecting us. He did invite us to come to Tenochtitlan in the first place."

More threats and reasonable arguments were exchanged before the main steward was called for. By then, Kuini felt like either killing someone or going away. Tenochtitlan's people, even its slaves, were incurable snobs. He began missing his mountains. Even the conquered Lowlands seemed like a better place to spend one's time around, now.

However, the main servant turned out to be more reasonable. Impressed with Coyotl's way with words, sensing someone of importance, the stocky man had allowed them to come in and even ordered food and a bath, to let them refresh themselves. Yet, he was quick to inform them that the Master was not in Tenochtitlan at the present, and he was not expected to return before the next market day or so. They would have to go away and come back then.

And so now, here they were, fed and clean, but with no place to stay in a completely strange *altepetl*, with Coyotl still recovering from his wounds and the sickness that had followed and the girl scared beyond any reason, curse the restless old bastard of Tenochtitlan's former Warlord into the first level of the Underworld.

Leaving Coyotl and the girl to rest back by the wharves, Kuini wandered the Plaza, trying to think. Should they leave the dangerous, unfriendly city and come back in a market interval? he asked himself, still watching the young warrior, who by that time had turned around and strolled away, deep in thought. The people with hidden clubs tensed and ceased talking, he noticed, trying to watch without being too obvious about it.

Was his father right about this *altepetl*? he wondered. Was it truly the place to start preparing the Acolhua uprising? It didn't seem that way. Tenochtitlan seemed too busy, too full of itself.

The thought of his father sent a familiar wave of anxiety down his spine. It had been almost half a moon since they'd left, and he had no way of knowing what happened in Huexotzinco ever since. Was his father still the Warriors' Leader, or was he forced to leave his position because of what he had done? Without the powerful presence of this formidable man, without his forceful arguments, Kuini could not help but see their deed in the true light, understanding that they had just fled, with the powerful man's active help and against the clearly expressed wish of the town council. *Oh mighty Camaxtli*, he thought, turning to walk back toward the wharves. *Please keep him safe.*

Deep in his reverie, he didn't notice going around the corner of a square building until he bumped into the same tall warrior he had watched earlier, walking busily back toward the Plaza.

"Watch where you are going!" growled the young man. He was about the same age, maybe a summer or two older than Kuini, broadly built and imposing.

"You watch it," said Kuini without thinking. Trying to make his mind work, he stared at the broad face and did not move when the warrior stepped closer.

"You *are* looking for a good beating, aren't you?" The deeply set eyes measured him, sparkling with rage.

"No. I'm looking for you to move your fat carcass and let me pass." He watched the warrior's hands clenching into fists, knowing he should swallow his pride and walk away. Only half a day in this hostile *altepetl* and he was being challenged for the second time.

"You dirty piece of dung! If you don't go away now, I swear I'll beat you senseless before killing you."

"Right here it would make quite a show," said Kuini, feeling better by the moment, despite his misgivings. "Why don't we go somewhere quieter?"

The warrior drew a deep breath, visibly trying to calm down. "All right. Wait for me behind the Tlaloc's temple, by the wall that is facing the marketplace."

Kuini shrugged. "I don't know where your marketplace is, and I have no time to wait. Either we go there now or you can run about your business. I have things to do."

"So do I, you cheeky foreigner. I wish I could kill you right now."

"Then let us go behind that temple of yours."

The warrior hesitated, his deeply set eyes measuring Kuini once again. "Follow me," he said curtly as a leader would to his warriors.

"Keep your orders to yourself. I'm coming with you, but I'm not following you!"

"Oh, I'll take great pleasure in killing you, you know? This city can do without uncouth foreigners."

Now it was Kuini's turn to clench his fists. "Maybe I won't wait to get to your quiet place. Maybe I will kill you right here and now, the way uncouth foreigners do."

"You wish!" Turning into a small alley, the young man hastened his steps. "Luckily, it would be just on my way. I will have to kill you in a hurry, though."

"Me too," said Kuini, watching his surroundings. He remembered losing his way on Texcoco marketplace three summers ago. "I should have told my friend that I'm going, but I suppose I can send you onwards and be back before he starts looking for me."

"He'll be looking for you in vain in a short while."

"Your chances to reach your destination are slim, anyway. Even should I decide to spare you, there are those people with clubs that seem to be as put out with you running around."

"What?" The young man halted so abruptly his sandals made a screeching sound upon the dusty pavement.

Kuini paid him no attention, but when the rough palm grabbed his arm, he shook it off violently.

"What people with clubs?" The youth didn't seem to notice,

glaring at Kuini, suddenly agitated and not as arrogant as before.

"Some people. Not warriors."

"Where are they?"

"And how, in the name of the Underworld, should I know?" Pleased with this unexpected reaction, Kuini allowed his grin to show. "I will kill you before they have their chance, anyway."

This made the youth snap back in control. "Let us get over with it," he said, resuming his walk.

For a few heartbeats they proceeded in silence.

"Not warriors you are saying?" asked the young man as they turned into another alley.

"No, not warriors. No topknots and no cotton cloaks." Kuini frowned. "But they did have clubs, and they did stare at you, so don't feel too good about it yet."

"Why were you watching me?"

"I was curious and this ugly *altepetl* of yours has nothing better to offer."

"Oh, you dirty piece of dung. I bet your Azcapotzalco is nothing but a pit full of excrement."

"I'm not from Azcapotzalco, but I've seen this *altepetl*. It's twenty times more dignified than this place. And the same goes for Texcoco."

"Oh, those losers. I bet the Acolhua *altepetl* looks pretty pitiful these days."

They rounded another corner, passing by a group of warriors with spotted cloaks. Uncomfortable with their open scrutiny, Kuini pressed his lips, remembering his misadventures three summers ago. Why did the damn Aztec Warlord, this uncle of his, go away in such a hurry, and where? His stomach shrunk at the sudden thought. Father! Father seemed to know the goings on in Tenochtitlan. Had the Warlord went to visit his brother in the Highlands?

"Almost there." Suddenly, the youth halted, glaring at Kuini, his eyes narrowing. "How do I know you are not leading me straight into the trap of those commoners with the clubs? How do I know you are not with them?"

Glancing at the broad palm tightening around the sword's hilt, still tied to the richly decorated girdle, Kuini glared back, now perturbed. The spotted cloaks were still in sight, and he could feel their curious gazes.

"I don't need other people to help me kill someone," he said, trying to sound lighter than he felt. "I'm not with those manure-eaters."

But the eyes of his rival flickered victoriously, as if detecting Kuini's uneasiness. "Maybe I'll just ask those warriors to finish you off while I'm going about my business."

Kuini felt the knot in his stomach tightening. "Why would elite warriors want to do your dirty work for you?"

"Because I'm no commoner like you." The deeply set eyes sparkled. "Because the elite warriors are obliged to defend royal family."

Oh, he should have listened to his instincts and kept away. "You are no royal family," he said, reading the answer in the derisively glimmering gaze. The warriors' glances burned his skin.

Involuntarily, he took a step sideways, to be closer to the nearby wall so it would protect his back. Not that he had any chance against the spotted cloaks. Maybe one, but not all five of them, aided, no doubt, by the arrogant, ugly bastard of the royal family.

"What is going on?"

One of the warriors parted from the group. Unhurriedly, he came closer, his frown light, not direful, not yet. The silence prevailed, interrupted by the distant clamor of the marketplace coming from behind the high wall. Kuini's fingers moved as if having a life of their own, untying the strings fastening his sword to his girdle. How stupid, he thought, clenching his teeth. Would he never learn to avoid unnecessary fights?

"Well?" The warrior studied him, eyes narrowing, gaze wandering down the line of tattoos adorning his jaw line. "Who are you? What are you doing wandering Tenochtitlan with this sword?"

Kuini just shrugged, not attempting to hide the way his palm shifted its hold on the carved handle.

"Oh, you little piece of dirt," growled the warrior, still half amused. "You are wishing to die, aren't you?" The rest of the warriors laughed and drew closer.

Making sure his back was protected by the sharp stones – even the walls of that city were cold and unfriendly – Kuini did not bother to answer. What was there to say?

Taking a deep breath, he brought his sword forward, holding it with both hands now, preparing for the frontal attack. He could see their faces clearly, the sweat, the scars, the tattoos – their designs alien to him – the spotted pattern of their cloaks. They were elite warriors, and there were five times too many of them.

His arms went rigid the way he gripped the handle of his sword, feeling the carvings. The touch of them made him feel better. He forced his muscles to relax, his eyes following the first warrior as the man untied his sword slowly, unhurriedly, enjoying himself.

"He is with me." It came from the tall youth, who still stood where he was, watching impartially.

The warrior turned to him. "And who are you?"

The youth raised his eyebrows, unbearably arrogant all of a sudden. "I'm Tlacaelel, the late Emperor's First Son."

A fleeting silence prevailed once again as the warrior's face changed from a skeptical surprise to the apprehensively narrowing eyes. The rest of the group peered at them, all ears.

"Where are your slaves and your guarding warriors, Honorable First Son?" asked the warrior finally. "You should not walk the city unprotected."

"Of course," said Tlacaelel, unperturbed. "I'm heading back to the Palace now." Still unbearably arrogant, he turned to Kuini. "Come."

This time, Kuini followed without a word, welcoming his companion's annoyingly highhanded authority. The warrior seemed as if about to keep arguing, but Tlacaelel's haughtiness had clearly left nothing to talk about. Still he felt their stares boring into his back.

Not daring to tie his sword back to his girdle, mind numb, heart racing, he didn't even ask himself as to the nature of their destination this time. Only when they turned another corner and he could hear no footsteps but their own did he allow his senses to shift to the young man walking beside him. Another First Son of another Emperor? The heir to Tenochtitlan's throne? No, it could not be true. Tenochtitlan already had an emperor, a mere child according to Father, and Father would know. If this youth was the first son, he would have become the emperor upon his own father's death, wouldn't he?

"You are not the First Son," he said finally as the clamor of the marketplace grew stronger.

"Of course I am." The lifted eyebrows of his companion made Kuini wish to smash the broad face into a bloody mess. Coyotl was the First Son, and the heir, and he was never arrogant or haughty.

"How come you are not the Emperor, then?"

The merry laughter was his answer. "You are such a provincial. It is not that simple, you know?"

"It is simple enough in civilized places like Texcoco."

"Oh, stop bringing up this stupid new province of ours."

Kuini clenched his fists. "Texcoco is not your province. This *altepetl* is more civilized, more beautiful, more magnificent than yours will ever be. Without your betrayal they would never have lost. They were victorious for more summers than your petty *altepetl* ever existed."

To his surprise, Tlacaelel did not take offense. "So you are from Texcoco, aren't you? I would never have guessed. You look like a Tepanec, and you speak like them. But your tattoos look completely savage." He shrugged. "Whatever the reasons, your Texcoco is our province now, and they deserved that. Pitiful losers and worthless warriors." The deeply set eyes measured Kuini once again. "So what are you doing here in Tenochtitlan?"

Taking a deep breath to control his temper, Kuini clasped his lips. "Nothing. I just came to look around."

"And?"

"And nothing. So far, I ran into too many hostile warriors and strange royal family arrangements." He studied his companion in his turn, taking in the broad, well-developed frame and the muscled arms. "If you were the First Son you wouldn't be going around looking like a warrior, picking fights. That warrior was right. You would be escorted and well protected."

"Would I?" Tlacaelel laughed again. "You obviously know nothing about palaces and royal families. The Emperor, his wives, and his heir are moving about escorted. The rest of the royal family can do as they please." The broad face darkened. "As long as they don't stand in someone's way."

"So which son is your current Emperor?"

"The second," said Tlacaelel lightly.

"Then why did the second son become the Emperor? Was the first one that unfitting?" Delighted, he saw the deeply set eyes darkening with rage.

"You are still pushing it, foreigner!"

"I'm curious."

"Well, you will have to go and figure it out all by yourself. Go back to the Plaza and ask the people around. I predict by the nightfall you will learn a thing or two."

Pleased with his companion's obvious loss of temper and, therefore, loss of dignity, Kuini grinned.

"Weren't we supposed to fight somewhere near your marketplace?"

Tlacaelel's glare made him feel vindicated. "Yes! I was about to kill you, and this place will do."

Knowing he should go away now while having a chance, Kuini glanced around, taking in the high walls separating them from the clamor of the marketplace. The square they stood upon, indeed, seemed fairly secluded.

"Yes, this place seems good enough."

No, he could not fight the temptation. The arrogant frog-eater was so sure of himself, and to get under his skin was a pleasure. He shrugged. To kill a royal family member was the stupidest deed of them all, but this whole day was such an aggravating disappointment. Nothing had gone according to their plans. They were stuck, lost, and his father's sacrifice seemed as if it were coming to nothing, after all. Watching the furious youth in front of him, he brushed his misgivings aside. It couldn't get any worse, could it?

Tlacaelel untied his sword with an admirable swiftness. Not wasting his time on any more talking, he attacked fiercely, surprising Kuini, who'd had hardly enough time to bring his sword up, blocking the mighty blow.

Their hands shook, pressing against each other, but the offspring of the royal family was quick to disengage. Eyes sparkling, he attacked anew, his sword smashing against the wall where Kuini had stood a heartbeat before. The sharp obsidian cracked but held on. The youth's sword seemed to be of a good quality.

Blocking another attack, Kuini pushed his rival violently, but did not use the chance to hack into the momentarily exposed side of the richly decorated cloak. Instead, he waited for the next onslaught, ready to block the blow. There was no need to kill this frog-eater, unless he had no choice. He could just tire him, humiliate him thoroughly, then leave. The youth fought well, displaying a good, aggressive style, but he clearly lacked any real battle experience.

One of the obsidian spikes cracked when another blow crashed against the stones Kuini's back had been propped on earlier. This time, he could not fight the temptation to land the flat side of his sword against the tall youth's ribs.

Tlacaelel gasped, but did not lose his balance. Taking a moment to catch himself, he attacked again as if nothing happened. No, this offspring of the royal family was not that bad.

Concentrating on his rival's sword, Kuini sensed more than saw a foreign presence. People came up the narrow alley. Listening to the hurried footsteps scratching the pavement, he saw Tlacaelel's gaze losing its concentration. Their swords still locked, still pressing, they looked at each other. An imperceptible nod and he allowed his eyes to leap toward the newcomers.

Of course those footsteps belonged to the commoners with the clubs he had seen on the Plaza earlier. He was hardly surprised. Forming half a circle, they stood there, watching the fight, somewhat at a loss and apprehensive. Three of the five held their clubs openly now, while the other two clutched onto long obsidian daggers.

"Go away," said Tlacaelel imperiously. "Off with you before any of you get hurt. I won't be repeating myself."

Kuini watched the leading man frowning as though deliberating about his next move. The others tensed, watching their leader.

"Those are the admirers of yours I told you about earlier," he said quietly.

It had the desired effect. Tlacaelel straightened his shoulders abruptly, now obviously taking in the half-circle-formation and the openly held clubs. His nostrils widened as he took a deep breath.

"Then you'll have to wait until I'm through with them," he said in a low voice. "Unless you are a coward enough to join them."

Kuini grinned. "No, I'll wait for my turn."

However, he knew he had no choice, so when his former rival stepped forward, not wasting his breath on any more talking, he watched the attacking men, seeing one of them drawing aside, obviously planning to attack the royal back. Tlacaelel had not enough sense to press against the wall, making sure his back was protected. Those were things one learned while fighting in real battles, reflected Kuini. They didn't teach them that in *calmecac*.

Tlacaelel attacked suddenly, with a great vigor, just like he had with Kuini, and the first man with the club took an involuntary step back. The sword slipped against the club, slicing the man's thigh. The superficial cut made the commoner hesitate as his attention slid to his injured leg, but the immediate thrust of the sword sent him reeling, crashing against the nearby wall, not wounded but gasping and disoriented for a moment. If not for his companions, the man would have been done for, reflected Kuini, watching the other two pouncing on the tall youth, forcing his attention off their groaning companion.

The heavy gazes of the other two men still on him, Kuini let his instincts decide, jumping forward, making them scatter. Those two had neither swords nor clubs, still, armed with their daggers they presented a threat, especially for a man busy fighting alone, with his back unprotected.

The owners of the knives had not much fighting spirit in them, scattering against another of Kuini's attacks, so he turned his attention to the fight in the middle of the square. Tlacaelel seemed as though doing well against two of his attackers, but the third man, abandoning his club and clutching onto his dagger, charged toward the youth's unprotected back.

Hindered by the sword he could not let go of in favor of the wild leap, Kuini threw himself forward, colliding with the man. Losing his balance, he clutched onto the man's wide frame, whether to stop the knife from pouncing or in order to stabilize himself, he didn't know. His bulky rival wavered and together they fell, with the knife slipping off, clattering against the dusted stones.

Kicking viciously, Kuini jumped up, not attempting to go after the knife, his own sword still clutched in his right hand. He saw the man on the ground twisting, pouncing in an attempt to reach his dagger, and this time it was no effort. One blow, then another to silence the screams, and he was free to look around again.

Tlacaelel, pressing against the wall – at least the man had had enough sense to do that – seemed to be in control of the situation, still attacking. Yet, two of his rivals were very much alive, although bleeding, with one of the knives' owners joining in. The other lay motionless in the dust.

Shifting his grip on his sword, Kuini rushed forward, attracting the attention of both clubs owners, unintentionally so. He ducked the onslaught of the first man, then pushed the other one with his shoulder, kicking at the man's exposed shins at the same time. That neutralized his rival for a heartbeat, allowing Kuini to concentrate upon the first man.

Not waiting for the attack, he hacked his sword viciously, sending it flying in a beautiful half circle, to bury itself into the man's shoulder, cutting through the muscles of the upper arm, breaking the bone with a disgusting crack.

The force of the blow sent his victim flying sideways, to crash onto the dusty ground, still numb and not understanding what had happened. It took him a heartbeat to start screaming and another heartbeat for the blood to burst unrestrained, pulsating wildly, splattering the nearby wall.

Breathing heavily, Kuini straightened up. All eyes were on the man, gaping. Even Tlacaelel stared. Briefly, his gaze shifted to him, wide-eyed, but were quick to return to the screaming man. Bettering his grip on the familiar carved handle, Kuini raised his arms, preparing to deliver the final blow. There was no need to prolong this man's agony, enemy or not.

He heard the muffled sound of a club hitting the ground. The second club owner rushed forward, weaponless and pale. Incredulous, Kuini watched the man kneeling beside the wounded, clutching the half severed arm with his trembling hands as if trying to connect it back where it belonged, the dirty hands covering with crimson, turning brownish where it mixed with the dust.

"Get away from him," he said, still finding it difficult to understand. "He is a dead man."

The commoner did not move, did not raise his head. "We have to stop the bleeding," he muttered as if talking to himself. "If he stops bleeding, he may live. There is this healer woman, by the spices stall, in the food alley. She does wonders." The muttering of the man grew incomprehensible with his hectic attempts to push the crimson mess together, to close it around the brighter stiffness of the protruding bone. The screams of the wounded grew, and he fought faintly as though trying to escape his companion's ministrations.

"Who sent you?" Tlacaelel's voice made Kuini jump. He hadn't noticed the tall youth coming nearer.

The kneeling man shivered and did not look up. "Please, let me take him to the healer," he whispered, now just trying to cover the pulsating flow with both hands. "He is my brother. The healer can help."

"Tell me who sent you, and maybe I'll let you live." Towering above the man, Tlacaelel shifted forward, threatening. "But tell me quickly."

The taut, colorless face looked up. "No one. We just thought you were rich. Saw you fighting here..."

Kuini felt more than saw the young man's glance. "You were

watching him on the Plaza," he said. "I saw you. All five of you."

The screams grew fainter as the wounded man's limbs began to sag and the grip of the other man tightened. "We were given five cocoa beans," he whispered without looking up this time. "To kill you. I don't know the men who gave them to us, but we asked no questions. You can't say 'no' to so many beans. They promised another five if we were successful."

"I can't believe it! Dirty, stinking, disgusting manure eaters!" Making a visible effort to control his temper, Tlacaelel growled. "Take this thing wherever you like, and if I encounter you another time you are a dead man, even if I see you just walking the city." He turned to Kuini. "Come."

Taking a last glance at the kneeling, grief-stricken man and his dying brother, Kuini followed, not asking questions this time, but noticing that the man with the knife had long since disappeared.

"Who are you?" asked Tlacaelel curtly as they headed down another alley.

Shrugging, Kuini slowed his pace. "I need to go back to the wharves," he said.

The tall youth stopped. "You fought well." He frowned. "Not against me but against them. Who are you?"

Kuini stood the penetrating gaze. "No one of importance."

The deeply set eyes narrowed. "It doesn't seem that way. And anyway, you saved my life, so, as much as I dislike it, I owe it to you now."

"You owe me nothing. You would have dealt with them anyway. When I fought this little scum with his pitiful knife, you dealt with four men and stayed alive."

"No," said Tlacaelel impatiently. "I saw what you did in the beginning. The little piece of dirt would have stabbed me in my back." His frown deepened. "You saved my life."

Kuini shrugged. "So, do you know who paid so many beans to these people?"

"Yes, I have my suspicions." The tall youth looked around. "Come with me. The Warlord may want to take a look at you. He is always after good warriors, even though you are a Texcocan."

"The new Warlord?"

Tlacaelel's eyebrows flew up, his annoying arrogance returning. "We have no new warlords, not to my knowledge."

"You had another one a few summers ago," stated Kuini tersely.

"Oh, the old Tepanec? Yes, he was quite a man. But he is not around now. He sailed away, gods-know-where."

"Yes, I know."

The pointed eyebrows climbed higher. "How would you know that?"

Annoyed, Kuini glared back. "I just know."

A skeptical grin was his answer. "Well, are you coming or not?"

"No. My friend is waiting for me by the wharves, and we still need to find a place for the night." He shrugged. "I don't think they will let you bring me into the Palace, anyway."

Tlacaelel's face darkened. "I'm not going back to the Palace. Not after this." He took a deep breath. "The old Tepanec was right, and I'll do what he said this time."

Kuini remembered the broad, sunburned, wrinkled face of the Aztec. "So he keeps telling the royalty what to do," he muttered, grinning. "It is so much like him."

Tlacaelel's stare brought him back to his senses. "You can't possibly know this man."

Annoyed once again, Kuini shrugged. "There are too many things you don't know, strutting around your pretty Palace."

But this time, Tlacaelel just laughed. "You are something, you know? A funny foreigner who thinks the world of himself because he knows some influential people here in Tenochtitlan." He slowed his steps once again. "Listen, come with me. You have nowhere to stay anyway, and I'll be spending my time keeping low until the old Tepanec is back." He shrugged. "You can bring your friend too, but only if you promise he is not as wild as you are. Two of your type might prove somewhat difficult to handle."

Kuini hesitated, letting the offense pass this time. "I can't bring my friend anywhere near Tenochtitlan's authorities. He also needs to keep low, come to think of it."

"Why? What has he done here?"

"Nothing. It is his first time in Tenochtitlan too, but they won't like to know he is alive and well." He measured his tall companion with a glance. "A sort of your trouble."

Tlacaelel narrowed his eyes. "Texcoco nobility," he said, making it a statement.

"Well, sort of, yes."

"Oh, it's getting interesting. Where is he?"

"Show me the place you'll be staying, and I'll go and fetch him." Watching his surroundings, Kuini shrugged. "I have to ask him first, anyway."

"All right, follow me."

Letting out a sigh of exasperation, Kuini had followed the arrogant royal offspring for the fourth time through this eventful afternoon. This might be a contact that could prove helpful after all, he thought, hurrying to keep up, glad that he did not commit them before seeking Coyotl's advice.

CHAPTER 4

Pressing against the damp stones of the wall, Dehe let the warriors pass, watching the litter that followed them with some interest. Too scared to feel any real curiosity, the wooden construction carried by sturdy-looking men still attracted her attention against her will. She tried to imagine a person, a real human being, carried like some kind of merchandise in such wooden curtained seat. *What were the people's legs made for if not for walking?*

The crowds around her paid the palanquin little attention, mainly put out with the necessity to move off the road, as it seemed. Afraid of them too, she pressed closer to the cold stones, her palms sweaty, heart thumping. Why had she sneaked out all alone this morning?

She bit her lips, knowing the answer. She wanted to show *him*. She wanted to make him worried. And also, they needed things, food and maybe some clothes. Through the past half a moon, hiding and taking care of the Lowlander, she'd grown used to thinking of herself as one of them, taking care of their needs in the woods of the Highlands, improvising on their food and their shelter. The attempt to try to do that here too, in this huge, frightening *altepetl* seemed logical at the time. Well, what else was she supposed to do in the long cluster of buildings with so many rooms and open grounds that one could have lost one's way wandering through them, surrounded by so many weapons and tools? What was Kuini thinking bringing them to this place?

Scowling, she remembered the way they had arrived on the damp, noisy island through the previous dawn. To watch it bearing down on them, her stomach turning, chest hurting, having difficulty breathing, but whether from awe or from fear she didn't know, was frightening, so she just curled at the bottom of their canoe and wished they would never reach the land.

The fleeting excitement, the sense of a nearing adventure she had felt when Kuini and the Lowlander agreed to take her along, evaporated quickly, letting the bad feeling prevail. From the morning of their arrival she felt terrible, watching this hard, cold, aloof *altepetl*, with its main pyramid towering against the brightening sky and the multitude of low, wooden buildings lining the shores. It had an indifferent, cold air about it, and although she had never seen an *altepetl* in her entire life, she felt this was the way those cities should be – cruel and cold, a fitting place to breed bad, ruthless warriors.

Then there was the incident on the wrong wharf. She had almost fainted, watching Kuini arguing with those vile violent men, getting ready to fight them. She was about to jump out, to try to help him somehow, not knowing what else to do, but luckily, the Lowlander solved the problem. It made her marvel at the way the tall Acolhua managed to talk everyone out of fighting, smoothly and authoritatively, making them listen. Oh yes, this Lowlander was all right. She was glad she had the opportunity to save his life back in the Highlands.

Well, from that stressful incident it did not get any better. The clamorous roads and alleys packed with busy, pushing people made Dehe nauseous, and the beauty of the former Warlord's spacious dwelling, after they had managed to get in, only made her feel worse. Full of colorful mosaic and beautiful furniture, it impressed upon her sense of her smallness and her worthlessness, the derisive glances of the servants relaying to her most clearly that she was nothing but a barbarian, not worthy to mar such a place even as a meaningless slave. Relieved when they left, she hoped they would go straight back to the wharves, to quit the accursed *altepetl* at once.

Well, they did go straight back to the wharves, but then Kuini had decided *to sniff around*, was the way he had put it, with the Lowlander as reluctant to go away. They had wanted to leave her in some secure place by the lake, but before she could start arguing, making them angry with her, the Lowlander grew pale and his face covered with sweat. He was not well, not yet. So it came down to Kuini leaving them both upon the small shore with enough shade, disappearing into the noise of that hostile city for a whole afternoon, making her fret and near panic. The Lowlander tried his best to reassure her, but it didn't help, as he himself was clearly almost as worried. Oh, he was a nice man, this heir to the Texcoco throne. He was nothing like the cruel, heartless Acolhua warriors.

She shivered and forced her thoughts off her village and the horrible morning of more than three summers ago, trying to make her heart calm, clutching her sweaty palms, pushing the pictures her mind still drew too vividly away. It was in the past. It never happened. Her man was a fierce warrior, who would never allow the nightmare to return, and his friend was as good. No, she would never relive that horror again, never. Unless they stayed in this accursed *altepetl*.

Clenching her teeth, she forced herself to look around, trying to remember what had made her come here all alone. The previous evening, of course. The fretful waiting upon the wharves had resulted in Kuini coming back before the dusk, scratched and dust covered, with his cloak torn but beaming, pleased with himself. Oh, could he not move around for half a day without getting into a fight? She rushed toward him, hoping to relax in his embrace, but he just caressed her shoulders, flashing a fleeting smile at her – one of those unguarded smiles of his, the ones that always made her heart melt – and proceeded to talk to the Lowlander at length, keeping his voice low.

Deliberating for a long time, they discussed the possibility of some troubles in Tenochtitlan's royal palace, finally getting up and going back into the city, beckoning her to follow. Oh, but she wasn't their slave. She was Kuini's woman, wasn't she? Was she not entitled to know what their plans were?

And it only kept getting worse. With darkness they had arrived under the high walls, sneaking in through a small, unguarded gate. Some wandering between the multitude of low buildings, and here they were, entering one of the doorways, greeted by an imposingly tall, broad, young man, with a pleasant face and deeply set arrogant eyes. She didn't like this warrior from the first sight, and the way his eyes widened while resting on her only made it worse.

"What's with the slave?" The youth called out, turning to Kuini. "You said nothing about this kind of entourage. Fancy bringing maids to *calmecac*."

"She is with us, and she is not a slave," said Kuini, shrugging, seemingly unperturbed. "I just forgot to tell you. But Dehe is quiet, and she'll give you no trouble."

The tall youth's frown deepened. "No slave? Than who, or *what*, is she?"

"She is just a girl, and she'll make no trouble," repeated Kuini, now impatiently. "I think you should be more interested in meeting my friend." Eyes glimmering, he watched their host as if expecting something.

The tall youth measured the Lowlander with his gaze, eyes concentrating. "I'm honored to meet you," he said slowly, studying Coyotl's face.

"The honor is all mine,"' answered Coyotl smoothly, his old, dignified self again, the afternoon exhaustion gone, or well hidden. "It's not every day one meets the First Son of the Great Emperor."

"Thank you." The youth's eyes narrowed. "I gather you are of a noble blood, as well."

Coyotl did not let his smile show, but it sparkled in the depth of his glittering eyes. "Yes, and come to think of it, we are related. My mother was the half sister of your powerful father."

This threw their host off his arrogant self assurance. "And which sister was that?" he asked, wide-eyed.

"The one that was given to the Acolhua Emperor more than twenty summers ago."

"Oh, I see. It is a great honor, indeed. I wasn't expecting to entertain such a high company. I wish I could greet you in the Palace." The young man's polite words did not match his tightening lips and the darkening gaze. "You should have told me," he said stonily, glancing at Kuini.

"Would it make a difference?" Kuini's eyes turned narrow and cold.

"Maybe. Maybe not. But you should have told me." The deeply set eyes returned to Coyotl. "I wasn't aware you were alive."

"Many people are not aware of that," answered Coyotl lightly, but his eyes, too, went blank and flinty.

"Where have you been for the past few seasons?"

"Safe with my friend." The Lowlander's grin was still light, still non-committal.

"Safe with that one?" The tall youth laughed and the tension broke. "Spending just a little time with your friend this afternoon made me wave my sword more than I'm normally required to in a market interval."

"Then you should go out on campaigns," commented Kuini, laughing in his turn. "You fight well, so your sword could be put to use, and not against marketplace rats."

"The Warlord will take care of that as soon as all sorts of situations are solved." The youth's smile widened. "Come on in, let us see if we can get some food for you two, and a couple of mats. We will stay here, in *calmecac*, until the old Warlord is back, or until the current one thinks of a way to use us all." His eyes sparkled amusedly. "I know it's a strange way to greet you into Tenochtitlan, oh Honorable Heir to Texcoco throne, but one day I hope to be able to pay you more honors."

Safely forgotten and still angry over the 'she is just a girl' comment, Dehe saw Coyotl smiling broadly. "When I finished my *calmecac* training more than three summers ago, I never thought I'd be returning to it one day. What a nightmare! Will they wake us before dawn, yelling and shouting, ready to slap the three of us into obedience?"

Smirking, they proceeded into another corner, sinking onto mats, leaving Dehe to stand there near the entrance to bite her lips and fight the tears of anger from showing. He hadn't even made sure she was settled and all right, leaving her to her own devices, too busy with his newfound friend. *Just a girl!* But she was his woman, and she had saved his friend's life.

She watched the tired looking old man bringing in a tray with plates and simple looking cups. The fleeting glance he gave her made her struggle against the tears more difficult. But for the scary *altepetl* outside those walls, she would turn around and run away.

"Here, let me get you some food." She refused to raise her head, but *his* voice made her stomach flutter with anticipation.

"I'm god," she said stiffly, swallowing hard to make the tears go away. "You don't have to worry about me."

"I'm not worried, but we will have to settle you somewhere, won't we?" His arm wrapped around her shoulders lightly, propelling her toward another corner with mats. Well away from theirs, she noticed. "You must be dead tired. So just eat and go to sleep."

"I'm not tired!" She stared into his face, taking in the paleness, the smeared dust, the dried blood upon his right cheek. "You look worse than I could ever dream to look. You should go to sleep, not me."

His eyebrows flew high as his frown spread, making him look younger in his bewilderment. "Are you all right?"

"Yes, I am! I'm all right. I'm always all right. Am I not just a girl who is making no trouble?" Breathing heavily, she stared at him, welcoming the confrontation.

His frown deepened and his eyes changed their expression. "Yes, Dehe, you are a girl that is making no trouble," he said stonily. "Go to sleep."

Thrusting the plate into her hands, he turned around and went back to his friends, his paces long, his torn cloak swirling. She stared at it, wishing to have something to throw at him. Something heavy, or maybe sharp, she thought, clenching her teeth. Something that would make him feel as bad as she felt.

So her night dragged on, with them talking for what seemed like half of it, sometimes serious, sometimes laughing, sometimes dropping to mere whispers, glancing around carefully.

She made her point in not going to sleep, not trying to conceal her sitting there, listening and watching. They would have to throw her out by force to make her stop listening. But, of course, they didn't bother to look in her direction at all, forgetting all about her presence. Oh, she should have let the Lowlander die!

"So your mother was Huitzilihuitl's first wife, even before he became an emperor?" The Lowlander's voice rang softly in the dimly lit hall. He half rose in order to reach for the plate of tamales, which Kuini had made sure to place right next to himself.

"Yes," said their host idly, sipping from his cup, indifferent to the food. His name was Tlacaelel, Dehe was quick to learn. "She was the first, but this did not last. The Tepanec woman would not tolerate any competition."

"Tell me about it!" cried out Coyotl, sinking back onto his mat. "My father had one such, too. A terrible woman." He shook his head. "Such a hag. Luckily, my father had enough sense to put her aside."

Tlacaelel's eyebrows rose high. "It depends on what you call 'enough sense'. It did not do him any good in the long run."

Coyotl's face darkened. "What happened has nothing to do with it," he said stiffly, the tamale in his hand forgotten.

Kuini, half lying on his mat, devoured his share of tamales with an obvious pleasure.

"Those are good," he said as though unaware of the momentary tension that prevailed. "I missed good food. The best we could do through the past half a moon came to various berries and roots." He made a face. "That poor rabbit the heir to the Texcoco throne hunted quite skillfully notwithstanding. The stupid thing was so thin its meat hardly made us feel any better."

"Well, that's why I managed to catch it," Coyotl's grin was reluctant, but wide. "It was so starved it had no strength to run away."

Tlacaelel roared with laughter. "You two seem to have quite a tale to tell. So that's what you've been doing, hiding in the woods since the Tepanec second invasion?"

"Well, sort of."

"And the savages didn't catch you?"

Dehe caught her breath, watching Kuini's face turning to stone.

"The Highlanders hospitality was beyond any reproach," she heard Coyotl saying stiffly. "Those people treated me well. They are impeccable people." A reserved smile dawned. "I came to love the Highlands, actually. I would have stayed there but for a few complications."

Tlacaelel stared at the Lowlander, losing most of his previous lightness. "You do mean what you say, don't you? You did spend your time in the Highlands? It's unbelievable!" He studied his guest, wide-eyed. "How come they didn't kill you right on the spot? I would think they would sacrifice you on the altar of one of their barbarian gods before you could say 'Azcapotzalco'."

"Maybe because they are civilized enough to sacrifice captured warriors and not fleeing youths," said Kuini stiffly, his voice low, ringing eerily in the semi-darkness. "Maybe they could teach Tenochtitlan's people a thing or two."

Tlacaelel's eyebrows jumped high. "And what are you getting all warmed up about? Did you grow that fond of the Highlands, too?"

"Yes, I'm fond of that place. Living there for most of one's life can do it to a person."

"Oh, so that's where your manners are coming from. I should have guessed, with those tattoos and that wildness of yours." He peered at Kuini, and even from her far corner Dehe could see his eyes sparkling challengingly. "Well, I didn't mean to be rude. I suppose some Highlanders are all right."

"All of them are all right, and all of them are civilized!"

But Tlacaelel just laughed. "Oh, don't you turn all indignant on me. If you want to go back to what we were doing when we got interrupted on that square, you'll have to wait for the morning."

"We can get back to it right here. There is more than enough space and plenty of moonlight," growled Kuini, shifting as if about to get up.

"Ever tried to spend some time without looking for fights?" Tlacaelel shrugged and didn't change his position. Shaking his head, he reached for a plate of vegetables, then made himself comfortable again. "You two are touchier than the Emperor's wives. Try to relax, both of you. Here in Tenochtitlan you will hear many unpleasant things about both of your homes. Get used to it." He shrugged. "Or go back."

A silence prevailed, interrupted by buzzing mosquitoes.

"We don't know yet why we came to Tenochtitlan," said Coyotl finally, voice low. "We were supposed to talk to your former Chief Warlord, see if we could be of any help. Maybe he needs good warriors. Maybe he was just bored, dragging us out here for nothing." He picked a small tomato, studying the round fruit but not attempting to eat it. "I honestly don't know why we came here anymore."

Tlacaelel grinned. "Oh, the former Chief Warlord is a deep frog-eater. If he told you to come, then he has a good reason, and you will be put to a great use." The deeply set eyes squinted. "He is going to use me, too. That's why he went to the trouble of smuggling me out of the Palace. I should have listened to him sooner. That would have spared us that stupid fight behind the temple." His grin widened. "He is up to something, this old Tepanec. He doesn't like seeing Tenochtitlan ruled by the daughter of Tezozomoc. He doesn't want us to become a Tepanec province, peacefully or otherwise. He thinks we can do better independently. And being a Tepanec himself, he goes about it blatantly and arrogantly, not bothering to conceal his intentions." The grin disappeared. "I shall be like him when my time comes. You don't have to be an emperor to do great things, to be remembered as a great man."

"Maybe you'll still make it as an emperor," said Coyotl quietly. "You are the First Son."

Tlacaelel's laughter rolled between the plastered walls, light and unconcerned. "You may cherish those ideas, oh Heir to Texcoco throne. You have no one waiting in line, and should your people throw the Tepanecs' yoke, you will be the one they'll be looking up to. But me? Oh, no. I won't get into this struggle. Too many influential people with great clout and the necessary blood are coveting the reed-woven seat in the main hall in Tenochtitlan's Palace. I have a fair idea who our next Emperor will be, and I have no intention of crossing this man's path. I will do great things my way. I won't be an emperor, but I will be remembered."

Fascinated, Dehe leaned forward, afraid to miss a word. This youth meant what he said, and somehow, she knew he was right.

This one would make a name, and he would be remembered.

Forgetting her anger, she watched them, their faces strange in the flickering light of a single torch, beautiful like stone statues coated with gold, so different and yet so alike, three great men that were destined to change history.

She caught her breath, mesmerized, trying to understand. Those were just forceful, vigorous, restless youths, yet suddenly she knew, with all the clarity of foresight, that the three of them would do many great things, change the world as they knew it, each in his own way, but together, always together.

Hugging her elbows, suddenly cold in the warmth of the night, she moved back, pressing against the wall and closing her eyes. What would this trio do? And would she be offered a part in any of it? Would her Highlander keep her? Would he make her his woman for real?

Shivering, she opened her eyes; sought his face in the shadows. He was still there, still deep in his thoughts, a young man and not a golden vision, not anymore. The magic was gone, and she breathed with relief. It was frightening to know the future. It had never happened to her before.

"So, I suppose we just wait here for our mastermind to come back," said Kuini lightly, breaking the spell. *Were they under the same breath of magic she felt?*

"Yes, we'll stay here, and we will wait for him to come back. He actually organized me to help the veterans with their *calmecac* lessons. He thought it'd help me to pass the time." Tlacaelel chuckled. "None of us expected such a highborn, or high-spirited, company." His eyes flickered toward Kuini. "Exotic and high-spirited."

The Highlander's laughter rang as lightly. "Don't push it. I wouldn't want to rob the future generations off the great man to revere and learn from." He drank from his cup. "Don't they have a decent flask of *octli* anywhere around here? I'm growing tired drinking this water."

"Not in *calmecac*, man. Don't you remember your days in school? One drop of *octli* and you are beaten and expelled and what-not." The generous lips stretched into a smile. "But come to think of it, you are free to run around the city, unlike the two of us. So maybe you can take care of this business tomorrow. Go out and get us some decent drink."

"Send your slaves, oh honorable first son!" growled Kuini, grinning. "I'm not your servant. But I may go out while you two are teaching the fat, pampered kids of the nobility how to wave a stick. I want to take a good look at the Palace."

"Why?"

"No reason. Just want to study this ugly *altepetl* in case we will stay here for good."

"Oh, spare me another homesick litany about the beauty of Texcoco," cried out Tlacaelel. "He lectured me on your *altepetl* until I truly wanted to kill him, you know," he said, turning to Coyotl. "Just to make him shut up."

Kuini laughed. "He won't tell you that he tried to make the spotted cloaks do this for him. So much bravery left me almost breathless, I'm telling you."

But there was something in the Highlander's face that made Dehe concentrate. Narrowing her eyes, she peered through the darkness, trying to see what his eyes held. Why would he try to sniff around the Palace? And why did she think it was of any importance?

"Speaking of relatives; Coyotl's favorite sister was given to your father a few summers ago," Kuini was saying, still breezy and amused, but his eyes clung to the tall Aztec's face, openly expectant.

"My father has many wives. Too many to count, and one is not supposed to be looking at any of them." Tlacaelel stretched, then picked another tortilla, dunking it lazily in the bowl with spicy sauce.

"But she was a very exalted Acolhua princess," insisted Kuini. "You should remember someone like that."

"Oh, the Second Wife?"

"Oh yes, Iztac Ayotl would be made a Second Wife at the very least," cried out Coyotl, animated for a change. "She deserved to be the First Wife, though. She is impeccably noble, and well educated and trained. Did you happen to meet her?"

"No, of course not. But they say she is very beautiful and very haughty."

"Iztac Ayotl is anything but haughty." Looking at Kuini, Coyotl laughed. "Isn't she?"

An indifferent shrug was his answer, but Dehe saw the Highlander's eyes turning blank and unreadable.

"People change, you know," she heard him saying, his voice just a little too calm, too indifferent. "There is a difference between being a princess and the emperor's wife. Maybe she learned to like her high status."

Tlacaelel shrugged, wiping the remnants of the sauce off his chin. "With the Emperor's Chief Wife, other wives do not have that much status. They all keep very low and quiet."

"What happened to them upon the Emperor's death?"

"Nothing. What should happen to them? Some stayed; some were given away."

"Was the Second Wife given away?"

Stomach turning, Dehe watched Kuini leaning forward, as if trying to read the answer in his companion's face. She clasped her palms tight, suddenly warm and sweaty as opposed to her previous feeling of being cold. *He wanted to know about that haughty princess. Why?*

"I really don't know. Ask the old Warlord. He knows everything."

"It would be wonderful to meet her again," said Coyotl dreamily. "It was never the same without her."

But all Dehe could see was the way Kuini leaned back against the wall, his face closed, lips pressed into a thin line, eyes dark, staring into space, wandering unknown distances.

Her anger rose once again, here in the crowded marketplace as intense as it had back there, in the dimly lit warriors' hall. Clenching her teeth tight, she pushed herself away from the safety of the wall, stepping back toward the road. Oh, she was not a burden, not a *girl that is making no trouble*. She was a person, and she could take care of herself. And when he found that she was gone, he would be sorry.

Picking her way carefully between the multitude of mats and

stalls, jostled every now and then, she went on stubbornly, not bothering to mark her surroundings. In all her life she had never lost her way, always remembering the places she had passed, being those forest's paths or town's alleys.

Her fear began calming down, and, looking around, she noticed that not only people were plentiful in this place. Food, clothes, and jewelry piled all over the alley, crammed upon the mats or arranged prettily, sparkling in the midmorning sun. Eyes wide, she began stealing glances, and then, giving in, she gaped openly, amazed at those unbelievable riches. So much of everything!

Still not sure enough of herself to stop and peer closely, she turned into a smaller alley in an attempt to escape the crowds. Here, the aroma of cooked food enveloped her, making her stomach churn. People squatted or sprawled on mats, in the shade of the high wall, talking idly or throwing beans while eating and drinking. No one paid her any attention.

Reassured, she slowed her steps and watched the sweating old man toiling above a steaming pot. Neatly, the man fished out small bundles of something wrapped in maize husks, placing them on a wooden plate, oblivious to the scorching heat.

Fascinated, Dehe watched him working as the man from the nearby mat got up.

"Let us see what you've got here, old man."

"The best tamales you ever tasted," grinned the stall owner, interrupting his activity to unwrap one of the bundles. His nimble fingers picked the steaming tamale, dropping it neatly onto a smaller plate.

"I'll have another one for my companion," said the other man.

"Next time wait patiently until I'm done," the cooking man grunted, complying with the request. "I'll have the rest of my tamales burned because of you."

"Oh, I bet a cocoa bean you'll find a way to force those burned tamales on your other customers," laughed the man, heading back to his mat.

The old man cursed, returning back to his steaming pot. "Those will cost you more," he called out more loudly. "It'll round your whole meal to a whole cocoa bean, so don't bet any of it before you pay me."

"What a thief!" The man with the plate dropped beside his companion, grinning broadly. "You can go on dreaming about those cocoa beans, old man. I don't see any warriors or other nobility around your stall." He caught Dehe's gaze. "Here, maybe this little slave came here with a bag full of beans. Didn't you, girl?"

Frightened, Dehe took a step back, but the man's attention shifted back to his plate and the bowl of thick sauce upon another tray. Breathing with relief, she turned to go, glancing again at the steaming pot. The spicy aroma tickled her nostrils. Having been too angry to eat on the previous evening, she had slipped away well before dawn, before any chance of getting her morning meal. Oh but how she wanted *him* to wake up and find her gone. He may have not paid her any attention on the previous evening, but he did come to cover her with a blanket later through the night. She had pretended to be fast asleep, hoping he would recline beside her and try to wake her up, but he just caressed her hair fleetingly and went back to his mat, leaving her with her eyes shut, and her heart thundering in her ears. He did care for her, he did, even if just a little!

Another man neared the stall, picking a tortilla from the side tray. Leaning against the wooden pole, he consumed it unhurriedly, deep in thought.

Dehe hesitated. Could she just pick one for herself too, the way this person did? The grumpy old man seemed to take this sampling of his goods kindly.

She took another hesitant step, then another. It was hot beside the stall because of the fire raging under the pot. The owner paid her no attention, busy unwrapping another tamale.

The delicious aroma enveloped her, making her stomach constrict. She swallowed, took a deep breath. The man that leaned against the pole finished with his tortilla and picked another, his eyes brushing past her indifferently.

Resting her hands upon the stall, she almost shut her eyes before reaching for the plate. The tortilla felt cold against her palm, dry and crispy, not especially fresh, not like the tamales the old man was fishing out of the pot.

Heart beating fast, she wrapped her fingers around it, afraid to breathe. The cracking of the fire under the pot grew fainter, and the clamor of the alley seemed to retreat.

Then, all at once, the noises were back, and her heart made a wild leap against her ribs as a hand grabbed her wrist, crushing it in its stony grip. The wild pull made her slam against the rough wood of the stall, pressing her chest to it, making her gasp for air.

"You little piece of dirt!" hissed the old man. "You were trying to steal my tortillas and in the broad daylight, you little whore."

Unable to breathe, Dehe just stared at the round, wrinkled face as it swayed in the blurry air, making her nauseous.

"Did you think you could get away with that, eh, you dirty piece of meat?"

"I think she did." The man by the stall laughed. "She looks *that* desperate."

The noises began coming back as her heart picked a tempo, together with the flooding panic. She fought the man's grip, but his fingers tightened, digging into her skin, making her cry out.

"You useless, stupid, dirty slave," the old man went on, almost spitting into her face. "You will pay for this, you dirty whore. You will pay for this dearly."

"Come, old man," said the other one, still laughing. "Let her have that tortilla, it's cold and useless anyway."

"And how is she going to pay me for it, eh? How?" The owner whirled at his customer, eyes ablaze.

"You know, she is a cute little thing, and there are many ways even for an old bag of bones like you to get pleasured."

Feeling the grip on her wrist lessening momentarily, her panic welling, overwhelming, Dehe hacked the nails of her free hand into her captor's wrinkled palm. The plate of tortillas slid along the wooden surface as the surprised owner cried out. Momentarily at a loss, he tried to catch his scattering goods, thus releasing the pressure of his fingers for a heartbeat. And a heartbeat was enough.

Pulling her hand hard, she wriggled out of the man's grip,

avoiding the palm of the other man as he tried to catch her shoulder. In one leap she was back upon the road, dizzy and free. Not wasting her time looking around, she dashed down the alley, oblivious to the shouts and the people happening on her way. The clamor was back, along with the pressing crowds. She didn't pay them any attention, racing up another alley, then another, hearing only her heart thundering in her ears. People yelled at her, but it only made her run faster. She needed to get away from this place. She *needed* to find a shelter.

At some point, her instincts made her turn into yet another smaller alley, but as she did this she bumped into a broad man with bundles tied to his forehead. The man cursed violently. Unable to straighten up under his burden, he shoved Dehe with his elbow, pushing her with such force she went sprawling into a heap of baskets on the nearest mat.

Half stunned, she struggled to get to her feet, her head reeling, senses on fire. The old nightmare was back, with those violent, hostile people closing on her just like back then, in her village. She could almost smell the odor of blood and the burning flesh, could hear the screams of the people. *They were going to catch her again! They were going to hurt her!*

She tried to get up, but her limbs refused to move, suddenly heavy and as if paralyzed. The sky above her head went gray, swirling nauseatingly, with only the thundering of her heart and the man's frightening yelling penetrating her mind.

"Move on, you bulky lump of meat," called a deep female voice, stopping the current of curses. "By your yelling one might think you've been attacked by a bear, not bumped by a tiny little girl."

"The stupid thing almost made me fall, and who would pay for this pottery if it would break, eh, you filthy witch?" The man's voice rose once again.

"Nothing was broken, so move on before I put a curse on you until you will never deliver your stupid bundles undamaged."

The noise grew fainter.

"Are you all right, girl?" The wide, round face of a woman swam into Dehe's view.

She blinked, trying to concentrate, wishing the strident noise in her ears would go away, let her understand the woman's words.

"Here, drink this." A hard pottery cup was thrust against her lips. Startled, she drank obediently, although most of the water ran down her neck.

"You shouldn't have been hurt that badly, the way you crashed into my baskets," went on the woman. "Did you hit your head?"

Swallowing the last of the water, Dehe felt the world slowing its spinning. The woman's narrow, slightly crossed eyes radiated warmth, staring down at her, reassuring.

"I'm sorry," she whispered, still nauseated. It was difficult to form words.

"Oh no, it's not entirely your fault," said the woman smiling, revealing a row of large, brownish teeth. "This uncouth piece of useless meat pushed you so hard, it's a wonder you didn't go straight through the ground into the Underworld, breaking all my baskets on your way." The woman chuckled. "As it is, you seem whole, and so are most of my goods. So just help me gather what spilled out, and you may go." The woman's coarse palm took hold of Dehe's shoulder, pulling her into an upright position. "But watch where you are going, girl. Don't run that heedlessly, no matter how urgent your errand is."

Shrinking from the touch, Dehe struggled to get back to her feet unaided. She couldn't stand anyone touching her, not yet.

The woman's eyes narrowed. "You are still not that well, girl. Sit down. Stay where you are."

Grateful to get a moment of respite, Dehe hugged her knees, breathing deeply, trying to make her heartbeat calm.

"Here, drink this." The cup thrust into her hands was smaller this time. "It'll help to make you feel better."

The spicy beverage burned her throat and she coughed, embarrassed. She had never drunk *pulque* before.

"I'm sorry," she repeated, returning the cup. Glancing at the woman, she took in the oddly crossed eyes set in the broad, wrinkled face. The calm, penetrating gaze made her drop hers quickly.

"So tell me, what was so urgent to make you run the way you did?"

Dehe clutched her knees tightly. "Nothing. I was just... I just need to go back... back to... to my people."

"With your hands empty?"

Watching the woman's eyebrows raising, Dehe frowned. "I don't understand."

The woman laughed heartily. "Girl, you are not fooling me. Something is wrong with you, and I'm now curious to understand what it is. Slave girls are sent to the marketplace to buy things." The crossed eyes narrowed. "Or to deliver something clandestine. Is that your thing? Is that why you've been running up this alley, pale and frightened as though the lowlifes of the Underworld were after you?"

Dehe blinked, trying to understand.

"Did you deliver your message? Is your mistress waiting for you now?"

"My mistress?"

The woman frowned. "You must have hit your head when you fell." The amused gaze slid up Dehe's face, inspecting her briefly. "You are a strange girl."

This time Dehe managed to get up. "I'm sorry," she said again. "I don't understand what you are talking about. I think I better go."

The woman got up as well. "First, help me pick up the seeds you spilled while crashing into my baskets. Then you can go." She pointed at the colorful mess. "Put the roots of *chichipilli* into one basket, and *tlalamatl* into another, but make sure to blow on them, to make it clean and to ward off any disrespect." Kneeling beside another mess of leafs, she went on, now muttering mostly to herself, as it seemed. "Luckily, I didn't grind the *cocyatic* leaves this morning, but the *itzcuinpatli* I'm afraid will have to be thrown away."

"The leaves of *itzcuinpatli* are so rare," exclaimed Dehe. "You can't just throw them away."

"Oh, so you know your way around herbs," the woman's smile was almost victorious. "I knew it!"

"I… yes, I do."

"How well?"

Dehe hesitated. In this strange, hostile *altepetl* she should probably not tell anything about herself, she thought, avoiding the slightly amused gaze of her rescuer. She had better leave as quickly as she could, to find her way back into the protection of her Highlander and his friend, and that arrogant warrior they had both grown so thick with. And yet, the open condescension of the woman hurt.

"I learned for many summers, from the best healer of our village," she said, embellishing the truth.

"So what do you do when a person complains of pain in his head?"

"You make him inhale the dry herb of *cocoyatic*, or you grind it and put it in his nose. It makes him sneeze out the bad phlegm, or bleed to get rid of the unneeded blood."

The woman lifted her eyebrows, surprised. "Well, well. And what about…" She hesitated. "*Quechpucaoaliztli*, a swelling throat?"

Feeling better with each passing moment, Dehe allowed herself a calm smile. "You rub the sick person's throat with root of *cococxihuitl*, to make him vomit. Then you make him drink water with a little *aacaxilotic*."

"Interesting. I never rub a person's throat with *cococxihuitl*, though. I use this herb for another purpose." Smile wondering and not condescending anymore, the woman knelt to pick up the rest of the herbs. "So, that's what you do for your owners. A pity you are a slave. I could use you, girl."

Freezing, Dehe looked up. "I'm not a slave!" Staring at the woman's doubtful face, she remembered that back in that dreadful alley, by the food stall, people also said something to that effect.

"You can't be anything but a slave, girl. Don't lie to me."

She felt her anger rising along with her fear. "I'm not lying to you. I'm not a slave."

The crossed eyes blinked. "Then what are you?" Studying Dehe thoughtfully, the woman frowned. "You are obviously not

from here. You are too scared, too wild-looking, and your accent
is dreadful. You can't be anything but a recently acquired slave.
How long has it been since you arrived in Tenochtitlan?"

Picking up the dry, brownish leaves with great care, Dehe met
the questioning gaze. "I came here on the previous morning, but
I'm not a slave. I came with a man. He is a warrior, and he has
taken me to be his woman."

The woman laughed outright. "You have a great imagination,
girl! No warrior would take you into his household, not even as a
concubine." She smiled broadly. "Believe me, I know. The Aztecs
are incurable snobs."

"He is not an Aztec, neither he nor his friend."

"Who is he, then?"

The sudden curiosity in the woman' eyes made Dehe pause.
"He... he is not from Tenochtitlan."

Shaking her head, the woman turned back to her baskets. "You
are a lousy liar, girl. But you do have knowledge." She paused,
frowning. "If you are not in a hurry to go back wherever you
belong, you can stay here and help me. I won't pay you, but I will
make sure you get a good meal and maybe some passable clothing
if you prove useful." A skeptical side-glance made Dehe feel
naked. "This torn gown makes you look savage. Unless your
owners are really poor, they should not let you go around looking
like that."

"I'm not a slave!" exclaimed Dehe, jumping to her feet. She
glanced at her gown. The old leather was worn, colorless, and torn
in some places, but it was clean. She had made sure to wash it in
the lake while waiting for Kuini on the day before. "My dress is...
it's all right. It's a good dress."

The woman watched her, eyes laughing. "Oh, so your warrior
is not complaining?"

"No, he is not!" It was difficult to utter this through her
clenched teeth.

"Then I suppose he won't mind you staying here for the day."

Biting her lips, Dehe hesitated. She could stay and help this
woman. Hadn't she been promised food and maybe some clothing
in return? It would be nice to dress prettily, and to spend a day

doing what she loved instead of watching Kuini enjoying himself with his Lowlander and the haughty Aztec, paying her no attention. She grinned. Oh, he would worry when she didn't come back through the whole day.

"Yes, I want to help you," she said, meeting the amused gaze.

"Well for now, make sure the baskets are arranged. Spread them upon the mat prettily. We want all those women with their shopping baskets to stop by, even if they did not come here looking for spices and herbs." Her benefactress winked. "You'll be surprised how many pretty, rich ladies are willing to leave their cocoa beans here, going away with the best of my ointments."

"Cocoa beans?"

"Yes, of course. What do you think they pay me with?"

"I don't know." Dehe busied herself with the large basket, sorry for not keeping quiet. The woman's open amusement was annoying. Cocoa beans? The man by the dreadful stand of tortillas talked about those beans too.

"Sometimes, of course, the girls pay me with something else – rare foods, pretty bracelets," the woman was saying as she squatted comfortably, picking a small bowl, busy crushing dry chili leafs into it. "But the nobility are always carrying enough beans to buy this whole alley. Do you know that even the Empress sends her slaves here from time to time?" The crossed eyes sparkled proudly.

Dehe's stomach tightened. "And the Second Wife?" she asked without thinking.

"The Second Wife?" The woman frowned. "Our Emperor has no wives yet. He is still very young."

"Oh," Dehe almost breathed with relief. So there was no second wife, no Acolhua royal princess that made Kuini's eyes sparkle. She must have misunderstood them last night.

"Or did you mean our late Emperor?" The woman seemed unable to stop talking as she worked on. "Oh, this one had many wives. What a good ruler he was, so wise and just. And fruitful, too. Many of his offspring inhabit the Palace these days. Most of his wives bore him a child. Had his life not been cut short, he would have fathered half of Tenochtitlan." The woman chuckled, looking up mischievously. "Even that haughty Acolhua princess of his."

Dehe felt her stomach shrinking once again, the basket suddenly heavy in her hands.

"If people knew half of the secrets one gets to discover while dealing with herbs." Laughing, the woman searched through another basket. "This Palace is a nest of wild bees," she muttered, not looking up.

"This Acolhua Princess," asked Dehe, her throat dry. "She never bore a child to the Emperor?"

"No, she did not. But once an unfamiliar maid came looking for a certain potion." The woman's eyes glimmered victoriously as she looked at Dehe. "A very certain potion, if you know what I mean. Well, I'm sure this slave had an Acolhua accent and she clearly belonged to the Palace." Chuckling, the woman turned to watch two well dressed ladies nearing their corner. "For some reason our haughty Texcocan did not want to bear a child. A strange wish if you ask me, unless it did not belong to the Emperor."

Dehe watched her getting to her feet, nimbly and gracefully for a woman of such advanced age and ample girth.

"Grind those leafs until it turns into powder." A bowl was tucked into Dehe's hands. "Then do the same with the pine nuts before you mix it with lime water from this flask. If you do this well, girl, you will have earned a good meal." All smiles, she turned to the chatting women. "What can I do for you, pretty ladies, this morning?"

CHAPTER 5

It was already well into the second part of the night when Iztac climbed down the wall. Working her way along the ledge, she pitted her face against the night breeze, enjoying its coolness. The night had always worked its magic on her, improving her mood, making her feel light and careless.

Not that her life was that bad now, with her nighttime excursions to Chimal's chambers. She was careful not to do it every night, no matter how strong the temptation. The boy needed his night sleep. He had the Emperor's duties to attend to every morning. But her? Oh, she would sleep well into the midday, ignoring the wondering glances of the other two women, her fellow minor wives. Or minor widows! Why didn't the court bother to give away those two? she wondered irritably. The silly women were such a nuisance!

Almost two market intervals had passed since that first time that she had climbed Chimal's window, desperate and at a loss. Two market intervals of cheerfulness. Oh, her life had improved a thousand fold since that night. Whatever the young Emperor did or said, no one bothered her with any more marriage proposals, and the Flaying Festival went and passed, with no warlords trying to take her anywhere.

She grinned to herself. Oh, that boy had more to him than the Empress and the whole court had thought. He was smart, and he was cunning. He would make a good Emperor when older.

The visits to his room also provided a much-longed-for diversion. They would talk and laugh and play a bean game, and he would tell her everything about what went on in the Palace and in the city. It was nice to know what was going on. This time she had stayed so late, because it took him ages to explain to her how the engineers planned to bring water to Tenochtitlan. He kept searching for words, trying to describe the earthen ditches lined with clay, the way they would carry the water all the way up through a construction crossing the lake.

She had had a hard time believing him. It didn't seem possible. But he said that the main problem was to obtain the Tepanec permission to use the springs of the mainland. The engineers of Tenochtitlan could deal with any challenge given a chance, and now, it looked like this chance may be given to them, as the mighty Tepanec Emperor said yes. She remembered the way his eyes flashed proudly, victorious. They would be drinking fresh water from the mainland's springs soon.

Impatient with her uncomfortably long skirt, she jumped down, having reached the lower part of the wall, her feet bare, relishing the touch of the soft, slightly damp earth. Bending to put her sandals on, she thought about that construction. How would they make the water flow uphill?

Pushing her hair out of her face, she straightened up and winced. Something moved in the darkness. Leaping to her feet, her heart thumping, she saw a silhouette parting from the shadow of a nearby cluster of trees. Clearly visible in the light of the dying moon, the man neared her slowly, unhurriedly, his thick arms folded upon his broad chest, his warriors' lock standing out proudly, not concealed by a heavy headdress this time, a derisive smile stretching his lips, flickering in the narrowed eyes. *The Warlord!*

Iztac took a step back; felt the damp stones of the Palace's wall.

"Well, well," he said quietly. "I would never believe it had I not seen it for myself. When I bribed a slave to follow you, I never expected to find out something like that. I only wanted to meet you in private, to talk to you. But, oh glorious gods, I never thought the Acolhua princess was *that* ambitious." He shook his head, the corners of his mouth turning downwards in an inverted sort of a grin, derisive and appreciative at the same time. "You will stop at nothing, will you, pretty princess? And he is just a boy!"

Speechless, she stared at him, not understanding his words, overwhelmed by a sense of acute danger, by an overpowering urge to run away.

"Well, Princess," he said, still shaking his head. "Come. We need to talk." His formidable palm came out, taking a hold of her shoulder, not aggressively but firmly. "Come."

She shook his hand off. "I'm not coming with you!" It came out hoarsely, more of a quiet shriek.

He smiled and did not attempt to recapture her shoulder. "You are coming, Acolhua Princess. You are smart enough to understand that right now you have no choice." His hand dropped. "I won't hurt you, but I do need to talk to you. And if we keep talking here, under the Empress's side of the Palace, you may find the consequences of this conversation not as favorable as they might be." The eyes of the man grew stonily cold. "Follow me, Iztac Ayotl." Now it was a warlord speaking.

They made their way silently, away from the accursed wall, diving into the protection of the dark gardens. Careful not to touch her, he walked beside her, keeping close. Ready to catch her should she try to run away, she reflected numbly. Her mind seemed to stop working, along with her heart. As though both just went still. She concentrated on her steps, trying not to trip over her sandal's strips. She hadn't had time to tie them properly.

"Well," he said, halting beside a pond, away from a grove of thick trees. *Away from a possibility of being overheard?* "Here we can talk." He measured her with an amused glance. "So Princess, what do you have to say for yourself?"

She met his gaze. "Nothing! I don't have to tell you anything."

"Oh, proud and fearless. I like that." He folded his thick arms across his chest once again. "It takes some spirit to plan what you've been planning. And more spirit and courage to implement that." His gaze flickered. "Oh, the Tepanec noblewomen are ambitious, and they stop at nothing to get what they want. Moral or immoral makes no difference to them, eh? You and the Empress are not so much unlike each other. I never realized that before. And you do share the same royal blood. Interesting."

The breeze brushed against her face, giving no pleasant sensation. Her skin seemed to turn numb.

"And I kept wondering," went on the amused voice, unperturbed. "The priests took their omens and no wedding could be held through the Flaying Festival. The gods were against it. Such clear omens." He shrugged. "The Empress was the one to offer me this alliance, but now she seemed to forget. Was it possible that the boy has some influence over his mother? Is he a cunning boy?"

Oh, so Chimal had managed to find a way to use the priests, thought Iztac randomly. How clever. She never bothered to ask him, but she should have, she realized. And how did he manage to convince his mother? The ruthless woman would never fall for this trick, unless she was convinced it was for the best. Oh but what did he tell her?

"Well, now I do have some answers, don't I?" The narrow eyes watched her, flickering. "The boy wanted my future Chief Wife all for himself. He wasn't prepared to share the favors of the haughty princess who wouldn't stop from climbing his terrace at nights to make him happy." The amused grin was back, stretching the thin lips. "But he is so young, our Emperor. How old is he? Twelve? Thirteen? Can he perform?"

She gasped, finding it difficult to get enough air. "How dare you!"

The Warlord burst into a hearty laughter. "The question is how dare *you*, pretty princess. You were the one to seduce the young emperor. Not me."

She glared at him, her urge to sink her nails into the broad, smirking face overwhelming. The narrow eyes glimmered, returning her gaze, challenging. Without realizing it, she took a step forward, her hand leaping up as if on its own accord, landing against the sharpness of his high cheekbone, making a smacking sound. She felt the impact of the blow running down her palm, warming it.

Staring into his face, she saw the narrow eyes widening, their amusement vanishing, replaced by a flash of anger. As he caught her arm in his crushing grip, she came back to her senses and tried to squirm free. The memory of the Texcoco marketplace and the Aztec warriors surfaced, washing her whole being with a latent wave of fear. She remembered the blows; remembered the panic, the acute sense of helplessness, being hit for the first time in her life. And this time there was no handsome Highlander to come to her rescue.

She fought as he jerked her closer, hard put to keep her balance. His smell hit her nostrils – a surprisingly clean, masculine scent, mixed with the spicy aroma of *octli* and hot beans.

His body pressed against hers, hard, intimidating, his grip crushing her arms. Fighting the overwhelming panic, she forced herself to face him, to stand his blazing gaze.

This seemed to cool him. He studied her more calmly, breathing heavily, gritting his teeth.

"Don't you dare to do that again," he growled after a while, not releasing her. "Do you hear me? No one, not even a haughty princess, will dare to touch my face."

She still stared at him, speechless.

His grip on her arm tightened, grew unbearable. "Do you understand me?"

She nodded, unable to move her lips, so tightly were they clasped.

"I swear I'll kill you if you try to hit me again," he repeated. "And also don't try to run away. Do you understand?" He shook her violently. "Answer me!"

She just nodded.

He backed away slowly, and she leaned against a tree, trying to control the shaking. Her legs trembled so badly, she could not trust them to support her. Clasping her palms, she crushed them against each other, her teeth rattling.

He seemed to be having a hard time calming himself down, as well. Leaning against another tree, fists clenched, he studied her with none of the previous amused derisiveness, his eyes dark and narrow again.

"You are a wild beast, Acolhua princess," he said after a while. "It could be good and bad at the same time." He seemed to be talking to himself now. "I thought you were just one of the minor wives, a meaningless woman. I wanted you for your noble blood, although you are a very pretty thing. But, gods, how wrong I was."

She swallowed to clear her throat. "I won't be your wife, chief or minor!"

"Oh no," he said hurriedly, his amusement returning. "I won't have you now, either."

"Then what do you want?" Genuinely surprised, she gazed at him, now that the immediate threat seemed to be over, finally able to see him clearly, an interesting-looking, formidable man.

He peered at her as if deliberating. "What I want might be more difficult to achieve. You seemed to have more than your share of courage, and you clearly have even more ambition than that." He pursed his lips. "But can I trust you?"

"Trust me to do what?" Breathing the fresh night air helped, letting it flow through her body, spreading its calm.

"With your Acolhua roots you must be frustrated with Tenochtitlan's current policies," he murmured as if talking to himself, ignoring her question.

She licked her lips. "I hate what you did to my people, yes."

"Your people are of no importance now, Iztac Ayotl," he said coldly. "Your father was stupid enough to lose this war. In this aspect, Tenochtitlan profited greatly. The tribute your *altepetl* is paying helps to develop our own *altepetl*. It is put to a great use."

"My father lost because your people betrayed him—" She began hotly, but he raised his hand.

"Let us not waste our time talking history. Your people lost, yes, because my people chose to side with the smarter, more cunning, more powerful nation. Yet, it was not that simple. My brother, your husband, our previous Emperor, did not want to do this. Did you know that? He wanted to throw our fate with your people. He talked to me, his Chief Warlord, asking for my advice. Both I and his former Chief Warlord, that arrogant Tepanec who served my father so faithfully, told him to stay neutral, to keep away from this war. Yet, his Chief Wife thought differently, and she had many creative ways to make him do her bidding. Even when it stopped working, she knew what to do."

Hating the way her gaze leaped around, making sure no curious ears were lingering within hearing distance, she dropped her gaze, embarrassed, studying her broken fingernails, instead.

"You can help us change Tenochtitlan's policies." His voice reached her, hardly audible, but firm.

"How can I do this?"

"Oh, there are many ways. You seem to have quite an influence on our current Emperor, more than you seemed to have on the previous one, your lawful husband." The sparkle in his eyes made her grind her teeth. "And we may need to use your climbing skills, too."

She peered at him. "For what?"

"Well, we'll see, pretty princess. I have to talk to some people first, see in what ways we can use you." His gaze hardened. "Remember this. I know your secret now. Should the Empress discover what you've been up to, you would be put to death. You will die quicker than my brother, Huitzilihuitl, but maybe not as painlessly." A one-sided grin appeared. "You see, I want you to help us of your own free will. You have nothing to lose and everything to gain, if you think about it. Yet," the grin disappeared, replaced by the stony gaze once again, "yet, you should remember that I know your secret now, and should you prove disloyal or uncooperative, I will not keep it." He shrugged. "I won't ask you to do anything shameful in return. You can be sure of that. You can keep entertaining the Emperor as far as I'm concerned." As she glared at him, furious again, he added, "Oh, don't try to convince me you are climbing that boy's terrace to talk to him. He would not be so possessive about you otherwise. He would give you to me with no additional thought. You must make him very happy indeed, pretty princess. But I don't mind. Maybe the boy deserves to get what he wants, too." He shook his head. "It may all work out for the best. So now, go back and try not to get caught. I would advise you not to visit the Emperor for some time. To make sure you are safe. You seem to be a smart woman. I bet you will figure it all out and will know what should be done by the time we meet again, be ready to help us of your own free will." He straightened up. "When I send you a word, come and meet me with no delay. Remember that your free will may not be enough."

CHAPTER 6

Kuini disliked the man from the first glance, the moment the warriors' leader strolled into the room – broad, thickset, arrogant, halting by the doorway, eyeing the squatting people skeptically, even accusingly as if doubting their right to be there. Those who crowded the spacious warehouse, indeed, shifted uneasily, and the few warriors eating and playing beans jumped onto their feet.

Folding the thick arms across his chest, the man acknowledged their greetings with a slight nod, his gaze not thawing. The cloak upon his broad shoulders fluttered with a draft.

"Who is this manure eater?" whispered Kuini, safe in doing so, crouching in their far corner, between scattered chests. He made an effort to go on chewing his tamale as if nothing happened.

"Has to be someone of importance, with this cloak and all the jewelry," breathed Coyotl. He wiped his mouth, having finished with his food. "Ten warriors? I wonder why such a big thing is moving around on foot."

Kuini watched the warriors who had poured in after the man, halting in the doorway. His fingers found the rope tying his dagger to his girdle and it made him feel better. Oh, they should not have agreed to come here without their swords, he thought, should not have agreed to wander this marketplace disguised as just youths of no importance.

The memory of Tlacaelel bursting upon them only this morning, sparkling with excitement, anything but his composed derisively arrogant self, made him smile.

"The old Warlord is back in the city, and he wants to meet you, Acolhua scum," he had said, grinning. "It seems our *calmecac* days are over. Oh, now that the old frog-eater is back, we'll see some action. I'm prepared to bet my inheritance on that."

"I thought you nourished no wild ideas concerning your inheritance." Coyotl shrugged lightly, but Kuini could see his friend's guarded gaze and the tightening jaw. He was unsettled by the news, attempting to conceal it by light jokes and their usual baiting.

"So, what's now? Where are we going?" Sharing the excitement of the tall Aztec, Kuini narrowed his eyes against the strong midmorning sun.

"*He* goes to meet the old leader on the marketplace. The Warlord sent two warriors to guide him there, and to keep him safe." The pointed eyebrows lifted in the typical challenging way. "*You* stay here, and do whatever you like. He said nothing about you."

"I'm coming!" Kuini glared at the tall youth, suddenly sick with impatience and in no mood for their usual bantering. "The former Warlord will want to see me, you can be sure of that."

But Tlacaelel just shrugged, refusing to be taken out of his unusually shiny mood. "Do whatever you like. If you can, try not to pick a fight with our former warriors' leader, Highlander," he added, turning away, still laughing.

And so, before the sun reached its zenith, they had found themselves rushing through the maze of the alleys, following the warriors, tense and uncomfortable with their lack of knowledge as to their destination, but still elated. Things were finally beginning to happen.

Gazing around, Kuini tried to suppress his grin. After almost two market intervals, he had come to grips with the busy island city, not disgusted with its purposeful self-centeredness and the lack of elegance anymore. Even the perpetually damp air did not haunt his nostrils the way it did on the first day of their arrival.

He grinned. Tenochtitlan was no Texcoco, but it had its own peculiar charm, although he still hardly knew the city. Despite the declaration to his friends, he did not bother to venture outside, fascinated with *calmecac* and its life. Working alongside ever-busy Tlacaelel, Kuini had found himself enjoying his unusual tasks, sorting out endless collections of weapons, making the classes ready for different lessons of the day.

Priests and veteran warriors behaved cordially toward their unexpected guests, asking no questions. Whatever Tlacaelel said to justify the presence of the two foreigners was, apparently, enough. They went wherever they wanted, receiving no hostile glances. *Calmecac* seemed like an island of tranquility in the stormy river of this gushing, busy *altepetl*.

Feeling more and more confident, Kuini began entering the classes under this or that pretext. Lingering, he would listen avidly, fascinated, with history lessons most of all, although the lectures on the use of different weapons were as captivating.

Youths of various ages filled those various buildings. Wide-eyed and well-behaved, they seemed eager to learn, paying their elders and betters an appropriate amount of respect. No, they were not the fat, pampered aristocrats he had half expected to meet.

Learning about the wandering past of the Aztecs, and the eagle and the prophecy, Kuini felt his stomach twisting uneasily. Here was a whole island of fierce, industrious people convinced of their own supremacy as a nation and their glorious destination to rule the world. They seemed to truly believe the claim that they were chosen by Huitzilopochtli, that strange god of theirs, sincere in their intention to take over their proposed duties one day.

He had brought the subject up with Tlacaelel on one of their cozy evenings, and was surprised by the tall Aztec's response. Not amused in the least, Tlacaelel said that yes, the Mexica people were definitely chosen, and yes, they were readying to fulfill the prophecy.

When pressed, he became somewhat evasive, trying to be light about it, responding with his usual amused aggressiveness to Kuini's baiting remarks. Yet, the whole conversation left Kuini uneasy, and lying awake at night, he thought that his father may have been wrong about the Tepanecs, but not in the way everyone assumed. The real enemy to the Highlanders might not have been the Tepanecs, and not the historical Acolhua foe, but this fierce nation of the emerging Mexica Aztecs, bubbling with energy and purpose.

He also learned a great deal about his uncle, and this knowledge had him bursting with pride. Tlacaelel liked to talk about the formidable man, recounting his historical campaigns, but more often he was inclined to dwell on the wonderful way Tenochtitlan's first Chief Warlord had organized the whole Aztec warrior force and its hierarchy of ranks, developing the naval warfare and the land-born invasions as well.

"He is the smartest, fiercest, most fearless frog-eating bastard that ever lived," Tlacaelel would exclaim, his face alight and lacking his usual amused haughtiness for a change. "Before him, we were just a small nation of unorganized warriors and peasants. Yes, fearless and brave to the point that even the mighty Tepanecs were reluctant to go on their raids without asking Tenochtitlan's warriors to join; but still just a wild, unorganized bunch. But now, oh, now we are a force to be reckoned with, growing stronger with each passing day. These days no nation around the Great Lake would do anything without taking us into the account. And all thanks to him, that wild, unpredictable Tepanec with his unordinary ways and his different thinking."

"Oh, yes," muttered Coyotl, face darkening. "And you, people, are playing your beans well, making all those strong neighbors come courting after your favors, switching sides faster than an emperor's wife would switch her garments."

The deeply set eyes flashed fiercely, but before the tall youth could say something sharp, Kuini, by now used to the sudden enmity springing up between the two royal offsprings, asked nonchalantly, "How did this man organize the naval force? What did he do?"

"Oh, well," Tlacaelel frowned, making a visible effort to calm down. "He put the engineers up to developing those long, sturdy boats that could carry ten warriors and more and still float freely. Then he ordered a large amount of those to be built. He trained warriors to fight while still on the water, just in case. He said we are an island nation, and should, therefore, be able to fight by whatever means and in all sorts of conditions. People didn't like some of his changes, but my grandfather, Revered Acamapichtli, always let him have his way. And now, here we are, controlling our waters and all the trading routes around it." He glanced at Coyotl angrily. "Now go on and say that if not for the Aztec treachery your people would be controlling most of the trade still."

Coyotl shrugged, in control of his temper once again. "I don't care for your trading routes."

"We saw this kind of a boat when we first arrived here," said Kuini, more from a genuine interest than to prevent another clash. "It was monstrously big. How can it float at all?"

"It can. The engineers made sure of that. Trust the Warlord to frighten the life out of them to avoid this kind of a failure." Tlacaelel grinned reluctantly, obviously still smarting about the insult. "Itzcoatl, our current Warlord, is trying to double their amount. Just in case."

"In case of what?"

"In case of all sorts of things." He lifted his eyebrows, glancing at Kuini. "Why don't you go out and see what's happening. We, Coyotl and I, are stuck here, but you are free to roam. Why do you spend your time listening to the priests teaching children?"

Kuini shrugged. "Because that's what I want to do now."

"Very brave and efficient of you, Highlander."

"And very smart too, Aztec."

They grinned at each other, unperturbed, used to this sort of exchange. And yet, he did get to tour the city one day.

Shaking his head, Kuini suppressed his grin from spreading, thinking about the wide roads and twisting alleys, packed with people. And about his unexpected guide. Dehe, of all people! Oh but this girl kept surprising him. A small, frightened mouse on the day of their arrival in Tenochtitlan, the silly girl who had needlessly dragged after them, turning into a complete burden, was gone, replaced by a vital, confident, pretty thing, busy earning her daily meals, spending her time doing gods-know-what.

He shook his head again, grinning. No, this girl was something.

When she had disappeared on the first dawn of their arrival in *calmecac*, he considered going into the city looking for her, not too keen on the idea. His day being so full of the strange, but fascinating, *calmecac* activities, he knew his chances of finding her in that busy *altepetl* were slim. So he had shrugged and put her out of his head. Whatever happened, if she got herself into a trouble, he could not help her out. She should never have come with them in the first place.

However, she had returned in the evening, clean and dressed nicely in a simple, unadorned blouse and a long skirt, her hair combed and her eyes shining proudly, seeming as if she had grown in stature, back to her brisk, confident self of Tlaxcala Valley. Amused, he watched her, relieved that she was all right after all. But she behaved as if she didn't want to talk to him, and he was too tired and too busy, glad to avoid this sort of confrontation. Whatever she had done did her good, so when she kept disappearing dawn after dawn, explaining nothing, glaringly independent, her head held high, he had shrugged and let it be.

"What about the girl?" asked him Coyotl after a few days, when they squatted in the shadow, checking a pile of would-be swords with no obsidian blades attached to the polished wood.

"What about her?"

"Where is she spending her time?"

"I don't know."

"Aren't you supposed to know?"

Kuini shrugged, searching through the pile for cracked shafts as they had been asked to do. "Why should I?"

"Well, she helped us tremendously when we were in trouble." Coyotl paused, frowning. "When I was in trouble," he corrected himself. "And she thinks she belongs to you, you know."

"She may think whatever she likes," grunted Kuini. "I have no time for this."

"You shouldn't have let her come with us if that's so."

"Oh, I told her not to. She wouldn't listen." He looked up, angered, but mostly by the knowledge that his friend was right. "How can I take care of a woman when we do not even have a place to stay? And anyway, if she was patient enough, she would be waiting quietly for us to solve our problems. But, as it is, she chose to do whatever she does, and if it keeps her busy, than all three of us are well off."

Coyotl shrugged and returned to the long shaft he had been busy cleaning with a maguey cloth. "She is a good girl, loyal and clever. She saved my life, or at least helped you to save it. That's why I think she deserves better treatment. Unless you don't want her, and, in that case, we should make sure she gets back to her mountains safely."

Kuini fixed his gaze on the pile of fake swords. "Oh well, I'll talk to her, and if she wants to go back, I'll take her there, but only when the old Warlord is back. I don't want to miss anything because of the annoying *cihua*." Clenching his fists, he welcomed something to focus his anger on. "Why are women always so clingy, so needy, so eager to get in your way? I will have to drag all over the Lowlands and the Highlands, missing important happenings, because the stupid *cihua* insisted to come along, curse her into the worst parts of the Underworld!"

But when she did not return for more than a few days, he had found the thoughts of her invading his mind uncomfortably often, interfering with his concentration. He did treat her badly, didn't he? So when on one early noon she appeared at the building they had come to regard as their own, hesitating at the doorway, he leaped to his feet and rushed toward her, ignoring Tlacaelel's derisively lifted eyebrows.

"What's his thing with the slave?" he heard the Aztec asking behind his back, the grin in his voice obvious.

As he propelled her back outside, he heard Coyotl saying quietly, "She is not his slave."

"A concubine?"

The strong light poured on them, sparkling off her neatly combed, braided hair. He noticed her blouse was new yet again, brightly colored, setting off the golden shade of her slender shoulders in most favorable of ways.

"Are you all right?" he asked, at a loss.

Her eyes peered at him, dark and unreadable. "Yes, I'm well."

"Well, you disappeared and..." He lifted his hands helplessly. "We didn't know what to think."

She looked at him searchingly. "You wanted me to come back?"

"Well, yes, of course."

"I just didn't know..." She swallowed, and he saw her fingers crushing the fringes of her pretty blouse.

"Where have you been? You look well."

The color washed her cheeks all at once, turning her slender face into a darker shade of gold.

"Oh, these clothes," she said, smoothing her skirt nervously. "I feel so strange wearing them. It's not as comfortable as my gown, but no one is staring at me now."

"Where did you get those clothes?"

"On the marketplace."

"How?"

"Kaay bought them for me, like she promised."

He stared at her. "Who is Kaay?"

"Oh, Kaay is a healer. And not just a healer." The girl's eyes sparkled proudly. "She is a great healer. Everyone is looking for her help and advice. Even the Palace's dwellers are sending their slaves to buy her ointments and potions."

He watched her animated face, remembering the morning he had woken up in her makeshift home for the second time, after a night of lovemaking, after making her a woman. Back then, the change in her had been immense. And pleasing. The haunted, pitiful creature was gone, replaced by a sparkling, pretty girl, full of promise and expectation. He had considered coming back the next night, he remembered, hoping to postpone his and Coyotl's journey.

He blinked, his curiosity welling along with his excitement. Yes, now again the frightened, badly dressed, clingy creature was gone. Even her cheeks seemed to fill and there was a beautiful glow to her skin now.

"Why are you staring at me like that?" she asked, frowning.

He shook his head. "Why would this healer woman buy you clothes?"

"Because I help her. I work for her, every day." Her eyes lit proudly once again. "At first I was just arranging things and helping her to make everything look pretty. But now she trusts me with making medicine as well. And she promised to teach me how to make rare ointments and other things I didn't know."

"So that's where you've been spending your time." He looked at her incredulously. "Working in the marketplace?"

"Yes. Is there something wrong with that?"

"No, not at all. It's just... strange. I didn't expect you to get that busy."

Now her eyes drew darker, having a familiar spark to them. "You expected me to sit in that far corner for days, keeping out of your way, didn't you? Just a girl that makes no trouble." Even in her anger she looked pretty, not the panic stricken, frightened thing of their first night in Tenochtitlan, but a high-tempered, attractive girl that would not be put in her place by a few cutting words. If he did this, she might turn and leave, and suddenly he didn't want her to do that.

"Listen, I'm glad that you found something to do and that you enjoy it. When the old Warlord is back we may know more about our plans. And we will have a better place to stay, too."

"In that great house of his?"

"Maybe." He frowned. No, it would not work. She would not be allowed to stay there without him, and he was certain to be busy elsewhere. "We'll see about it when he is back," he added, narrowing his eyes.

"Oh well." She shifted her weight from one tiny sandaled foot to the other. The tip of her tongue slipped out, licking her full lower lip.

"Do you have to go back to that healer of yours?" he asked.

"Yes, I do. She will be expecting me back after midday."

"I'll take you there." Resolutely, he glanced into the semidarkness of the building, still hearing his friends' quiet voices. "Let me just tell them."

And now, watching the thickset leader talking to the warriors, Kuini found it difficult to suppress a grin, remembering the way her face transformed once again, glowing with pure childish joy. Oh, she was changing so fast – girl, woman, forest creature, insignificant, then suddenly attractive, reliable and always there, then in a matter of heartbeats disappearing, turning evasive, a precious thing to be tamed and used carefully.

Oh, and she was a wonderful guide, too. Leading the way through the maze of alleys, she had made him follow her, never bothering to mark their surroundings but never erring regardless, talking all the while, breathless and excited. Apparently, she had learned a great deal in these two market intervals spent on the marketplace. From the prices on food to the Palace's gossip, she had related to him mounds of information.

Tenochtitlan was prospering, she had told him in a breathless rush. The prices stopped climbing since the Acolhua Lowlanders lost their war and the markets filled with plenty of new items to buy and to sell. Foreigners, tourists and traders flooded the city, making it crowded but cheerful, bubbling in contentment. The new emperor, just a boy really, intended to build the construction to bring fresh water into Tenochtitlan, having received the blessing of his grandfather, the Tepanec Emperor. The main engineer was reported to start the preparations.

He watched her sparkling eyes, fascinated. They said the main engineer was seen running all over the mainland, she said, waving his rolls of bark-sheets, followed by so many workers and other engineers that they looked like an invading party of warriors. Kuini could not suppress his chuckle, imagining this picture.

The Empress was, of course, the one who ruled Tenochtitlan now, wielding much power over the other island and Tenochtitlan's sister city, Tlatelolco, although this other town had its own ruler and a council of the elders, she went on.

She would hardly stop for breath, bubbling with excitement, but this state suited her, making her so attractive he could not fight the temptation, catching her in his arms for a fleeting kiss in a seemingly quiet corner. Of course, he had wanted more, but remembering their unsuccessful first attempt to make love in the woods and her fright and the need of preparations, he did not attempt to push it further than a few wandering kisses, although she melted into his arms, content and deliciously soft.

"Come back to *calmecac* tonight," he had told her hoarsely, suppressing his need. "I'll make sure we sleep alone."

She beamed at him from below, her eyes glowing, dominating her slender face. "You will wait for me? You will not spend another night talking to your friends or thinking about the Second Wife of the late Emperor?"

He felt like taking a step back, his excitement evaporating. "What do you mean?"

She watched him, suddenly wary and apprehensive.

"What are you talking about, Dehe?" He made an effort to unclench his teeth.

"Nothing. I just thought... I thought you might like this princess. I thought..." Her voice trailed off, eyes growing frightened under his heavy gaze.

He swallowed. "What do you know, Dehe? What did you hear?"

Her eyes grew darker as her lips tightened. "I heard many things. I know that this woman had not been faithful to the Emperor, and I know that she took a medicine to prevent her child from being born." She took a deep breath. "I also know that you think about her and that now, because of her, you are angry with me. And it is not right and not just. You should not think of this evil woman..."

He took a step back, clenching his fists to stop his hands from trembling. "You don't know what you are talking about," he said, controlling his rage with an effort. "You repeat some stupid gossip like some stupid market girl. But if I ever hear you mentioning Iztac Ayotl again, I swear I will kill you. And I mean it, Dehe. Never talk about her again, not with me, nor with anyone else. I don't want to hurt you, but I will if you say anything like that again. Do you understand?"

She stared at him, horrified, her eyes enormous in the paleness of her face, glittering with unshed tears. He took a deep breath, then another.

"I'm sorry," he said finally, uneasy at making her so frightened. "I shouldn't have threatened you, but you should never have said what you said. It's filthy gossip. Stupid, dirty, rotten nonsense." He shrugged. "Of course, I won't hurt you. Stop looking so frightened."

The tears ran down her cheeks now. He saw her clenching her teeth as if trying to hold them back, but they kept pouring, silent and huge. Gaze fixed on him, she just stood there, again forlorn and desolate, a small, helpless creature that he had hurt carelessly, without a need. How had it come to that?

Taken by compassion, just like the first time by the river, he stepped closer, squeezing her thin shoulders between his arms.

"Don't cry, Dehe," he said helplessly. "I didn't mean to hurt you."

But as she pressed closer, burying her face in his chest, he felt his stomach as tight as a wooden ball, his anger still alive. Was it true what she said? Had Iztac Ayotl did any of these things?

He could feel the girl trembling, fighting the tears. "Can I still come back tonight?" she whispered.

"Yes, of course."

But he knew he wouldn't touch her. Not tonight. Not after this.

The raising voices tore Kuini out of his reverie, bringing him back to the warehouse full of pottery and chests and overturned tables, among strange warriors, eating and playing beans, facing aggressive newcomers. He returned his gaze to the thickset leader in the doorway as the man walked in unhurriedly, the escorting warriors lingering at the doorway.

"Well, where is our noble Acolhua guest?" asked the man, his gaze encircling the dimly lit space, resting upon their corner.

Kuini felt more than saw Coyotl rising to his feet.

"Greetings, Honorable Leader," he heard his friend saying, standing there calmly, composed, facing the man, neither submissive nor aggressive. The Lowlander's tension could be detected in the clasped jaw, in the overly straight shoulders, yet Kuini was sure he would be the only one to see these signs. His heart squeezed with pride. Oh, Coyotl would not beg for help. He would receive his due with dignity and pride.

The man came closer. "It's a pleasure to meet you at last, young heir to Texcoco throne." The narrow eyes sparkled with a flicker of amusement. "I wish we could meet under more favorable circumstances. This place..." The man's lips quivered derisively as his gaze encircled the cramped dusty room. "Oh, I'm sure the Acolhua royal family was used to better surroundings."

"I'm not complaining," answered Coyotl, still calm.

The man's grin widened. "Oh, I suppose a few seasons among the savages would do that to a prince."

This time Coyotl winced. Kuini watched his friend's fists clenching. "True. I enjoyed the hospitality of the Highlands for more than a few seasons. Those people treated me well. They are no savages."

The warrior raised his eyebrows, unperturbed, yet, his grin lost some of its amused spark. "Well, I suppose this attitude was the one to keep your heart from being dumped on one of their barbarian altars," he muttered, shrugging. The gaze left his guest's face, shifting toward the warriors. "Out. All of you."

Kuini watched the men hurrying to obey, their cloaks swirling, not concealing the long swords attached to their girdles. He wished they hadn't left their weapons at *calmecac*.

"What are *you* waiting for?"

The barking question made him wince. His eyes leaped back toward the leader, meeting the man's blazing gaze.

He blinked. "What?"

"Are you deaf? Go away. Now!"

Kuini didn't remember leaping to his feet, but somehow he was not squatting anymore. Staring at the broad, furious face, he took in the wide cheekbones, the bushy eyebrows, the blazing, narrow eyes.

"You won't tell me what to do. You are not my leader." He was surprised to hear his own voice still steady, hard put to control his limbs, which were trembling with rage.

The man's eyes narrowed. "I will tell you what to do, and I'll do it for the last time," he said, ominously calm. For a heartbeat he stared at Kuini, then shrugged, turning to Coyotl. "Tell your warrior to go away in a hurry, before I cut him here and now. I'm repeating myself only as a courtesy to you, Netzahualcoyotl." He grinned humorously. "You'll be provided with a new guard to keep you safe."

Curious to see Coyotl's reaction, Kuini did not dare to take his eyes off his adversary. The dangerous bastard looked fit to attack any moment, his thick fingers playing with the ties fastening his sword. Kuini ground his teeth, thinking about his pitiful dagger.

"This man is my friend, not my warrior," he heard Coyotl saying, his voice still calm, but with an obvious note of uncertainty creeping into it.

The leader's gaze deepened, growing unbearably cold. "It doesn't matter who this man is. I sent all my men, *friends and warriors*, away. And with all due respect, I'm a more prominent person than you are, oh honorable, but displaced, heir to Texcoco throne." The bushy eyebrows rose. "Are you sure you wish to start your relationship with Tenochtitlan with a bad, ugly incident? Do you know who I am?"

"You are the Chief Warlord of Tenochtitlan." Coyotl swallowed, then glanced at Kuini helplessly. "Please," he said so quietly it came out almost as a murmur. "Please, wait for me outside. We should respect these people's customs. Please."

Kuini took a deep breath, the air seeping through his clenched teeth with difficulty. With an effort, he took his eyes off the man in front of him, made himself disregard the derisively twisting lips.

"I'm leaving only because you asked me to," he said to Coyotl. "I'll be outside."

There was a movement by the doorway and another group of people poured in, talking loudly. Well, not all of them were talking, but only the man in the lead, his cloak flowing down his wide shoulders, his head held high, his warrior's lock standing up proudly, although there was evidently not much of it left. Oh, how could one forget that arrogant, challenging bearing? Kuini just stared.

The old Aztec Warlord came in, crossing the dusty, dimly lit space in a few long paces, his large, widely spaced eyes narrowing, taking in the tension.

"I see you already met our honorable guests," he said lightly, addressing the other Warlord.

"Oh, yes, I did." There was a light friendly tone to the Warlord's voice now.

The large eyes of the Aztec twinkled, lingering on Kuini. He saw the generous lips quivering, stretching into a grin. "And they already gave you trouble."

The Warlord roared with a sudden laughter. "Oh, yes, they did that, too."

"Typical." The Aztec grinned and came closer. "My nephew would not be himself if he did not get into trouble the moment he arrived in this or that *altepetl* that is foreign to him."

"Your nephew?" exclaimed the Warlord, clearly taken aback. "Is this youth your nephew?"

"Oh, yes. The wildest of the Highlanders and the fiercest of the Lowlanders." The Aztec laughed, turning to Kuini. "So how are you, Nephew?"

"I'm all right," muttered Kuini, having difficulty unclenching his teeth.

"What did he do?"

"Quite a few unforgivable transgressions. But now that I know his blood connections, I'm not surprised," said the Warlord good-naturedly. "I should have guessed." He sobered. "Well, shall we proceed? I suppose now that I know who this youth is, he can stay."

"Oh, so he refused to leave." The Aztec made it a statement. "No. If you wanted a private conversation with the heir, you should have it. Come," he added motioning to Kuini. "We'll be waiting outside."

The Warlord frowned. "Won't you join our conversation?"

"Call me if you need me. I'll be outside, by that stand of tortillas."

The clamor of the marketplace pounced on them as they came back into the world of the blazing sun.

"So, you refused to leave? Rudely at that, I suppose," said the Aztec, leading their way up the narrow alley.

"He didn't ask," muttered Kuini, following. "He was ruder

than me, and he talked about savages most of the time."

"I see." The older man glanced at Kuini, his eyes twinkling again. "Well, he is the Chief Warlord of Tenochtitlan. He can talk however he likes."

"He is not my leader. He cannot tell me what to do."

The man's grin widened. "I wonder how you survived among the fighting forces of the Lowlanders with that attitude of yours." His eyes narrowed against the stall with hot tortillas piling on it, before leading their way to a cluster of mats at the shade of a wide-branched tree.

"Well, it's good to see you again, boy," he said, squatting comfortably.

The owner of the stall rushed to their side, carrying a tray with a flask and two cups. Pouring slowly, obviously lingering, he eyed his guests with an unconcealed curiosity.

"Leave the flask here," the Aztec gestured with a measure of impatience.

In the daylight, he looked different, older and paler, more wrinkled than Kuini remembered. The man had thinned, he suddenly realized, studying the brown skin that hung vacantly upon the sharp cheekbones. Only the widely spaced eyes had not changed, sparkling with the same arrogance and pride, softened by a well familiar, mischievous twinkle. His stomach twisted. The man did not look well.

"So, now tell me what you've been up to during these past three summers," said the Aztec, lifting his cup, his grin widening again. "Naturally, I would be most interested in the first two of those summers."

Kuini returned the smile, sipping his *octli*, enjoying its taste, relaxing with every gulp. "It was an interesting experience. Azcapotzalco looked good. I think we could have taken it.'

"Not a chance!" his companion called out hotly. "Acolhua warriors are not fierce enough, and your leader was nothing but a stupid emperor."

"I agree about our leader. He took his time, lingering around Tollan for days, instead of rushing toward Azcapotzalco as if a pack of hungry winter wolves were after him. Stupid, I think. By the time we arrived, they were ready, closing the roads leading to the city."

The large eyes narrowed. "You would rather approach this *altepetl* from another direction?"

"Well, yes." Kuini hesitated, somewhat embarrassed. This man knew everything there was to know about warfare. If he thought Azcapotzalco could not be taken, then that was that.

"Which one?"

"The one opposite to the lake. You see, they did expect us to roll down those hills the moment that battle was over. And then, after giving them so much time to prepare, we took the wide, well-beaten road like we were stupid traders." He shrugged. "They had so much time to prepare I wonder why they did not try to ambush us."

"They must have been stunned by their losing that battle at Tollan," said the Aztec, watching Kuini with some appreciation. "They are not used to losing battles. Let alone so near the Capital. I was stunned too, you know. I never expected to hear about the Tepanec warriors losing battle after battle. I could have understood the failure of their ill-prepared first invasion, but I never expected them to go on losing for the whole cycle of seasons." The man shook his head. "Tezozomoc's mind must have been losing its sharpness. He is such an old man. I wish he would die already."

"How old is he?"

"Oh, he is old, very old. Must be a hundred summers or more. He was about your father's age when he came to rule, and it was more than two times twenty of summers ago. I was about your age when it happened. My father was a Chief Warlord, and he made sure Tezozomoc came to inherit, because some influential people wanted to see his older brother upon the throne. There was a terrible mess, and the whole capital was in turmoil, but my father prevailed, alone against many." The man's eyes sparkled proudly. "He was quite a man. I worshipped him. Still, I was stupid enough to make matters worse for him, getting into a bunch of trouble, doing all the wrong things." The large eyes cleared, sparkling amusedly. "Hard to imagine, eh?"

"Not that hard." Kuini smiled, perfectly at ease. No, it was actually easy to imagine that man getting into a whole bunch of trouble.

The Aztec laughed. "You cheeky bastard!"

Another flask of *octli* was brought, along with a plate of freshly rolled tortillas.

"I'm famished," said the older man, grabbing the food. "Try to run all over your mountains when you reach my age. I wish your father had chosen to join people closer to the Great Lake's shores." The dignified head shook. "And all this only to learn that my brother did not wait for my counsel, and that you two were already safely on your way here. What a waste of time and energy!"

Kuini caught his breath. "Have you met Father?"

"Yes, I did." The man looked up calmly. "I wish we could spend more time together, but in the current situation neither of us could entertain each other in our homelands."

"Was he..." Kuini swallowed, finding it difficult to utter the question. "Is he well?"

"Yes, he is well, if that's what you wanted to know." A grin stretched the generous lips, but this time it did not reach his companion's eyes. "Or did you want to know if he is still the Warriors' Leader?"

"Yes." Kuini cleared his throat, hearing his own voice breaking. "Yes, I want to know that."

The mirthless grin widened. "What do you think?"

He swallowed once again. "He is not."

"Of course." The Aztec resumed his eating, suddenly cold and accusing. "He went to desperate measures to save you two, stupid hotheads that you are. He paid the price you were supposed to pay. You didn't expect your deeds to go unpunished, did you?"

Shivering, Kuini felt the soft summer breeze penetrating his bones. He clenched his fists tight. "Is his life in danger?" he asked, fixing his gaze upon the crude surface of the low table.

The Aztec's voice softened. "No, he doesn't think so, and I agree with him. He is an extremely capable, formidable man. He can handle this situation. But in his age people are expecting to sit down and enjoy the fruits of their life-long labor, especially powerful, successful people. Your father deserved it more than anyone, you know that?"

"Yes, I know that." The pattern upon the rough wooden table seemed to blur, mixing with each other. He blinked forcefully, refusing to look up.

"Well, boy, I'm not accusing you of betraying your father," said the Aztec finally, in a kinder voice. "I know how you must feel. Like I told you, I did my share of stupid deeds at your age, and I know you did want to take the responsibility." He drank thirstily. "Your father is an outstanding man, and he can weather this storm and come out of it unharmed. His spirit is high, and he is very proud of you and expecting much from you in the future. So get it out of your head for now." The man leaned forward, placing his palms upon the table. "I gather you didn't waste your time skulking around Tenochtitlan, did you? Tlacaelel seems to think highly of you and your friend, and to impress this haughty imperial offspring takes skill. It seems that you started making right contacts even before I could push you in that direction. Impressive, very impressive."

Reluctantly, Kuini lifted his gaze, meeting the amused, well-meaning eyes. "So, what now?" he asked, feeling better by the moment.

"Oh, now? Now you wait."

"Wait for what?"

"For a certain matter to be resolved." Another tortilla was devoured. "On the other hand, your friend is the one that will have to wait." The man's affectionate gaze rested on him with an obvious satisfaction. "You've proven yourself a good warrior with obvious leading capacities. I'll arrange for you a place in the nearing campaign into Zacatlan, and I'll make sure your leaders are aware of your abilities and your family connections. You'll go far, boy, you will Mark my words."

"Where is Zacatlan?" ask Kuini, his heartbeat accelerating. A campaign, at last!

"Oh, it's far enough into the southwest, much farther than you ventured on your previous adventure. A misty, mountainous area. You'll find it interesting, I predict."

"And what about Coyotl?"

The man shrugged. "He may be allowed to join this campaign, too. Depends on how he handles his friendship with our young Emperor. Depends on quite a few events that should be taking place through the next market interval or so." His gaze clouded. "The Palace is boiling, and I wouldn't like to see any of you near the royal enclosure now."

Kuini studied his pottery cup. "After the Emperor's death, what usually happens to his wives?"

"I don't know. They live on, I suppose, if not given away to other rulers." The man chuckled. "I heard of places where the wives would be sent onward, to accompany their masters into the afterlife."

"So Huitzilihuitl's wives were given away?"

"Some of them, yes, I'd assume." There was a wondering note to his converser's voice now. "Obviously not his Chief Wife, but some of the minor wives are still there. Which one are you curious about?"

"None of them!" Refusing to meet the amused gaze, Kuini reached for his cup of *octli*. "I just remembered that Coyotl's favorite sister was given to Huitzilihuitl. If she is still here, he would be happy to meet her, I suppose."

The amusement in the dark eyes deepened. "Oh, now I remember you getting into a trouble over some princess. Was that the same favorite sister?"

"No!" Kuini clasped his teeth tight, fighting to keep the agitation off his face. "It was another princess, and I did not kidnap her at all."

The Aztec still peered at him, his amusement spilling. "I now remember you disappearing night after night, going out of that window the moment everyone would fall asleep." He shook his head, then sobered all of a sudden. "Forget it, boy. Forget it all together. I think I've already given you this advice before, but I'll repeat myself. Don't chase princesses or emperors' wives. It's dangerous and unnecessary. There are some chances one should not take." He shook his head again, his frown deepening. "Echoes of the past. I also came once to Tenochtitlan, chasing a princess. It was a hideous affair. I won't wish it on my worst enemies, let alone my favorite nephew. There are plenty of girls out there, and I'll make sure you get your pick while you are here in Tenochtitlan. Just don't come near the Palace."

Kuini stood the penetrating gaze, his heart beating strongly, unevenly. "I won't do any of it. You got me all wrong."

Relieved, he saw a warrior heading toward their table.

"Honorable Leader, would you please come to meet the Honorable Warlord?" asked the man, and the Aztec's gaze lost its intensity.

"Of course," he said, rising to his feet, dignified and unhurried, but his face paled and his lips were clasped tight, as if it took him some effort to get up. "Wait for me here, Nephew," he added, stressing his last word.

The eyes of the warrior widened, and Kuini was hard put to suppress a grin. Well, well, he thought. He was the nephew of the powerful former Warlord of Tenochtitlan. Not bad, not bad at all, come to think of it.

He watched the stall owner returning with another tray, nimble and servile.

"Would you like to drink more *octli*, Honorable Master?" he asked, and Kuini could not hold his laughter anymore.

Honorable Master, of all things!

"Yes, bring another flask," he said as imperiously as he could. "And more of those rolled tortillas."

Seeing Coyotl coming out of the wooden structure, hesitating, blinking against the strong sun, he waved.

"Help yourself, Revered Emperor," he said, reclining upon his mat. "Those tortillas are good, and the *octli* is of the best quality."

Coyotl dropped onto the opposite mat, where the Aztec had squatted earlier. "You look mighty pleased with yourself."

"It's the food. Those tortillas are good!"

His friend's eyes twinkled. "And the *octli* smells good, too. How much did you drink?"

Kuini choked with laughter. "A few cups, *father*. Am I allowed to get more?" He poured two goblets until the bright, whitish liquid spilled. "Here, get some. Your sour face gives me indigestion. Was that arrogant dung-eater so unbearable?"

Coyotl shot a careful glance around. "Well, he was not easy to handle. But I think he is all right, actually. He knows what he wants, and he doesn't go around it."

"What does he want?"

"Pretty much what your father said." Coyotl reached for a tortilla, eyeing it thoughtfully, as though deliberating whether to eat it or not. "Most of our time he spent making sure I'm aware of the fact that they are doing me a great favor and that I'll be expected to repay all their kindness. As if I couldn't figure it out all by myself." His face twisted. "Your father did it too, but unlike the Aztecs, he and his people saved me. They gave me shelter, and I owe them much anyway, even should they decide not to help me anymore. But the Aztecs? They did nothing but betray me and my people. Without them I wouldn't be in this mess. So I'm not sure how much gratitude I should feel now that they have decided to act decently."

Pushing the cup across the table, Kuini straightened up. "Drink *octli* and relax. You need them now, so you will have to suppress all this anger and be your charming, easygoing self again."

"Oh, what a fine adviser!" cried out Coyotl, picking his cup up. "You almost started a fight with the Chief Warlord of Tenochtitlan the moment we met the man."

"Oh, don't remind me. What a filthy bastard!"

"Oh, yes. And he was so deliberately rude."

"I know. That's why I couldn't help it."

Coyotl frowned. "Anyway, what do we do now?" he asked, addressing his untouched tortilla.

Kuini shrugged. "We rest and eat and have a good time until the things are settled here. The Aztec said we showed up too early."

"The Aztec?" Coyotl's eyes twinkled. "That Tepanec uncle of yours, you mean."

Kuini shot his friend a rueful glance. "Yes. The dear Tepanec uncle of mine."

"You two got along pretty well, actually, judging by your

mood. It can't be just *octli*."

"Look, he is all right. He is a great man. It's just that I can't think of him in those terms. Not here in Tenochtitlan." He poured them more *octli*. "Although, I would give anything to see the face of that manure-eating warlord again, when the Aztec introduced me as his nephew. Gods, that was a sight worth seeing." He chuckled. "Tlacaelel will be flabbergasted, too."

"I wondered why you didn't tell him of your Tenochtitlan's connections before."

Tossing his tortilla aside, Kuini shrugged. "I don't know. I guess I wasn't sure if he could be trusted, and also, I wanted him to talk to us more freely."

"Oh, you are a deep one!" Elevated from his previous gloomy mood, Coyotl roared with laughter. "But the Warlord, oh gods, he didn't see it coming. Even though, he recovered well; said with your temper and insolence he is not surprised at this family connection. Come to think of it, he is right. You do look like that man, but worse than that, you sometimes act like him as well."

"Oh, shut up!" Half amused, half irritated, Kuini banged his cup against the table. "What are they doing there, anyway? What takes them so long?"

Coyotl's eyebrows climbed up. "Conversing privately."

"In that warehouse?"

"Yes."

"I want to know what they are talking about." Surprising himself, Kuini jumped to his feet with such suddenness he had a hard time keeping his balance.

"Sit back down, you crazy adventurer. You will never get near enough. There are plenty of warriors strolling all around that building." Coyotl hand locked around his arm. "And if you get caught trying to eavesdrop it'll be the end of us."

"I won't get caught, and I think we should know more about their plans. We are not their tools. They may think that we are, but we are not. I want to know why we came here too early; what should have happened that has not; what we are expected to do afterward."

Coyotl's grip on his arm tightened. "Stop yelling and sit

down," he hissed. "You know very well all that and more. I told you all about my conversation with your father." The Lowlander's frown deepened. "You are so edgy since we entered Tenochtitlan, and this is plain crazy. This *altepetl* is doing something to you, but what we need is exactly the opposite. We need to keep calm and be careful and wise, not to pick fights, drink *octli*, and run all over the marketplace like children. What's gotten into you?"

Kuini pulled his hand back. "Nothing. I want to know what's going on, that's all. I'll be back shortly." Looking around, he grinned, seeing a small side alley spreading to their left. "Stay here until I'm back."

Before his friend had a chance to try to stop him or continue preaching on carefulness, he charged down the narrow pathway, his heart pumping with excitement.. He'd had enough carefulness for one day, and he did want to know what was going on, what both wily warlords were planning, even though the general gist was clear to him. Spending two market intervals with Tlacaelel, he learned all about the brooding in Tenochtitlan, with some of its most prominent citizens unhappy with the Empress's policies, which made the Aztec island into just another province of Azcapotzalco.

Yet, was it really true? Were the warlords about to kill the Empress, the late Emperor's Chief Wife and the current Emperor's mother, Tezozomoc's favorite daughter? And what happened to the rest of the late Emperor's wives?

Light-footed and lightheaded, he rushed down the alley until another pathway spread to his left. Taking that turn, then another, he reached the warehouses from behind, a whole cluster of them. Not playing with idea of sneaking through the doorway, he recalled a row of small openings near the roof, definitely unguarded.

Slowing his pace, he watched the passersby, his blood boiling with impatience. When the alley momentarily cleared, he scaled the wooden wall, rolling onto the craggy roof, hoping that no one had noticed him doing so. To leap between the tiles and the gaps between them seemed like the best of courses until reaching the one that, according to his calculations, belonged to the warehouse of his destination.

A silence prevailed. Nearing the edge, he listened. Muffled voices seemed to reach out. Clinging to the wooden border, he went down the ledge, then listened again. The voices carried more clearly now. He caught his breath.

"You can't delay this raid into Zacatlan." The Aztec's voice uttered, low and strained.

"I can't leave Tenochtitlan now." The warlord's voice rasped angrily.

"I know. Unless you want to postpone the whole thing."

"Can't do that, either. She is becoming less and less cooperative. She has been running this fresh water project without consulting me, although I was the one to suggest it in the first place. She sent the delegation to Azcapotzalco without letting me know, and she's been acting independently ever since."

"Is she suspecting something?"

There was a heartbeat of silence. "I don't think so." More silence. "She must have just thought it through, realizing that I can be a threat to her son after all."

This time the silence lasted for longer period of time, having a heavy quality to it.

"I think that the offer she made, with that Acolhua-Tepanec princess for a Chief Wife, had brought her back to her senses," said the Warlord after a while.

Kuini felt his grip slipping against the rough ledge, his palms sweaty, heart making wild leaps inside his chest.

The Aztec's voice rang calmly, unperturbed. "It would make sense. Curious that she didn't realize that before. She must have been desperate making sure her son would inherit."

"Oh, yes, that she was. Filthy *cihua*!"

"So, when do you plan to get rid of her?"

More silence. "It proves more difficult. Her slaves are afraid of her more than they are afraid of the wrath of gods. The whole Palace seems to be under her palm."

"Is it so difficult to kill someone?" cried out the Aztec, and Kuini stifled a nervous laughter, remembering the killers Texcoco Emperor had sent against this very man. It had, indeed, proven difficult to kill someone. "Were I a little younger…"

The Warlord's mirthless laughter shook the air. "Oh, I'm sure you would go straight ahead, hacking the Empress with your sword."

"Oh, don't make me reflect on the glorious past," The Aztec chuckled. "Once upon a time, I climbed one of those Palace's terraces, to make one bad empress behave. It was a mad deed, and I still don't know how I managed to get away with that." He hesitated. "I didn't kill her, though."

"Who was she? Not my father's Chief Wife, surely!" Kuini could imagine the Aztec's grin, as the Warlord's voice grew lower. "I'm sorry you didn't kill her. She was a vile woman."

"Another *cihua* of Azcapotzalco's royal family."

"Oh, yes. Those are usually ruthless and highly ambitious." The current Warlord paused. "There is more than one such in the Palace these days, I came to discover."

"Oh?"

"My Acolhua-Tepanec bride-to-be, the late Emperor's Second Wife."

"This girl? She is nothing. A meaningless princess."

"That's what I thought. But the pretty *cihua* is cunning and ambitious. Apparently, she had planned for many summers to come, and she would stop before nothing, believe me. Such a wild beast!" A short silence prevailed. "She may help us."

"Why would she? I imagine she may hate the Empress, of course. But what would she gain?"

"More than you think. And anyway, I can force her into helping us should she prove difficult."

"I daresay I don't want to know how."

Another silence. Kuini grew aware of his cramped muscles as he hung under the roof, beside the row of smallish openings, his body so tense he could imagine it breaking into twenty little pieces should he fall off this wall, the way a hard pottery would break. He unclenched his teeth with an effort.

The silence in the dimness of the warehouse hung.

"We'll solve this one way or another before the next market day," said the Warlord finally.

"I'll send the word to my people. And I'll send you some warriors too, so you can pick the best fitting ones."

"How about the Acolhua heir?"

The Aztec's voice did not change. "He can't be of use to us in this. He'll have to wait until the deed is done."

"And that nephew of yours. He is a highlander, isn't he? I can use him in the Palace."

"No!" The Aztec's voice rang sharply. "I don't want him to be involved in any of this. He is a good warrior. He'll prove useful in the raids on Zacatlan."

"He needs to learn a civilized way of behavior."

"He fought with the Acolhua Lowlanders, so he knows perfectly well how to behave."

The voices grew lower as though the speakers were drawing away. Kuini pressed closer, hoping to hear more. He *needed* to know. What he had heard was painfully not enough.

A creak of a wooden screen being removed confirmed his conclusion. They were moving out. Hurriedly, he made his way back toward the roof.

By the time he reached the tortillas' stand, the mats in the shade of the tree were empty, but he could see Coyotl's tall figure lingering at the head of the alley, with both warlords standing nearby, conversing idly, like people who had just met. They all turned their heads and watched him dubiously as he neared, sweaty and fighting for breath. The Aztec's eyebrows crawled up in an amused question, while Coyotl's dark gaze and the Warlord's disdainful grin made Kuini uneasy.

"Speaking of civilized behavior," muttered the Warlord, turning back to his companion. "It was a delight to see you, Old Friend," he added, addressing the Aztec. "I wish you would accompany us on our nearing campaign."

"Oh, it would be a rare pleasure," said the Aztec as politely, but his eyes sparkled with mischief. "I wish my health would allow it. But I'll send you the best of my warriors, so you will be able to choose the ones who will suit."

"I appreciate that." The Warlord nodded and turned toward the waiting litter.

"Honorable Leader!" Kuini felt like taking a step back the way they all whirled at him. He hesitated. "With your permission, I wish to apologize for my previous behavior."

The narrowed eyes of the thickset man bore at him amidst the deafening silence.

Kuini swallowed. "What I said to you was unacceptable, and I apologize for that. It will never happen again."

"All right, warrior," said the man after another heartbeat of staring, his eyebrows lifted high. "Anything else?"

"I would be honored to be among the warriors you would select for your personal use in the Palace." He blurted it out in one breath, knowing that it was now or never. The heavy silence around him was nerve-wrecking.

Now the man looked genuinely surprised. The corner of the thin mouth lifted in a slightly amused grin as he glanced at the Aztec, a silent question in his widening eyes. Then his gaze returned to Kuini.

"Why would I do this, warrior?"

He fought the urge to take a deep breath. "I'm good in all sorts of warfare, traditional and less-so."

The gaze boring at him hardened, then deepened. "Well, if your Honorable Uncle does not object, you may present yourself along with the other warriors he'll send," said the Warlord, turning away. "But one slip, one rude answer, one incident of disobedience, and you'll be sent back in disgrace. *If* you are lucky."

His paces heavy and firm, the thickset man headed for his litter amidst the lingering, uncomfortably heavy silence.

CHAPTER 7

Iztac rubbed her eyes against the strong midmorning sun. Had she slept late again? Yawning, she refused to get up, the silly chatter of the other women reaching her from the adjacent room. Stupid *cihuas*! Why wouldn't they go out, stroll the gardens or do something useful? Why did they have to be around, chirping on and on like a pair of silly birds?

She pressed her palms against her forehead. The heavy sleep gave no relief to her tiredness. Had it been only a few days since this terrible night and her conversation with the Warlord? It seemed like a lifetime now.

She didn't go out during these days and nights, and every time a less familiar slave would enter their quarters she would jump, her heartbeat going wild. *Had he talked to the Empress already?*

There was no telling what the filthy Warlord would do, but one thing was certain. That man would do nothing that wouldn't serve his goals. So she might be safe as long as he felt he could use her. *To do what?*

She pressed her fingers against her skull, trying to ease the headache. He wanted her to help them change Tenochtitlan's policies. Them? Who were those people? And how did they propose to go about changing the Palace's policies? Shivering, she remembered that the last time such policies were changed, the Emperor, her husband, had died and the Aztec warriors joined her people's enemies. So what could be changed this time?

Her heart missed a beat. Was another emperor destined to die? Were they expecting her help in disposing of Chimal? Oh gods, but she needed to talk to him, warn him, somehow; find a way to keep him safe.

Pushing her hair off her face, she snatched her blouse, frowning at its crumbled, badly wrinkled state as it lay there on the floor, where she had dropped it before falling asleep. The stupid maids could have picked it up. As she tied her sandals' strips, the light footsteps of Ihuitl, her fellow minor wife, interrupted the silence.

"Iztac-Ayotl, where are you going?" asked the young woman, standing at the doorway, her eyes open wide, her face fresh, her figure a pleasant sight to look at, plump but curving in all the right places.

It's none of your business, you fat cihua, thought Iztac, ignoring the question, busy with her sandals.

"You've been acting strangely, you know?" continued the girl. "Are you well?"

Iztac straightened up, eyeing the fresh, round face in front of her. The large eyes reflected no malice, gazing back, widely open as though genuinely concerned.

"I haven't been acting strangely. Why would you say that?"

"Well, sister, you know. You keep to this room, and you sleep all day long, than you turn over and over until the sun comes up. And you don't go out at all. It's strange, if you ask me. You used to sneak out all the time." The girl's large brown eyes twinkled. "At nights, too."

"What?"

Ihuitl laughed with an open delight. "Did you think we wouldn't notice?" Hurriedly, she took a step back, her face draining of any trace of merriment. "You don't have to get angry, Iztac Ayotl," she mumbled. "We told no one."

"No one but all the slaves and everyone else willing to listen to your stupid gossip," hissed Iztac. "I can't believe you spied on me!"

"I did not!" cried out her companion, taking another step back. "I just saw you leaving our sleeping quarters from time to time." Her eyes glittered with tears. "You are so unfair! I could have told anyone, and I didn't."

Taking a deep breath, Iztac tried to calm down. "Well, don't talk about it. Not even with your silly friend." She bit her lower lip, angry with herself for feeling sorry for the stupid *cihua*. "Don't cry. I'm sorry for yelling at you. But it's important you talk to no one about any of it. Do you understand that?"

The young woman nodded, stifling a sob.

"Good. Now let me pass. I have to go."

"Can I come with you?"

"What?" Already over the threshold, Iztac turned abruptly.

"I want to come with you. You are always busy out there, doing interesting things. I want to do it, too."

She felt like laughing. "No, Ihuitl. Believe me, you don't want to be involved in any of this. It's not interesting, and you wouldn't enjoy it." She shrugged. "I wish I could avoid being involved."

"I don't believe you." Over her brief spell of sobbing and fright, the young woman peered at Iztac, her eyebrows creating a single line around the glitter of her eyes. "You go out and do things, the way a man would do. I want to be like that, too. We do nothing but eat and talk and stroll the gardens, and now we are not even wives anymore. I'm growing fat!"

"Don't talk nonsense!" Against her will, Iztac laughed. "You are not fat, and you'll be a wife again soon enough."

Her companion snorted. "You will be a wife again, but not me. I'm nothing, just a granddaughter of the dead ruler of Cuauhnahuac, a mother of yet another prince. Nobody needs me. I'm expected to live here quietly and to raise my son well. Nothing more." She shrugged, then smiled suddenly. "You will be given to the ruler of Tlacopan, they say."

"What?" She felt the air leaving her lungs all at once. "Who said that?"

"I don't know. I just heard that." The woman pressed against the doorway, frightened again. "Don't get angry with me. It's not my fault."

"Tlacopan is a Tepanec city! They can't give me away to the Tepanecs!"

"Why not? The Tepanec Empire is huge. Azcapotzalco is ruling the world, and Tlacopan is also a large and influential city. What's wrong with being sent there? I wish they would send me to

Tlacopan."

Iztac stomped her foot. "No. This is just too much. First the Warlord, and now this? I won't have it. They can't force me."

The young woman stared at her, openly awed. "Can you refuse?" she gasped.

"I don't know. But I'll be dragged out to Tlacopan screaming and kicking if they try to force me!" She hit the wooden pole of the doorway and winced with pain. "I don't know if they can do it, but I won't go tamely. I won't. Oh, I hate them so!" She pushed her way past the stunned woman. "I'm going to see the Empress!"

"You can't," gasped Ihuitl behind her back. "Iztac-Ayotl, wait!"

But she rushed past their sitting room and down the long corridor, oblivious of the staring servants and the warriors guarding the entrance in this left wing of the Palace.

The afternoon sun welcomed her, soft and caressing, yet she didn't notice any of it. Past the ponds and the groomed cluster of trees, she almost ran up the broad, well-swept alleys, the same way she would go at nights. Servants scattered out of her way, startled. She didn't slow her pace. Should she slow down, should she allow herself to think, she would lose her courage, would never dare to confront the Empress, she knew. And it had to be done, it had to! She was fed up. She could not prevent their attempts to give her away, one after another. She needed to stop these for good.

How? Grinding her teeth, she did not allow this question to enter her mind. Somehow, it had to be done.

The other wing of the Palace swarmed with people – servants, scribes, warriors. She slowed her pace and looked around attentively. Maybe she could talk to the Warlord if this man happened to cross her path. Her eyes scanned the warriors, searching for the imposing headdress or at least his tall, thickset figure. Yes, he would be willing to help her. He needed her.

The gazes of the warriors guarding the entrance made her uneasy. A servant blocked her way. "What can I do for you, Honorable Mistress?"

"I'm here to see the Emperor," she said as imperiously as she could.

The man frowned. "The Emperor is busy," he informed her after a heartbeat of awkward silence.

"Then I'll wait." Mustering the remnants of her courage, Iztac straightened her gaze. "I'm the late Emperor's Second Wife. You can't deny me entering this side of the Palace."

An imperceptible shadow passed through the man's eyes. "I know who you are, Honorable Mistress. Yet, even a noble person such as yourself cannot appear before the Emperor looking like that." His gaze slipped over her wrinkled clothes and her hastily smoothed hair.

She followed his gaze. "Then send for a maid to bring me better clothing. And make her hurry. I have to see the Emperor urgently."

The man looked around. "Please, follow, Honorable Mistress."

The polished stones of the stairs were hard against her feet, and it took her an effort to keep her back straight. What would she tell to Chimal, if admitted into his revered presence? With all his advisers, scribes, and servants, and the Empress herself listening, how could she talk to him?

A small, prettily furnished room greeted them with its cool, plastered walls, welcoming in their brightness.

"Please, make yourself comfortable here, Honorable Mistress. Your maids will be sent for."

"When will I see the Emperor?" asked Iztac, sensing a trap.

"You'll be informed, Honorable Mistress," was her non-committal voice answer, as the man retreated past the doorway.

She paced the small space nervously, crossing it back and forth, back and forth. Her maids would be sent for, and they would try to take her back. Of course, she would not be admitted into the Emperor's presence upon her demand. She had not enough power to stand up to the whole Palace.

Smashing her fist against the reed podium helped, if only a little. She wouldn't go away tamely. They would have to drag her off, and then, maybe Chimal would hear about it and do something. And she had to see the Warlord, too. This man could be her ally. He needed her help, and if he wanted to be rid of the Empress without harming the Emperor, she would help him with an open delight.

A look out of the small opening in the wall rewarded her with the sig of the large patio not far below. The urge to sneak out welled. She should not have stormed the Palace the way she had. It was a stupid impulse. She would never be allowed to see Chimal, gaining nothing and losing much.

As her ears picked the sound of nearing voices, accompanied with unhurried footsteps, she willed her limbs into calmness, listening intently. The rustling of the long embroidered skirts promised the worst, and when whirling around in time to see the Empress's tall, imposing figure blocking the doorway, she was barely surprised.

One heartbeat, then another. Nothing happened in her chest as she stared at the strong, broad face, taking in the calm, the mild irritation, the slight amusement, the expression of a predator annoyed by an insistent insect, yet not overly so. Her gaze glued to this woman's face, she heard the maids rushing about, arranging an appropriate seat – a wide reed stool, padded with cushions.

"Leave us," said the Tepanec woman calmly, her gaze resting on Iztac, cold and unwavering. "Have a seat, girl." A curt nod indicated the smaller, unpadded stool. "So, what do you have to say for yourself?"

Clasping her palms tight, Iztac said nothing, the effort of standing the heavy gaze taking most of her strength. *Where had she heard this question before?*

The plucked eyebrows lifted as the Empress's eyes measured her with a glaring lack of true interest. "You are looking no better than a laundry maid. Am I to assign special slaves to make sure you are going out dressed and groomed properly, in a way fitting a noble princess and the Second Wife of the late Emperor?" The feathers of the high headdress rustled disapprovingly as the imposing woman shook her head. "I would be happier with you being sent away from this Palace, still you cannot keep this sloppy appearance in Tlacopan's royal court. There you will be representing Tenochtitlan."

"Am I not to be given to the Chief Warlord?" blurted Iztac,

unclenching her teeth with an effort.

The woman's eyes flickered. "No, girl. You will be spared this shame. The Warlord was not good enough for you. It would have been stupid to waste a princess of your exalted origins on the descendant of a slave. This man will not be our Chief Warlord for much longer."

"I won't go to Tlacopan!" Taking a deep breath, Iztac relaxed, feeling better for saying it aloud at last.

The eyes peering at her hardened. "Of course, you will. You are offered no choice."

The staring contest seemed to last forever.

"Don't try my patience, girl," said the Empress at last, her voice low, almost growling. "You are a woman of no significance. Your birthright is the only excuse that justifies the cost of keeping you. It would be a terrible waste to give you away to any unimportant province ruler. That is why we took our time to find a suitable court." The gaze of the woman calmed. "Tlacopan is the most important *altepetl* after Azcapotzalco, and its worthwhile ruler seems to be delighted to make an alliance with us. This marriage will straighten our ties with the Tepanecs. Now, with our ongoing water project, we will need much support from all the surrounding communities of the mainland. Don't you want to see my son, our Emperor, succeed in this great undertaking? He seems to be very fond of you, unusually so."

Poor Chimal. She licked her lips, her tongue as dry as the earth in a drought. "I want him to succeed. But I won't go to Tlacopan. I won't live in any of the Tepanec cities."

The Empress's face darkened. "You have no choice."

"Yes, I do. I refuse to go. You will have to drag me there in force, and it will not look pretty. Tlacopan's ruler will not be pleased."

"I can have you killed, you know that?" It came out as a growl.

Clasping her palms tight to stop them from trembling, Iztac leaned forward, feeling better than she had in moons.

"Then do it! I don't care. My life is worthless, anyway. I don't want to stay here, in Tenochtitlan, either. This court is a farce, and this city is ugly and unworthy. Texcoco, despite what the

Tepanecs have done to it, in spite of your shamelessly heavy tribute, still has all the might and the majesty. You could never take it away from my *altepetl*, and Tenochtitlan will never be half as beautiful or as important. This city is full of upstarts. It's trying to belong so desperately, but none of you know how to do it. So you are making fools of yourselves by turning yourselves into groveling slaves of the Tepanecs, with no shame and no dignity." She jumped to her feet, her fists clenched. "I hate you, I hate all of you, but I despise you more than anything!"

Glad to be able to say it all at last, she didn't care how loudly she was shouting, seeing the Empress leaping to her feet with a surprising agility for such an imposing woman. Out of instinct, Iztac ducked and the bejeweled palm, shooting toward her cheek, missed its target, brushing against the top of her head. Breathing heavily, she straightened up and stood the glare of the woman, ready to evade another blow. Or maybe to take it proudly and with no fear. The slaves, pouring back into the small room, halted at the doorway, awestruck.

The Empress's hand shook, stopped in midair. "One more word, and I'll have you killed," hissed the tall woman, almost spitting with rage. "You will stay here for now, and you will not be allowed to go out. You'll be guarded until I summon you, and you'd better come back to your senses by then, you insolent brat. There are many ways to be rid of your filthy presence in this Palace and none of them pleasant, save for your going to Tlacopan all smiling and happy." The dark eyes bore into Iztac, burning her skin. "I can even arrange you being sold into slavery. Think about that, girl, before you'll continue trying to stand up to me. I can do even that, and no one will know what happened to you. Not that there would be many people asking questions, with you being so meaningless, so unimportant, so unpleasant even to your fellow minor wives. Think about it, girl. Think hard."

The rustling of the richly embroidered skirt died away, but the Empress's voice could still be heard from the corridor, giving instructions to the slaves that were left to guard the door.

Her body trembling, paces unsteady, Iztac went toward the opening in the wall, peering out of it again, seeing nothing this time. Could the dreadful woman truly do that? Sell her as a slave? No, she could not. Or could she? And the other possibilities were no more pleasant.

Her gaze focused, taking in a group of warriors that were strolling by, shielding their eyes against the strong high-noon sun. There had to be a way to find the Warlord. She had to talk to this man, and urgently.

Narrowing his eyes against the blazing sun, Kuini hesitated at the top of the staircase, reluctant to dive into the unmerciful heat of the early afternoon. The wide, sheltered patio and the spacious gardens spread beneath his feet, quiet and utterly deserted. The whole luxurious dwelling of his uncle seemed to be abandoned, its inhabitants, masters and servants alike, hiding in the coolness of the plastered walls.

For a heartbeat he considered going back to the beautiful set of rooms provided to him and Coyotl to enjoy themselves, to sleep and eat and do whatever they liked for the duration of their stay in Tenochtitlan. The elaborately carved panels and statues, the beautiful mosaics upon the floors beckoned. So much space, so much luxury. Not that he expected anything less from this powerful uncle of his. Oh, this man knew how to live, and he evidently did not bother to conceal his riches.

Another heartbeat of hesitation resulted in him heading down the stairs. He was tired and his head ached, yet he could not fall asleep the way this whole household seemed to do, the way Coyotl sprawled now upon the soft, cotton blankets, wandering the world of the dreams.

No, to him no amount of soft mats and covers seemed to help. He just kept turning over and over, his mind abuzz with thoughts. What he did on the marketplace was wrong, rude, careless, even dangerous. He should not have gone eavesdropping, and most certainly, he should not have pushed himself into the Warlord's dubious enterprises, in the rudest of manners and against his uncle's wishes. Oh but had it made the dignified old man angry!

Scowling, he remembered the way the Aztec had talked to Coyotl, curtly and matter-of-fact, stalking off toward his litter, sparing not a glance to his nephew. Still lightheaded by the elating effect of *octli*, Kuini had shrugged his uneasiness off back then, brushed it aside, not paying attention to his friend's admonitions. So they all, including Coyotl, were angry with him, so what? He may get his chance to sneak into the Palace without climbing its walls, and that's what was truly important.

Yet, now the effect of the *octli* was wearing off, and his uneasiness grew in proportion. There had to be a way to talk to the Aztec, to make him understand. The old man did not deserve such treatment, not after everything he had done for his nephew, after the affectionate, well-meaning conversation on the marketplace.

Two slaves passed him by, carrying buckets of water, heading toward the low mushroom-like structure of a steam bath. *Who would take a bath in such heat?* He followed them, deep in thought. A swim in a pond would be a welcome thing. There had to be a pond somewhere between those well-groomed flowerbeds and trees.

"Who is in there?" he asked.

"The Master," muttered one of the sweating men, bent under his heavy load.

"Oh!" Kuini halted abruptly. Here was his opportunity, yet suddenly, he preferred to be elsewhere.

Hesitating, he watched the men going in. Another slave came, carrying a clean, cotton cloth. The Master was clearly about to finish his bath. Kuini glanced at the gardens, contemplating a hurried retreat into the safety of the trees behind the wide path.

Still undecided, he watched the Aztec's imposing figure appearing at the low doorway, the proud head bending in order to pass, the wide shoulders seemed difficult to squeeze through the narrow entrance. Looking pale, but greatly refreshed, the man stood there, still naked, making the low structure behind him look small, his brown chest and shoulders wet and glittering, wrinkled, well-muscled, sporting multitudes of scars, aged but mighty –

Camaxtli, the old god of hunters and warriors.

The fatigued eyes rested upon Kuini, turning colder, radiating an unconcealed animosity. Oh gods, but he should have gone while having a chance.

"What do you want?" ask the man curtly, turning to take his loincloth from the hovering slave.

Kuini swallowed. "Nothing. I was just passing by."

"Oh, then go on."

Numbed, Kuini watched the strong fingers tying the loincloth, snatching a plain cloak from another slave.

The dark gaze rose, lingered, still cold but with an unmistakable twinkle accompanying it this time. "Feeling quite stupid, aren't you?"

"No." Kuini felt his lips numb, moving with an effort. "But I think I should explain myself."

"Come." The man nodded to the slaves. "Bring the food to the pond."

Diving gratefully into the shadow the densely planted trees provided, Kuini followed the wide back, heading up the well-swept path, his heart beating fast. The road narrowed, then widened again, running between islands of blooming flowerbeds.

"Women love those things," said his host, glancing at the colorful beauty. "I can't see its worthiness. Meaningless things, a waste of time."

"How many wives do you have?" asked Kuini, feeling obliged to respond.

"Not many. Three wives, a few concubines. Nothing to boast about." The older man grinned. "Plenty of sons, though."

"My father never took another wife, save my mother."

The Aztec laughed. "Oh, it runs in the family. Our father also took no woman save our mother. Peculiar habit." He turned onto another, smaller path. "Your mother gave your father enough strong, healthy sons. Not every woman can do this. So I suppose he chose wisely, after all." The man shrugged, chuckling. "He followed her quite a long way. I'm glad it worked out for him."

By the large pond the man halted. "We'll make ourselves comfortable here," he said, sitting on en elaborately carved wooden seat with an obvious relief, his face pale, glistening with sweat.

Kuini studied the mosaic adorning the edges of the pond. "It's beautiful," he said. "I wish my people would build things like that."

The Aztec shrugged, lifting his eyebrows. "So what do you have to say for yourself, Nephew?"

The pieces of the beautiful mosaic lost some of their vivid colorfulness. "I... I want to apologize first—" began Kuini, but a hearty laughter cut him short.

"Save your breath. I've heard those fake apologies before." His uncle's voice shook, taking a higher note. "*Oh Honorable Leader, it was unacceptable. It will never happen again.*" Another outburst of laughter. "It was very touching, you know, but I can do without this pretended humility. Get to the point."

Kuini ground his teeth. "I mean it most sincerely," he said, hearing his own voice ringing stonily, low and strained. "It's true, I was not sincere with the Warlord, but I do owe an apology to you."

"Why do you want to get to the Palace?"

"I... I want to be involved in whatever will happen. I want to help."

"How do you know what will happen?"

"My father, he was honest with Coyotl. He told him what he'll be dealing with. He gave him a choice." Kuini took a deep breath. "He didn't want him to be a tool. He wanted to give him a chance to decide for himself, to be a part of it with his eyes open."

"Your father is an outstanding man."

"Yes, he is." His stomach twisted at the thought of his father.

"Still angry with him?"

"No, not anymore."

The Aztec's one-sided grin held none of its usual irony. "It's about time."

Kuini studied the mosaic once again, not seeing any of it.

"And how did you know I was going to send my warriors to the Palace? I don't think your father had this information to share with you, or your friend."

Aware of the blood rushing into his cheeks, Kuini lifted his gaze, and to his enormous relief, saw a group of slaves nearing, carrying mats and trays.

"Leave us," said the Master curtly as the mats were placed and the contents of the trays – a bowl of roughly cut vegetables, a plate of tamales, and two flasks and cups – were arranged. "Help yourself," he added, addressing Kuini, his large, brown hands picking at the bowl full of greenish, unappealing-looking sticks with an obvious lack of enthusiasm. "Well, nephew, I'm not sure I want to hear more of your 'you've got me all wrong' protestations. I'm afraid I've got you too right. Now," he raised his hand before Kuini had a chance to sound his protests, "I don't want to hear your explanations. You have obviously decided to do stupid things, and it would be stupid of me to try to talk you out of it. So spare me your passionate speeches."

For a heartbeat a blissful silence prevailed as the man bit into a long greenish stick, his face twisting. "Disgusting stuff," he muttered.

"Why do you eat this?" asked Kuini, mostly to take the conversation off his motives for breaking into the Palace.

"Health troubles." The Aztec shrugged. "I'm an old man, you know? Should have died on the battlefield, a death of heroes. Instead, here I am, watching over young hotheads, taking baths in the middle of the heat, eating disgustingly healthy, trying to prolong the inevitable." The wide brow creased with a frown. "I've already covered most of the distance of my Path of the Dead. There is not much left to walk. Still, one tries to prolong the way when his time is nearing." He shrugged again. "Warriors should die before they grow old."

"We need the old men, too." Kuini shifted uneasily, curiously unsettled at the thought of parting ways with this man. "What would we do without their wisdom?"

The Aztec laughed heartily. "You don't seem too eager to use this much-praised wisdom, do you?" He poured for himself, then filled Kuini's cup from another flask. "So, you want to be involved, and you know the Warlord is willing to use you, because you are a highlander with some unusual skills." The generous mouth twitched with an open amusement. "Well, you made the first move, smoothed the matters with the Warlord as best as you could, and now all you need is my agreement, because the Warlord won't use you without it."

"No!" Fighting the urge to jump onto his feet, Kuini peered at his converser, anxious to convince. "I didn't come to talk to you because of that. I came to talk to you because I felt bad, because I shouldn't have done what I did, not in front of everyone, because you were always good to me. I do want to use your wisdom. I know you are right, and I should join this war in the south. It's just…" He clenched his fists tight. "It's only a market interval, and the campaign won't start until then, anyway. But I didn't come to talk to you because I wanted you to make it easier for me to get to the Palace. I didn't!"

The man's face cleared as he nodded. "I see. Well, I didn't mean to accuse you of trying to manipulate me. You are a straightforward boy. Always have been. With all this hot temper and stupid impulses, you always said exactly what you thought. I remember that about you most clearly from our Texcoco adventure. Yet," the broad face closed once again, "yet, there is one thing that is unacceptable and should never happen again." The man did not raise his voice, but it rang out as cold and as hard as obsidian striking another glassy surface. "You dared to listen to my private conversation. You did it intentionally, and you went to great pains to do it. It will never happen again! Do I make myself clear? Should you dare to eavesdrop on me one more time, you will never be able to enter Tenochtitlan. I will not have you killed, because you are my brother's son, but you will never be able to show your face anywhere around the Lowlands. Do you understand that, *Nephew*?"

Bereft words, Kuini just nodded, his throat dry.

"Well, as long as it's clear, you can do whatever you like. I'll send you along with the people I intended to present to the Warlord." The twinkle was back, sparkling out of the dark eyes. "I'll even make an offering to the gods so they'll watch over you and maybe even help you survive this market interval, for you to be able to join the projected campaign in Zacatlan."

Relieved, Kuini drank his water. It tasted good.

"Thank you," he muttered. "I promise not to do anything rash, and I promise to be helpful."

"Be careful of the Warlord. Do not underestimate this man. He is dangerous, ruthless, and extremely capable. Do not play games with him. He is a good friend of mine, but it will make no difference to him as far as it concerns you. He won't feel obliged to keep you from harm, and he will hurt you without a second thought should you make him angry. He is not overly fond of you as it is." The broad face closed. "And don't get caught alive whatever you do. These days the Palace is full of despicable people. They would stop short of nothing to get the information out of you before finishing you off."

Kuini shivered. "Then it's important to do what you think should be done," he asked, studying the carvings upon the table.

"Yes. It is." The Aztec shrugged. "Still, I would leave youths like you and your friend out of it." He emptied his cup, grimacing. "Disgusting, sweetish brew!"

"What is it?" asked Kuini, glad to switch topics.

"Hot water with honey, imagine that! The healers insisted I drink sweet things, and, unbelievably, it helped. So I'm to drink either this or a sweetened chocolate and eat disgusting nopal-cactus and bathe like twenty times a day. What a life!" The man shrugged. "But it helped. Before that, I was a mess. I'm telling you, boy, make sure to die prettily on the battlefield before you grow old." He chuckled. "But don't rush with any of it, either. Not through the next market interval, at least."

CHAPTER 8

It was not even midnight, and the opening in the wall was painfully small. Still, Iztac tried her best to squeeze through it, landing on her feet carefully, making no sound.

Dashing for the nearby group of trees, she looked around, watching the deserted patio and the occasional people who walked the well-swept pathways, holding torches or guided by the generous light of the moon.

In such early part of the night, it would be difficult to get to the guard houses, where the warriors were most likely to congregate, where her chances of locating the Warlord were greater. She sighed. Most likely, he wouldn't be there, and she had no idea where he lived. Probably not in the Palace at all. Still, she had to give it a try.

Pitting her face against the slight breeze, she enjoyed its cooling touch, her tiredness welling. Since the high-noon and the hideous interview with the Empress, she hadn't been able to rest, pacing her small prison from one brightly painted wall to another, pausing only occasionally, to look out of the window.

No one entered her room, and it was a relief. Although hungry and thirsty, she had preferred it that way. Behind the tightly-shut screen she felt safer, the voices of the guarding slaves reaching her, but barely. With the nightfall she stopped her pacing and listened more carefully, until the light snores reached her. Then she dashed for the window, realizing she should have been waiting for midnight, knowing she could not.

The moonlit ground was soft under her feet. She tried to remember the way toward the gates. In the Texcoco Palace the guards' quarters would be located among the buildings nearest the openings. Careful to keep to the shadows, she followed the main alley, enjoying the night air. Oh but she needed to take a bath. And to eat and drink properly. Did the vile woman intend to keep her like that for days, until she gave up on her struggle? She cursed softly.

A group of men swept by, glancing at her curiously. She glared back at them, surprised with their open scrutiny. *Who did they think they were?*

One separated from the group, came closer. "What are you looking at, pretty girl?" he asked, eyes sparkling.

She gasped. "How dare you?"

The rest laughed. "How dare you talk to pretty maids, man?" Someone chuckled.

The man frowned, then decided to join their merriment. "Please, allow me to apologize, oh honorable slave girl."

Angry with their laughter, she turned around and resumed her walk, but the man caught her elbow. "Not so fast, girl."

"Get your filthy hands off me!" she hissed, pushing him away forcefully. Caught by surprise, the man stumbled, releasing her elbow for a heartbeat, and she dashed away, disappearing into the shadows.

Breathing heavily, her heart beating fast, she reached the outer buildings near the wall and the western gates. Groups of warriors congregated around a long, wooden construction. Reluctant to approach them after her previous encounter, she tried to pick a tall, thickset figure among the moving silhouettes. The warriors came in and out, talking quietly, their swords tied to their girdles, their cloaks swirling. Finally, the whole group moved away, their paces long and forceful.

She came closer, moving toward the low, moonlit staircase, now empty and abandoned. Inside the building, people were talking, but their conversations died away as she entered.

"What's that?" gasped someone.

In the dim light of a few torches she could see maybe half twenty of warriors, crouching near the entrance, drinking from gourd cups.

"What are you looking for, pretty thing?" asked one of the men, lifting his cup.

She took a deep breath. "I need to see the Warlord."

"The Warlord?" Their laughter matched the merriment of the cheeky people who had tried to detain her. *What was so funny about what she said?*

"This one has high aspirations," said another warrior. "Palace's guards are not good enough for her."

"Is he right, pretty thing? Won't you make us happy first, before going on searching for the leaders?"

"Listen," she said, trying to hold onto her temper. "I need to see the Chief Warlord urgently. Where can I find him?" She frowned at their grins. "He will be very put out if you don't help me. He sent for me."

One of the warriors shifted, patting an empty space beside him.

"Come, sit here and drink some *octli* with me," he said amidst the cheers of his companions. "Then I'll tell you how to find any leader you want, you greedy little thing."

She took a step back as another man began to get to his feet.

"No, don't run away!"

Their voices rang out behind her back as she made her way out, jumping the low stairs and running back into the darkness. No, it was hopeless. She bit her lips, stifling unwanted tears. How could she go about looking for the Warlord when everyone she came across thought her to be a slave, wanting to laugh at her, to use her, to do her harm? She cursed. Filthy bastards, each and every one of them.

She watched another group of warriors nearing the building, not daring to come closer to see if the Warlord was among them. Now what? Back to her small prison with no meals? No, she could not go back.

Resolutely, she turned on her heels. If not the Warlord, then she could go and talk to Chimal. She measured the sky. It was nearing midnight, so maybe he would already be asleep and alone.

Deep in thought, she headed toward the main alley. What could Chimal do? Not much, as it seemed, yet, it was worth a try.

He was a smart boy, and he wanted her for himself. He would certainly try to prevent another attempt to give her away, and maybe he'd be successful, just like the first time.

Still deep in thought, she didn't notice the men until she bumped into one, a sturdy, thickset fellow with bushy eyebrows, clearly visible in the generous moonlight. Recognizing him as one of the slaves that had been there through her interview with the Empress, she leaped backwards, her mind in a jumble, her instincts deciding for her.

"That's her!" cried out another man, rushing toward her, blocking her way.

The sturdy slave caught her arm, but she squirmed out of his grip, her heart pounding wildly. With the second man blocking her way once again, she tried to dash toward the dark trees, but, although his attempt to grab her was not crowned with success.

"Go away, you filthy slaves!" she hissed, more outraged by their attempt to catch her than frightened by being detected. "Don't you dare to lay your filthy hands on me!"

Both men hesitated.

"You should go back," mumbled the sturdy man, unsure of himself. "The Revered Empress will be enraged. How did you get out?"

"I'll go back when I'm ready to go back. Now go away."

"You have to come with us now. The Revered Empress will have our skin for this."

"She'll have your skin anyway, because I'm not going back quietly, and you can't make the whole Palace aware of what happened. So just leave me alone, and I promise to come back soon." She looked at the tall man sternly, sensing his indecisiveness. "You don't want to lay your hands on the Second Wife of the late Emperor," she added forcefully.

It seemed to work, as the man took a step back. Her whole attention on him, she didn't notice warriors coming up the path.

"What is going on?"

Startled, she looked back, her heart pounding.

"This woman should be in the Palace now," said the slave hurriedly. "The Revered Empress did not allow her to go out."

One of the warriors snorted. "Then take her away!"

"She wouldn't come," muttered the man, dropping his gaze.

"Oh, this is getting funnier and funnier." Another warrior laughed. "Do you want to make us do your dirty work, slave?" He came closer and Iztac was not quick enough to avoid his grabbing her elbow. "Here, take your prisoner."

She squirmed, fighting the tightening grip, not wasting her energy on talking this time. There was no point in talking to warriors.

The man pressed her closer. "Stop fighting, stupid *cihua*!" he hissed. "Go where they want to take you."

Choking at the distinctive smell of hot spices on the man's breath, she kicked at his shin and heard him cry out. "You filthy rat!"

She ground her teeth as the strong fingers tightened around her elbow, digging into her flesh.

"Let me go!" she groaned, hacking his arm with the nails of her other hand.

He pushed her violently, and she ducked, trying to avoid the blow of his rising fist. It brushed past her shoulder, and she stumbled but didn't lose her balance. Momentarily free, she darted aside, but the other man, one of the slaves, caught her across her shoulders.

"Let her go!"

The tall, broad-shouldered figure of the newcomer was among them so suddenly it seemed as though this warrior sprang out of nowhere. The violent shove at the slave who was holding sent the man sprawling into the bushes, dragging her with him. She waved her arms trying to catch her balance, and was grateful for her rescuer's supportive hand catching her shoulder, pushing her behind his back.

"What are you doing?" hissed the first warrior, thrusting his face forward.

"Nothing. Do you know who this woman is?" There was a distinctive accent to the man's voice, the accent that made her heartbeat accelerate, although it pounded insanely as it was.

"Some filthy slave making trouble."

"No, she is not, and you don't want to be involved in this. I came here with the Honorable Warlord, and he wants to see this woman, so you better be off before he finds out what went on here."

Still safely behind the man's back, Iztac tried to slam her mind into working. The Warlord sent this warrior to fetch her? But how did he know? Had the men in the guard house told him she was looking for him?

"Are you sure?" asked the second warrior.

"Yes. And you better be off before he finds out what happened. I promise not to tell him."

Her rescuer turned to the slave, who still lay sprawled in the bushes and whose companion, apparently, had long since disappeared. Yet, what he said to the man and what the man had answered back was lost on her entirely, as her eyes took in the warrior's profile, the wide cheekbones, the neat line of tattoos. Now his accent made sense.

Her heart made a strange leap inside her chest, cast itself against her ribcage, then went absolutely still. The world swayed, wavered, and for awhile she was busy making sure she wouldn't fall. By then, he had finished with the slave, and they were alone, surrounded by the silvery darkness.

As if in a daze, her eyes took in his dark, widely spaced eyes staring at her, the uncertainty lurking in their depths, engraved upon the wide, handsome features. He had changed, dramatically at that. But for the tattoos and those eyes, she might have thought she had been mistaken after all, taking the other warrior for him because of the darkness. The slender boy with the long, uncut hair had disappeared, giving way to a tall warrior with a wide, generously padded with muscles chest and shoulders, his cloak sliding confidently down his back, his hairline shaved neatly above the broad, weathered face. Even the turquoise piercing under his lower lip was gone, replaced by a small round scar.

"Are you all right?" he asked quietly, and his accent made her feel better.

She cleared her throat. "I think so, yes."

"Why were those men attacking you?"

"I'm not allowed to leave the Palace."

His smile flickered, reassuringly familiar – a sparkling, mischievous grin. "Some things never change."

She caught her breath, finding it difficult to keep calm, her stomach churning. "No, it's different now."

His smile did not waver. "Different Palace, different ruler, different circumstances, but you are still sneaking away, getting into trouble."

She narrowed her eyes, annoyed by his amused confidence. "And what about you? Did you come here legally this time, or will they drag you into the court first thing in the morning?"

He shrugged. "Who knows what will happen in the morning, but for now, I'm here legally, serving the Chief Warlord himself."

"The Chief Warlord?" She shivered. "So he *did* send you to fetch me?"

He frowned. "No, of course not. I used his name to get rid of those manure-eaters without the need to fight them. Don't want to pick a fight in the Palace on my first evening here. The dirty Warlord would be only too eager to catch me doing that, to make an example out of me." The large eyes sparkled contentedly. "He doesn't like me."

"Take me to him."

His amusement fled all at once. "Why?"

"I need to talk to him. I sneaked away for that reason."

His face darkened. "So he won't have to force you into helping him." It came out as a statement, an open accusation.

"What do you mean?"

"Just that. He thought he would have to force you, but I see you are too eager to give him all the help he wants."

She watched his dark, questioning gaze, her anger rising. "You understand nothing of it."

"I think I understand more than I want to."

Clenching her fists tight, she felt her nails sinking into her palms. "You know nothing. You don't care what it was like to live here for all those summers. You just went away, to become a warrior, to have a good time, forgetting all about your promise. And now you dare to accuse *me* of something?"

She glared at him, seeing the tightening jaw, the thinly clasped lips.

"It was not precisely like that," he said quietly.

Stomach twisting, she stared at him, taking in the wide scar upon his forehead, another one twisting down his sharp cheekbone, the pain reflecting in the depths of the dark eyes. Of course it was not like that. But then, how was it?

"Come. I'll help you to find the Warlord," he said in that same quiet, toneless voice, turning away.

Her stomach hollow, she followed him as he walked toward the looming Palace, keeping to the shadows, careful to make no sound. The breeze rustled in the trees above their heads, bringing back memories she had not allowed to surface since coming to Tenochtitlan. Back then, she had been the one leading, young and hopeful and sure of herself, excited by the adventure, knowing what she wanted, even if vaguely. But now? Now he led the way, tall and strange, not a boy anymore but a warrior, an almost foreign presence, strong and masculine, maybe even dangerous.

She felt him by her side, and it made her thoughts swirl, rushing about in no sort of an order, like a bunch of panicked squirrels. He was so tall now. She remembered him being almost the same height as her. She hadn't needed to stand on her toes to kiss him. Yet, now her head was hardly reaching his cheek, and his paces were firm and pliant, his body tense, alert, his large, brown palm swaying easily, not far away from the ties of his obsidian sword. A warrior!

"I think you better wait here," he said when the wide staircase of the main entrance loomed ahead. "I'll try to make him come out." His eyes avoided her gaze.

"Will they let you in?"

"Yes, I was there before sneaking out. Before running into you."

"Why did you sneak out?"

He just shrugged, still avoiding her gaze. "Wait here."

She watched his tall silhouette heading down the path and up the staircase, stopping to talk to the warriors guarding the entrance, his posture radiating easy confidence. But then, wasn't he always like that? Even as a runaway highlander boy.

She clasped her palms tight, forcing herself to breathe evenly. She needed to concentrate her thoughts, to think of what she'd say to the Warlord. The handsome Highlander from the past should not interfere with her plans.

It took them a long time, but finally they came out, two broad, confident figures, hesitating at the top of the staircase, conversing with the warriors once again. They descended in a leisurely manner, and she found it difficult to curb her impatience. Why should they make her wait?

The bushy eyebrows of the Warlord crawled up as he saw her, the smile playing upon his lips, curling downwards.

"Greetings, Honorable Princess," he said quietly, not trying to conceal his open amusement. "What a delightful surprise. I would be less astounded to see the Moon Goddess manifesting herself before me, than seeing you here, and in such a state."

She narrowed her eyes. "I needed to talk to you."

"Of course." His smile did not waver. "I was about to send you a word asking for this honor." He glanced at the Highlander. "What are you waiting for, warrior? Go away."

She saw the familiar dark eyes flashing with rage. The effort of holding onto his temper was evident in the young man's tight jaw. "I will escort the Honorable Princess back after you finish," he said.

The Warlord lifted his eyebrows. "You will do so if you are asked to do so, warrior. Now go, and don't make me repeat myself." The thickset man shook his head, clearly displeased. "Wait by the staircase."

She watched the Highlander turning abruptly, even his swirling cloak reflecting his rage. Oh yes, he was right. The Warlord did not like him.

"Insolent bastard," muttered Itzcoatl, following her gaze. "Unruly, but resourceful. A perfect replica of his uncle." The man shook his head, his gaze concentrating. "Well, Princess, tell me what happened. Are you all right?"

She tore her gaze off the drawing away figure. "I waited for you to send a word," she said, at a loss as to how to proceed.

"And?"

She took a deep breath. "I... I want to help. As long as the Emperor doesn't get hurt."

The man's grin did not reach his eyes. "I would never dream of hurting our Emperor."

"Do you promise that nothing will happen to him?"

"Yes, I promise. Our boy-emperor will go on ruling as if nothing happened."

She peered into his eyes, unable to read the dark, heavy gaze. "Then I'm willing to help," she said finally, not reassured.

"Why did you look for me with such urgency?"

"I... I had a row with the Empress with morning."

He smiled appreciatively. "A row with this woman? You have guts, girl. What did you argue about?"

"She wants to give me away to the ruler of Tlacopan. And, well, I told her I won't have it, and... I told her some other things, too. And now I'm locked in the small room of this side of the Palace, forbidden to go out."

The Warlord frowned. "Oh, that is not good! I need you on the best terms with the Empress. I want you to be her friend. I want you to share her morning meals."

"That is impossible. I'll never shares meals with this woman. I hate her!" She swallowed. "And she hates me, too."

"Then I can't use you." He turned around and watched the Palace as if about to leave.

"She told me you won't be the Chief Warlord for much longer now."

That made him turn back so fast his warrior's lock swayed. "Why would she tell you this?" he asked, eyes flashing. "Why would she discuss with you something like that?"

Fighting the urge to take a step back, Iztac stood his glare. "When she told me that I was to be sent to Tlacopan, I asked her what happened to her previous marriage proposal. This was the way she came to talk about you."

"What did she say?"

"Just what I said. Also that you are not good enough for me."

She could almost hear the man grinding his teeth. His blazing gaze grew more difficult to stand with every passing heartbeat. "Filthy *cihua*," he muttered through his clenched teeth.

"I want her dead," she said quietly, surprising herself.

That made him come to his senses. The dark gaze cleared, focused. "Well, then the first thing for you to do is to make peace with her. I need you to get back to your quarters, so I'll be able to communicate with you easily. I can't send you anything when you are stuck in this side of the Palace, guarded and clearly ill-treated." His gaze measured her fleetingly, making her aware of her disheveled appearance.

"I can try," she said after a while. "How do I let you know when I get back to my side of the Palace?"

"Is there a maid you can trust?"

"No."

He signed. "Then I'll send the Highlander to watch over you. The cheeky bastard should be able to handle this."

She bit her lips, trying to conceal her excitement. "Yes, he'll manage."

"How do you know?"

"I don't." She shrugged. "But you said he is resourceful."

"Then I'll send him to take you back, and the first thing in the morning you act humbly, beg for an audience with the Empress, then beg some more to get her forgiveness. Tell her you'll do whatever she wants. Ask her to teach you good manners. Try to cry or something." He eyed her sternly. "You clearly don't know how to do this, to cry or to act humbly, but you will have to try very hard. Remember, you are to make friends with her. You have to share one or two of her morning meals in the next few days."

She peered at him, the sound of his voice suddenly stony and ominous, making her cold, despite the warmth of the night. What would she have to do through her morning meals with the Empress? Oh, wasn't that clear? She shivered.

"I'll try to do this," she said, dropping her gaze.

"Look at me!" She felt him drawing closer, catching her shoulder, squeezing it, not painfully, but firmly, his face looming above hers, dark and menacing. "I trust you, girl, but don't underestimate me. If you try to play games with me, if you try to switch sides, you will regret doing this. I'm no less ruthless than the Empress, whatever the ambitious woman might think or assume. I will have you killed with no second thought."

Her heart beating fast, she took a step back, freeing her shoulder with a sharp movement of her own.

"Don't threaten me," she said, not afraid anymore, but angry. She had had enough of people grabbing or threatening her through this whole evening. "I'll do what you want only because it suits me. I'm not one of your warriors, so don't give me orders or threaten me, or even touch me!" She stared back at him, suddenly so furious her whole body trembled. "And I can be just as ruthless, so if Chimal gets hurt, you will regret it, too. If something happens to him, I'll find a way to get back at you, even if it'll be the last thing I'll do in this World of the Fifth Sun!" Clasping her lips tight to stop them from trembling, she glared at him, drawing convulsive breaths.

The narrow eyes peering at her narrowed even more as he watched her with an almost genuine interest. Then his lips twisted, stretching into an appreciative smile.

"Fair enough, Iztac-Ayotl," he said. "Fair enough." He watched her for another heartbeat, then turned around and went away, his paces long and firm, unruffled by their confrontation.

Frozen, she watched his wide silhouette crossing the moonlit patio, stopping by the staircase, talking to the Highlander. Wishing to know what they were talking about, she knew she couldn't have heard even had they been standing next to her. Her heart pounded in her ears wildly, insanely, interrupting with her ability to listen. Drawing one convulsive breath after another didn't help in trying to calm her trembling limbs. Her head was spinning, and she leaned against a tree, exhausted. This entire day was just too much. She should not have gotten out of her sleeping quarters this morning.

The Highlander was coming back, his paces long and soundless, like those of a forest cat. An ocelot. A jaguar. She had never seen this magnificent forest creature, but she'd heard plenty of stories, and this was how she imagined it would move, light and springy, ready to leap aside, or to pounce, should a danger appear.

Mesmerized, she stared at his broad face, studying its sharp lines, enhanced by the mysterious thread of tattoos, taking in the prominent nose and the outline of the generous lips. Like in a dream, she studied his face as if trying to memorize it.

He stared back at her, wide-eyed. "I'm to take you back now," he said finally, licking his lips.

The thought of her small, airless prison and the confrontation of the next morning made her stomach turn. "I need to wash up first," she said and saw his eyes widening, then deepening, glittering darkly in the silvery moonlight.

"Of course," he said, his voice low and throaty. "Where?"

"There is a pond…" Realizing how it would sound, she paused abruptly. "It's not what you think!"

He narrowed his eyes, then shrugged. "Lead the way."

The walk beside him, keeping to the shadows of the trees, brought back the memories in such force she found it difficult not to stumble over fallen branches. She led the way now, and he followed quietly, reserved and on guard, just like then, three summers ago. A lifetime. Back then, she had resolved to make love to him, but he wouldn't have it at first. He had made sure she wasn't using him before agreeing to take her. Oh, how proud he was, this wild, battered boy, who drew such beautiful pictures and who would kiss her in a way that made her head spin.

"Do you still draw on bark-paper?" she asked, mostly to take her thoughts off the other memories.

"Sometimes," he said. "But not much. On campaigns you have neither time nor *amate*-paper." She could feel him shrugging in the darkness. "When we spent that winter in the Highlands, after Texcoco fell, there was plenty of time, but not enough paper."

Her heart missed a beat. "You and my brother, you mean? Was Coyotl with you there, in the Highlands?"

"Of course."

She brought her palms to her burning cheeks. "You saved him!"

"No, not really." He grinned. "You know how he is. Made himself liked before I had a chance to introduce him properly. No one had enough time to entertain the thought of cutting him up on one of our altars." His chuckle wafted in the air, soft, comfortable, caressing. "Such a prominent Lowlander. The appropriate gods must have been disappointed."

She could not stifle a giggle. "I'm sure your warriors made it up to your gods with enough Tepanec blood."

He sobered. "Well, no, they did not. The Tepanecs have kept to the Lowlands so far, not venturing into our mountains. So it has been relatively quiet since Texcoco fell."

"Then how did you become a warrior?"

He looked at her, surprised. "I fought with your brother. We've been all over the other side of the Great Lake, laying siege on Azcapotzalco and all that." His voice rang proudly. "It was something."

She caught her breath. "You've been to all those places?"

"Well, yes. There were plenty of towns and villages out there. We even took a few, and then we put a siege to Azcapotzalco that lasted for almost a market interval."

"What did it look like? Azcapotzalco, I mean. As stupid and as ugly as the Tepanecs themselves?"

He grinned. "No. It's a beautiful *altepetl*, as far as we could see. There was this hill, a good vantage point, where one could see the city quite well. I also wanted it to be ugly, but it was not. It's very large and very pretty, beautifully planned, as though carved out of stone, sprawling everywhere you look. Their Great Pyramid is so huge it's towering to the skies. Then there is this avenue lined with so many pyramids and temples one's head spins. And I probably haven't seen a half of it."

She frowned as they halted by the edge of the small pond. "So what? Texcoco has a Great Pyramid, too. And the avenue with temples. Don't you remember? You were mighty glad to see this avenue when we were looking for our way out of the marketplace."

He turned at her, eyes glittering. "I remember. It took us ages to find the Plaza, and you made me steal tortillas."

She wrinkled her nose. "I was hungry, and you had no cocoa beans."

"You had no beans, either."

"I wish there was another stall over here. I'm dying of hunger."

He beamed at her. "Don't tell me you'll make me steal from the Palace, now."

"Maybe. Why not? I'll wait for you here." Sitting upon the stone border surrounding the pond, she busied herself arranging her skirt, avoiding his gaze. The soft material felt wrinkled and dusty under her palms, and there was a tear right under her girdle.

He came closer and towered above her, his eyes still amused, yet some heaviness lurked in their depths, now. "I won't go all the way back there. You should have told me earlier."

She took a deep breath, her limbs suddenly weak and feeling as if out of control. "I didn't think about it before." It came out helplessly, a stupid phrase with no meaning. She bit her lips, trying to force her mind into working. "But it doesn't matter. I'll get a meal in the morning, I suppose." More meaningless information. She wanted to bite her tongue off.

He said nothing, just stood there with this heavy gaze resting upon her, throwing her mind into a jumble, making her limbs liquid. But for the water behind her back, she might have tried to back away, if for no other reason than to make her mind work properly.

"So what else has changed?" he demanded, the intensity of his gaze not lessening.

Frantically, she searched for something to say. If only her heart would not beat so loudly, she might have thought of a proper answer.

She needed to get up, she knew, to face him and to answer him. However, her legs would not support her, so when he took hold of her shoulders, pulling her up gently but firmly, she felt almost grateful.

Yet, his hands did not release her once she was up. Another heartbeat of hesitation on his part, and she was very close, propped against his chest, enveloped in his warmth and the clean masculine smell of his. No hot beans, and not even *octli*, but the warm scent of a young body, firm against hers.

His lips were soft and assertive as they sought hers, just the way she remembered his kisses, forceful, demanding. She felt her own lips responding, and then it all made sense, and she clung to him, delighted in his touch, relishing the feeling of his skin under her palms. Gasping with surprise, she felt him picking her up, carrying her toward the protective darkness of a nearby cluster of trees. The moonlight faded, and she felt sorry for it, hardly able to see him.

"No," she said firmly, pushing his hands when he pulled her skirt up. "You have to take it off."

His smile flashed at her guiltily out of the darkness. "Yes."

It took him time to remove her clothes, and she felt his fingers trembling with impatience, so she helped him, happy to be free of the wrinkled, dusty, sweat-soaked cotton.

The breeze rustled in the tree tops, caressing her body, cooling it off, taking away the filthiness of this whole day, cleansing her. Then his caressing hands warmed it, bringing it back to life.

His body was firm against hers, strange and familiar at the same time, and her body welcomed him, receiving its warmth readily, trembling with pleasure. The time stopped and disappeared, and there was nothing but them and the darkness and the rustling trees above their heads.

"You were right," he whispered some time later, as they lay there spent, breathing heavily, still clutching onto each other. "This is the way to make love. All the rest is just lying around – a waste of time."

She raised her head and watched him, finding it difficult to make out his features in the darkness, longing to be back beside the moonlit pond. "Did you lie around often?"

He grinned. "No. Not really. And most of the times it was a disappointment." His grin disappeared. "You see, when you sample a goddess, you are in trouble, because no mortal woman can compare to that, no matter how she, or you, would try."

She nestled against his shoulder, satisfied. "I'm not a goddess anymore, if I ever was. Just a piece of merchandise to toss about, to offer to this or that needy ruler. And they are not even that eager to use me. They just need me to decorate their women's quarters." She shut her eyes against the suddenness of the pain. "I wish I had known you would come one day. It would have made it all easier. I would have had something to wait for."

His arms tightened around her. "Was it that unbearable?"

She didn't answer but pressed closer, fighting away the insistent tears.

"Do you want me to take you away now?" he asked quietly, his words brushing against her cheek.

She swallowed the sobs. "I wish it was possible!"

"Why not?" His finger slid around her breasts, leaving pleasant sensations in its wake. "We'll get dressed, climb over the nearest wall and be gone. I'll steal a canoe or we can try to get away through one of those causeways if we can find our way there."

"And then to your Highlands," she said dreamily. "To hunt and cook and climb canyon walls and make love. Plenty of love." Brushing her palm against his side, she felt another scar under her fingers. "But you are a warrior. You will dump me there to go away on your campaigns."

He tensed. "Well, that how it works. But it's not that bad. I'll be back often. And my family will look after you in the meanwhile."

She laughed. "Oh, yes. They are used to taking in highborn Lowlanders by now. The whole royal house of Texcoco will move to the Highlands in the end."

He pressed her closer. "Stop laughing. I'm serious. I don't like you being involved in this mess. This Palace is dangerous. More than you think."

"How would you know?"

"I know." He fell silent for a while. "I listened to your future husband talking to my uncle. It is not pretty what they were planning, and I want you out of it."

She blinked. "My future husband?"

"Yes, the Warlord."

His body was now tense against hers, and she threw her arm across his chest, towering above him, beaming at him, hard put not to laugh.

"Then you know nothing yet, you jealous, lusty warrior," she said triumphantly. "You know nothing at all. It's more dangerous and more complicated than you think, and I would rather have *you* out of it. They are mad, the people of this Palace, mad and power-hungry, and some would stop at nothing to achieve their goals." She beamed at him. "And I'm to be given to the ruler of Tlacopan. The Warlord is old news."

He stared at her. "Tlacopan? But it's a Tepanec province!"

"Oh, yes. Tenochtitlan is strengthening its ties with the Tepanecs all the time. They will be the best Tepanec province ever one day."

"Unless…"

"Yes, unless. And that's why we can't just run away. Not now. Maybe later, after it's settled. After this matter is solved, one way or another."

He tried to get up, but she pushed him back, climbing on top of him.

"Forget it. Forget it all. It's our night, and we won't let them ruin it."

She felt him stirring, and it made her feel powerful. Confident and elated, not concerned with her lack of experience anymore, she let her instincts guide her, to tell her what to do. She was his goddess, the mighty Goddess of the Moon, the only one capable of giving him pleasure. All those women he must have taken through his campaigns were powerless, meaningless, nonexistent. His eyes told her that, peering at her out of the darkness, wide-open and expectant, enthralled, awed, worshiping her.

Oh, she would take him to the realm of the gods, she thought, giving in to the wave of her own pleasure, and she would make sure he would want no other woman.

CHAPTER 9

Dehe watched the Warlord, fascinated with the way the man stood there, his thick arms folded, legs wide apart.

The shadowed patio seemed to be crowded almost to bursting, dotted by low tables, covered with plenty of mats, full of maids rushing among the guests, graceful women, balancing their trays. Smells of hot, spicy food spread everywhere, brought to the gardens by the soft afternoon breeze, but Dehe felt no hunger, still replete from the earlier, midmorning meal.

This reception was clearly thrown for Coyotl's sake, although Kuini's uncle's mansion looked as if it was used to throw many such parties, with those pretty, playful maids, and the soft music flowing from the invisible sources in the depths of the gardens.

What riches, she thought, shifting her weight from one foot to the other, her gaze drifting back to the grim-looking leader. She studied him more carefully, safe in doing so in her cozy niche behind the bushes. Not invited to come near the noble gathering, she was still allowed to go around as she pleased. So, she watched them, having nothing better to do. It was either that, or going back to the small room she had been given. Or back to the marketplace and Kaay, but this would cut her off from them completely, put an end to any hope of seeing Kuini again. And, although he had left on the previous evening, telling her to stay here until he came back, flashing at her this fleeting, surprisingly light, smile of his, she didn't leave as she wanted to do, but stayed to endure a long, lonely night full of misgivings.

He'd gone to the Palace, she knew. And he was unusually excited about it. Oh, he went to see that filthy princess who was not even faithful to the Emperor and who had made him scream at her, Dehe, for telling him the truth, threatening to kill her. Her! The woman who was faithful to him and who helped him every time he needed help.

Clenching her teeth tight to stop her lips from trembling, she blinked away the gathering tears, concentrating her gaze on the Warlord, who had, by now, been approached by their host. Another impressive-looking man, another dangerous bastard, although this one was much older and more dignified, with his broad face wearing an arrogantly good-natured, perpetually amused, expression. Oh, he reminded her of a well fed jaguar, sitting there with his tail moving slightly, licking his fur, not paying you much attention, not especially dangerous as long you kept him fed and made no sudden movements.

"So, this is where you have been spending this last half a moon!"

The hearty laughter of a tall, thickset warrior in a richly decorated cloak attracted her attention, drawing it to another group. She watched Coyotl and Tlacaelel coming toward the flowerbeds near her bushes, walking the path that had clearly led into the depths of the gardens.

The warrior joined them, still laughing. "And here I've been wondering."

Tlacaelel shrugged, careful and reserved, not his usual derisively confident self of their days in the *calmecac*. "I wonder who else has been wondering."

"Oh, yes. All sorts of interesting people must have been jumping to all sorts of conclusions." The warrior grinned, unperturbed. "But none of us came to guess correctly. Not even those who assumed you might have been busy joining your ancestors." The man's grin widened. "Nor had we any chance to imagine the nature of your company." Turning to Coyotl, the man measured the Lowlander with a calmly inquiring gaze. "So, the honorable heir to Texcoco throne, how did you find our *calmecac*'s hospitality?"

"I have no reason to complain," answered Coyotl, seemingly composed and at ease, but Dehe could see his unnaturally straight shoulders and his tense back.

Tlacaelel's deeply-set eyes sparkled with the familiar, challenging amusement. "He is not picky these days. He grew used to spending his time in all sorts of places."

"Well, a few more days in *calmecac* and I would flee back to the Highlands," retorted Coyotl, smiling.

As all three men laughed, Dehe pressed deeper into the bushes, letting the small army of servants pass, unwilling to be discovered.

"I might have gone with him, you know," declared Tlacaelel, leading the way up the alley. "I did my five summers in *calmecac*, like everybody else. No exceptions, not like our precious Emperor."

The warrior nodded, then measured Coyotl with a glance. "You've been to Texcoco's *calmecac*, haven't you? In spite of you being the heir."

"Yes, of course. Only four summers, though. I was fifteen when the trouble with the Tepanecs broke, so it was the end of school for me."

"Lucky you!" Tlacaelel's eyebrows climbed high as his face twisted in a mocking distress. "I did my time until I was seventeen, and then a year of shield bearing. The Empress made sure I was given no exceptions." He shrugged, his face losing some of its good humor. "She was careful to make sure neither me, nor anyone else, harbored any ideas regarding my birthright."

The warrior measured Coyotl with a glance. "So, I hear you did not have a bad time among the savages of the Highlands? They treated you well, I'm told."

"Yes, iI was treated well up there in the mountains." Straining her eyes, Dehe watched the Lowlander shifting uneasily, glad that Kuini was not anywhere around to hear that. "They are no savages, those people. And they will help me when the time comes."

"Help you to do what?"

Coyotl winced. "I don't know. I guess I can always go back there, to live. If something goes wrong."

This time it was Tlacaelel's turn to laugh heartily. "Don't

bother to get all cagey, Texcocan. Not in this house. Those people around here," the young man gestured toward the patio. "Most of them are not happy about what's going on in Tenochtitlan. And as you see, those are important, influential people. They would know right from wrong. They are smart and ruthless, and they would stop at nothing, but they have the best interest of Tenochtitlan in their hearts." His crooked smile widened. "Just like you, they are waiting for the right time. Although, their chance should come earlier than yours. Unless your Highlanders are really many and strong."

Coyotl licked his lips. "The Highlander's War Leader wants Tezozomoc dead before he considers anything," he related finally.

"It shouldn't take much longer." The other warrior shrugged. "Most of us also would not mourn the passing of this particular ruler. Neither his nor any of his progeny."

What progeny? thought Dehe, watching Coyotl as the Lowlander glanced around.

"So what now, oh honorable brother of our mighty war leader?" asked Tlacaelel, giving their new companion a challenging look. "I don't want to go back to *calmecac*. Two market intervals were more than enough."

The brother of the Warlord, thought Dehe, following quietly. That would explain the man's proud bearing and his richly decorated, spotted cloak. There was also the similarity in the overly broad shoulders and the narrowly squinted eyes, although this warrior seemed younger and less important.

"You can't go back to the Palace, either. Be patient and wait for my brother's word, unless you are eager to follow the footsteps of your father."

Tlacaelel's eyes clouded, while the warrior grinned.

"How did we get to such a dull subject?" he said, turning to Coyotl. "I looked you up because I wanted to hear about your adventures on the Tepanec side of the Great Lake. Tell me all about it, would you?"

They beckoned the slave, who rushed forward to refill their cups, then proceeded down the path. Nervous and tense, Dehe followed, welcoming the light breeze and the shade of the thick trees, her back breaking out in a cold sweat. These gardens were no forest. She could be caught any moment, and what would she say if questioned? She was here thanks to the Lowlander, her status unclear, her presence in this beautiful mansion an effrontery to everyone, to the slaves of the house in particular. Oh, how she hated their openly questioning derisive stares.

She should have gone back to the marketplace and Kaay, she knew. Kuini was in the Palace, abandoning her without a second thought, happy to let his friend take care of her. The annoying Highlander! She shut her eyes in order, to stop the tears. He hadn't touched her since that ugly incident in the marketplace, a few dawns ago, and now he was in the Palace, trying to reach that haughty Acolhua princess, curse his brown Tepanec eyes!

The fragments of their conversation reached her, but she didn't listen, bored with the tales of yet another Lowlanders' campaign. She'd heard enough of that when wandering with them through the woods, on their way to Tenochtitlan, and in the *calmecac*, too. Tlacaelel had been curious, wishing to know all about the terrain around Azcapotzalco and the earthworks that had blocked the access to the great city.

"You should have surprised them from the other side, from the hills with no good road," said the warrior, unknowingly repeating what Tlacaelel had said a market interval ago. "Of course, they expected you to come by the main road, with your warriors lingering at Tollan for days."

"I know," admitted Coyotl grimly. "My friend kept nagging at me with that, too. But, back then, we were surprised with our victory. No one expected that the Tepanecs would just go on losing battle after battle. My father didn't plan to try to take Azcapotzalco, so this siege opportunity came as a surprise."

"He didn't make much of it."

"Well, he did more than the others!"

The Warlord's brother raised his eyebrows. "So why are you here? To try to grab a chance that may cross your path?"

Irritably, Coyotl proceeded down the well-swept alley. "I don't know why I'm here. I liked it in the Highlands, you know. I would stay there for good." He shrugged. "But their leader thought I should be here, making friends with your Emperor. Or worse." He turned to face both men. "I hate being dependent on others to decide what I should do. Your brother and the former Warlord are playing their games, and they are using us without bothering to explain, to let us know. And I hate that! I would probably do whatever they want anyway, but I would rather be aware of what is expected of me, what is at stake." Clenching his fists, he turned away. "My friend went into the Palace, to be in the middle of the action, and I should have accompanied him, instead of getting angry with him for acting stupidly."

"Who is that friend of yours?"

"Just a friend. A boy who has been with me since it all began."

"His friend is a wild jaguar," contributed Tlacaelel. "A valuable ally, and a good man to have by your side, but you will have to get used to all sorts of unexpected escapades, and you will never know what he will do next."

"What is he doing in the Palace now?"

"That's the thing. We have no idea!" Amused, Tlacaelel kicked a pebble and watched it rolling toward the edge of the small pond. "Maybe he is busy solving our problems all by himself."

"I hope not!" Clearly upset, Coyotl picked up another pebble, throwing it toward the flickering water, hitting the mosaic adorning the other side of the small pond.

"So, you two want to see some action, I gather." The warrior strolled toward the edge of the pond and stood there, legs wide apart, watching both youths through his narrowing eyes. "Want to sneak into the Palace tonight?"

Coyotl turned abruptly. "Is it possible?"

"Oh, yes." The man's eyes flickered. "With my brother's permission, that is."

"Yes, we want to do that," said Tlacaelel firmly.

Fascinated, Dehe strained her gaze, studying the calm, level eyes, unable to read their expression.

"Let's find our host, then."

Coyotl shifted uneasily. "The former Chief Warlord, you mean?"

"Yes, the man who has bothered to give you shelter and to

throw this reception for your sake," said the warrior, suddenly irritated. He frowned, then shrugged. "Wait for me here."

Along with the two youths, Dehe watched the man's sandals raising clouds of dust, his paces strong and determined, his wide back disappearing up the groomed alley.

"I bet his suggestion was not as spontaneous as he made it look," muttered Tlacaelel. "I'm sure both Warlords will be here shortly. They are as thick as two beans in a boiling pot these days."

"Do you trust them? All of them?" The Lowlander's voice was low and held some urgency.

But Tlacaelel just shrugged. "The Tepanec, the former Warlord, is beyond doubt. Every warrior of Tenochtitlan would follow him with their eyes covered and one of their hands tied behind their backs. No warrior will question this man's integrity. He is a great leader and a good man, ruthless and unpredictable, but not with his warriors." The youth paused. "Also, he has no claim to the throne. No claim whatsoever. Which can't be said about our current Honorable Leader."

"The current Warlord?" Coyotl's eyes seemed about to pop out of their sockets. "He can't."

"Of course, he can. He is the son of the Revered First Emperor, even if an illegitimate one. He has the blood. He has the ambition."

"So do you."

"Me?" Tlacaelel laughed. "I wish I had half of his power and resources. He is more than forty summers old, and he has been the warriors' leader and a sort of an adviser for more than half of that time. I will not be the one to cross his path, and I don't envy our current emperor-boy. Without his mother's protection, he will be like a small mouse between the mature jaguar's paws." The mirthless grin widened. "Me? I will settle for the life of a leader and an adviser."

"Will he dare to remove your current Emperor?" whispered Coyotl.

"Probably. Although, I think he may want to wait a little with that, until the Tepanec ruler is dead."

All ears, but aware of the light music seeping from the patio, Dehe saw both Warlords nearing. Oh yes, Tlacaelel was right. It didn't take them a long time to arrive.

"Greetings, Honorable Leaders," she heard the young man saying, lowering his head with just the right amount of deference when the prominent men deigned to pay them attention.

"Greetings, young man."

Like when she saw him for the first time, their dignified old host made Dehe's skin crawl. Yes, definitely a jaguar, a dangerous animal, good natured but only because it was fed and in peace with the world. She got the feeling he would find it easy to turn into a ruthless killer if provoked. Oh, Kuini had some of his uncle's qualities, she realized, her stomach tightening at the thought of the Highlander. Another untamed beast.

The current Warlord just nodded curtly, paying the youths no more attention than to his own brother. His name was Itzcoatl, Obsidian Serpent, remembered Dehe, liking the sound of it.

Kuini's uncle grinned. "I see you've shown our Acolhua guest of honor around, while I've been neglecting my duties as a host." The gaze of the former Warlord dwelt on Coyotl, calm and unperturbed, but in the depths of the well-spaced eyes Dehe could see an amused, slightly challenging twinkle. "I've been entertained lavishly while visiting Texcoco Palace, and it was inconsiderate of me not to return the honors."

Surprised, she watched Coyotl wincing, his face losing some of its color. "Oh, well, yes," he muttered, dropping his gaze.

The man enjoyed the uncomfortable silence for only a heartbeat. "So, what have you been up to?" he asked, turning to Tlacaelel.

"We wish to be of help, Honorable Leader," said Tlacaelel, obviously knowing better than to try to go around the issue.

The older men exchanged glances, but the gaze of the current Warlord did not thaw.

"You'll be of help, but later on," said Kuini's uncle, shrugging.

"We want to help now," insisted Tlacaelel. "The happenings are affecting us directly. Our fate will be decided by the outcome, and we both want to be involved."

Their host's gaze lost some of its lightness. "You will be involved when we think it's time for you to get involved."

"Actually," said Itzcoatl, frowning, deep in thought. "I can use them now. Their names, if nothing else, will add the necessary clout should the events take an undesirable course."

Kuini's uncle pursed his lips. "They will be unnecessarily exposed. If something goes wrong they will be executed first, quietly, or possibly with a great pomp."

"This is the risk we are all willing to take."

"You have no choice, but they do."

The Warlord raised his eyebrows. "We all have choices, and these young men indicated their willingness."

"The outright taking of power may damage your name beyond repair." Shrugging, the older man turned to watch the flickering pond, seeing none of it, as it seemed. "The council of the elders won't stand for it, and those districts wield much power. More than our royal house cares to admit."

"I know that." The Warlord grunted, his grinding teeth making a screeching sound. "I keep this option as our last resort." He glanced at the two youths as if suddenly remembering their presence. "So you want to be involved, eh?"

Dehe could see Tlacaelel swallowing, nodding stiffly, at a loss for words for a change. Coyotl did the same, clearly as uncomfortable.

"Keep it as your absolutely last resort," repeated Kuini's uncle, clearly displeased. "Try everything you can to make it look like a natural thing. She managed. So should you."

"You have much faith in my power and resources," retorted the Warlord.

"What about that princess of yours. Has she proven too difficult?"

"Oh, that one." The Warlord's eyes sparkled. "The wild *cihua* is actually eager to help, but she is a mess. Managed to get herself into a fight with the Empress, so she is of no use to me now." He shrugged. "An interesting type. Your nephew is keeping an eye on her, to let me know if she manages to do something."

The old man's face twisted as if he had eaten something

incredibly bitter. "I knew it," he growled between his clenched teeth.

"Knew what?"

"Nothing. I wish the young hothead had stayed in his Highlands."

"Don't underestimate him. He is quite useful and is clearly capable of extricating himself from all sorts of situations."

A dark gaze was Itzcoatl's answer, but Dehe could not listen clearly anymore, her heart thundering in her ears, making her limbs tremble.

"Is this the Acolhua princess, the Second Wife of the late Emperor?" Coyotl's question made her heart stop.

Tlacaelel rolled his eyes, while the two older men stared at the young Lowlander, startled and clearly displeased.

"Yes, future emperor of Texcoco. We were talking about the late Emperor's Second Wife, one of your numerous half-sisters," said their host, his voice freezing. "Does this fact change anything for you?"

Coyotl stood the stony gaze. "No," he muttered, then cleared his throat. "I... I just wanted to know. I apologize for my outburst."

To Dehe's disappointment, yet to Coyotl's obvious relief, the warlords turned around and began walking up the path, back into the world of the blazing sun.

"I'll bid my farewells now, Old Friend," Itzcoatl was saying. "I hope to bring you good news in the very near future."

Kuini's uncle's grin was openly skeptic. "I'll make a generous offering."

"Don't bleed yourself to death." The Warlord laughed. "But your presence in the Palace may be of help, so if you manage to get an invitation to visit there tonight or tomorrow, I'll be a happier man." He sobered. "The warriors will be encouraged, especially the veterans."

"I'll be there."

Dehe watched the tall, imposing figure diving into the shadowed patio, conversing with his other guests lightly, like a person without a single worry.

"You two, come along," said the Warlord curtly, circumventing the patio once again.

CHAPTER 10

The Empress reclined upon soft cushions, breaking her fast with a plate of sweetened tortillas. At her feet, a small slave girl crouched with a bowl of water and a cotton cloth, washing the royal feet, massaging them gently and carefully.

"Well, Iztac Ayotl, don't waste my time. Tell me why you insisted to be bidden into my presence?"

The imposing woman finished with her tortilla, and another maid rushed forward, hurrying to clean the royal fingers, sticky with honey.

"I wanted to apologize," said Iztac, taking a deep breath. "My behavior on the previous day was unacceptable."

The dark gaze rose, rested on her, coldly contemplative. "Is that all?"

Iztac felt her stomach churning, but whether from hunger or fear she didn't know. "I will go to Tlacopan, and I will make no trouble."

The large eyes bore at her, burning her skin. "I don't believe you, girl," said the woman finally, taking her gaze off and reaching for a cup of a chocolate drink. "You are lying. A night in that room have clearly not broken your spirit, although, you are quite anxious to convince me to the contrary." The heavy gaze was back, measuring her thoughtfully. "You even look better than I've seen you in summers. Pleased and satisfied, like a slave who had gotten away with stealing the mistress's meal for herself. What is your game, Acolhua princess?"

Fighting for breath, Iztac stared back, feeling a stony fist griping her insides. Limbs numb, she tried to think of something sharp to say, something that would conceal her bottomless fear. Something offending and insolent, so the dreadful woman would not look so pleased with herself.

She bit her lower lip, trying to gather the remnants of her rage, the hatred she had always felt for this woman. Yet, this time the usual feeling refused to surface. Although exhausted from lack of sleep, tired and hungry, she found it difficult to keep her happiness at bay, the memories of the wonderful night invading her mind, uninvited. The pond, and the moon, and *him*, so beautifully built, so forceful, so demanding. Oh but they had stayed at their secluded clearing until the night had faded and the darkness had threatened to turn gray, taking away its protective cover. Reluctant to part, they took their time getting up, still holding onto each other, exhausted from too much lovemaking, but willing to cuddle, and touch, and talk some more.

She hadn't thought two people could make so much love in one night. She thought it was a short process to get over with, but obviously, she was wrong. He would hold her close and they would talk, but then his hands would wander again, and surprisingly, her body, exhausted and satisfied, would react, expecting more pleasure, greedy and just as demanding.

She also wanted to know everything about these three summers they were apart, so resting between their wild spells of lust, she had made him tell her everything, amazed by his revelations. A demented, mad storyteller could not make it sound more insane, she decided, finding it difficult to believe that the former Chief Warlord of Tenochtitlan was his uncle, his father's only brother. She had listened to his account of the two brothers' encounter with held breath, trying to imagine the narrow pass in the mountains, and the two fighting forces, with him, just a youth of fifteen, wounded, exhausted, and confused, trying to make it right, not knowing what was coming. Hugging him tight, she relived with him those desperate moments, stunned and indignant, just like he was. They should have told him, of course they should have! He was right to be angry with them.

"So, with all this hatred for the Tepanecs, you are half a Tepanec," she whispered, finding it hard not to laugh. "And me too. And I hate them as much. Oh, we are such a mess."

But then he would laugh and kiss her again, and she would forget all about their origins and the troubles of their people, giving in to yet another wave of the most exciting pleasure in the whole World of the Fifth Sun.

The birds had already begun to chirp when he helped her squeeze through the small, round opening in the wall, back into her prison, to pretend she had spent a lonely, desperate night there. Lightheaded, she had promised to meet him the next night at the same pond. Then, still smiling, she had fallen asleep, not bothering to take off her dirtied, torn, sweat-soaked blouse or skirt, oblivious to the passing of time, sleeping through the first part of the day, well into the early afternoon.

However, when she woke up, still happy and surprisingly refreshed, although weak and dizzy with hunger, she remembered the Warlord's plan and so called the slaves and demanded to be taken to the Empress. And here she was now, standing before the horrible woman like the last of her maids, not bidden to sit or make herself otherwise comfortable, enduring the scrutiny of the cold, hostile gaze.

"It's so strange the way you look now, girl." The Empress's voice cut into her reverie. "So pale, dirty and disheveled, but somehow glowing. What did you do in this small, silly room of yours?"

Iztac clasped her teeth tight, welcoming the rising wave of rage. It helped to suppress her fear. She opened her mouth, trusting that something sharp and offensive would come out on its own accord. Then she remembered. The Warlord's words surfaced, came to the front of her mind – *you act humbly, beg for forgiveness, try to cry or something.* For Chimal's sake, and for the Highlander's, and for her own sake, too.

With an effort she dropped her gaze, giving in to the wave of dread, afraid of the unfamiliar feeling. She had never allowed herself to feel helpless or desperate. The only time it had happened was when she had run away to the Great Plaza of her beloved *altepetl*, when a market interval had passed and he had not come as promised. The black pit she had fallen into back then was dreadful. It took her moons to come out of it, and she swore not to allow herself to fall there again.

Yet, now she made an effort, letting the unsettling sensation in, to well, to envelope her, to sweep her along the cold sea with nothing to cling to, no grip, no foothold. Truly frightened, she bit her lips, fighting the welling tears, then she remembered again and made another effort to let go. She had to cry and act humble. She had to do it, and the realization that in her current state it should not be that difficult made her feel better.

Which ruined the whole thing. The tears stuck somewhere near the surface, refusing to come out, and she wanted to curse aloud. The silence was nerve-racking. She had to say something. Anything.

"I'm sorry," she muttered, eyes firm upon the floor, unwilling to see the satisfaction in her rival's eyes. "I don't know what to say."

Surprisingly, it did the trick. In the middle of the sentence her voice broke, her breath turned convulsive, and suddenly, the tears burst, beautifully abundant. Sobbing, she refused to look up, feeling the wetness running down her face, her nose behaving strangely as if all of a sudden she had a cold.

She tried to remember what other girls would do while crying. The minor wives used to cry a lot, especially while having rows with each other. They would cover their faces and sob or wail in the most annoying of manners. Although Ihuitl would cry quietly, like an offended little creature. She was the nicest of them all.

Hurrying to cover her face and sobbing with relish, Iztac dared to peek through her fingers. The Empress sat straight now, frozen as if turned to stone, astounded, mouth half open. *It worked!*

Pleased with the effect, Iztac considered casting herself onto the floor, the way one of the other wives would do, but then decided against it. The floor tiles looked hard and cold, and her body was battered from all the lovemaking of the last night.

"What are you waiting for?" she heard the Empress saying. "Bring her something to sit on. And water to wash her face."

One of the maids rushed forward. "Please, Mistress," she whispered, hesitating beside Iztac. "Please come."

Obediently, Iztac followed, letting them place her upon a mat, taking the cup thrust into her hands. The water tasted good. She drank it all, then finally dared to raise her gaze, glancing at her adversary as the woman sipped her chocolate, watching the scene, calm, in control once again. Carefully, Iztac dropped her eyes, wholly immersed now in her role in the play. Her hands, holding the cup, shook, and she let it show, exaggerating their trembling.

"Well, it was a surprise. I never thought I'd live to see *that* happening." The voice of the Empress vibrated with amusement. "So, proud Acolhua princess, I gather you don't want to be put to death or sold into slavery, do you?"

Iztac shook her head, gaze firm upon the floor, teeth clenched tight against the rising wave of anger. *What did she care what the vile woman thought?*

"I said it before. You have some spirit, but you are not a strong woman." A wave of a bejeweled hand summoned another maid. "Take her back to the minor wives quarters, and make sure her maids lead her to the baths and get rid of her current clothes." The woman wrinkled her nose. "These should be thrown away, not even taken to the laundry slaves. A princess cannot go about looking and smelling like that. Maybe in the former Texcoco court it was allowed, but not in the respectable Palace of the Mexica people. In Tlacopan, in the immediate proximity of the Great Capital of the Tepanecs, even the meanest maid would not be allowed to stroll royal grounds looking like that."

The familiar wave of anger helped Iztac to remember her mission. She raised her eyes, blinking, trying to summon the tears back. Those would not come, but her vision was still blurred, and she hoped her appearance was pitiful enough.

"Revered Empress," she said, making an effort to make her voice tremble. "You are right. You were always right. I want to behave like a princess. I want to be more like you. I should have listened to my mother, your revered sister, when I had a chance. I wasn't even sent to serve my time in the temples. I wish I was. Please!" In a spurt of inspiration, she clasped her hands in front of her chest, imploring. "Please, show me how to be a good princess, a good Emperor's wife. Please, teach me."

The usually squinted eyes of the woman widened in a genuine surprise. "You keep surprising me today, Iztac Ayotl," the Empress said, shaking her head, her lips quivering. "I don't have time to run a school for wild princesses and unfitting minor wives. I have a growing empire to manage until my son will be old enough to lift that burden off my shoulders."

Oh yes, try to convince me you will let him do just that, thought Iztac, her heart twisting with pity, as always, when thinking of Chimal.

"Can I spend some time around you, then?" she asked, making an effort to keep her expression as pitiful as before. "Can I share your morning meal with you? I wish to see how a great empress should behave. Maybe it'll help me to learn to be more like you."

The woman's grin widened, turning downwards in an open amusement. "I find it hard to believe one night of a poor treatment changed you so much, Acolhua princess. You are nothing but a misguided girl, aren't you?" The Empress shook her head again, her narrowing eyes reflecting her doubts. "Yet, your mother was my half-sister, and I suppose I should try to help. Present yourself here tomorrow, at midmorning, looking your best. And I mean, your best, Iztac Ayotl! Not just clean, but pretty and well groomed. Then I'll decide if you are worthy of sharing my meal." The topaz bracelets sparkled as the broad hand lifted in dismissal. "Now go."

Having difficulty keeping her triumph at bay, Iztac rose to her feet, thankful for the supportive hands of the maids. "Thank you, Revered Empress," she said, proceeding with her role, almost enjoying herself. "You are so kind to me. I don't deserve it."

And that was a perfect performance, she decided, walking away, leaning on the maids, exaggerating her state of exhaustion. So, the Warlord thought her incapable of acting humbly in order to achieve her goals? Oh, the arrogant man should have seen her now. Hi9ding her smirk, she tried to imagine his narrow eyes widening, filling with mocking appreciation. Oh but she needed to send him a word right away. The next midmorning meal might be their only opportunity. The Empress was not a fool.

Walking down the corridors, paying no attention to the

wondering gazes that were shot at her from every direction, Iztac shivered, realizing for the first time how dangerous what she was doing could be. She could very well die trying to get rid of the Empress, and while only a day before she came to this side of the Palace, angered, ready to fight, not concerned with her safety in the very least, she didn't want to die now. Not anymore. Not after the previous night.

His face materialized before her minds-eye, broad and strong, as though chiseled out of marble, adorned with that alien pattern of tattoos. Other warriors may also sport tattoos and lip plugs, but his were different, foreign. They set him apart, even if his unruly behavior, his independent thinking would not. Could she lose him again after yet another wonderful night of lovemaking, just like the first time?

Blinking against the strong afternoon light, she clasped her palms tight. There was no point in thinking about it now. First things first, and now she had to find a way to send the Warlord a word. Hopefully through him, her handsome Highlander.

Crouching above a bubbling pot, Dehe watched Kaay covertly as the heavyset woman paced the floor, back and forth, back and forth. Her benefactress's lips were clasped tight, and the rim of her gown swayed angrily every time she turned around to hurry back toward the opposite wall. In such a small cane-and-reed cabin she was forced to change her direction quite often.

The brew began to simmer, forcing Dehe's attention back to the fire. Stirring it carefully, she kept her thoughts on the medicine, and the healer, and that strange looking house, anything but on what preyed on her mind.

"Don't stop stirring it, girl," said Kaay irritably. "Don't let it boil. Concentrate on what you are doing."

"It's not boiling. The fire is too small to make it boil. I made sure of it."

"Still, you have to put all your attention on this. If you miss the right time, the medicine will be no good. And if it's spoiled because of you, I will throw you out and will never let you come here again." Not her usual unperturbed, amused, gossipy self, Kaay turned around, resuming her pacing.

"I won't miss the right time. I never have," said Dehe calmly, not offended, used to the woman's shifting moods by now.

After almost two market intervals, she'd grown to like the famous healer, and she knew that the strange Mayan liked her back. By now, she'd learned that the unfamiliar accent and the foreign name of her employee were those of the Mayans, mysterious people from the distant southeastern lands, people who thought that beautiful women should have crossed eyes and who thought themselves more civilized even than the people of this *altepetl*. How strange!

Always talkative, Kaay had told Dehe all about those mysterious lands and the way she had arrived in Tenochtitlan as a young girl, sold into slavery by her own family who hadn't approved of her strange ways.

"Our whole village was afraid of me," Kaay had told her one evening, when they worked late into the night preparing a large amount of medicine one of the old customers expected in the morning. "They thought I was a witch, with all sorts of powers. Superstitious lot." The woman's eyes sparkled derisively. "But I liked it. I liked being feared. Yet, I never thought my family would try to get rid of me."

"That is awful!" Busy grinding pine raisins, Dehe frowned, thinking of her own family. "How could a mother be so cruel to her daughter?"

The Mayan shrugged. "Oh, they couldn't go against the whole village. And they were afraid, too." For some time she was silent, tending the fire, deep in her thoughts. "But it all turned out for the best. My skills brought me plenty of fame among these island barbarians. I love my life."

"Don't you miss your family, your people?"

The woman's laughter was hearty and full of mirth. "They are all dead by now, girl. I'm an old woman. Didn't you notice that?"

"But didn't you want to have a family of your own? Even here, in Tenochtitlan?" insisted Dehe.

"Who said I hadn't had a family?" The woman's eyes clouded momentarily, then cleared. "But it's another long story, and I have you now, the mysterious little thing to take care of and to pass my knowledge on to. I'm glad you were pushed onto my baskets on that strange day two market intervals ago."

Not liking this particular memory, Dehe smiled nevertheless. Indeed, the woman had treated her that way, she reflected, watching her benefactress pacing now from wall to wall, impatient and tense. Like a daughter, or at least a favorite niece, kind and firm, teaching, admonishing, but also spoiling, taking a great pleasure in buying her new clothes and sometimes – a tasty treat. The woman let her sleep in her cabin and actually fussed over Dehe's lack of appetite in the mornings. Yes, she acted like a wise, witty aunt, but now she was as tense as a female coyote about to have cubs.

"What's wrong?" asked Dehe finally, taking her pot off the fire. "Why are we here, boiling brews instead of selling our herbs on the marketplace as always?"

The woman turned back, not slowing her pace. "You ask too many questions, girl."

"I asked only this one." She stood a direful frown, not dropping her gaze. "I'm not stupid, I know something is amiss. You act strange, almost scared, and you're as tense as a coyote that is about to give birth."

"Watch your tongue, girl!" The woman paused, measuring Dehe with a skeptical glance. "You are growing too bold." Standing there with her hands on her hips, challenging, she grinned without mirth. "And I'm not the only jumpy one around, come to think of it. After you went away on that morning, two dawns ago, you are not yourself, either. Don't you think I didn't notice? You are all nervous and angry, and also sad. What did your warrior do? Took another market girl?"

Dehe caught her breath, not ready for this attack. Clenching her teeth tight, she returned her attention to the cooling pot. "I need to pour this into another bowl," she said, pleased to hear her voice steady and matter-of-fact.

Kaay's mirthful mood evaporated once again. "We may not need it at all, if the dirty warlord will not send anyone to pick it up." Her lips tightened. "I wonder if he went to that stupid woman down the alley, that old bag that pretends to know things about herbs. The dirty lump of rotten meat could offer him cheap medicine but nothing that will do a real work."

The woman went on, but Dehe stopped listening. *The Warlord?* She tried to curb a sudden wave of excitement.

"Why don't you send it to him?" she asked, her voice almost trembling. The woman just stared, so Dehe went on in a breathless rush, "You are sending ointments to the houses behind the Plaza, and you sent other potions too, to those corners of the loose women behind the colorful wall. So why not do it this time?"

The Mayan flopped her hands in the air. "Are you simple in the head, girl? This is not an ointment of those noble ladies behind the Plaza and no potions of the pleasure girls. Who will deliver this thing for me, eh? Who can be trusted to do this?"

"I can do this."

"What?"

Her palms were sweaty, and she clasped them tight to stop them from trembling. "I can take it and keep it safe until it's delivered. You just have to tell me how am I to enter the Palace. If the guards let me in, I will manage to find the Warlord, to give him your... medicine."

The crossed eyes narrowed as the lips of the Mayan pressed into a thin line. "Even if you manage to get into the Palace, you will never be able to find the man."

"I know what he looks like."

"You?"

Dehe took a deep breath. "Yes, I met him only this morning."

The Mayan frowned. "You are lying again, girl!"

"No, I'm not. I never lied to you. Everything I told you was true." She resumed her stirring. "He is tall and very broad, and he is squinting his eyes most of the time. His name is Itzcoatl, and he has a brother who is also leading warriors. And he is a great friend of the former Warlord. He visits his dwelling often and feels at home there." She took another deep breath. "And I know why he needs your help, too. I even know that he is going to force the Second Wife, the haughty Acolhua princess, into helping him."

Kaay's jaw dropped, and her eyes seemed as if about to pop out of their sockets. "Who *are* you, girl?" she asked hoarsely.

Pleased with her small victory, but afraid she might have pushed it too far, Dehe stood the piercing gaze. "I never lied to you. My warrior, he is involved in this, and I want to help. Help you and help him. You can send me to the Palace, and you can trust me to find the Warlord. I will deliver your potion, and I will bring his payment back to you. You trusted me before. Why not now?"

The dark gaze bore at her, glowing eerily. Then the shadows cleared off the wrinkled face.

"Oh, you are a deep little thing," said Kaay, and now there was a slight amusement to her voice. Shaking her head, she turned around and went toward the bubbling pot. "So you want to help, eh? Well, it can be arranged. But do you realize the risk you will be taking?" She scooped a spoonful of the brew and studied it carefully, blowing on it to help it cool. "I'm not sure it's worth risking your life for, but I daresay you will not listen to my advice this time. You are after something, girl. Your heartfelt '*I want to help*' isn't fooling me." Taking the pot off the fire, she placed it on the earthen floor. "So let me think it over." The dark, thoughtful eyes rested on Dehe, making her shiver. "And we will also need to find a pretext to get you into the Palace with no trouble."

CHAPTER 11

The breeze grew stronger toward the late afternoon as the sun hurried to kiss the treetops. Iztac leaned over the terrace's railing, pitting her face against the new gust, enjoying its cool touch. Scanning the people drifting down below, she strained her eyes, searching for a familiar figure.

He was assigned to keep an eye on her, but, of course, he would not do it openly, she reasoned, pushing her irritation down. So, she would just have to go out and look for him.

Raising her palm, she made sure her elaborately woven tresses were still in place, pulled high, held by obsidian pins and decorated by feathers. It felt strange to have her hair out of her face, her neck exposed, enjoying the touch of the cool breeze, too.

It was good to be clean again, she decided, sliding her fingers against the polished obsidian of the pins. She had spent what seemed like a lifetime in the steam bath, coming out reeling and dizzy, but reborn. Returning to the minor wives' quarters, she paid no attention to the gaping women, who were, as always, huddled together, feasting on sweetmeats and chocolate drinks, their silly children nearby.

Fat rats, she thought disdainfully, proceeding into the sleeping quarters, where she ordered a meal, then sent for every maid responsible for the grooming and well being of the noble ladies. Imperiously, she ordered them to bring her a variety of clothes and took her time going through the offered garments, finally settling for a sky blue, boldly cut blouse with a richly decorated girdle sparkling topaz. Then, she let the other maids tend her face, applying oily ointments to her skin and a little yellow to her cheeks. The slave responsible for tending hair toiled for what seemed like half a day, combing Iztac's tresses, fighting the entanglements, rubbing it with plenty of oil and some indigo to make it shine before braiding it and pulling it together.

No one said a thing, no one commented as to the advisability of such an investment for the regular evening with no reception in sight. The other women gaped, but dared not to ask questions, scattering out of her way. Even Ihuitl kept well away, gazing at Iztac with those huge, liquid eyes of hers, wondering and obviously at a loss. Well, thought Iztac, turning around and heading back into the minor wives sitting quarters, the silly woman would do.

Most conveniently, Ihuitl was alone, fanning herself with a feathered fan and watching her only child, the small serious boy of about ten summers named Moctezuma.

"Come, let us stroll the gardens," said Iztac, halting at the threshold.

The round face peered at her, taken aback. "Iztac Ayotl, you can't go out looking like that."

"Why not?"

"The way you are dressed and groomed you should be carried in a litter, wherever you want to go."

Iztac laughed. "Stop being silly, Ihuitl! I dressed prettily because the Empress was angry with me for being sloppy all the time. That's all. I wanted to show the old hag."

The young woman gasped, and her eyes darted around, haunted and afraid. "You should not talk like that, Iztac Ayotl," she whispered. "The slaves will tell on us."

"Then come with me to walk the gardens. You've been sitting here the whole day, haven't you?"

The young woman rose to her feet obediently. "Well, yes. Somehow the time went by, and I was worried about you, too, when you didn't come back yesterday." She frowned, her gaze searching Iztac's face. "Will you tell me what happened, where you spent the night and then most of the day?"

"Maybe. Maybe I'll tell you some of it, but hurry up. I want to be back before it's dark."

Ihuitl's child looked up but said nothing, returning to his small, wooden planks of an elaborate construction. She remembered Chimal at the same age, when she had first arrived at this Palace, sneaking away to play with her, to run around or toss a ball. Ihuitl's son was too serious, too thoughtful for a boy, and he was free to do whatever he liked, unlike the late emperor's heir.

Her stomach twisted at the thought of Chimal. He was still a boy, only thirteen summers old, open and trustful, but unable to play around anymore, carrying the weight of the large *altepetl* upon his shoulders. He depended on his mother, he trusted, and maybe even loved the dreadful woman, and she, Iztac, was about to take her from him. Shaking her head violently, she pushed away the disturbing thoughts. One thing at a time.

"Come," she said briskly. "If you don't want to grow fat, you should walk every day."

The servants looked at them, surprised, but fell in step with them naturally, almost unnoticeably, keeping a respectable distance.

Iztac frowned. "Tell your maids to leave us alone."

Ihuitl gaped again, wide-eyed.

Irritated, Iztac stopped in her tracks. "We are not going into the city or anything," she reasoned, taking a deep breath. *Patience,* she thought, *patience.* "We are perfectly safe in the Palace's gardens."

As the young woman turned to talk to the servants, Iztac watched the surroundings. There were many people – nobles, warriors, scribes, and servants – walking the paths, unhurried and at ease, enjoying the nearing evening and the coolness it promised. She caught their gazes lingering upon her, appreciative, even awed. Unused to this sort of attention, she shifted uneasily, straining her eyes in an attempt to see the familiar handsome face. *He* would be surprised too, she realized, her stomach tightening with anticipation, her palm sneaking again to make sure the obsidian pins held.

"So, will you tell me what happened?" Ihuitl's voice broke into her thoughts. "Did you talk to the Empress?"

"Well, yes. And it was anything but pleasant. Don't do this when your time comes."

The young woman blinked. "What did she do to you?"

"Oh, nothing. She locked me in a small room, with no baths and no food, and told me to think it over." Iztac shrugged, amused by the open dread in her companion's eyes. "So, today I told her that I had thought it over, and that I won't make any more trouble. And that was that."

"And she just let you go back?"

"Well, you know the Empress. She made some difficulties. I had to convince her that I meant it. I had to cry and make pitiful noises."

"You? Cried?" Ihuitl's eyes almost popped out of their sockets.

Pleased with herself, Iztac laughed. "I did it well, actually. You should have seen it. All the sobbing and the stupid sounds. The maids didn't know what to do, and the Empress was aghast." She put her palm on the young woman's shoulder, propelling her down another alley. "Come, let us go on. People are staring at us."

"That's because you are dressed like that. This color makes you look stunning. If I was as pretty as you I would never go around in those rags you used to wear."

"I'm not pretty, and I wish I could go about dressed comfortably. This skirt is too long, and this blouse is cut so low I feel that my breasts will fall out any moment."

That made Ihuitl laugh. "That's how it should be, sister. Men should look at you and think all sorts of dirty thoughts. Like that warrior over there."

As she followed the young woman's nod, she already knew it would be him, so her heartbeat accelerated even before she met his gaze, his eyes wide open and gaping, staring at her. Shivering, she returned his gaze, her breath caught.

He looked different by the daylight, older and more of a stranger, not a youth worshipping a goddess, but a man, a powerful warrior full of desire. His eyes, dark and intense, reflected what he wanted to do to her. All the wonderful things and more, she knew, her stomach fluttering at the memory of the night. She took a deep breath, tearing her eyes off him with an effort.

"I want to talk to this warrior," she said, ignoring the

scandalized look upon Ihuitl's pleasantly round face. "We are allowed to talk to warriors, aren't we?"

"I don't think so, Iztac Ayotl," mumbled the young woman. "Why would we want to talk to the warriors?"

"I want him to do something for me."

She hesitated, racking her brains for a reasonable excuse. They were surrounded by so many people, and some of them were still staring at her. Oh, she shouldn't have dressed like this.

"Well, let us go on with our stroll. By the ponds it should be cooler," she said fighting the urge to drag the silly woman away by force.

Glancing back, she tried to signal him with her eyes, seeing the intensity of his gaze lessening, a hint of a smile stretching his lips. Allowing her own smile to show, she turned around, but another clamor caught her attention. A large group of people proceeded along the main alley, warriors followed by servants. In their midst the thin figure of Chimal was hardly visible, the magnificent feathers of his headdress swaying, making him looking smaller than he really was. The Palace's guards leading the way frowned, urging the people to step away, impatient and not especially polite.

"Move, warrior," barked one of them, and she saw the Highlander's eyes darkening, flashing with anger. His jaw tight, he stared at the warrior for a few heartbeats before stepping away, purposely slow.

"The Emperor," breathed Ihuitl. "What is he doing on our side of the Palace?"

Iztac watched Chimal walking on, concentrated, listening to the impressive-looking men beside him. He also looked changed, another stranger. She hadn't seen him for a whole market interval, and their recent encounters occurred in his sleeping quarters, with him being nothing but a boy, a companion to toss beans and chat. In his Emperor's regalia he looked more forbidding, not a child to play around with and tell him what to do.

"Come, Iztac Ayotl." She felt Ihuitl's plump arm pulling her away. "We should clear the Emperor's way."

Taking a step back, she felt the softness of the dry earth

beneath her sandals. The entourage was very near now, the warriors clearing the way off the walking by, frowning.

"He is just a boy," she heard Ihuitl muttering, the young woman's voice lacking its usual affability.

Surprised, Iztac glanced at her companion, taking in the level eyes and the shadow crossing the pleasant face. "What do you mean?"

"Nothing," said Ihuitl hurriedly. "Nothing at all."

People pressed all around her, trying to see the Emperor – not an everyday occurrence, even for the Palace's dwellers. Oh yes, Ihuitl has a reason to grudge Chimal's occupying of the wide woven chair, realized Iztac taking another step back. After all, her own son was only a few summers younger and just as legitimate.

Turning her head, she saw the Highlander's wide shoulders pushing his way toward her, politely yet firmly. A few more steps backwards and felt her skin prickling at the sensation of his nearness.

His lips brushed past her ear. "What can I do for you, beautiful princess?" he whispered, and she knew his eyes would be flickering with laughter.

"Many things," she said, keeping her voice low.

"It would be my pleasure."

She tried to keep her smile from showing. "I daresay it would be."

Daring to glance at him, she saw his smile narrowing, filling with meaning.

"But first," she whispered, leaning closer. "Find the Warlord. Tell him that I did as he asked, and that I was successful. Tomorrow I'm to share her meal, and it will be our only chance. Tell him to send me whatever he wanted tonight." She paused, out of breath. "Tell him exactly that."

She felt him tensing by her side. Smile gone, he frowned, eyes narrowing with suspicion.

"You have to do it," she said urgently, when he kept looking at her, silent. "You promised the Warlord to keep an eye on me, to report to him. You have to do it now."

"I don't always keep my promises," he said, voice unnaturally low. "I don't want you to be involved in this."

She felt the warmth spreading through her chest, making her stomach flutter. He was concerned with her safety. He cared nothing for Tenochtitlan or the Tepanecs, sparing not a thought for the empires around the Great Lake. Alone in this entire city, he cared for her. If only the people surrounding them would disappear!

Unable to resist the temptation, she put her palm on his arm, felt the warmth of his skin.

"I know," she said. "And I promise to be careful, to keep myself from harm. For you."

Aware of the heavy, uncomfortable silence, she turned away. People were looking at them, puzzled. The group surrounding the Emperor halted, parting a little, allowing a clearer look at Chimal, who stopped and was staring at her wide-eyed, his sharp cheekbones taking a darker shade, his eyes wide open and awed, but also grim, questioning.

"Iztac Ayotl," he called out, the frown not sitting well with his delicate, gentle features.

Struggling to compose herself, she took a step forward, meeting his offended gaze.

"Greetings, Revered Emperor," she said, painfully aware of the stares.

He blinked, not used to this formal communication, not with her. "How are you?" he asked finally.

"I'm well." She forced a smile. "I trust you are well, too."

His frown deepened. "Yes, I'm well, but..." He hesitated. "I haven't seen you for a long time."

"Well, yes, of course." She fought the urge to look around. *Why wouldn't anyone say something, anything, a word that would break this awkward silence?* "I would be delighted to pay my respects to you, Revered Emperor," she said finally, hoping he would receive her message.

Indeed, he brightened visibly. "Yes, do so!" It came out boyishly, in a way unfitting for the great ruler. "I'll be waiting."

Oh gods! As if the fact that the Emperor stopped to exchange pleasantries with his late father's Second Wife was not enough.

She bit her lips. "It will be such an honor for me."

At least the dirty Warlord was not there, she thought, clenching her sweaty palms. Oh, the vile man would have a hard time restraining his laughter, remembering her climbing down the Emperor's terrace. Some respectable visits!

He hesitated. "I want you to come." Biting his lips, he looked around helplessly. "I want you to come along."

People gasped, held their breath. The advisers beside him looked scandalized and flabbergasted at the same time, while the rest of his entourage just stared.

"I..." She glanced around helplessly, aware of the profound silence. "Well, of course. You are too kind to me."

One of the advisers, a plump heaviest man dressed in a beautifully embroidered gown, shifted his weight from one foot to the other. "But, Revered Emperor, you can't—"

"I can, because I want it so!" said Chimal, sounding imperious at last. He looked at the rest of his followers. "Shall we proceed?" he added, stepping forward but making a space for her beside him.

Falling into step with him, she glanced back, seeking the Highlander in the crowds. Yes, he was still there, his lips clasped tight, eyes dark, concentrated, obviously calculating, weighing the circumstances. Catching his gaze, she shook her head, looking at him pointedly, hoping to convey her message. *The Warlord, talk to him,* she thought fervently. Oh gods, why didn't she stay inside the peacefulness of the minor wives quarters?

Before turning away, she noticed a thin, pretty maid peering out of the crowds, staring at her with huge offended, furious eyes.

The guard house was abuzz with activity, spitting out agitated groups of warriors and receiving clusters of animated newcomers, instead.

"Where is the Warlord?" asked Kuini, stopping a man who had burst out of the low building.

The warrior measured him with a dubious glance. "Who knows?"

"I need to find him urgently!"

"Well, then go and look for him." The warrior shrugged and walked away briskly.

Kuini cursed and hesitated, watching the surroundings. Something was amiss, he knew. While this place had been quiet and well organized yesterday when he first arrived here, now, it seemed to be babbling with an unspoken agitation.

He contemplated returning to the Palace and maybe trying to talk his way in. There must be a way to know what that slimy emperor-boy wanted from Iztac. That scene in the gardens seemed bizarre. An emperor stopping to talk to one of his father's minor wives, with the most awkward conversation at that, looking at Iztac as if accusing her of something, as if she was supposed to come and chat with him on her own, with her growing more uncomfortable with each uttered word. The whole incident did not make any sense, the demand that she should come along less than anything else.

Deep in his thoughts, he turned around and almost bumped into a tall, thickset man.

"Watch it, warrior!" the man growled.

Kuini measured him with a glance, taking in the richness of the man's girdle and the spotted pattern of his cloak.

The cold gaze measured him back. "Who are you?"

"No one of importance." As the man stepped forward, Kuini held his ground, refusing to move back. The filthy manure-eater was no simple warrior, yet Kuini was accountable to the Warlord and no one else.

"You insolent brat," said the man angrily. "You are lucky I'm too busy to bother teaching you good manners. Run along before I decide to do so."

His instincts urging him to follow the sensible advice, Kuini hesitated. "I will go about my business when I'm ready to do so," he said finally, narrowing his eyes against the man's glare.

From the corner of his eye, he saw a familiar tall figure appearing at the doorway of the low building. Carefully, he glanced in that direction, his attention still on his angry adversary, his senses honed, ready to evade a sudden blow should the man decide to attack.

"Oh, you will regret this, warrior," hissed the man, but before he started untying his sword, a merry laughter reached them.

"I see you already met our infamous Highlander." Tlacaelel's voice trembled with mirth.

The thickset man turned abruptly. "Don't tell me this insolent rat is the friend of the Texcocan."

"Yes, he is. And he is a friend of mine, too." Tlacaelel grinned widely. "And I told you he is an untamed beast. More of an ocelot rather than a rat, though, I would say. We've been gossiping about you," he said, turning to Kuini. "The other day."

Still tense from the confrontation, Kuini forced a smile. "I'm glad to see you. Didn't expect to run into you here, though." He caught his breath. "Is Coyotl here?"

"Oh, yes. The Texcocan is in there." Tlacaelel motioned toward the building. "We didn't expect to find ourselves here, either, but our leaders were afraid we might grow bored."

The thickset man shrugged, not amused. "I haven't seen you so happy and unconcerned, Tlacaelel, for quite a while." He eyed Kuini coldly. "And you, keep away from me. I don't like your type." They turned to watch as the broad figure of the Warlord appeared at the head of the pathway. "Go inside, you two. After I talk to my brother I'll tell you in more detail what is expected of you."

Brother? That would explain the man's haughtiness, thought Kuini, seething. He caught Tlacaelel's frown, and it made him feel better. The proud First Son clearly did not like being ordered about by this man anymore than he, Kuini, did. Stubbornly, they stayed where they were, watching the Warlord bearing on them.

"What is this gathering for?" demanded Itzcoatl. "What are you doing outside?"

Tlacaelel hesitated. "I thought to look around, Honorable Leader. It's perfectly safe here."

"No, it's not. Get inside." The Warlord glanced around. "Where is the Texcocan?"

"Inside the building."

"You should be there, too." The man made a visible effort to moderate his tone. "And you? Why are you here?" he demanded turning to his brother.

"The warriors are gathering in the guard house, and I wanted to make sure everything is as it should be," said the other man hastily, losing some of his previous haughtiness.

"Good." The squinted eyes of the Warlord cleared, but his eyebrows still created a single line beneath his forehead.

"And what do *you* want?" The dark gaze of the Warlord rested on Kuini

"I... I was looking for you." Kuini licked his lips. "Honorable Leader."

"What for?"

"I have a message to deliver."

"Oh." The dark eyes opened wider, showing a flicker of an interest, before the Warlord motioned with his head. "You two go inside and stay there. Make yourselves useful. Talk to the warriors, make a good impression. I'll join you before the darkness."

Tlacaelel shrugged and this time complied with the request, with the Warlord's brother giving Kuini a hostile glance and stalking away, too.

"Tell me what does she want."

Kuini shifted uneasily. "She said she was successful. She is to share the morning meal tomorrow." He hesitated. "She thinks it may be her only chance, so she wants you to hurry. To send her whatever you wanted to send."

The dark eyes clouded. "The clever *cihua* is good. She keeps surprising me."

"She is no *cihua*." He wanted to shut his mouth with both his palms, the gaze the Warlord shot at him making his stomach tighten.

"No *cihua*, eh? What's your story? Do you know her well?"

Kuini stood the penetrating gaze with difficulty. "No. I just kept watching over her as you asked."

The raised eyebrows were his answer. "Well, stay around for a while. Don't go anywhere until I call for you. Go inside. Spend some time with your Acolhua friend. He is here, apparently willing to take a part in the happenings. When I send for you, take whatever is delivered and go to the minor wives' quarters. Deliver her that by any means. I don't care how, but don't get caught."

Kuini shifted uneasily. "She is not in the wives' quarters now."

The Warlord looked surprised. "Where is she?"

"She is with the Emperor."

"What?" The broad man seemed to grow in stature, his eyes flashed. "Filthy *cihua*! What is she doing there?"

"The Emperor insisted. She didn't want to go. It was all very strange."

"Oh, yes, I'm sure she didn't want to go."

The bitterness of the Warlord's tone startled Kuini. This, and the man's unexplained rage. He studied the blazing eyes, then remembered that she was supposed to be given to this man.

"The Emperor insisted," he repeated, feeling obliged to defend her honor.

"Had he not, she would climb his terrace at night," muttered the Warlord, then shook his head as though trying to get rid of his anger. "Go to the rest of the warriors, and wait there for my instructions."

"I can watch the Palace and let you know when she comes back."

The man exhaled loudly. "I wish it was that simple. I'll go and look for her in the Palace. You wait here." The dark eyes narrowed. "And no independent enterprises. Do you hear me? I'm still not sure about you, so watch your step."

Reluctantly, Kuini went toward the building, deep in thought. Why was the Warlord so upset with her going with the Emperor? Was he afraid of betrayal? Had he intended to kill the Emperor, too? He frowned. Iztac should be taken away from this mess, the sooner the better.

In the semidarkness, the warriors, about twenty of them, were spread loosely, sprawling or squatting on mats, drinking *octli* and cracking nuts. Finding it difficult to see, Kuini strained his eyes, hesitating.

"At last!"

At the far corner, the familiar, slender figure sprang onto his feet, and he breathed with relief.

"We've been here since the early afternoon, and I kept waiting for you to show up." Coyotl's smile was broad and unconcerned.

"I had no idea you would break into the Palace, too," said Kuini quietly, uncomfortably aware of the listening warriors. "Don't you want to go out and breathe some air?"

"Can't do that," said Coyotl cheerfully. "Apparently, you have more rights to be here than me."

"That's a novelty." Kuini could not stifle a chuckle. "Where is Tlacaelel? Is he with you?"

"Oh, yes, but he went off to sniff around. Come. I want you to meet someone, and you look like you could use a cup of *octli*."

"That's a certain bet! And if you have something to eat I would be overjoyed, too." He hadn't eaten or slept properly through this whole day, busy keeping his watch over her, and suddenly, he felt weak with hunger.

"We have a pile of tortillas over there."

Ignoring wondering glances, Kuini followed, suddenly elated. Food, *octli*, and time with his best friend! What else could one ask for? Oh, how elated Coyotl would be upon hearing that Iztac was still here, just the same girl, wild, unruly, and with her spirit unbroken.

"Here, make yourself comfortable."

The tortillas were fresh and still warm, and Kuini sank onto one of the mats with relief, welcoming the respite, delighted to have his friend along. Oh, Coyotl would be overjoyed to hear about Iztac.

"Listen," he said devouring his tortilla and reaching for a narrow flask. "You wouldn't believe if I told you…"

At once, his sense of well-being evaporated. The annoying leader from the outside neared them, following Tlacaelel and two other warriors.

"Not this manure eater again," muttered Kuini, part of his mind calculating his way out of the building should the man start a fight and maybe be backed by the rest of the warriors.

Giving him a wondering look, Coyotl rose to his feet. "Greetings. I'm delighted to introduce you to my most faithful friend, a great warrior and a future leader."

"All that, eh?" The leader's eyes sparkled unpleasantly, his smile openly mocking.

Coyotl raised his eyebrows in surprise. "Have you two met before?"

"Yes, they have," contributed Tlacaelel, eyes sparkling.

"When?" Coyotl's gaze leaped from one face to another.

"Not long ago."

"And?"

"And nothing." The Warlord's brother shrugged. "I may hold a different view on the bright future of your friend." He turned to leave. "Stay here until I come to fetch you all."

His steps were heavy on the wooden floor.

Coyotl dropped back onto the mat. "What was that all about?"

"Our Highlander has a peculiar way of striking up friendships." Tlacaelel laughed. "Although, in that case I might understand you, you know. This man thinks too highly of himself." He reached for an empty cup. "But his brother is the Chief Warlord, so we have to be nice to this piece of dung, too. Not that he'll reach this exalted position himself. He will not, mark my words."

"I wish he would die in the most shameful way to prove you right," growled Kuini. His appetite gone, he stared at the half empty plate. "Stupid lump of rotten meat!"

"Be careful with him and the Warlord," said Coyotl quietly, his frown deep. "I wonder how long we'll be stuck here, doing nothing. I would rather spend my time at your uncle's pretty house."

"We very well may be stuck here until dawn and longer." Tlacaelel lowered his voice. "The Warlord changed colors when he spotted me outside. Before the message of our wild friend took his attention away from me." He turned to Kuini. "What did you tell him?"

"Nothing. Nothing of importance."

"Oh, yes, I'm sure it was just an idle talk that made the

Warlord send us away in an indecent hurry." The deeply set eyes narrowed. "Stop being all cagey. We are together in this."

Kuini watched the tall youth thoughtfully. "I'm not cagey. I just don't really know what he wants me to do."

"You've been keeping an eye on the Second Wife." Tlacaelel grinned, obviously pleased with Kuini's open surprise. "What? You thought we wouldn't hear about it? This Palace has no secrets, Highlander. You better remember this."

Unsettled, Kuini made an effort to compose himself. "Well, that's what the Warlord wanted me to do before."

"And your dear uncle was not pleased to hear about that, too." The Aztec's eyes twinkled. "Must have been boring to keep an eye on the silly woman, unless you got to watch her *all* the time. They say she is a beauty, but a cold, haughty *cihua*."

Kuini clenched his fists, his rage sudden and surprising in its intensity. "She is none of that!"

Tlacaelel's grin was wide and full of satisfaction. "None of that, eh? So did you get to see the more pleasant sides of her?"

But now it was Coyotl's turn to become indignant. "This is my sister we are talking about!"

"Yes, and my father's second wife. We are all related to this paragon of beauty and virtue." He chuckled. "Except for her loyal bodyguard, who may have seen the nicer sides of her, hence his tired looks and his bad-tempered outbursts."

"If you don't stop talking about her," growled Kuini. "I will shut you up with my fist, I swear. I don't care if it'll create a scene."

Sipping from his cup, Tlacaelel reclined on his mat as comfortably as he could, eyes twinkling.

"Have you really seen her?" asked Coyotl.

His worry returning with a double strength, Kuini nodded.

"And? How is she?"

He took a deep breath. "She hasn't changed."

Coyotl leaned forward. "How?" he asked eagerly, eyes shining in the semidarkness.

"Wild, beautiful, in trouble."

Coyotl's smile vanished. "What trouble?"

"The same trouble as ours."

"Can't we keep her out of it?"

"I tried. She wouldn't listen."

"She remembered you, eh?"

"Yes, she did." He stared at the plate of tortillas, seeing nothing.

Tlacaelel frowned. "I don't remember if I've met her at all, but none of my father's wives were wild. His Chief Wife would not tolerate anything like that."

"She may not survive the Empress." Surprised to hear his own voice low and strained, Kuini tore his gaze off the wooden plate. "The Warlord is determined to use her, and she is as eager to help. Unless we manage to get in first, somehow."

"Climb the Empress's terrace and kill her, eh?" Tlacaelel's eyes twinkled again.

Kuini ignored the sarcasm this time. "According to your former Chief Warlord it can be done."

"Oh, that Tepanec could do anything and get away with it. But he is old. And we are not him." Another ironic glance at Kuini. "But you can go ahead and try."

Kuini ground his teeth. "What I do is none of your business, but if you go on talking about Iztac Ayotl we'll soon be back at our hand-to-hand on the marketplace. I don't care that we are friends now."

"Tempting," said Tlacaelel, unperturbed. "And although it may save the filthy Empress's life, I'll be pondering your generous offer."

Coyotl sprang to his feet. "I'm tired of you two biting at each other like two *calmecac* boys when serious matters are at stake! I need a break." Fists clenched, he stormed off, halting by the entrance to stare into the thickening dusk. The few warriors that were in the building followed him with their gazes, puzzled.

"He is right, you know." Tlacaelel's lips twisted amusedly. "It's just that there is something annoyingly cheeky about you that makes one want to put you in your place most of the time."

Kuini shrugged. "It goes both ways."

"I know, I know." The deeply set eyes measured him once

again, their twinkle gone. "What did the former Chief Warlord, that dear uncle of yours, do that impressed you so much?" The pointy eyebrows climbed high. "That was an interesting family connection that you didn't bother to share with me through our *calmecac* days." He shrugged. "Anyway, I don't recall any dead Empresses during his time. Or Emperors, for that matter."

Kuini frowned. "I'm not sure, but I overheard him once saying he climbed the Palace's terrace to make one bad empress behave. He said it as a joke, but I think he meant it. He seems like a person who climbed his share of terraces in his lifetime, so why not the Empress's?"

"What did he do to her?"

"I can imagine plenty of things."

"Which empress was that?"

"Your Warlord seemed to think it was the Revered Acamapichtli's Chief Wife."

"Yes, it would make sense. The Tepanec is too old to mess with the current Empress, and my father was not as fond of him as Revered Acamapichtli was." The youth grinned. "I remember how incensed he was over the Texcoco incident. Instead of getting angry with the Acolhua Emperor for trying to hunt his own Chief Warlord down, he blamed the Tepanec for not handling the matter well. He didn't dare to replace him right away – the Tepanec held too much power over the warriors and many others – but he was angry with him ever since."

Kuini grinned against his will, remembering those days, the hurried flight down the coast, the cheerful arrogance of the Aztec Warlord, then the Highlands and the revelation.

He shook his head. "This man is something out of the ordinary. There are no people like him anymore." A shrug seemed to be in order. "Still, we can try to do it. It can't be that difficult. If only he was as fit as back then, he would have helped us greatly. Or just done it all by himself."

"Did you know him back then?"

"Yes, I did."

"But it was summers ago. You were just a boy."

"Fifteen summers old, yes."

The deeply set eyes measured Kuini once again, challenging but not condescending. "As much of a troublemaker as you are now, I bet. Well, then what do we do? Should we go and talk to your revered uncle, asking for guidance on climbing terraces?"

"How do we get to him? He is not in the Palace."

"He promised the Warlord to try to make it here tonight."

Kuini tensed. "Is he coming here?"

"It seems that way."

"I wish he would hurry."

Tlacaelel narrowed his eyes. "You really mean it, don't you? You would just go and try to kill the Empress, I believe. Gods, people like you are an asset if they are successful and used correctly. But it's a big 'if'."

"No one will use me!"

"You may be surprised." The youth's grin widened, became unbearably smug. "They use you and me, and that Texcocan friend of yours. But it's all right. I don't mind being used if it serves my goals. I'll use my share of people when my time comes."

Kuini watched the strong face, fascinated against his will. "Are you going to try to make it into the Emperor's chair?"

"No. Not in the near future, anyway. I have a fair guess who our next Emperor will be, and I don't want to cross this man's path." He shrugged, his grin deepening. "But I'll get to the real power, never fear."

Coyotl came back, refreshed and in good humor once again. "What? You didn't kill each other yet?" His eyes laughed. "So, what do we do?"

"We wait for the Warlord," said Tlacaelel firmly. "I'm not going to argue with him. Not over this."

Kuini sprang to his feet. "You can wait all you like. I'm going to look for him."

"Will you come back here?" Coyotl's deep frown made him look older.

"Yes, I will. We have to do something, and it has to be done tonight."

"We?" Tlacaelel's voice rang eerily in the deepening dusk. "I beg to disagree, oh Honorable Leader. You can do whatever you like, tonight or tomorrow, but you won't drag me into your wild schemes. Go and save your princess alone."

Surprised by his own lack of rage, Kuini just shrugged, making his way toward the fresh breeze of the outside.

CHAPTER 12

Dehe stood the Chief Warlord's heavy gaze, her heart fluttering with fear. She remembered watching this man earlier through the day, intimidated by his impressive width and aggressive bearing. Yet, back then she had been safe, hidden behind the bushes at Kuini's uncle's spacious dwelling, not forced to face this man, watching him getting angry with the Lowlander and the young haughty Aztec, instead. She was invisible and safe, having every right to be where she was. Oh, she remembered the lifted brows and the twinkling eyes of Kuini's uncle when they had informed him of her existence. Again just a girl who makes no trouble. But this time she didn't feel too bad about it, uncertain of anything anymore.

"You what?" The Warlord's cold, squinted eyes measured her dubiously.

"I… I have to give you… give you something," she stammered, clutching onto her basket.

"Who are you?"

She swallowed, but her mouth was too dry to bring a relief. "Kaay sent me. The healer from—"

"Shut up!" His threatening gaze cut her off before his words would. "Go away, and wait for me under that terrace."

Turning so abruptly his cloak swirled, he stormed off, back toward the polished stairs of the Palace's entrance, leaving Dehe standing there, legs trembling and unable to move. Oh gods, Kaay was right, she should never have ventured into the Palace.

However, it was so easy in the beginning. Oh but how surprised she had been with the swiftness and the easiness with which she had gotten inside those formidable walls. One moment outside, following her guide – the woman Kaay had sent to accompany her – nervous and tense; the next in, walking through a narrow gate together with a small flow of other commoner-looking people carrying things. She clutched onto her basket laden with avocados, not daring to look at the warriors guarding the entrance, but they had barely paid her any attention, busy talking between themselves.

Encouraged, she had dared to breath once again, but then the woman measured her with a dubious glance and told her that from there she was on her own, and so her fears returned, only to calm down again as she proceeded along the groomed roads, drawing no attention.

Grateful to Kaay for making sure that she was dressed nicely, in a pretty maguey blouse and skirt, with her sandals clean and her hair washed with indigo, combed and braided, fastened by a colorful string, she went on, hiding a smile. Kaay even forced her to smear some yellow cream on her cheeks and then threw a pretty necklace around her neck. And, while feeling uncomfortably pretentious to be dressed up like a princess, Dehe could not hide a smile. *He* was somewhere in that Palace, and if she was lucky, she'd meet him there. Oh, he would be really surprised, and his eyes would sparkle again with desire, as had happened to him from time to time.

However now, taking a deep breath and forcing her legs to stop trembling, she knew why Kaay had made this effort to dress her nicely. Maids rushed all around, but they all looked like well-off ladies that would frequent the marketplace. None were dressed in the plain maguey the market girls wore with pride.

The terrace the Warlord pointed at was wide, protruding out of the wall, not very far from the main entrance. How beautiful, she thought, walking there slowly, her heart still fluttering. The dusk colored the solid stone walls into a darker shade, hiding the cracks, making them look smooth and perfect, like a wooden toy, polished and covered with paint. Like the things Kuini would carve out of scattered pieces of wood every time he would grow bored or restless throughout their journey over Tlaxcala Valley.

She loved those carvings of his, picking up the ones he would throw away, careless and indifferent to his own art. The Lowlander knew she was collecting them, and he had told her once that he thought she was right in doing this.

Again she looked up. People rushed all around her, maids dressed in the same fashion, or more important looking men holding scrolls. And warriors. Many warriors. Too many. Hastening her step, Dehe hurried past the wide stairs, eager to dive into the relative safety of the Palace's wall and the terrace.

The clamor around her grew, and she glanced back in time to catch a view of a large group proceeding along another wide, perfectly swept road. The warriors' cloaks swirled arrogantly as they walked ahead, clearing the way, calm yet forceful, making the passersby move aside. Behind the warriors proceeded middle-aged men dressed in colorful garbs, sparkling with rich jewelry.

Afraid, yet curious, Dehe watched them, her eyes drifting toward the middle of the group, and the young boy almost hidden under a colorful, evidently heavy headdress. Yes, of course the strikingly beautiful woman was still by his side, walking tensely, her step constricted by the showy, sky-blue skirt, her hair pulled high in elaborate tresses, sparkling with obsidian pins.

Dehe's stomach tightened, and her fear gave way to the familiar surge of rage. Oh the skinny she-wolf, she thought, biting her lips. The dirty, rotten piece of meat. The infamous late Emperor's Second Wife, no doubt, she knew, choking with hatred, her eyes brushing over the matching blouse that set off the golden skin of the young woman, revealing much of its creamy smoothness. Displaying it all, as generously as the last of the marketplace whores!

Oh, she remembered the look on Kuini's face just a little earlier, when she had been wandering the Palace's grounds, looking for the Warlord, relieved to find out she was blending with the crowds.

Grinding her teeth, she rememeber how her heart leaped when she suddenly saw his unmistakably wide shoulders. She stared at him, hoping to catch his eye, expecting his surprise and his joy at seeing her there, but his gaze was glued to the slimy whore in the blue dress, along with the rest of the people around them. They all stared at her. But of course! The dirty princess shouldn't have bothered using the blouse at all the way her breasts threatened to pop out of it.

And then, when Dehe was still struggling to convince herself it was just a coincidence, the emperor-boy came along, and while everyone turned to gape at him, she saw Kuini making his way toward the dirty piece of meat in blue. And then they were whispering, thinking themselves safe, but some people glanced at them, especially a roly-poly woman the princess had previously been standing beside.

Oh, it did give her satisfaction, to see the Highlander's eyes turning dark, flashing angrily, but as she began feeling better, hoping the slimy rat would annoy him into leaving for good, the cheeky woman began whispering soothingly, touching his hand just as the Emperor-boy turned to look at her, along with the rest of the Palace's people.

Fighting for breath, Dehe had watched the princess changing colors and Kuini tensing by her side, looking as if about to step forward and shield her from Tenochtitlan's Emperor and his entourage. She fought the tears from showing, but those were not the tears of grief but of anger, she knew, and the thought of another small jar of Kaay's brew she was careful to bring along with the one entrusted to her gave her enough strength to go on looking for the Warlord.

"I told you to wait under the terrace!" The hissing voice tore Dehe out of her reverie, making her jump back. Pressing against the damp stones of the wall, she peered at the grim face of the Warlord, her heart thundering in her ears, interrupting with her ability to listen. "Where is what you were supposed to give me?"

She tried to reach for her basket, but her hands trembled so badly she could not bring it up to search through its contents.

The Warlord's face softened. "There is no need to get that scared, girl. Just give me the damn thing and be off."

She clenched her teeth tight and managed to reach for the small jar, buried deep between avocados.

"Kaay said to be careful," she mumbled, offering him the

unpainted pottery. "It spills."

"And you've been shaking the whole stupid basket like a maid making a chocolate drink." He shook his head, but his face was slightly amused now, wearing this same, somewhat kinder expression. "Now ran along, girl, and don't stare at the Emperor the way you did just now. Remember your place."

She watched him walking away with the long, forceful paces, the jar small and invisible in his large weathered palm. Taking a deep breath, she let the slight breeze cool off her burning face. So now all she had to do was to find her way out of the Palace. Not a difficult task. Many servants were still rushing about, flooding the alleys and the passageways.

Carefully, she stepped away from the safety of the wall, clutching onto her basket, afraid to draw attention to herself. It should now have been filled with avocados only, an innocent cargo, but for the other jar she had smuggled in when Kaay was busy arranging her clothing.

She shivered, then looked up. The richly dressed group had long since broken, with the Emperor-boy already mounting the wide stairs, his pleasantly round face agitated, the frown not sitting well on the gentle, still child-like, features. What had the vile princess told him to make him so upset? wondered Dehe, scanning the alley with her gaze, looking for the sky-blue spot in the colorful river of moving people.

Sure enough, the tall woman was still there, standing in the middle of the road, oblivious to the passersby and their stares, not bothered by the fact that she was blocking people's way. Two women, clearly maids, judging by their bearing and the simplicity of their clothing, talked to her, but the haughty princess paid them no attention, staring ahead, frowning, biting her lips.

Oh, she didn't look that beautiful with her face so troubled, thought Dehe. Her nose was definitely too long, and the creases crossing her forehead made her look older. Kuini should have seen her now!

"Move along, girl!" A woman's voice tore into Dehe's thoughts, making her heart jump once again. She looked up. The broad, sweaty face of a maid crinkled with laughter. "Stop dreaming. Those avocados should reach the kitchens before they rot, shouldn't they?"

"I... well," Dehe stared at the woman, lost for words. "I should be going, yes."

"Use the wooden stairs, right behind that terrace," said the woman briskly. "Those will bring you straight to the kitchen slaves. But hurry up. They should have finished already with the preparations of the evening meal, and they'll be mighty upset with you bringing your avocados so late."

"I... thank you. I'll do that," muttered Dehe.

The narrowing eyes looked at her with a measure of interest. "You are new, aren't you? Come. I need to speak to the main cook anyway, and we can grab a nice, warm tortilla on our way."

Wincing, Dehe fought the urge to break free as the woman took a firm hold of her arm, steering her back toward the terrace. She could go to the kitchens and give them the stupid basket. There was no need to make a scene over it. She was still relatively safe.

"Oh, they must have bought you just recently," went on the woman, as if unable to stop talking. "Didn't they?"

"Yes, they did." Glancing back, Dehe saw the princess still standing there undecided, ignoring the imploring speeches of her maids.

"Minor wives wing, isn't it?"

"I'm sorry, I don't understand."

"You were bought to serve one of the minor wives." The woman smiled with superiority, clearly enjoying herself and her ability to read people. "You obviously know nothing about this side of the Palace."

"Oh well, yes. The minor wives." Dehe's heart seemed to stop for a moment. "I was bought to serve the Second Wife."

"Oh, the Acolhua princess. You are lucky. She is easily pleased." The wooden stairs creaked under their feet. "Those princesses are the worst, usually. A spoiled capricious lot. But the Acolhua girl only wants everyone to stay out of her way and leave her alone. Such a strange princess." The woman dropped her voice and looked around carefully. "She had a bad row with the Empress only the day before. She was lucky to make it back to her side of the Palace alive."

"What row?"

"Oh," the woman's eyes sparkled. "They say it was something, the way they yelled at each other. Like two market women. But the Empress has the power, while all the Second Wife has is the spirit."

A wave of heat pounced on them as they passed the threshold, crossing into a long, spacious room. Fires burned under many clay pots and desks, held in place by large stones, and the room was incredibly hot, full of smells, some deliciously spicy, some revolting and burned.

A sweaty man bumped into them.

"What are you doing here?" he demanded angrily. "What do you have?" He grabbed Dehe's basket. "Stupid *cihua*, what's with those avocados? What are we to do with them in this part of the night, eh?"

Fighting her panic, Dehe clutched onto the basket, her thoughts on the small jar buried at its bottom.

"Easy on the girl," called the woman, seemingly not deterred by the unfriendly welcome. "She is new, and she didn't know. Give him your avocados, little one," she added, turning to Dehe. "There is no need to be scared. Kitchen slaves are always a rude, angry lot." Her eyes sparkled teasingly toward the sweating man.

"Oh piss off, both of you," the man cried out, grinning.

"Not before we have gotten something to chew," retorted the woman.

"Oh, you'll get a good beating first, you insolent *cihua*," the man said as he laughed, turning toward one of the tethering disks. While he grabbed a large, crumbled tortilla, Dehe saw her chance. Breath caught, eyes almost shut, she rummaged through her basket, smearing her hands with the sticky greenish pulp. The small jar felt sleek against her fingers, but she clutched onto it desperately, pulling it up, trying to conceal it under her palm.

"Here, have some leftovers that I would have to throw away anyway," said the man, tossing a crumbled tortilla at them.

The woman caught it deftly, still laughing. "What a skinflint. Come, girl. Leave your basket here, and let's get out of this smelly cesspit."

"Oh, you just wait and see what you'll get in your next meal," the man called after them.

The deepening dusk enveloped them in its cooling embrace, and Dehe felt her taut nerves calming.

"Now run to your mistress, girl, and stop looking so tense. This Palace is not a bad place. You could have done worse."

"Yes, thank you." This time she found enough courage to straighten her gaze and smile. "Can you please tell me how to find the other side of the Palace? I don't remember my way."

"Oh, it's easy, silly girl." The woman put her arm around Dehe's shoulders, propelling her towards the road. "You just follow this alley. Run all the way up, then turn when it turns. And of course use the side staircase. Don't you try to go up the main entrance." Eyes laughing, she pushed Dehe slightly. "And now run along and try to remember your way next time. And stop being scared. You'll do all right. The Second Wife is no Empress. She is nice, and is as messed up as you are."

Stomach tightening, Dehe swallowed. "I'm not sure she is so nice. I heard she is arrogant and haughty. I heard she does things she should not."

The woman laughed, unperturbed. "Oh, she certainly does things she should not. But she is not a bad person, and this is what matters to us, the servants. She won't be mean to you; she never has been mean to her slaves." Her mirth growing, the woman put her palms against her hips. "She might punch you if you say mean things about her. She did this to one of the other wives. Hit her so hard, the silly woman crushed a podium on her way down, so they say." Now the woman's whole body trembled with laughter. "This princess is something. Fancy picking fights with other noblewomen, the Empress included. But she is nice to her slaves, so just serve her meals and clean her clothes and stay out of her way." Her long, shapeless skirt swishing, Dehe's guide whirled around. "See you later, pretty girl."

Shivering against the breeze, Dehe peered through the deepening twilight. She only needed to follow the road for a little while, then turn right into the smaller alley, heading toward the narrow gate. She never got lost, never. The silly woman was so easy to manipulate.

Her fingers tightened around the tiny jar. But if she followed the road, going along with its twists, and then used the side staircase, she would get to the other side of the Palace without much trouble, according to that woman. And then, and then... Oh but the dirty princess had no right to grab his hand.

Iztac peered at the thickening darkness, welcoming the freshness of the night. The soft breeze caressed her bare neck, sliding down her shoulders, fluttering the rims of her long uncomfortable skirt. She hadn't bothered to change into more comfortable clothes since she'd come back to her side of the Palace, to stand on the terrace stubbornly and watch the darkness descending.

Dizzy with exhaustion, she refused to come in, oblivious to the pleadings of Ihuitl, who kept studying Iztac with her large, liquid eyes wide open and expectant. As if she, Iztac, were about to perform an exotic dance or do some other magical thing.

Annoyed, she sent the young woman in almost rudely, craving to be left alone, needing this solitude badly. Oh but she needed to think things over, to understand. In the span of a few dawns, and after the unbearable boredom and idleness of three summers, her life had suddenly taken a sharp turn, offering her more adventures than she seemed to be able to handle. First, the Warlord catching her climbing into Chimal's rooms, assigning his own dirty interpretation to her deeds; then, the Empress threatening to kill her or sell her into slavery if she would not go tamely to Tlacopan, to be given to the governor of the influential Tepanec province; next, her resolution to help the Warlord to be rid of the Empress, and of her own free will, of all things. Why, she had almost begged the vile man to let her help.

She ground her teeth. How had it come to this? And, of course, on top of it all, him, the Highlander, coming back from the past, as handsome, as attractive as ever. More than ever! But at the worst of times. What should she do about him?

The dream of running away belonged to two innocent children in the Palace of Texcoco. They were not children anymore. Had he only appeared only a market interval earlier, before the despicable Warlord had caught her climbing the Emperor's window...

A market interval!

She clenched the stony railing of the terrace so tight she could not feel her palms anymore. He was always late, always missing the right timing. A market interval ago she would have left without looking back. But now? Oh, now she had obligations. She could not leave Chimal all alone in this Palace, surrounded by sneaky people like his mother or his Chief Warlord, or all those sleazy, smooth-talking advisers of his.

Shuddering, she remembered their wondering, disapproving glances as she walked beside him, uncomfortable and ill at ease. Of course, he shouldn't have invited her to accompany him. Of course, it was out of the ordinary, inappropriate, even scandalous. Still, he was the Emperor, and it was none of their filthy business.

Recalling that walk along the Palace's well-groomed alleys, she frowned. Chimal was so edgy and restless, so awkward as he tried to talk to her politely, clearly yearning for all those people around them to disappear. And if she'd seen it, they'd seen it too. Nosy bastards.

Trying to help, she asked him general questions, but it only made him more frustrated. Finally, as the main entrance of the Palace grew nearer, he stopped.

"Please, wait for me by the stairs. I want to talk to the late Emperor's Second Wife," he said imperiously, but his voice had a pleading ring to it.

"But your Revered Mother is expecting you to attend her evening meal," argued a paunchy adviser.

"It will take only a few heartbeats," pleaded Chimal, disconcerted even more. He glanced at Iztac, as if trying to pull together the last of his courage. "Please wait by the staircase," he repeated more firmly.

Uncomfortable under their stares, Iztac gave him a fleeting

smile, proud of him for standing his ground. The army of his attendance went away, but their gazes burned their skins nevertheless, now from a barely respectable distance.

He glanced at her again, then shifted uneasily, studying the ground under his feet.

"What did you want to talk about?" she asked finally, counting the heartbeats. The time was trickling away.

"I don't know." He looked up, frowning. "Many things."

"Like what?"

"Why don't you come at nights anymore?"

She shrugged. "I visited you only a market interval ago."

"It was more than a market interval," he muttered, his frown deepening. "And I needed to talk to you, and you did not come."

"I could not. Your Warlord saw me climbing down your terrace."

"He did?"

It was difficult not to laugh at his surprised, gaping face, a gamut of emotions chasing each other across his pleasant-looking features.

"It's all right. He promised not to tell anyone."

"But he did! I think he did."

Now it was her turn to gap. "Why? What do you know?"

He dropped his gaze once again. "About a market interval ago Mother asked me about you."

"What did she want to know?"

"She said... Well, she said all sort of things. I don't know." His shoulders sagged, and he seemed to be shrinking, trying to hide inside himself.

"What, Chimal? What was it all about?"

He refused to meet her gaze. "I told her I want to take you to be my Chief Wife."

Oh gods! She felt like running away.

His gaze flew at her, angry and pleading at the same time. "You told me to act like an Emperor and not like a frightened boy."

"Yes, of course, but I didn't mean for you to pick a fight with *her*!" She brought her palms up, then forced her body back into calmness, aware of the stares. "Was she furious?"

"Oh, yes, she was. She called you all sort of names, and then she told me to get it out of my head, because you will be given away soon."

Tlacopan, of course! So that's why she was being sent to the Tepanec province.

He was peering at her, eyes pleading. "I don't know what to do about it, Iztac Ayotl. She wouldn't talk to me about you anymore. And I tried, I swear I tried!"

Forcing a smile, she pushed her fear back with an utmost effort. "I'll take care of it. Don't worry."

"How?"

"You'll see."

He looked up at her searchingly. "Don't be angry with my mother. I'll find a way to convince her. She'll let me take you to be my Chief Wife. I'm sure she will." He shifted his weight from one foot to the other. "She has so many things to worry about. She helps me so much. I could never do anything without her."

Iztac felt her throat going dry. It was not the time, nor the place to get into this discussion. The stares of his advisers and followers scorched her skin.

"Do you love her?" she whispered.

His eyes widened. "Of course! She is my mother."

And now, recalling this awkward conversation in the quietness of the dark terrace, she shut her eyes, trying to contain her welling dread. She was about to kill his mother! He loved this horrible woman, he trusted her, he needed her, and she, Iztac, his best friend, was about to take her away from him.

Unclenching her palms with an effort, she jumped as a pebble landed beside her, rolling, clattering over the stone floor. Heart beating fast, she picked it up, studying its uneven shape. A lonely torch behind her back flickered, as another pebble rolled by.

Fighting a sudden smile, she leaned over the railing. The darkness was thick and the gardens below quiet, partly lit by a faint moon. Straining her eyes, she tried to pick out a shadow.

A silhouette moved, and her heart leaped, recognizing the wide shoulders and familiar broad steps, his warrior's topknot swaying in the soft breeze. Hands trembling with excitement, she fought the tight material of her skirt, struggling to tuck it up, to make her climb down easier. She could not even lift her leg to go over the railing in the stupidly fancy dress.

His silhouette disappeared beneath the terrace, and she held her breath. Would he try to climb up? The silence enveloped her. Even the bushes adorning the alley froze, not rustling with the breeze anymore.

She listened intently, counting her heartbeats. Twenty, two times twenty, three times. *What took him so long?* Leaning over the railing as far as she could without risking a fall, she heard the sound of a sandal slipping over a stone. She didn't dare to move. Another twenty of heartbeats, then some more.

When his hand clutched the stony parapet firmly, she realized she was holding her breath. Anxious, she leaped toward it, in time to see him jumping in, light and sure-footed, as graceful as a jaguar.

His arms pulled her closer, enveloped her in their embrace, strong and demanding. She could feel his chest rising and falling, his breathing stabilizing gradually.

"You shouldn't have climbed here," she whispered, raising her head, her lips brushing against his face.

"I know."

His arms tightened around her as his lips sought hers. As always, his kiss took her breath away, making her limbs weak and out of control, interrupting her ability to think. Melting into his arms, she closed her eyes, wishing to let go. They were still alone on that terrace, and she needed him badly.

Another gust of wind made the bushes beneath rustle, and she broke the kiss abruptly, startled.

"We can't. Not here," she whispered.

"I know."

She could feel him tensing, the muscles of his arms tightening, fighting for control.

"You should have waited for me to come down." She brushed her lips against his neck, sensing his immediate reaction and feeling powerful because of that.

"I don't want you to endanger yourself anymore," he whispered hoarsely, pulling away but not releasing her, not yet. His eyes twinkled in the darkness. "Also, you would never make it in this fancy dress of yours."

"Oh, yes?" She moved away, leaning against his encircling arms. "It took you half a night to get here. I started to think I imagined you trying to stone me earlier."

He laughed. "I've never climbed this terrace before, and it's dark. I had to be careful." Suddenly, his eyes sobered and the smile left his face. "Have you climbed this wall often?"

"Sometimes. Why?"

"The Warlord. He said you would climb the Emperor's terrace." His frown deepened. "It was all very strange. He was upset, even angry to hear you were talking to the Emperor this evening, and he said you would climb his terrace if you could." The piercing gaze bore at her. "What did he mean?"

She broke away from his embrace and leaned against the railing. "Don't you start this nonsense, too!" she said sharply, then lowered her voice back to a whisper. "Chimal is just a boy. He has seen hardly twelve or thirteen summers. He doesn't lay with women. And he is the only friend I have in this Palace."

She could hear him chuckling, but still she peered into the darkness, refusing to look at him.

"So the Warlord thought you were lying with the boy? How ridiculous!" She could feel his body trembling with laughter. "It explains a lot. He thinks you are a devious Tepanec monster-woman, like the Empress herself at the very least."

She pursed her lips. "That's what he thinks? Good. I hope he is afraid of me."

But he sobered all at once. "This man is not afraid of anyone, and he is dangerous. You should keep away from him. And from all of it. Let him change the things. He should be capable enough to do it. Don't put yourself into a danger on his behalf."

She tensed. "Did he send something for me?"

"Yes, he did." His voice was so low she had difficulty understanding his words.

"Let me see."

The small pottery jar felt warm in her hands. She brought it up. The slight odor reached her nostrils.

"What does it do?"

"I'm not sure I want to know." He leaned closer to study the jar. "Careful with this thing."

The smooth, oval container fit her palm, strangely pleasant to touch. She shook it lightly. "It feels like water. Or some sort of a drink." She smelled it again. "It smells strange."

"Stop sniffing it! It may work from great distances or something. I don't like any of it."

She caressed his arm gently. "It will all be well. You'll see. Tomorrow it will be over."

"Maybe the Warlord—" He fell silent, and she could feel him tensing by her side.

"What happened?"

He moved away in a smooth, catlike movement, sliding along the terrace's railing, as soundless as an Underworld spirit – one moment beside her, the next gone.

She caught her breath, glad to feel her heart going still. It gave her better ability to listen. Yet, she heard noting. Not even his steps. He was still somewhere around, according to her senses, but whether he moved or not she didn't know.

"What is it?" she whispered.

"Quiet!"

A shutter cracked, moving with the wind. Below the terrace, dry leaves rustled on the small gravel. The usual sounds of the late evening. She had heard plenty of that over the summer nights spent on that terrace.

He materialized back from the darkness, startling her.

"Coyotl said your name meant Jaguar."

"Well, yes." His eyes still peered in the direction of her rooms.

"I can understand why. You move like that magnificent creature. You make no sound, and you are just as dangerous."

His lips stretched into a contented smile, but his gaze still concentrated upon the darkness behind her back. "Yes, I like my name."

"What happened? What did you hear?"

"Someone was listening to us. We weren't alone for some time."

She felt it like a stony fist, tightening around her entrails, squeezing it. "Who was it?"

"I don't know. Someone who can move really quietly." He hesitated. "Not a warrior. A much smaller, light-footed creature."

Suddenly, she thought of the slave girl she had seen earlier, when coming back to her side of the Palace. A small, wary creature that stood at the bottom of the servants' staircase, staring at her, Iztac, in the way no normal slave would dare to look at the late Emperor's Second Wife, with a strange mixture of fear and animosity. Were the slaves angry with her, too? She had been too busy to think about it, but now the memory surfaced.

"You should go," she said firmly. "It is not safe for you here. If I'm caught outside, I'll get into trouble, but it won't be serious. I've been caught before." She thought of the Warlord grabbing her arm, permitting himself to threaten her, the Emperor's Second Wife. Shaking off the memory, she peered at him. "But you will be executed, if caught on the minor wives' balcony."

He was still listening to the darkness. "I'll go," he said absently. "But I'll wait for you by the pond." His gaze concentrated, peering at her, again turning heavy and demanding. "Come there as soon as you can."

"Yes, I will," she said, her throat dry. "Near midnight."

CHAPTER 13

The ground around the low building and the patio was lit brightly, the almost full moon aided by a few flickering torches. Warriors strolled or congregated in groups, animated and wary, unbecomingly so.

Had it been a clearing in the woods or the river it would make more sense, reflected Kuini watching the two leaders arguing at some distance, the feathers of the Warlord's headdress rustling in the breeze. The feeling of a battle about to commence was strong in the air. He had participated in enough of these to recognize the signs.

"What are they arguing about?" he asked Coyotl, who stood there as tense and as apprehensive as the rest of the warriors.

The Lowlander shrugged. "Isn't that obvious?"

"No, it's not." Kuini shifted his weight from one foot to the other, regretting coming here. He should have headed straight for the pond.

"The Warlord seems eager to do something rash with all these warriors he has, and your uncle thinks we should wait and be patient." Coyotl grinned humorlessly. "The current Warlord is the leader, but the former one still has plenty of clout with the warriors. They seem to worship him, according to Tlacaelel, and to my own observations."

"Where is Tlacaelel?"

"Wandering around, too restless to stay still. Just like you."

"And the dirty manure-eater, the Warlord's brother?"

"He is here, busy making sure everyone is ready. For what? Well, that's another question." Coyotl's eyes twinkled. "He hates your guts, doesn't he?"

"It goes both ways."

"Why? What happened between you two?"

"Nothing. He is just a pompous piece of dung who thinks the world of himself. I hate those types."

"You do have a wonderful ability to make enemies in high places."

Kuini spat into the bushes. "Give me a break!" Studying his sword, he ran his fingers between the obsidian spikes, feeling the carvings. This always made him feel better. "I hope the Warlord will prevail. It could be interesting to fight in the Palace."

"Against whom?"

"Other warriors, I suppose. I don't care. I just want to do something. Maybe to kill the Empress along the way. I still think we can climb her terrace and make everything easy for everyone."

This time Coyotl laughed loudly. "I'm surprised she is still alive. Since you wandered off this evening, I thought Tenochtitlan was about to lose its most famous connection to the Tepanecs." He measured Kuini with a quick side-glance. "What did you do?"

"Nothing worth mentioning." Kuini's gaze brushed past a group of nearby warriors. Although seemingly immersed in the idle talk, their gazes wandered again and again toward the arguing leaders. "They should not argue this way. It doesn't look good. The warriors don't feel reassured."

"No, they don't." Coyotl pursed his lips. "So what are your plans?"

"I don't know. I wish they had decided on some action already. I wish they would sort their problems out before dawn breaks." *Before the dawn. Before she is forced to go into the jaguar's lair*, he thought. He watched his uncle's impressively wide back. "He knows what he is doing, though. The Warlord should have the sense to listen to him."

Coyotl shrugged and said nothing. Oh, the Lowlander looked atypically angry and frustrated, reflected Kuini, glancing at his friend. He didn't like to drift with the current. He was raised to be an emperor, and he had been forced to follow other people's manipulative moves for far too long, tossed between Huexotzinco and Tenochtitlan, waiting for all sorts of leaders to decide how to use him.

He touched Coyotl's shoulder, his eyes still on the arguing leaders. "It'll all be well, you know? You will be an emperor one day, yet. And not just an emperor, but a great one. And all those summers of being tossed around will remain nothing but a memory."

"I like your prophesy." He could hear a smile in Coyotl's voice. "And with you for my Chief Warlord, we will take the whole Tepanec Empire. All *altepetls* and towns around the Great Lake. But not the Highlands. Never the Highlands."

"Yes, the Highlands will have to take care of themselves." He watched the warlords talking quietly, calmer than before. *Had they agreed on the best course, at last?* "Let us see what is going on."

Not needing to coordinate their action, they drifted closer to the talking men.

"She will make a move soon," the former warlord was saying, his voice firm, but calm, sure of himself. Kuini's heart squeezed with pride. Oh, his uncle was a man of unlimited authority and resources, a person no one would dare to overlook. "Be patient."

"I trust your judgment, as always, but my heart is not tranquil. It tells me that an action would be our best course. Yet," the wide shoulders of the Warlord lifted in a shrug. "Let us do it your way."

The widely spaced eyes of his uncle rested upon Kuini, amiable even if lacking their usual twinkle.

"It's good to see you, Nephew," he said as ceremonious as always while around Tenochtitlan's people. It would have been "boy" had they been alone now, and the twinkle would be there too, reflected Kuini, realizing that he had missed this man's company.

"Thank you, Honorable Uncle," he said.

The man frowned. "Where is the First Son?"

"He accompanied a group of warriors on their regular route around the Palace," said Coyotl.

"And what do you do with unruly youths?" exclaimed Itzcoatl angrily. "I told the young hothead to wait inside."

Kuini saw his uncle grinning, unperturbed, while Coyotl said hurriedly. "He promised to be careful. He knows what he is doing."

"Oh, that one always knows what he is doing," muttered the Warlord, not pacified in the least.

The former warlord's grin widened. "Well, then you'll have to run along and find him. Only you, Nephew," he added, when Coyotl made a movement to take the offered scroll. "It's not safe for you here yet, Acolhua Heir." Turning back to Kuini, he tucked the scroll into his hand. "Find the First Son. Tell him to bring this to his uncle, Honorable Quatlecoatl. Accompany him and keep him safe."

The rolled piece of bark-paper felt heavy in his palm. "I will, Honorable Uncle. Thank you for your trust." He didn't need to look at Coyotl to feel his friend's splash of irritation.

Suppressing a shrug, he hurried off, his frustration welling. How long would it take him to find Tlacaelel and then to accompany the First Son on his errand? Too long, undoubtedly, and she would be waiting by the pond. She may have been making her way there in these very moments.

He ground his teeth. He could have rushed on, delivering the note all by himself, had he known this Honorable Quatlecoatl and his whereabouts. He should have gone straight to the pond, instead of detouring by the congregating warriors.

To his endless relief, Tlacaelel's unconcerned voice reached him as he crossed the wide road. The tall youth was back, or maybe he hadn't gone on any route at all.

"Highlander, what are you doing here among us, boring mortals?"

Kuini found it difficult to hide his grin. "Looking for you."

"Oh."

Tlacaelel's companions measured Kuini with wondering glances.

"Well?" The deeply set eyes measured him too, challenging.

"Well, would you come with me?" Taking in the warriors' frowns, he clasped his lips tight. No, he would not use any honorable titles. He had never done it before. Coyotl did without humble reference, and so would this highborn Aztec.

After a heartbeat of deliberation, Tlacaelel grinned crookedly. "Of course, Honorable Warrior. You do me too much honor."

Clenching his teeth, Kuini let the remark pass.

"Well, what is going on?" asked the tall Aztec as they began walking briskly into the night.

"The former warlord wants you to deliver a message."

"Oh, is he here?"

"Yes."

"Good. Now we'll see some action."

"I wouldn't be so sure about that. I gather that Itzcoatl is all for storming the Palace at last, but my uncle keeps him from doing this."

"Your uncle, yes, I keep forgetting. You were such a manure-eater for not telling me, happy to let me run away with my tongue all these days back in *calmecac*."

The open resentment of the First Son made Kuini feel better. "I counted every time you called him a dirty frog-eater. I remember every one of them. And all the rest, too. I wonder what he would say about it."

"Oh, you are such a pain! Why don't you go back to guarding royal wives instead of bothering decent people?"

"When I see a decent person around here I promise not to bother him. In the meanwhile, have this!" Grinning, Kuini thrust a scroll into his companion's hand. "You should give it to some honored Quatlecoatl. Do you know where he is?"

"Quatlecoatl?" Tlacaelel slowed his steps. "What does that frog-eater have to do with any of it?" Heading toward the moonlit patch, away from the road, he unfolded the scroll carelessly.

"Aren't you going to deliver it?" asked Kuini, taken aback.

"Yes, I am." The tall youth squinted his eyes, peering at the thin piece of paper. "But I want to know what I'm delivering first."

It took him some time to decipher the roughly drawn symbols, but Kuini didn't mind. Yes, they should know what was going on.

"Well?" he asked, when the tall youth straightened up, returning to the road.

"Well, your dear uncle seems anxious to ensure Quatlecoatl's support of their case."

"Who is this Quatlecoatl?"

"He is one of my numerous uncles. One of the many children sired by Tenochtitlan's First Emperor."

"Acamapichtli?"

"Yes, Acamapichtli. Nice of you to keep a count of our emperors."

"That wasn't easy. They are dying fast, your emperors," stated Kuini, incensed with the youth once again.

But Tlacaelel laughed, unperturbed. "That's why I won't be an emperor. I will live a long life, and I will influence events, but not from the emperor's chair. I will be remembered, and not because of the title. You just wait and see."

"Nice plans. I wish you luck with those. But I'll take your word for it, as I will be too busy with my own life to keep an eye on you."

The Aztec grinned. "It won't be as long or as fruitful as mine. You are picking fights too easily. You will die young."

"I've survived so far, but your concern is very touching."

"Actually, I will be sorry to see you die. You would be an excellent man to guard one's interests. Good warrior; maybe a leader even. But mostly, a man for all sorts of extraordinary missions. I would be glad to use you when I'm older and more important."

"You just try to use me once!"

But the Aztec laughed merrily. "One day I will. If you live long enough."

Kuini shot his tall companion a direful look, but in the darkness he wasn't sure his message was received. *Dirty, arrogant bastard,* he thought. *You are so sure of yourself, but you will be put down one day.*

The Palace's walls loomed ahead, dark and unfriendly. It would be difficult to climb those, he reflected. It was too dark, and they needed to keep quiet. Iztac's terrace was challenging enough, and it was lit generously by the moon.

He frowned, suddenly annoyed with the thought of Iztac

climbing these walls. The emperor was just a boy, but the way he looked at her this afternoon was not innocently boyish. How old was the little bastard? She said twelve or thirteen summers. Old enough to cherish all sorts of dirty thoughts about her. He was not too far away from that age to forget.

"What we are looking for?" he asked in order to take his thoughts off the slimy emperor.

"A small side entrance." Tlacaelel peered into the darkness. "Behind that far corner."

"I'll wait for you outside."

"Suit yourself."

The tall youth disappeared, only to slink back after a while, cursing beneath his breath. "It's guarded. Filthy manure-eaters!"

Pleased with the First Son's loss of his perpetual composure, Kuini raised his eyebrows. "Why shouldn't it be guarded? It's a Palace, for gods' sake. For a future great leader you think simply."

The glance Tlacaelel shot at him should have burned his skin. "Servants' entrances are not guarded, not usually. But how would *you* know this?" He took a deep breath, trying visibly to calm down. "Well, we'll have to check the one on the other side of the Palace."

"Is your uncle's quarters somewhere around here?"

"Yes! That's why I'm so upset. He is right there." Pointing at the small balcony on the first floor, Tlacaelel cursed some more. "Right above our stupid heads, with those filthy stairs leading almost straight into his quarters."

Kuini studied the small balcony. "We can climb it."

"What?"

"Climb the balcony. You know, go up the wall. Don't you know how to climb?"

"No, I don't, wild boy. Emperor's sons are taught many things, but they are not taught to climb walls like stupid lizards. Noble people don't do this."

The thought of Iztac sent a warm wave down his stomach. "You think you know it all, but you may be surprised."

"What, your Acolhua friend can go up and down those bricks? Texcocans are a strange lot."

Kuini smirked. "So the pampered Emperor's son who cannot climb a small, stupid wall is about to go back, with his message undelivered."

In the darkness, he could hear Tlacaelel grinding his teeth and he tensed, ready to leap aside should the youth try to hit him. They had shared much through the two market intervals, wavering between mutual respect and friendly animosity, still, with the filthy Aztecs one never knew.

"You can climb it and deliver the note," said Tlacaelel finally. "But the trouble is, he doesn't know you, and if you think I'm haughty then you have never met a haughty royal offspring before. He will never have it, a wild Highlander climbing his terrace. Oh, what a mess."

Kuini eyed the beams of the wooden structure sheltering the patio. The rope tying one of the poles seemed to be loose enough to pull it off with no trouble. "You know what? We'll get up there together. Just let me get this thing."

Having no time to struggle with the rope, he took out his knife, cutting the ties, making sure the beams weren't shattered loose.

"Here, tie it around your waist or something." He tossed his loot toward the gaping youth and turned to study the wall once again.

"You are not suggesting..." Tlacaelel's voice held none of its usual confidence.

Kuini paid him no attention.

"You are insane," he heard the Aztec muttering as he grabbed the first bulging stone. "Completely insane."

It took him no time to reach the stone railing of the lone balcony, pulling himself up, throwing his body over it. The night breeze cooled the sweat off his face, with no need to wipe it with his hands.

Not daring to make a sound, he pulled at the rope, hoping that Tlacaelel would get his message and would know what to do. The useless son of an emperor should be able to climb it with him, Kuini, holding the rope, stabilizing him and taking some of his weight off. The aristocratic brat should manage.

Leaning forward, he watched the young Aztec panting,

clinging to the bulging stones, seeking other protrusions. The thought of Iztac climbing one of those walls surfaced, spoiling his mood once again. He remembered the way she would sneak out of her rooms in the Texcoco Palace, graceful and sure of herself, an elegant, long-legged, beautiful creature.

He frowned. Why would she climb the Emperor's terrace? What did they do in his rooms?

Tlacaelel slipped, and he felt the rope cutting into his palms, as he held onto it desperately, cursing his clumsy companion. The precious royal offspring would not break his neck falling from such a low height, but his crash would create much noise, attracting the attention of the warriors guarding the side entrance.

"Gods, you are useless," he muttered as the youth rolled over the railing, falling onto the stone floor.

"Shut up," groaned Tlacaelel. He picked himself up, breathing heavily, his warriors' lock askew and his arms scratched. "I can't believe you talked me into doing this."

"So, what now?"

"Now I go in and deliver the note." The youth smoothed his hair, then began brushing the dust off his shoulders. "I'll be lucky if he doesn't take me for a commoner and call for the royal guards right away." He looked up. "You wait here."

"Don't give me orders." Kuini peered into the dark rectangle of a doorway. "Are the Emperor's, or the Empress's, quarters somewhere around?"

"Oh, you are impossible," hissed Tlacaelel, stepping toward the doorway. "Just wait for me here." Before disappearing into the darkness, he glanced at Kuini. "If you are not here by the time I'm back, I'm leaving without you."

"Suit yourself!" But the tall silhouette of the youth had already been swallowed by the gaping darkness.

Kuini looked around, wondering which floor the Empress would occupy. The first or the second? Most probably the second. Still, he could look around, couldn't he? He must have some time, and if the occasion presented itself, he could kill the vile woman, saving Iztac from all this trouble.

The passageway was dark and deserted. Maybe he could

manage to kill the Emperor along the way too, he thought, sliding down the quiet corridor, making no sound. The annoying boy pissed everyone off, that much was obvious. From Tlacaelel to both the Warlords, the boy-emperor did not please anyone. And he had the gall of looking at Iztac the way he did.

The splendor of the inner corridors pounced on him, reminding him of Texcoco and its Palace before the first Tepanec invasion. Same polished, glimmering wood lining the walls, same elegant tiles adorning the floor, same smoothness of the statues.

He followed the first corridor into yet another, then another, counting the turns, trying to carve the way he walked into his memory. It was so quiet he might have thought the Palace was abandoned but for an occasional murmuring behind the closed shutters. He would never find the Empress's quarters without peeking into one of the rooms.

Voices burst upon him, giving him barely enough time to dive behind a stone statue of a beautiful serpent. Heart thumping, he listened to the warriors passing by, talking hurriedly, their voices low.

"It doesn't make any sense," a man was saying, coughing. "To walk those corridors? And in groups? Really!"

"Would you shut up? You'll wake the whole Palace." Another voice rasped, so near Kuini held his breath. "The Empress is touchy, and she will have you killed for waking her up."

"Well, we are nowhere near her quarters, so stop yelping like a wounded coyote," retorted the first man.

"We are heading that way, you stupid lump of meat!"

Kuini let his breath out as the voices began drawing away. His cloak was soaked with a cold sweat, and he shivered, although there was no draft. Another statue beckoned. He could dash for it, and then for another, following the path of the warriors.

Holding his breath, he did just that, sliding from statue to statue, keeping the colorful cloaks in sight. Stupid, stupid, stupid! He could do nothing with warriors patrolling the passageways, still he went on, drawn down the corridor as though against his will.

When they halted beside a large doorway, he was squeezed

behind a golden statue, its touch smooth and pleasant against his cheek. The warriors talked between themselves until another pair neared them, coming from the opposite direction.

Kuini cursed silently. No, they didn't seem as though about to go anywhere, and them being reinforced didn't help. He could have tried to kill those two, taking them by surprise, but with more warriors he had no chance.

When one of the pairs squatted beside a small podium, he began easing away, in a hurry to leave before the other warriors headed in his direction, blocking his way back to the balcony. Tlacaelel was sure to be back by now, wondering, cursing and muttering angrily.

Turning around, he caught his breath. A woman stood there, clutching onto a small tray, staring at him, her eyes huge and round, her mouth gaping. For a fraction of a heartbeat they just stared, before he darted past her as she began screaming in an annoyingly high-pitched, screeching voice.

This time he bolted away with no reservations. The carved wood and the statues swished by, turning into a blurry line, as the heavy footsteps resounded down the corridor, still far behind his back, the only sound that mattered. Dashing into another corridor, then another, he let his senses guide him, smelling the breeze and the scents of the night outside the magnificent building. He didn't care which terrace or opening, he only needed to reach the outside.

Something swished by his ear, and he doubled his efforts, turning into another corridor, colliding with someone. The unsuspecting man, clearly a slave, carried a large basket, but it went flying as Kuini pushed him aside, to crash against the wall.

Oh, he could not have asked for a better diversion. The warriors' curses reached him, but those were accompanied by flying missiles, and as he dashed for the small opening, he knew he may have a chance.

Tlacaelel's broad face jumped into his view as he charged toward the parapet, grabbing the youth's shoulder, pulling him along.

"Jump!" he breathed, not releasing his grip, although, the

Aztec fought to free his arm.

"What in the name…"

The voices grew, and as he slipped over the railing, he saw Tlacaelel's eyes narrowing, filling with comprehension.

Their fall was short and not really dangerous, still, they rolled over the slope, scratching their limbs, breaking some bushes along their way. Tlacaelel cried out but was quick to silence himself.

"Quick!"

Jumping to his feet, he felt rather than saw the Aztec doing the same, wavering and cursing. Quickly, he caught his companion's upper arm. Half limping, half running, they charged toward the cluster of nearby trees, the loud voices carrying from the balcony, giving them strength to run faster.

CHAPTER 14

"Iztac Ayotl, please come to bed."

The voice of the plump woman made Dehe's heart go still, as she huddled in the shadows of the smaller room full of mats and cushions. Her hand jumped, and the contents of the jar almost spilled, the precious drops splashing over the reed podium. Taking a deep breath, she slunk deeper into the shadows, although both women made no sounds indicating their intentions of heading back inside.

The angry footsteps went on, resounding against the stone floor of the other room, back and forth, back and forth.

"Please, stop running around like an incensed ocelot." The woman's voice rose. "Iztac Ayotl, please!"

"Go to bed, Ihuitl. I'll come in, in a little while." The angry paces went on.

"No, you won't. I know you won't. What is wrong, sister? Please tell me. I've never seen you so upset."

"I'm not upset, I'm thinking. I need to think things over. Many things." The voice of the Acolhua princess shook. "Everything is such a mess, and I hate it!"

"What mess?" The other woman's voice dropped to a whisper, and Dehe held her breath trying to overhear. "Is that the Empress?"

There was a fleeting silence, and Dehe slipped back toward the podium, remembering the flask.

"Yes, her too. But everything else is a mess also. Everything, just everything! I wish I could run away."

"Back to Texcoco?"

"Maybe. Or maybe further away." The princess's voice took a bitter note. "As far as the Highlands. Right up the Smoking Mountain, where no one will find me."

"Oh, you are silly." Ihuitl's laughter held a measure of relief.

"You think I'm joking, eh?" The sound of the footsteps died abruptly. "Well, I'm not! I could go there, you know. I could do it right now."

Pouring the contents of the jar into the high, narrow flask, Dehe bit her lower lip so hard it bled. *Oh, the filthy rotten she-wolf,* she thought, choking with rage. *You will see no Highlands. Oh, no! You will die in this accursed Palace, and you will never touch him again.*

"Iztac Ayotl, stop talking nonsense. You are scaring me. What's in this jar you are clutching onto?"

"Nothing. Go to bed, Ihuitl. I'll see you in the morning, before going to share the Empress's meal."

"Oh, such an honor." The young woman paused, and Dehe stopped shaking the flask, afraid to be heard. "Will the Emperor share this meal, too? He was strange with you this afternoon. I didn't know you knew him so well."

"I played with him when he was smaller and not yet an emperor. He is a nice boy."

"He peered at you as if he were in love with you, you know? And he made you go with him to the main entrance."

"He is a child, Ihuitl!" said Acolhua princess tersely. "He is not in love with me or anyone else."

"He is thirteen, sister. He'll be allowed to take a wife soon."

"Well, he won't be allowed to take me."

"No, probably not. But he can want it, can't he?"

The angry paces were back, resounding loudly against the stone tiles. "You are the one talking nonsense now."

But the young woman just laughed. "And the handsome warrior? The one you were whispering things to when the Emperor was busy staring? Is he too young to desire you, too? You almost shone when you whispered to him, and you did touch his hand. I saw it. And the Emperor and his advisers saw it, too."

The furious pacing stopped once again. "See? This is the mess I'm talking about. Everyone seems to see everything, and everyone wants me to do things, and I don't want to be pushed around anymore!"

Dehe sniffed the contents of the flask, pleased with her rival's loss of composure. *So you are not that sure of yourself anymore, you filthy rat,* she thought, placing the flask back onto the tray and arranging the cups prettily around it. *Oh, they all saw you making a fool of yourself, and you had no right to grab his hand.*

"Listen, Ihuitl. Go to sleep. I need to think it all over. I need time. I need to be alone. I'll talk to you in the morning." The strained voice softened. "You are a good friend, you know? I never thought a girl could be a friend, but you are a friend, and I love you for that."

"Oh, Iztac Ayotl, you honor me too much." The young woman's voice shook. "Oh, you are the best friend I ever had."

Silly women, thought Dehe, ready to slide back into the shadows. She eyed the tray dubiously, contemplating her next move. If it stayed here the other wife was more likely to drink from it, while the filthy princess would go to the pond like she had promised *him.*

The tears threatened to spring anew, and she bit her lips, trying to banish the memory of the dark terrace earlier on, when he had climbed it to cuddle and kiss and whisper things, with the skinny Acolhua she-wolf clinging to him in a very unprincess-like fashion, telling him that he should not be here while melting into his arms, making him kiss her only more ardently. Oh, it was not fair! He was hers, Dehe's, man. He was a Highlander. He did not belong in Tenochtitlan, with his highborn friends and the lusty emperor's wives.

Snatching the tray, she was about to sneak out of the back door when a maid came in, carrying an armload of embroidered cushions.

"What are you doing here, girl?" The maid stared at her, and Dehe had a hard time steadying her cargo in her trembling hands.

"I... I was..." She licked her lips, trying to think of something to say.

The woman frowned. "Are you simple in the head? What are you doing running around the honorable ladies quarters at night?

Who sent you to bring this tray here?"

"The woman... from the kitchens downstairs... she told me..." She clenched her teeth to stop the rest of the words from coming out. That woman was from another side of the Palace. "I thought... the refreshments..."

"At night?" The maid shook her head and proceeded to spread the cushions all over the mats. "Go back to the kitchen slaves, and tell them to leave the mistresses alone. Tell them to eat their stupid tortillas themselves."

Springing to her feet, the woman stopped her tirade as the plump Ihuitl came in, her face troubled. "Honorable Third Wife," she whispered, kneeling.

The young noblewoman paid them no attention. Frowning, she took off her diadem and let it fall onto the floor.

"Help me undress," she said, dropping onto the cozy pile of mats.

As the maid rushed to do as bidden, Dehe took a careful step back.

"What do you have on that tray, girl?" The large eyes rested upon Dehe, cold and indifferent. With only the slaves and no highborn princesses around, the cute, silly woman was no longer silly or cute.

"Ah... err... refreshments..."

"Oh, good. Serve me some."

Not daring to breathe, Dehe come closer and knelt as she'd seen the other maid do.

"Those are cold and barely sweetened," complained Ihuitl. "Go back and bring the warm, fresh tortillas. And be quick about it." She sighed. "Pour me some water first, and then go to the main room and see if the Second Wife wants some of those. She likes her tortillas crispy, so she may want one of those."

Dehe's hands trembled so hard, she had a hard time managing the flask. As the water drops splashed all over the tray, the woman made a face, while the maid snatched the flask rudely.

"I wish they wouldn't put every newly acquired girl with the kitchen staff," muttered the maid, pouring the drink. "Here, take this back to the kitchens and try to be more useful next time. I apologize sincerely, Honorable Mistress," she added, turning to the Third Wife and dropping her eyes once again. "I will warn the kitchen slaves most sternly."

"Yes, do that." The noble lady stretched luxuriously. "But first, let her see to the Second Wife. Bring her the tortillas, girl, and be graceful about it."

"Yes, Honorable Mistress," muttered Dehe, unable to believe her luck as yet. Hardly feeling the weight of the tray anymore, she rushed into the outer rooms, her heart beating fast. At last!

"Honorable Second Wife." She halted abruptly, her heart missing a beat. The spacious room was empty, dark and abandoned in the flickering light of a single torch.

"What now?" The impatient voice came from the terrace.

Her tension welling, Dehe made her way past the threshold, almost stumbling over the elegantly laid stones adorning the doorway.

"The Third Wife," she said hoarsely, then cleared her throat. "The Third Wife wanted me to bring you this."

The tall woman turned her head. "I'm not hungry. Take it back." She peered at Dehe, then turned around, abandoning the stone railing she clutched to. "Aren't you the girl from the downstairs?" she asked, narrowing her eyes.

"I... I'm not. I'm new here. I was brought here only this afternoon."

"Oh, I thought I saw you before." The woman shrugged. She had changed into a loose fitting skirt and a blouse of mild coloring, and her numerous tresses now slid carelessly down her shoulders. "What do you have there on that tray?"

Dehe took a deep breath. "Tortillas and some water to wash it down."

"Water?" The woman laughed. "Oh, you *are* new here. Well, I never drink water. But give me a tortilla, and tomorrow make sure to bring a fresh chocolate drink first thing in the morning." Her smile widened. "And make it sweet, truly sweet. They always seem to skimp on the honey, so maybe with you here I'll finally get the drink as I want it."

"Yes, I will," mumbled Dehe, at a loss at this bout of

friendliness. "But won't you drink some water now, to wash the food down?"

"No, I won't. I hate water. You will have to learn to prepare sweetened drinks out of fruit juices, as I can't drink only chocolate. They know how to do it, so you will learn. But chocolate is my favorite, so be careful not to neglect this duty of yours."

Mesmerized, Dehe stared at the sculptured, beautiful face, her thoughts in a jumble.

The woman returned her gaze, then laughed once again. "Why are you staring at me? Do I look strange or something?" She frowned. "I do you remember you. You were staring at me earlier too, downstairs and in the Palace's gardens. It was you!"

The wave of latent fear washed over her back, covering it in a cold sweat. "No. It was not me. It must have been someone else." She felt her legs trembling, hardly able to support her anymore.

The woman shrugged. "Well, I don't care if it was you or not. They all stared and most of them were not as harmless as you are." She pursed her lips and looked as if about to curse. "Filthy lowlifes, all of them. I wish they would leave me alone." Turning back and peering into the darkness, the woman fell silent.

"Well, go away, girl," she said finally. "If you are so concerned with my welfare pour me a cup of your water, just in case. And leave the plate of tortillas here." She frowned. "Also go back inside and see if the Third Wife has already fallen asleep. Tell me right away, and then you can go."

It was well past midnight, when Kuini rushed toward the pond, avoiding the well-groomed roads and alleys. He didn't know if the maid who had seen him outside the Empress's quarters was capable of describing his general looks, but the stupid woman might have caught the sight of his tattoos. Who could tell if the Palace's guards weren't scanning the gardens in those very moments, searching for him.

The most sensible thing would be to go back to the protection of both the warlords and their warriors. Tlacaelel had told him so, commenting on Kuini's recklessness as they made their way hurriedly over the deserted gardens.

Leaning heavily on Kuini's shoulder because of the damaged ankle, the tall Aztec had halted abruptly upon hearing that some of the way he would have to make alone.

"You can't be serious," he cried out, balancing his weight on one leg. "I can limp back with no trouble, but you, don't tell me you didn't have enough adventures for one night. What, for the gods' sake, are you planning to do now?"

"Something I should have done instead of helping you run your errand."

"Oh, so the missions of our leaders are not good enough for you."

"They are good, but I have another thing to do."

"Something you can't share with any of us, eh?"

"Yes, something like that."

"Well, be careful. I should like to see you alive by the dawn break."

Curiously touched by the youth's open concern, Kuini grinned. "You take care of yourself, too. When I'm back I should like to see you your old annoyingly arrogant self again." He smiled. "You said you wouldn't, but you waited for me on that balcony."

The Aztec grinned back. "Well, I was busy pondering how to get down without your climbing abilities. It took time." He shook his head, his grin widening. "I never thought you would just send us both flying."

"I'm sorry. It was really my fault."

"Nice of you to admit that." The amusement was back, twinkling in the deeply set eyes.

"Shut up," said Kuini. "Will you be able to make it to the warlords with this stupid ankle of yours?"

"Of course. Who needs you?" The tall youth turned around, making an obvious effort not to limp. "Just come back as fast as you can. So you won't miss any action."

Oh, yes, he wasn't that bad, this haughty First Son of the dead

Emperor, thought Kuini, hurrying along the invisible paths, trying to remember his way. And he had waited for him, Kuini, to return, not abandoning him on the wrong side of the Palace. Yes, Tlacaelel was definitely a partner worth having by one's side.

The pond was lit more brightly than on the night before, and he shifted uneasily, reluctant to leave the safety of the darkness. Scanning the flickering water and the bushes around it with a glance, he relaxed, his eyes, as well as his other senses, telling him that it was abandoned. His heart missed a beat. It *was* abandoned. She was nowhere around the pond, either.

He came out carefully and scanned the area once again. There were footprints and trampled bushes and grass, but these signs might have been left by the daytime activities, or even from their previous night spent here. Thinking about her on top of him made his knees feel weak. Why hadn't she come as promised?

There might be twenty and more reasons, he thought, his anxiety welling. She may not have been able to sneak away. Yet, his senses whispered danger, and without noticing it, he began making his way back toward her terrace.

The moon shone too brightly and the night sounds were interrupted by the distant activities of the creatures not belonging to it. He thought of Tlacaelel and Coyotl, and the Warlord, and his uncle, and how displeased they all would be with him not coming back right away. Too many bets were thrown into this particular game of power. Who would rule Tenochtitlan, the Aztecs or the Tepanecs? But why should he care? Because of Coyotl, or because of his own powerful uncle? Or because his father thought it was important? Oh, why did life have to be so complicated at times!

Her terrace was darker than before, with no flickering torch and no slender silhouette leaning over the railing. It looked abandoned just like the pond, its stone railing glimmering coldly, arrogantly, reminding him that one shouldn't climb emperors wives' terraces unless one were looking for trouble.

Something moved in the shadows, and he froze, his heart going still. The moonlight hardly reached under the cover of the wide stones, but suddenly he knew that something was there, in the thickest of the shadows. Moving silently, disturbing no stone, he felt his palm sleek upon the hilt of his dagger.

The darkness enveloped him, but his senses were the ones to guide him until his eyes picked out a silhouette huddled beneath the wall. His hand clutching the dagger relaxed all at once.

"Iztac Ayotl!"

She just sat there, curled into a ball, hugging her knees, and as he rushed toward her he could see how her shoulders sagged desolately. Her gaze flickered at him out of the pale, puffy face.

"Iztac Ayotl, what happened?" he whispered, crouching beside her and pulling her into his arms.

"You didn't come," she sobbed, and he had a hard time restraining his heartbeat, while his hands pressed her tighter, containing her trembling. "I was by the pond, waiting and waiting, and you didn't come."

"I'm sorry." He stroked her hair, the stiff, oily tresses unfamiliar and unpleasant to touch. He loved the feel of her flowing hair. "I've been late. I know I should have gone there right away. But there were things I had to do. I'm sorry."

She lifted her face and peered at him, disheveled and messy, but still beautiful, still undeniably appealing, even with those streaks of yellow cream on her naturally golden cheeks.

"I know. I should not be such a cry baby. It's just... I just thought you would disappear again. Like back then, in Texcoco."

He felt his limbs going stiff. "I had no choice back then. If I could have helped it I would have been on the Plaza on time." He clenched his teeth. "I was there just like I promised. Only a few dawns after you had been sent away."

"You were?" She buried her face into his chest. "I'm so silly, and I hate being this way. I hate being pushed around. And I hate crying." She shivered. "This stupid crying makes me feel cold and dizzy."

He pressed her closer in order to stop the trembling. "No, it's not like you at all. What happened to that proud princess of Texcoco? That beautiful goddess of the moon who could climb like a lizard and who could make love like a real goddess, tiring her man into a state of complete uselessness."

She giggled. "You stayed useful last night. The goddess tried hard, but you did not cry for mercy. You held your ground like a real warrior, pleasing the deity mightily."

He pressed her tighter, because her trembling wouldn't go away. "It was a real feat. I never fought a harder battle." He frowned. "Are you really that cold?"

"No, I'm not. It's just that I feel strange. I shouldn't start crying. It doesn't do me any good. I didn't cry for summers."

"Did you ever? I find it difficult to imagine."

"Yes, I did. Once or twice." She nestled closer, as another shiver took her. "You asked me if I wanted to go away with you last night."

"Yes," he said absently, trying to think of how he would go about getting her up the wall of her terrace if she didn't feel any better.

"Well, I do. I do now. Would you take me away?"

He caught his breath. "Now?"

"Yes, now. I thought about what you said, and I don't want any part in what is going to happen. I want to go away with you."

The wind rustled in the nearby bushes, and he tensed for a moment, listening. Someone may have been moving there, but he couldn't tell for certain. To make sure of it he would have to leave her for a moment, distraught and cold, and she would feel even worse. He forced his thoughts back to her and to what she said.

"Yes, we can do this," he said, his heart beating fast. "We can smuggle you out of here and hide you in my uncle's house. Or, if he doesn't want to be involved in any of it, there is this girl on the marketplace. She can take care of you, until I'm done here. She is a wonderful girl, and a great healer, too."

With a twinge of guilt, he thought of Dehe. Would she agree to help, after all those things she had heard about Iztac?

"Can't we go to the Highlands now?" She lifted her face, peering at him, her trembling lessening.

"No, we can't," he said, caressing her cheek, not liking the touch of the yellow cream. "I have to go on helping my uncle and your brother. I can't abandon them like that. But it won't take long, judging by the Warlord's mood. This matter will be solved soon enough, and then I may be able to leave. You'll just have to be patient."

She made a face and looked again like a petulant child refused a sweetmeat. "Oh, you *are* a warrior. If you truly worshipped your goddess you wouldn't dump her on the marketplace, with some dubious girls you know."

"Oh, is that so?" He tried to stare her down but was finding it difficult to suppress his laughter. With her face smeared in a mixture of a yellow cream and dust, she looked anything but a goddess. "You look like some strange sort of a warrior yourself, you know. I swear I could see the patterns on this thing smeared all over your face."

She stuck an elbow into his ribs, hurting the fresh bruises from his fall off that balcony on the other side of the Palace. "You are pushing it too far, mortal. As soon as I feel better, you will feel my wrath."

"You stopped shivering."

"Yes, but now I feel like vomiting, and I don't want to do it in front of you. I drank a little water on my way out, and I wish I'd had the sense to drink the whole cup."

He shifted a little, his limbs going numb from taking her weight for so long. "Can you hold it in for a while? We can find some water on our way."

"Oh, yes," she said, unconcerned. "Women can do that."

Again his attention was drawn toward the dark bushes, his nerves prickling. Someone was there, watching them.

"Listen, we have to decide now. Wouldn't it be better if we haul you up there, so you can get some sleep and maybe feel better?"

"No, I'm not going back. You will be busy again, and when you find time for me I'll be safely away, given to yet another ruler."

"Then let us—"

A scream tore the darkness, a long, terrified howl. He jumped to his feet, his heart thumping, his hands pulling her up, although she seemed in no need of help. Another scream rolled tumbling down the balcony.

"It's coming from our rooms," whispered Iztac breathlessly.

"But it's not Ihuitl's voice."

They could hear the muffled footsteps of people running.

"We have to go now," he whispered, pulling her urgently. "Before they discover that you are gone."

"No, no." She resisted his grip. "I have to make sure Ihuitl is all right."

"You can't. If you go back now they'll know you were away."

Above their heads, rapid footsteps rushed out into the terrace, and more voices reinforced the clamor inside. The familiar screeching of the warriors' swords and clubs reached his ears.

"Come, we have to go, now!"

He pulled her deeper into the shadows as a pair of warriors rushed by, almost brushing against them in their haste. Not worried yet, he concentrated his senses, checking for an open path to charge for. He knew he could trust her to follow and to keep quiet when needed, remembering her fearlessness and her presence of mind back in Texcoco, or even here on the previous night.

His fingers untying his sword, just in case, he thrust his dagger into her hands, having no time to tie it back to his girdle. They needed to keep quiet just for a few more heartbeats. However, as another group of warriors rushed by, he felt her shuddering again, and then she swallowed hard and half coughed half groaned, her hands on her mouth. In the relative quietness under the terrace it made a strange sound, and then he knew all was lost.

The warriors halted abruptly.

"Who is there?" cried out one of them, charging into the darkness without any consideration.

Having every opportunity to kill the man, Kuini hesitated, still hoping to resolve it peacefully. He was in the Warlord's services, with every right to be here in the Palace. Was it not wise to try to explain should a good explanation occur to any of them?

"What happened?" he asked hoarsely as the man came closer, his face materializing out of the darkness. A few more silhouettes followed. He cleared his throat. "What is going on?"

"You tell me, you filthy intruder. Who are you?"

He would have liked to retreat a step, to keep his unprotected back against the safety of the wall, because of the way they surrounded him, yet with Iztac hanging on his arm, vomiting helplessly, he could not do even this.

"I'm with the Warlord's forces," he said, knowing it would not help him now.

"Is that not one of the minor wives?" muttered one of the men, stepping forward.

"Yes, she is sick. I have to escort her back to her quarters."

"You what?" They all peered at him as if he had been the one who was sick. Sick in his head.

Iztac coughed. "He is telling the truth," she groaned, her voice low-pitched and twisted. "He was asked to escort me back." He felt her tensing, taking some of her weight off his arm, and his chest tightened with pride at her courage. "Please, take me back, warrior," she added in a more passable voice, clearing her throat.

"I will escort you back, Honorable Mistress," said one of the men firmly, his tone suddenly wielding much authority. "You two, take care of this rat."

"No!" Her voice shook, and Kuini could feel her wavering, leaning back as the man took a step forward.

"Don't touch her," he growled and felt more than saw the other warrior thrusting his sword. Luckily, his sword was out and ready, otherwise he may have had difficulty parrying the blow, with her still leaning on him and making it impossible to leap aside. His favorite weapon took the impact, and he wavered but held on.

"Lean against the wall, but keep close," he hissed and yet again felt a surge of pride at her quick reaction.

The man disengaged, and now Kuini had had enough time to block the next thrust more comfortably, keeping the man's peers in sight, should they decide to join the fight. Having no space to maneuver, he went for the simplest trick. Pretending to give way under the pressure, with the victorious adversary focusing his attention, busy pressing his advantage, he twisted his sword suddenly, sending the sharp obsidians toward the momentarily exposed torso of the man.

Surprisingly, it worked. In a heartbeat the warrior was on the ground, cut so deeply he couldn't even scream.

There was a moment of stunned silence, before the other two attacked together, charging toward him, getting in each other's way. From the corner of his eye, he saw a small figure springing out of the nearby bushes, rushing toward them. It looked familiar, but he had no time to give it a thought, leaping aside to avoid the lethal touch of the razor-sharp obsidian while using the opportunity to land the flat side of his sword against the other man's exposed ribs.

Hearing the warrior's groan and seeing him wavering, Kuini turned his attention back to his other adversary, bringing his sword up in a swift movement, using its drive to the maximum effect. It slid against the polished wood of the other's weapon and made its way toward the man's shoulder, cutting it, but not as deeply as he would have liked to. The warrior sucked in his breath and retreated a step, ready to ward off another attack, although his face twisted as he tried to bring up his weapon.

Eager to finish his rival off, Kuini heard the hiss of the sword behind his back a fraction of a second too late. Throwing his body aside, out of instinct more than as a thoughtful reaction, he felt the powerful push and could not fight the force that sent him forward, to crash into his already wounded rival. They fell together, in a bunch of twisted limbs, but being on top of the man Kuini hurried to make the best out of his momentary advantage. Ignoring the tearing pain in his side, he sank his fingers into the man's throat, having no time to wrap his hands around it properly.

The man twisted, and it made the fangs gnawing at his backside redouble their efforts. Teeth clenched, eyes almost shut against the pain, Kuini pressed with the rest of his strength, his head spinning. He knew he would be cut from behind any moment now, yet he needed to make this man lose his senses, at least for a little while.

There was a noise behind his back, and as his rival began to slow his squirming, he paid the sounds of a struggle more attention, in his desperation smashing his fist against the stark face and then rolling away. Turning around with an effort, grinding his teeth against the pain, he strained his eyes, ready to evade a blow, wondering why none had come. Sweat rolled into his eyes, and he blinked, afraid to think of the agony pulsating in his side, the agony which bade him no good whichever way he chose to think of it.

He saw the third man struggling against someone small, who clung to his arm stubbornly, refusing to be shook, or even beaten, off. Like in a dream he watched the girl hanging there, her feet kicking at the man's legs. *Dehe? But how?*

He leaped to his feet, but the pain exploded, making him falter and grope the air in an attempt to steady himself. His hand caught the flimsy material, and then he was leaning against Iztac's slender form, her hands clinging to him, holding him desperately, their strength surprising.

"Oh gods, you are bleeding," she breathed, and he realized that the warm flow trickling down his thigh came along with the pulsating pain in his back.

However, before he could think of the way to reassure her, or maybe to take his weight off her as she seemed not very steady herself, they heard a smashing sound and a choking groan, and the small silhouette of Dehe went away flying, crashing into the wall with a loud smack.

The man cursed and turned back, his face twisted with rage, his sword raising again, very rapidly at that. Clenching his teeth, breathless with the effort, Kuini brought his sword up to fend off the attack, but his hands seemed to be powerless, and the blow sent him crashing back into the damp grass, colliding against his arm instead of his sword.

The new pain was so sharp, so paralyzing, he could not even cry out. It took his breath away. The air exploded with plenty of beautiful colors, but still he tried to move away in order to avoid the next blow.

Then the noises and the screams that were still cascading over the balcony faded, and he knew that his time had come. Sensing the man steadying himself, preparing for the final strike, he strained his eyes, pushing the pain away, wishing to go solemnly and with honor and not amidst this wild, unseemly agony.

The man seemed to appreciate that. His eyes cleared, peering down at Kuini with a solemn approval. His hands rose slowly, in a perfect movement, intending to cut neatly, to bring a clean, honorable end and no pain.

Their eyes locked, and Kuini took a deep breath, but instead of the right thoughts, instead of the image of the eastern sky paradise, the thought of Iztac invaded his mind, uninvited. She still needed his help to climb her terrace. With all the dizziness and the vomiting, she could not do it all by herself.

No, he thought. *Not yet.* But the sword was already beginning to descend, and he knew it was too late and he would just betray her anew, promising to take her away, then not doing it once again. He closed his eyes against the pain pulsating out of his arm, wishing he could at least have enough time to ask her for forgiveness. *Would he be able to do it while making his way toward the eastern sky?*

The air swayed again with many colors, but no respite to the pain came. And no oblivion. Instead there was a cry, a woman's cry. And the groan of a man. Then came the sound of a body hitting the ground. With an effort he opened his eyes, narrowing them against the swirling darkness. He could feel someone kneeling by his side.

"Give me that string!" hissed the familiar husky voice. "The one from your hair. Quickly!"

With the last of his strength he forced his eyes to focus, but where the warrior had stood earlier, his incredulous gaze took in Iztac, her eyes glazed, mouth gaping, the dagger he had tucked into her hand earlier, when he'd had no time to tie it back to his girdle, clutched in her trembling palms, glittering darkly.

"Come on!" Dehe sprang to her feet angrily, reaching for Iztac's hair, tearing off the beautiful, woven string, making her victim cry out. "Help me, for gods' sake, or he will die!"

These words worked. Iztac dropped beside him, disappearing from his view, disappointingly so.

"What... what are you doing?" she whispered haltingly.

"Stopping the bleeding."

As she grabbed his hand, he became aware of the pain. It rolled up and down his arm, like a burning flow, merciless and unrelenting, making his heart flutter. He tried to pull it off her hurtful grip, but she held him firmly, hurting him more and more.

"Talk to him. Make him stay awake."

The short order brought Iztac's haunted face back into his view. Twisted and very pale, it was not especially pretty, but he felt the pain receding all the same. Just the sharpest edge of it, but it made him feel better.

"Please, don't die. Please!" she whispered over and over, and he wanted to reassure her, but his lips were too heavy to move.

And then there were more voices in the distance, and a wave of latent fear washed over her face, making it look pinched and pallid, unpleasantly so. He wished she would calm down again.

"The warriors are coming!" Dehe's voice also lost the trace of her brisk confidence.

"Can you take him away, somehow? I can hold their attention for some time." Now Iztac was the one to talk calmly.

Dehe hesitated. "Yes, I can try. I just need a few more heartbeats to try to stanch the bleeding in his back." He could hear a frown in her voice. "Well, it can take a little more than that."

"I'll hold their attention. Take your time, then try to bring him to the warriors. You know, the royal guards, to the Warlord."

"Yes, I know where he is." Another heartbeat of hesitation. "After you are back in your rooms drink plenty of water. It will help if you vomit some more. Just drink on. And don't touch the water in the flask."

Busy trying to come to grips with the spinning world, he felt the heaviness of the sudden silence.

"You filthy *cihua*, you didn't!" hissed Iztac finally.

"It doesn't matter right now," answered Dehe, unabashed.

"After you save him, I'll have you killed, I swear." He found it difficult to recognize Iztac's voice, which now shook with uncontrollable fury.

"You can try." Another bout of silence, accompanied by burning gazes, he was sure of that. *What were they talking about? Why were they arguing?*

The agitated voices drew nearer.

"If you save him I may spare your life, but if he is dead..." Iztac's voice came from further away now. "If he is dead you will wish you had never been born!"

CHAPTER 15

The darkness was at its thickest, like always in the predawn time, and the chill filled the air with its pleasant freshness. Iztac pitted her face against the breeze, letting it cool her burning cheeks. Her paces were steady, even brisk, and she was pleased with the way she walked ahead of her captors, as if she were the one to lead them.

Not that the warriors, who had come to fetch her, were rude or demanding. On the contrary. Their politeness and apologetic manners were almost ridiculous. They were not supposed to feel so uncomfortable. The Empress was the one to send them.

Hugging her elbows against the new gust of wind, she forced her arms back to her sides. It may have been cold and damp, but hugging herself would make her look intimidated, scared, terrified, and she felt nothing of the sort, not now. Not after the hideous night. She was too numb to feel anything, because the world around her had gone completely insane. Nothing made sense anymore, so she stopped trying to struggle to understand. People were dying, everyone she cared for, thus Ihuitl's death came as no surprise.

She was going to die too, that much was obvious. But at least she was clean again, clean off dust and tears and the stupid creams, and the blood most of all. She was allowed to spend enough time in her quarters to wash herself as best as she could, but she wished she could have made it to the steam baths.

Shuddering, she remembered her rooms and the people, maids and servants and warriors, and Ihuitl, so calm and peaceful, but ridiculously gray, as if some Underworld creature had come and sucked all her blood at once, spitting it out in a sort of a fountain, to gush the way it had burst from *his* arm.

The tears were back, and she clenched her teeth so tight it hurt. He was probably dead by now, and, thus, may be watching her, before embarking on his short, glorious journey to the eastern sky paradise. Oh but she must make him proud of her. No more fear, and, certainly, no more crying. His goddess of the moon was a powerful, fearless deity deserving of his love. Oh, she would make him so proud he would go on loving her even in the warriors' paradise.

A pity she could not join him there, she thought, blinking the tears away. To merely die wouldn't help. She was a woman and a woman's only way to get any closer to that wonderful place of the warriors was to die giving birth to a child.

She shivered. She would have to conceive and then die, and it would take so much time and she would look just like him, bleeding and twisting in pain, but she'd try to be as brave as he was.

The tears threatened to take her in spite of her resolution, and she shut her eyes, desperate. *You don't think of his stark lifeless face,* she ordered herself. *And you don't think of all that blood.* So much blood! She hadn't thought that the human body had that much of the dark, sticky liquid in it. Neither had she imagined the way it could gush in such a powerful surge.

When she rushed to support him after he strangled that second warrior and was about to fall again, she felt it trickling, warm against her side, where his soaked cloak clung to her. But, oh gods, it was nothing compared to that flow that burst out of his arm, pulsating, anxious to break free.

The trembling was back and the nausea too, but she clenched her fists tight and made her nails sink deeply into her palms, the small pain taking the edge off the main pain. *Not now. Maybe later, but not now.* Now, she would think about something else. About that skinny little *cihua* tearing her favorite string off her, Iztac's, hair, so cheekily, so unceremoniously. But the way she tied it above the cut stopped the vicious flow, reduced it to a mere trickling. Like magic.

Who was this annoying little thing that had stalked her through this whole accursed afternoon? She recalled all the times she had seen this girl without noticing, when Chimal had made her to come with him, then back upon the stairs leading to her quarters, then bringing her the tortillas, a timid little creature, yet not timid at all, staring at her, trying to convince her to drink the water.

She cursed silently. Oh, the filthy, stinking, rotten piece of excrement! The disgusting slave had been trying to poison her, of all things! *Why?*

Not to mention the way she had fought that warrior, when Kuini was bleeding upon the ground, struggling against the other man. Why, the tiny *cihua*, hardly half of Iztac's height, fought like a wild ocelot, oblivious to the blows she'd had to take as the furious warrior tried to be rid of her. The man had to throw her against the wall, to render her half-stunned and half conscious, in order to free himself. The girl's bruised face and the torn blouse, and the blood that trickled out of her nose and the corner of her mouth, had testified to how difficult it was to be rid of her.

However, it helped. It gave the Highlander time to face the man once again, and it gave her, Iztac, enough courage to interfere when her time came. Her hand sneaked toward the fold in her blouse, feeling the knife tucked there safely, along with the small, smelly jar, the touch of the polished hilt and the glassy smoothness of the razor-sharp obsidian making her feel better, safer and closer to *him*. He had trusted her with his knife, and she had not disappointed him.

She remembered the strange feeling, like being in a dream, watching the warrior bringing his sword up, slowly, ceremoniously, and the way the Highlander stopped fighting, accepting his fate. She watched them for a heartbeat, and then she knew he was not ready, not yet. It was there, somewhere in the depths of his dark, bottomless eyes. No, he wasn't ready to die, and she had to stop it until he was.

And then the knife was alive in her hands, and her body moved of its own accord, and the feeling of it colliding with that man, the feeling of the blade sliding along the man's ribs, tearing the flesh, but not sinking, not yet, to plunge deeply only when it met no more resistance of the hard tissue, made it all perfect, a part of the ceremony. And then again, a heavy, warm body was pressed against her, seeking her support, soaking her blouse with more of the hot, pulsating flow, but this time it was a stranger, a foreigner, and so she pushed him away, letting the man fall, hit the ground heavily, to go still almost at once.

She shuddered again and forced her thoughts back to the present as the Palace's walls loomed ahead; the main wing of it with its intimidating dark terraces and the threatening dwellers.

"The side stairs, please, Honorable Second Wife," said one of the warriors, when she turned toward the stone staircase.

The servants' entrance? It was ridiculous. She gave the warriors a disdainful glance and turned to her right without a word. *What was their game?*

The steep, wooden stairs creaked under their feet, and she wondered how the slaves rushed back and forth on it every day, carrying things. *Why the side stairs?*

Had the Empress's sleep been interrupted with all this noise and uproar on the other side of the Palace? It was so very quiet here, compared to what went on in the minor wives' quarters.

Ihuitl dead!

She still could not entirely understand that. Why would she die, and why so peacefully? One moment alive, fussing around her, Iztac, trying to convince her to go to sleep, sending her a maid with tortillas…

She gasped. *The maid with tortillas!* The slimy *cihua*! She had had Ihuitl poisoned, too. That must be the reason. Oh, the poor thing must have drunk plenty of *that* water.

She ground her teeth. Oh, she would have the filthy rat flayed. She would see to that, and she would make sure the disgusting *cihua* suffered before she died.

The corridors were quiet, yet she could sense the tension mounting behind many of the closed shutters. Oh, yes, the Palace was very much alive, but not like their side, with all the deaths and the screams and the blood. She clenched her teeth so tight her jaw hurt.

A frightened maid burst upon them.

"Oh, please, please wait," she mumbled, covering her mouth and fleeing on down the corridor.

The warriors shifted uneasily.

"I'll have a slave bring you something to recline upon, Honorable Second Wife," said one of them.

Iztac's fingers tightened around the small jar, tucked into her girdle.

"No, there is no need."

Her feet hurt, and the nausea was still there, along with the dizziness. However, if she was made to sit, she might lose the last of her strength. If comfortable, she might start thinking about the meeting with the Empress, and worse yet, about what happened earlier, about *him.*

You don't think of him, she repeated over and over. *You'll think about it later, if you survive.* And if not, then what could be a better solution?

The sky began turning gray when she was led through the richness of the Empress's main rooms, passing along the expensive statues and the cozily arranged mats and cushions, seeing none of it. On into another set of rooms, then another. Where was the vile woman spending her night?

Sitting on a reed woven chair, the Empress peered into a spread sheet of bark-paper adorned by glittering topazes to keep the scroll from folding. Two terrified maids cowered in the shadows.

"Leave us," she said curtly, not raising her head from the scroll.

The warriors melted away. *Were they scared of that woman, too?*

"You two as well."

The maids disappeared as hurriedly.

"Well, Acolhua princess, what do you have to say for yourself now?"

The cold gaze rose, resting upon Iztac, piercing her skin. In the austere room, without the usual luxury, without the maids and the refreshments, the Empress appeared more imposing, more intimidating, more threatening. Iztac swallowed and said nothing, glad that the fear was taking her thoughts away from what preyed on her mind without any effort on her part.

"You know, girl," said the woman, folding the scroll carefully. "I think I will just have you killed and get it over with. We'll find another highborn bride for the ruler of Tlacopan. It will take some effort, but I can't deal with your insolence anymore, and you are worthless, anyway. It doesn't pay off to keep you. You were always a liability, but now you've just gone out of control." Her eyes narrowed. "So, aside from your wild escapades, aside from the despicable way you were courting the Emperor, aside from being caught with a warrior under your terrace tonight, why would you want to be rid of the Third Wife?"

Iztac fought for breath, taken completely by surprise. "I didn't kill Ihuitl!"

"Oh, please, girl. Spare me your protests of innocence. The only thing I could stand in you was your courage, your way of admitting the truth. Don't spoil it. Face the consequences of your deeds."

Her anger kept mounting, helping her to overcome her fear. "I would never kill Ihuitl. She was the only decent person in this whole Palace. I will not admit to something I didn't do."

The widely spaced eyes bore into her, mocking her openly. "And to what *will* you admit, haughty princess?"

"To nothing! I didn't do anything wrong. This Palace is a despicable place, impossible for a decent person to live in. It's no wonder everyone is dying here."

The woman rose to her feet. "Careful with your tongue, girl!"

Shrugging, Iztac kept quiet, her thoughts on the jar. It was tucked safely in the folds of her blouse, comforting. She had to support it with her hand to prevent it from falling, but she didn't mind. Its touch and the thought of its contents made her feel better, helped her to cope with the nausea and the dizziness; and the fear. There was no planned morning meal and, therefore, no cup and no flask to pour its contents into, had she had an opportunity to do this, still it made some sort of a weapon.

The Empress came toward her, her paces wide, unhurried, her richly adorned skirt rustling. Even in this predawn time and the privacy of her quarters the vain woman was dressed as though for the main reception hall, reflected Iztac. *Had she never rested?*

"So what was the Warlord's plan?"

This question caught her unprepared again. "I don't know."

"But of course you do." The widely spaced eyes glittered, amused, unconcerned. "There is so much activity around the Palace lately, especially tonight. Warriors running around as though preparing for an invasion. Oh, this man thinks he can outsmart me. Well, he can't."

Oh, so the Empress had her counter-moves, thought Iztac, mildly curious. If not for the attempts not to vomit, she may have liked to hear more. Water, she thought. The girl told her to drink plenty of water, and also to vomit all she liked. Would it make the Empress also vomit in disgust if she puked all over her perfectly polished floor? The thought made her feel better. Had she only managed to reach the other rooms, to vomit into this woman's mats and piles of pretty cushions.

The woman was still talking, telling something about the Warlord, smiling contentedly. Then Iztac's mind snapped into attention.

"So who was this warrior under your terrace? Had the Warlord sent him?"

"No!" It came out loudly, almost a shout.

"Oh, so it was just your private indiscretion." The dark eyes flickered. "He is dead, you know."

"Yes, I know."

"Too bad. He might have yielded interesting information if tortured."

She caught her breath. "Your people caught him?"

"My people are busy with more important things. They don't bother with dying warriors trying to get away." A grim half grin lit the woman's face. "Even if those commoners happened to enjoy the favors of the highborn princesses who should know better, they are still just that – unimportant commoners."

She felt the jar slipping under her sweaty fingers. Fighting for a better grip, she tried to think of something to say. "He would not tell you anything. He would die honorably, like the noblest person in the whole world."

"And you? Will you be as noble and strong under torture?"

"I..." She winced as her fingers brushed against the sharpened obsidian tucked in the girdle of her skirt, beside the jar. She had forgotten all about the knife. Trying to concentrate, she shivered as a cold gust of wind came from the half-closed shutters. "I will be like him, yes."

Her hands trembled badly, and she found it difficult to trace the glassy obsidian toward the smoothly carved handle. Yet as her palm locked around it, she felt infinitely better. The memory flowed in, trickling through her cold fingers, up her numb arm and into her dizzy head. She remembered the feeling well now, how it slid down the man's ribs, a short glide but one that tore the skin until able to penetrate into the vital depths of the warrior's stomach. She saved him back then, and she would save him now, too. His spirit should not take this mocking of his common origins. He was noble, nobler than the Empress herself.

Her hand came out, acting again on its own accord. She felt it pouncing from below, making its way firmly, strong and determined, unstoppable now. Momentarily caught in the mess of embroidered material, the knife cut through it neatly, before the familiar feeling was back. The tearing skin, the muscle, the stiffening body suddenly heavy against hers.

She watched the broad face changing, registering a genuine surprise. She had never seen this woman surprised, she realized.

The bejeweled hands came up, as though to strike her, or to push her away. She didn't know, didn't care. Her hand was one with the knife, having a mind of its own, pulling away then pouncing again, tearing more flesh.

It all came to her in waves, as if she were watching herself, or somebody else doing it, detached, just an onlooker. But when the weight of the body leaning on her became unbearable, she wavered and pushed it away, knowing that if she fell she would never be able to get up again.

The screams were what brought her back to her senses. Such a horrible sound. It went on and on, inhuman in its intensity just like the stench that hit her nostrils.

Her nausea grew, turning overwhelming, but she had to escape the stench and the horrible screams first, so, with the rest of her strength, she leaped toward the half opened shutters and squeezed through them, oblivious of the pain as they grazed her limbs. The freshness of the graying darkness beckoned, offering its calmness in exchange for the terrifying sounds and sights inside the small room.

Without thinking, she grabbed the bulging stones of the outer wall, allowing her body to guide her, her mind numb. She had never climbed this particular wall, yet, somehow, she managed to reach the ground quickly, charging for the nearby bushes, unwilling to vomit all over the clean paths.

Behind her back, the screams went on, terrifying in their inhumanness. As she caught her breath between the wild bouts of retching, she could hear those screams joined by other sounds. New wails, but not as terrifying, reminding her of the shouts that had spilled off her terrace earlier that night. *When she was still safely in his arms, planning to leave, to run away with him to his Highlands, or at least as far as the marketplace.*

She didn't try to hold the tears back, too spent and exhausted to try to be strong. Curling into a ball, she hugged her knees and rocked back and forth, letting the images of him fill her mind, knowing she would have to come to grips with his death sooner or later.

CHAPTER 16

"It can't go on like that, girl. You have to eat something."

Dehe winced, surprised by Kaay's voice as it rang behind her back. She hadn't heard the woman coming into the small, sunlit room, although the noise from the outside had not been as strong as it usually would be throughout the busy market day.

She glanced at the open shutters and then at the tray the woman carried. Unable to concentrate, she returned her attention to her hands. The water-soaked cloth was warming fast, too fast, so she took it off and dipped it again into the bowl of cool water beside her.

"I'm not hungry, thank you," she said, as she squeezed the cloth lightly, placing it back upon his forehead. "I wish he would cool off already. Why is his blood boiling so? His wounds have no smell."

"Because he is battling death, child," said Kaay gravely, not her amusedly derisive self, not anymore. "He has hardly any blood left. He should be dead already but for your insistence."

"He won't die," said Dehe through her clenched teeth. "I will keep him cool until he comes back to us, and then he will drink and eat and his strength will return to him."

"By that time you will die yourself, of pure starvation." Kaay shook her head. "Oh, girl, I wish him a quick recovery, mostly because his death will take you away, too."

Holding her breath, Dehe watched his chest as it lifted lightly, almost imperceptibly. Previously, through the night, he had struggled for breath, murmuring and sometimes talking and crying out, but now he has calmed, and she wasn't sure it was a good thing.

"Please, make another potion," she whispered, replacing the cloth once again. She wiped his chest, wincing at the heat it radiated. She could feel it burning her hands through the thin material. "Please, he needs to drink it again. He is getting hotter with every heartbeat."

"He can't drink this potion more than a few times a day." Kaay's voice was low and dull. "It'll kill him faster than his wounds."

"Then make something else. Please! He will die anyway, you say, so why can't we try all of your brews?"

"Oh, girl, you have much to learn. It doesn't work this way. But maybe I'll boil another root of *chichipilli*." To Dehe's relief the heavy footsteps drew away.

"Please," she whispered, leaning closer, brushing her lips against his dry, empty cheek. "Please be strong. Fight on. Please don't die." The tears were choking her throat and swallowed hard to keep them at bay. "Kaay is the best healer in the whole of Tenochtitlan. They all come to her, begging for her help and her treatment. But she doesn't help everyone. She is expensive. But she is now working so hard to keep you alive. Anyone else could die, but not you, never you. Please, don't leave me. Please, don't go away."

She wiped her face with the back of her palm, then squeezed the cloth once again, covering his forehead. Leaning carefully, she studied the ugly, crusted line that climbed up his ribs, coming from behind his lower back. It was dry and oozed just a little of the smelly substance, less than the day before, when he was brought here and after Kaay fussed with this wound for what seemed like all eternity, washing and sewing and pouring all sorts of brews and ointments into the red, frighteningly gaping opening.

The cut was vicious but not deep, she had told Dehe later. It did not reach the internal organs, cutting the muscle only. If it had, she wouldn't have bothered to treat him, she said, making Dehe choke with fright. It would be a complete waste of her time.

Satisfied, she shifted his left arm, careful not to disturb the two planks fastening it tightly between each other, leaving another crusted gash open to the touch of the fresh air. She studied it closely, then sniffed it for a long time. No, this wound was not rotting, either. It may have some slight odor, but this was mostly of the dry blood and all the smelly ointments. No, his wounds were clean, so all he needed was more rest and more potions to make him strong again.

She felt him shivering. His face, stark and thin and no longer calm, twisted and he muttered something, trying to raise his head. She put her arms around his shoulders, reassuring.

"It's all right," she whispered. "You are safe, and you are getting better. You will live. I will make sure of that. You can trust me. I will not let you die."

He did not open his eyes, but his good arm moved, seeking hers, the dry burning fingers closing around her palm, pressing lightly. It was difficult to battle the tears now.

"You will be well again," she whispered, her voice breaking. "I will make sure of that. You will not die. I will not let you."

The cracked lips moved but no sound came, and quickly he was back in his dreams, his face calming once again.

She resumed her treatment of the wet cloths, and it helped her to calm, too. The second dawn, she thought. It was the second dawn since that hideous night, when everything had gone so terribly wrong. Had she truly been there in the Palace, trying to poison the annoying princess? It seemed so meaningless, so pointless now. Why would she bother with this stupidity? Because of her, he was now battling the spirits of the Underworld. If not for the poison, if not for the other stupid emperor's wife, who had drunk her water so thirstily, none of it would have happened.

Yes, he may have run away with his filthy princess, but he wouldn't have left her, Dehe, behind. He even planned to make her host the stupid woman. She had heard him telling her that – 'there is this wonderful girl on the marketplace'. Not just a girl, but a wonderful girl. Oh, she was so angry with him for suggesting that back then, but now it felt silly. He was alive, and he would be unhurt but for her poisoning the other woman by mistake.

She remembered carrying him through the Palace's gardens. How, in the name of the Blue-Skirted Goddess, had she managed to reach the guard house, struggling under his weight? And then to convince his uncle to send him here to Kaay and not to the spacious mansion of the former Chief Warlord?

She had argued with the formidable man, and somehow, she had made him listen. He wouldn't have listened, probably, but he was evidently shocked and distraught, too. His face reflected his grief, although he tried to act briskly, matter-of-fact. Oh, the old man loved his nephew.

Smiling, she remembered the formidable man coming here, to this pitiful reed-and-cane house twice during the previous day, making Kaay ecstatic with excitement. He had brought so many cocoa beans, the healer's eyes almost popped out of their sockets, and she promised to make his nephew so well, the young man would never even remember what happened.

For half a day after that the old woman was busy planning her move into the better neighborhood, with a two room stone house and a wide workshop adjacent. As soon as the young warrior gets better, she had said. But her treatment of him hadn't changed, reflected Dehe, feeling a surge of warm affection toward the old woman. She had been doing her best already, for her, Dehe's, sake.

She caressed his cheek lightly, delighted to be able to do this. It was nice to have him all for herself, even if he wasn't aware of it at the moment. He would be well again, she told to herself, smiling now, the tears gone. He would not die, and he would be as strong, as vital, as unruly, as before.

CHAPTER 17

Itzcoatl sighed, shifting in his high woven chair, uncomfortable with this sort of a seating arrangement, as always. The side effects of his high office were these, to sit in the woven chair of the Chief Warlord and the Main Adviser and to ride in the palanquin all over the city. Quite a challenge for a born warrior. But a worthwhile benefit, nevertheless.

He straightened his shoulders and scanned the main hall once again. Such a large gathering. Delegations from many cities, towns and provinces came to express their condolences, to mourn the passing of Tenochtitlan's most prominent woman, the First Wife of the late Emperor and the mother of the current one. Even Azcapotzalco sent a highborn representative, as the remarkable noblewoman was the daughter of the mighty Tezozomoc, a favorite daughter at that.

Hiding his grin, Itzcoatl watched the delegation from Tlacopan nearing the dais and the reed-woven throne upon it. Had they only known the truth! He glanced at the Emperor, appreciating the boy's effort to look important. His face strained, pale and ashen under the magnificent colorfulness of his headdress, but serious and concentrated, the young Emperor listened to the flowery phrases, but it was obvious that his mind was not registering those, not fully. Instead, the boy's eyes wandered toward the place where the royal family members stood in a colorful crowd, where his father's, the late Emperor's Second Wife, stood rigid and still, also pale, but beautiful in her sky-blue garments and the light diadem.

What a woman, thought Itzcoatl, marveling at her beauty and

the way she stood there, so upright, so royal, so impeccable. Had he not known better, he would never believe what this woman was capable of, climbing walls, talking straight in a manlike fashion, and most of all, killing people in a way that made even seasoned warriors gape.

Oh yes, he had wanted this woman to help him get rid of the Empress; he was the one to push her there. However, what he had envisioned was quite different from what the wild *cihua* had done. By sending her the jar with the poison, he gave her an appropriate direction. Yet, even he was not prepared for the ghastly sight of the cut up Empress, stabbed again and again, her stomach torn to pieces, the spilling entrails leaking upon the polished floor.

No, he was not prepared for this, and neither were the rest of the Palace's servants, the ones who happened to see this. Warriors witnessed worse sights, yet those belonged to battlefields and not civilized *altepetl*s. Even the priests would cut their victims not as viciously as that.

Well, he, Itzcoatl, had hushed the affair, of course. Those who had seen, who had had to clean the Empress off the floor, were sworn to secrecy under the pain of death, and the word went out, informing the city of the regretful passing of the Emperor's mother, the late Emperor's Chief Wife. Yet, the sight of the cut woman kept haunting him because, of all people, he was the only one who knew who had done this.

Returning his gaze to the exquisite sculptured face, now so pale it looked as if chiseled out of lifeless stone, he tried to understand how such an innocent-looking thing could have done that. He knew she was pushed over the brink, pressed by the Empress and him, the Chief Warlord, her ambitions high, her options dismal. And yet...

I would like to posses this woman, he thought suddenly. *Despite the danger. Or maybe because of it. So much beauty, so much spirit. Had anyone awoken her sensuality yet?*

Not the late Emperor, for sure. This one had hardly touched her. And the current Emperor, the innocent boy, had not the slightest chance of doing that either, although he would try hard. The way he had looked at her, the way he had insisted on taking this woman to be his first wife, his Chief Wife, not wishing to wait for the mourning period to pass, showed how passionately he felt about her. However, this slip-of-an-emperor had not the slightest chance. He would not awaken this woman, and he had better watch his back. The new Empress of Tenochtitlan may prove stronger than the previous one.

He shrugged. Oh, he should be able to deal with it when the time came. So far, he had reached his goal. Tenochtitlan was free to start changing its policies, slowly and carefully, drawing, hopefully, no attention of the mighty Tepanec Empire. The old horror of the Tepanec Emperor should embark upon his journey through the Underworld soon, and by that time they should be ready.

His gaze sought the imposing figure of the former Warlord, standing among the advisers and the influential people of Tenochtitlan's districts that crowded the entrance, his shoulders wide and straight, his posture proud, royal-like. Tenochtitlan's First Chief Warlord, no more no less; the man who had helped its First Emperor to carve the basics of the rising empire.

And the empire it would be, thought Itzcoatl, suddenly shivering with a sense of a strange premonition. Tenochtitlan would be the capital of the mighty empire, and he would dedicate all his energies to advance it to this glorious future. The moment the Tepanec Emperor dies, he promised himself. Until then, the boy-emperor could rule safely. But only until then.

Feeling the gaze of the former Chief Warlord upon him, watching him with a genuine curiosity, as if reading his thoughts, he returned it, unafraid. *We are together in this Old Friend*, he thought. *You know well enough that the death of the Empress was just the beginning.* Amused and vastly relieved, he saw the imperceptive smile crossing the old man's lips. Oh yes, this man would help him. His goals went along with his, Itzcoatl's.

The Tlacopan delegation finished its flowery speeches and listened to the Emperor answering them politely, not stumbling over his words. The boy had learned diligently, taking his duties with a due seriousness. Without his mother's dominant presence, he may do quite well, provided his new Chief Wife approved.

Oh but he would do much to possess this woman, he thought again, watching her eyes light momentarily, losing their detachment. Following her gaze, he saw the warriors pouring in, escorting another delegation. From the conquered Acolhua lands, this time.

The tall figure of the Highlander caught his eyes. Haggard and very pale, the young man made his way carefully along the lined wall, heading toward his uncle, his cloak hanging vacantly upon his thinned shoulders, his arm, fastened in a sling, hindering his movements.

Oh, that one had more than his share of luck, and the gods were watching over him, thought Itzcoatl. Ten dawns ago he was as good as dead, with this slip of a girl, the one had who had delivered the poison earlier on, dragging him to the guard house, cut and bleeding so badly he had already been unconscious and gray. He should have bled to death but for the girl's good sense in tying his arm above the cut so tightly it stopped the bleeding. He saw the healers doing this sometimes, but never insignificant girls from the marketplace. Well, this saved the young man all right. This, and a certain amount of luck.

Curious, he watched the Emperor's Chief Wife following the Highlander with her gaze, her eyes alight, indecently so. The youth reached the crowd surrounding his uncle and halted, not trying to push his way in. Instead, he leaned against the wall, clearly exhausted, standing there with a visible effort, regaining his strength, peering at the Emperor's Wife, the intensity of his gaze even more scandalizing.

What was this all about? wondered Itzcoatl fleetingly, turning his attention back to the Tlacopan delegation. Had these two known each other? Oh yes, he remembered. He had made the Highlander watch over the princess, to be his, Itzcoatl's, connection to her. To force the wild *cihua* into the action more readily.

He raised his eyebrows. Had the wild beast taken his responsibilities too far? Well, having obvious qualities of his famous uncle about him, there was no wonder the young man managed all sorts of strange feats.

He shrugged. The delegation of Tlacopan was bidding their farewells, and Itzcoatl straightened his shoulders. Yes, the emperor-boy would do until the right time came, he thought. But only until then.

Fighting his exhaustion, Kuini leaned against the wall, pondering his possibilities. He had not been obliged to wait for all those delegations to finish their business. He had not been obliged to be here at all, not even sure he would be bidden into the Palace. Well, he was. Thanks to his powerful uncle and the Warlord, who now, obviously, wielded a thousand fold more power than before. Their names cleared his path like a magical spell, and so here he was, standing in the main hall, wondering why he had come.

People were murmuring all around him, whispering and talking between themselves, fascinated with the delegations and still upset with the mysterious death of the Empress.

He shifted his weight from one foot to the other. Ten dawns have passed since he had been to the Palace. They said it had been ten dawns. He didn't remember. Most of those days blurred into a foggy mist of heat, and cold, and pain, tortured with thirst but unable to drink, nauseated most of the time; forced to consume revolting potions, fighting to keep them down, exhausted, sweat covered, in pain most of the time. A hideous affair.

However, Dehe was there, always near and reassuring, smiling and calm, radiating her happiness, telling him how good he was doing, how much better he was since the day before. She knew he would heal and be his old self again, so he knew it, too. Sometimes she was accompanied by a strange old woman with huge piercings and crossed eyes, sometimes alone, but always there, *keeping him alive.*

He didn't want her to leave, not even for a heartbeat, so she never moved from his sight, holding him, giving him her strength. Thin and haggard, but glowing nevertheless, keeping him alive by the sheer power of her will.

His uncle came often, and also Tlacaelel and Coyotl, but he didn't want them to see him this way, not so filthy, and weak, and dying. He had told her so and she made them stop coming, standing up to those powerful people with the firm politeness of a person with a great will.

Taking a deep breath, he shook the unpleasant memories off. He had survived and healed, with only a sling around his arm, and the pain in the ugly twisted scar in his back and along his side to remind him of that night when he should have died. Those and the annoying exhaustion that made him want to rest after he walked ridiculously small distances.

A maid lingered nearby, seeking his gaze. "Honorable Warrior, would you please follow me?"

"Where to?" he asked, frowning.

The girl's pleasantly round face twisted. "Please follow," she repeated.

It took more of his precious strength to walk the corridor, trying to keep up with the troubled maid. The cut in his back made it difficult to remain upright most of the time.

"Please wait here, Honorable Warrior," said the girl breathlessly, moving the wooden partition of a small airless room.

"Wait for what?"

"The Revered Empress will be here shortly."

"Yes."

With difficulty he squatted upon a vacant mat, leaning against the wall, closing his eyes. The Revered Empress. So it was true, and she was going to be the next Empress of Tenochtitlan. Not a bad feat, even for the highborn Acolhua princess. Oh, she would make a good Empress, he decided, strangely untouched by the thought of her, empty. His heart had made wild leaps in his chest when he had seen her earlier in the main hall, sitting there, beautiful and aloof, clad in that same magnificent bright blue that set off her golden skin so favorably, yet wearing the royal regalia of the Empress. Not the Moon Goddess, but a cold, royal statue.

He shrugged, surprised with his own indifference. It was all in the past now, the wild dreams of the wild youth. Silly memories. Her and everything else. It was all in the past, to forget and to leave alone. Tenochtitlan, Texcoco, and the Lowlands, they were not his home; he did not belong here.

Her paces were light upon the stone floor, but he recognized them and opened his eyes in time to see her sliding in, a beautiful vision of gold and blue, striking but sad, with obsidian eyes clouded and uncertain.

"No, no, don't get up," she said breathlessly, rushing toward him. "You don't look well."

"I'm good." He got up stubbornly, clenching his teeth, waiting for the new bout of pain to pass.

She peered at him, the uncertainty in her eyes growing. "I needed to talk to you, but I could not reach you until you came to the Palace."

"I'm sorry," he said, forcing a smile. It was difficult to see her so helpless. "I couldn't come before."

"I know, I know. You were hurt so badly that night. I thought you were dead. They told me you were dead."

"Oh." He frowned, thrown out of balance. "Why would they tell you something like that?"

Her face fell. "Well, it was the Empress. You know…"

"Yes, of course. I should have guessed." He peered at her. "Did you?"

She stood his gaze but her eyes clouded, turned blank. "What do you think?"

"The jar I brought you?"

"No." There was a dull glow to her eyes now, something dark, not completely sane. He felt like taking her into his arms, but one couldn't do that to an empress.

"I'm sorry I couldn't help you," he said instead. "I wish I could have."

She shrugged helplessly. "It's all in the past now." Then her eyes lit. "But you are alive, and that makes it all worth it. I didn't believe the Warlord when I heard him saying that some dawns ago. I asked him straight away and he gave me this strange look, then nodded and stalked off." She grinned and there was a mischievous spark to her eyes, bringing back the girl from the Texcoco Palace. "I think he is afraid of me."

"Why would he be?" he asked, grinning back, feeling better by the moment. "Because you did what you did?"

"Well, yes, I suppose so."

"What did you use?"

"Your knife."

"What?" He gaped at her, seeking the signs of her teasing him. "My knife?"

"Well, yes," she said, smiling guiltily. "You gave it to me, and, well, I got to use it before, didn't I?"

He peered at her, reluctant to relive those memories which were, anyway, covered by a thick fog. "You used it, yes. You saved my life!"

She dropped her gaze and her smile faded. "I used it, yes. But I don't know how much it helped. That girl, she did most of it. She saved your life."

"No, you did this." Suddenly, he could remember her clearly, standing there in the darkness, her eyes glazed and the knife clutched tightly in her hands, wet and glittering. Reaching for her face, he felt her cheek smooth against his fingers, sending waves of familiar excitement down his stomach. "You are the bravest girl that I ever met."

Her lips quivered. "I wish I was…" Her voice broke and then, somehow, she was in his arms, trembling with suppressed tears, hurting his wounded hand. "I should have helped earlier, should have intervened before. Like she did."

"You did great," he murmured, stroking her hair softly, uncomfortable in the depths of the Palace. Had they only been by their pond, under the cover of the night. "You did wonderfully. You were brave, and you made me so very proud. Even before the fight, when you didn't leave but stayed to face them with me. You don't know how brave you are."

"I wish they had never found us," she whispered, pressing closer, her tears warm, soaking his cloak. "I wish we'd had enough sense to run away earlier that night."

He swallowed the knot that was tightening in his throat. "Yes, I wish we could have changed that. Or three summers ago, in Texcoco." He clenched his teeth against his frustration. "It always goes wrong, every time we try."

"Maybe one day it will go right." Her voice came out muffled, buried in his chest.

"Maybe one day."

"I can't leave Chimal all alone. He needs my support, against your Warlord most of all." She looked at him searchingly. "You understand that, don't you? It was not my choice, and I didn't want to be involved, but now I am responsible... responsible for what happened to his mother. And he loved her. He relied on her. I can't leave him all alone in this place. He won't survive it." Her words gushed out between convulsive breaths, impossible to stop, a wild current. "They are coveting his place, his high position, his right to sit on the reed chair. All of them! And he is just a child. He is trustful, and innocent. He should not have inherited. He is so young. But his mother made him the Emperor, so she could rule in his place, and he is stuck there now, trying to do his best. And they are all hateful, or envious, or just sneering because he is so young. I am the only person that he can trust, the only one who can try to protect him."

She stopped again, breathless and at a loss, and he pressed her to his chest, the knot in his throat tightening again. *You are the one needing protection,* he thought helplessly. *But you never made it possible, never let anyone keep you from trouble.*

"I understand, Iztac Ayotl," he said, stroking her hair. "I understand perfectly, and I accept. Please don't cry."

"What will you do?" she asked after a while, when the trembling was subdued and she broke free and busied herself trying to save what was left of the creams and colors applied to her face.

"I don't know. I haven't decided yet." He shrugged. "I lost my sword, and I don't want to fight without it. I know it's ridiculous, but I won't fight with another weapon. I need mine."

"But I have your sword!" She beamed at him. "I saved it. It's hidden safely in my chests, between my clothes. I took it out every now and then, and I studied the carvings. They are beautiful and so many. One can peer at its handle for days. When I thought you were dead..." Her face darkened. "Well, I...it helped me to cope with it. Those carvings, they made me feel closer to you, to your spirit. There is some magic about them, especially the one with the face of a jaguar. I would look at it and I would immediately feel better. I *knew* it was you." Embarrassed, she studied her palms, then looked up, grinning. "I'm not sure I'm ready to return it to you now."

His breath caught, he peered at her, feeling that he had never known her before, not for real.

"Iztac Ayotl, you are the most amazing woman in the whole World of the Fifth Sun," he said finally, his voice difficult to control. "I will never forget this, never! I will stay in Tenochtitlan, and I will guard you in every way I can. No harm will come to you as long as I live. Not if I can help it."

The way her face shone took his breath away. "Then all is well. If I can see you occasionally, then I can handle it all." She pressed to him fleetingly, then straightened her diadem. "If you stay in Tenochtitlan will you fight in the Warlord's campaigns? I wish you would become one of the Palace's guards, but I don't believe you would like that."

He laughed. "A Palace guard? Why not make me clean the Palace's rooms and cook?"

She giggled, then narrowed her eyes. "What about that girl?"

"I'll take her to be my woman," he said firmly, not liking the way her nostrils widened and her eyes flashed. "She deserves that much for everything she has done."

"Oh yes, she has done many things, that *cihua*!"

"She is no *cihua*. She saved my life, and whatever she has done to make you angry, she did only good things for me."

She took a deep breath, her lips pressed into a thin line. "Well, I wish you well in this undertaking. But be careful with your First Wife. Your guarding spirit has dark sides to her."

"As long as you are careful with your child of a husband, the mighty Emperor," he retorted, following her to the doorway, feeling light and elated.

The tiredness was still there, and the pain in his broken arm and the other wound, however, he knew these would go away soon. With Dehe's potions and a lot of rest, and most importantly, with his sword back in his possession, he would be able to join the impending raid to Zacatlan, embarking upon the path his uncle was eager for him to take.

Oh, he would not disappoint that remarkable man, he promised himself. He would turn into a great warrior, soon a leader, to make the old man truly proud. And by then Tenochtitlan would be ready to join the Acolhua people in their proposed rebellion against the mighty Tepanecs.

Oh yes, his father would yet lead the Highlanders down their mountains, and he would be there, waiting for him on the shores of the Great Lake, to join his forces with Coyotl and maybe Tlacaelel and the Warlord, and even his uncle, Tenochtitlan's former Chief Warlord. Oh, they would yet re-conquer Texcoco, and all those summers of waiting and indecision would be nothing but a bad dream.

AUTHOR'S AFTERWORD

But Tezozomoc's death was not as imminent as many of the provinces around had anticipated. It wasn't until 1426, after living for more than a hundred years and ruling for half of this time, that the mighty Tepanec Emperor died, leaving many sons to rule many provinces.

His death didn't plunge the Tepanec Empire into a chaos, as the conquered or oppressed nations expected. Tezozomoc's eldest son and his appointed successor, Tayatzin, seemed to be a reasonable man and a good ruler.

Yet, not everyone was satisfied with this arrangement. Maxtla, one of the other numerous royal offspring, appointed to rule Coyoacan, apparently began to think that the reew-woven throne of Azcapotzalco would suit his talents better than the petty province of Coyoacan.

Too busy to pay attention to the discontent offspring of the royal Tepanec house, Tenochtitlan faced its own problems. The water supplies. Though the first aqueduct was built successfully, carrying fresh water into Tenochtitlan all the way from the mainland and over the lake's waters, it also brought along much trouble. Built of clay and other inadequate materials, the water construction broke down alarmingly often, leaving the island with no fresh drinking water again and again. The Mexica engineers worked hard, fixing the problems, maintaining the important construction, yet the lack of appropriate building materials thwarted their efforts, this and the necessity to ask for the Tepanecs permission to do the repairs each time the need arose.

The relationship between the Aztecs and the Tepanecs began to deteriorate once again..

What happened next is presented in the fourth book of The Rise of the Aztecs Series, "**Currents of War**".

ABOUT THE AUTHOR

Zoe Saadia is the author of several novels on pre-Columbian Americas. From the architects of the Aztec Empire to the founders of the Iroquois Great League, from the towering pyramids of Tenochtitlan to the longhouses of the Great Lakes, her novels bring long-forgotten history, cultures and people to life, tracing pivotal events that brought about the greatness of North and Mesoamerica.

To learn more about Zoe Saadia and her work, please visit
www.zoesaadia.com

Made in the USA
San Bernardino, CA
31 March 2017